Scars of the Fawn

Beyond
Her Scars

NJ Colle

Scars of the Fawn is the first book in the "Beyond Her Scars" series written by Indie Author NJ Colle

Some scenes may be extremely upsetting to some readers, so reader discretion is strongly advised.

This story is recommended for readers 18+ years of age.

This story contains dark elements including:

- Explicit Language

- Sexual Assault/Rape of a Minor-Depicted on Page

- Sexual Abuse with a Foreign Object

- Racial Slurs

- Domestic Abuse-Emotional & Physical

- Gaslighting

- Attempted Murder / Graphic Violence

- Talk of Suicide and/or Self Harm

- Parental Neglect & Child Abuse

- Parental Loss / Sibling Loss

- Traumatic Events Including: Fire, Blood, Murder & Death

- Gun / Knife Violence

- Mature Themes / Explicit Sexual Content / Bondage

- Traumatic Birthing Event

Contents

Dedication

To anyone who has ever felt broken beyond repair,
Your salvation lies ahead...
You'll find it where you least expect it,
Within YOU...
Never, ever give up.

Prologue

The harsh fluorescent lights of the bus terminal flicker as dried leaves and discarded scraps of paper swirl around my legs, the thin fabric of my leggings doing nothing to protect against the frigid winds.

It's a cold night for running.

But the weather wasn't something I gave too much thought to when it came down to a choice between living and dying.

So I'm running... *again*. Trying to disappear.

I've escaped him before. I'll do it again.

Because I'm not dead yet and I'm not ready to give up.

Not. Fucking. Yet.

I tug my hoodie tighter around my body, curling further into myself when another cold gust of wind bites through the few meager layers of clothing I have—the clothes pulled from the evidence bag—still bloodstained, still damp. Not that it matters. The eternal damp chill of Britain at this time of year makes such discomforts irrelevant... I've survived worse.

Maria brought my things to the hospital for me; my purse, this hoodie and most importantly... *my bag*. My only real chance at escape. Hopefully I've saved enough cash to be able to put London—*and him*—behind me for good.

Like I said, I've escaped before, but those other times, I failed.

This time, I know what I need to do. I need to be more careful—smarter, if I want to stay off his radar.

This time, I'll do it right.

This time... *I have to.*

No cell phone. No credit cards in his name. No digital footprint. No way for him to trace me at all.

For what feels like the millionth time, I reread the crumpled letter gripped between my numb fingers.

The ink—spidery and frail—bleeds where I've touched the paper. Either the rain or my tears—probably both—having spread it across the page, the letters fading into watery pools of muted gray.

Not that I need to read it. I've memorized every word.

Just a few short paragraphs and an address. Written by someone who might be connected to me—by the one person who might have answers to questions I have yet to ask.

I tug at my zipper in a futile attempt to pull it up any further, the hoodie already zipped up as far as it will go, but it's no match against the chill in the air. So I try to sink myself deeper within its folds, my freezing cold hands disappearing into the hollows of my cuffs.

A shiver racks through my body and I wince at the flare of pain. The tug of my stitches, the perpetual ache of the bruises, cruel reminders of his brutality. The darker patches along my sleeves, a silent accusation.

I shiver again as another cold rush of air blusters past, stirring up a cluster of dirt and debris. I glare down at my hideous leggings, cursing myself for not planning my escape from hell a bit better.

I glance at the clock on the wall, the bus terminal quiet at this hour. A world emptied except for me and the occasional ghost passing through. If my research is right, I should have one more bus ride, then a few miles on foot, and I'll be standing on the doorstep of someone who may know who I am.

Or at least, who I was meant to be.

A lone couple drifts past.

Instinctively, I shrink back into the shadows, relying on the ebony fabric of my hoodie to cloak me. I turn my head, hoping they won't notice the purpling around my eyes, the pallor of my skin, the bandages barely concealed beneath my sleeves.

But they don't see me—don't likely care to. They just walk right by. Like everyone else, they're wrapped up in their own world, oblivious to me, my presence irrelevant.

Just like the rest of my life...

For most of my life, I've been a possession.

Never my own person. The daughter. The wife.

Cliché rules set in stone like:

Speak only when spoken to.

Be seen, not heard.

Eyes down. Don't talk back.

Sometimes, when I think about it, I have to wonder if there's a chance, I've never been a person at all.

If I've ever really even existed...

No. I don't think I have.

Not yet anyway...

The bus pulls into the station, the air brakes letting out a high-pitched sigh as it comes to a stop in front of me. A warm gust of acrid smelling diesel fumes fills my nose just as the doors fold open. Taking in a deep breath, I make my way up the steps.

I move down the aisle and settle into a seat, then watch the terminal grow smaller as the bus pulls away, taking me one step closer toward the next leg of my journey.

Chilled to the bone, the warmth of the bus feels divine, finally giving me a bit of a reprieve from the unrelenting cold. I rest my head back on the seat and let my eyes drift closed, grateful to be adding even more distance between myself and London.

And him...

Exhaustion starts to pull at my consciousness, the tug of sleep inevitable as some of the weight of everything finally starts to leave me. As my thoughts drift, I say a silent prayer, hoping this part of my life is truly over this time. That this version of me is finally gone for good—as surely as if the doctors had never saved my life.

I know, thirty years doesn't seem like a very long life. But when that life has beat the shit out of you almost every day for the last twelve and a half years, it can seem like an eternity.

I've spent far too much time wishing for it all to just end.

Too much time contemplating what it might be like if I just gave up—just gave in to my darkest thoughts. To let go. To give in to the demons, whispering of my salvation if I were to never open my eyes again, never take in another breath.

To let the darkness swallow me and usher me into sweet oblivion. Permanently taking me away from the fear, the pain... to a place where I could finally rest.

But no.

I'm not giving up. This can't be all there is for me. That letter tells me there's still hope. Still someone out there who could be my safe place to land.

I don't know what's next for me. I have no idea what I'll need to do, or who I'll need to become to survive.

But I will...

Survive, that is.

I'm determined to rise from the ashes of my personal hell.

Like a phoenix, I *will* arise anew.

The possibility of having a chance at a life without fear and pain lurking in the shadows at every turn, that distant glimmer of hope— just out of reach...

For now.

But can I survive on my own?

Will I be strong enough to keep my demons at bay?

Will I be fast enough to outrun him—for good this time?

As I finally let sleep pull me under, a soft wash of impending peace settles into me.

I suppose there's a certain poetic irony in escaping death on the same day you were born.

Happy birthday to me.

Chapter 1

Cain

"What do you mean she's gone?!"

My shout echoes through the hospital corridors.

"How could you lose her? She was unconscious—nearly dead! She can't have just vanished!"

The nurse futilely searches the room again, as if my missing wife is going to magically turn up in this tiny space.

"I don't know, Mr. Brentwood, I'm so sorry!" her face paling as she pleads. "The machines should have alerted us that she had removed her leads. I don't understand how she could have left without us knowing about it."

"I. Want. Her. Found!" I seethe, punctuating each word through clenched teeth.

Her eyes dart around the room nervously, tears welling up at my insistence and her obvious ineptitude, the sight of her wretched sniveling driving my rage nearly over the brink.

A woman's tears... weak, disgusting, pathetic.

It makes me sick.

Taking a step toward her, I draw my hand back, ready to strike.

She shrinks back, reminding me where I am. I drop my fist to my side, fingers clenching as I narrow my eyes at her.

"Never mind, you fucking useless bitch! I'll find her myself!" I spit at her, spinning out of the room, shoving an orderly out of the way, storming down the hall.

Incompetent fools.

And that fucking little cunt!

She thinks she can get away from me.

She should know by now, *I will always find her.*

She's managed to wriggle out of my grasp a few times before, but I would think the beatings she's received for her disobedience would be sinking in by now.

I guess another one will be in order once I get my hands on her again.

And you better believe, I will...

Chapter 2

Escape

Verdon-on-Wye is exactly how I had envisioned it—a picture-perfect English village, perched along the River Wye, framed by the rolling hills of the Forest of Dean. Oaks and conifers crowd the slopes, a dark green tide against the sky.

Buildings cling to the hillside in neat terraces, their small cottages—some thatched, others tiled in local stone—prim, proper, untouched by time. As an American, it's exactly how I had imagined the countryside villages in England would look.

A church spire rises above the rooftops, a quiet watchman over the village. But it's the manor on the hill that draws my eye—the biggest, grandest I've ever seen.

It stands apart, set back from the world, separated by rolling parkland. Regal, untouchable. It reminds me of the historical romance novels my mother used to read to me beneath the apple trees in the orchard back home in Connecticut—her British accent making each word, each phrase feel all that much more magical.

Tearing my gaze away from its imposing façade, I turn my attention back to the humbler street before me. It's early yet, and the village butcher shop is still shuttered, its painted sign promising farm butter and boar meat sausages. My stomach clenches, rumbling at the thought of food—at the memory of my last meal.

I shudder as unbidden; haunting images flash through my mind—*my bowl of soup smashing to the floor beside me. His iron grip, fisted in my hair, the toe of his boot connecting with my ribs.*

I shake my head, forcing myself back to the present.

No...he isn't here.

He can't hurt me now.

I flinch at the sound of glass smashing nearby, every nerve in me on edge—screaming *danger*! I spin, heart hammering, ready to run.

A skinny tortoise shell cat meows, blinking its bright golden eyes up at me as it pauses lapping milk from a broken bottle. It meets my gaze, its tail twitching with curiosity, gauging the stranger in its midst with cautious interest.

I blow out a shaky breath, "Hi kitty." I say, holding my hand to my racing heart and smile at the sweet little beast staring back at me. It studies me for a moment more before returning its attention back to the puddle of milk. I shake my head, silently chastising myself as I will my pulse to slow.

"Can I help you, miss?"

The deep voice behind me makes me jump.

Damn it! I'm shaking, my heart rate ratcheting up once again.

"Miss?" The voice tries again, closer now since I still haven't turned to face the newcomer.

I clutch my backpack tighter, holding it like a makeshift shield against whatever might come next, and steel myself before turning to face him.

I'm met with a pair of brilliant arctic blue eyes and a bright, disarming smile. My breath catches in my throat and I suddenly feel more shy than nervous as I take in his striking features. He's possibly one of the most attractive men I've ever seen in person. His jaw, chiseled, his sandy blonde hair, untamed.

My eyes track down his body, taking in his hulking size. His thick thighs are clad in denim—the knees muddied, his work boots worn and caked in dirt.

His huge forearms, lined with thickly veined muscles, hang loose at his sides beneath the rolled-up sleeves of a tan and beige plaid flannel that hangs loosely over a sage green t-shirt, stretched tight across the broad wall of muscles lining his chest.

His teeth seem impossibly white against his tanned skin, darkened naturally by long days spent working in the sun. His massive form towers above me, literally blocking out the rays of the early morning sun.

I swallow. Hard.

"I-I..." I stammer and clear my throat before trying again, frustration prickling. "I'm looking for Allbright's Bookshop."

His smile widens, lighting up his whole face.

"Allbright's? Well, if that's where you're heading, you're going the wrong way."

"Oh...," my shoulders drop, defeated.

He laughs loudly and I feel my cheeks heat as my confusion shifts to embarrassment.

"Hey now, no harm done."

His tone seems kind as he takes a step toward me, bending slightly in an effort to see my face, hidden within the shadows of my hoodie. But when his big hand reaches toward my shoulder, a surge of panic bubbles up in my chest.

I take a quick step back, tipping my chin down—tucking my head back further into my hood, my grip automatically tightening on the strap of my backpack.

"S-sorry. I...I really don't know my way around here yet."

A nervous laugh escapes me and I take another step back, trying to distance myself from him—from the questions that will likely follow if he gets a better look at the markings on my face.

He pulls his hand back, but his eyes stay on me, watching me for a beat, before he blows out a slow sigh, straightens back to his full height and strides past me.

"Come on then," he says, glancing back over his shoulder, the sun catching his eyes—the light making them sparkle crystalline blue, like shards of ice.

"This way... I'll show you."

I slowly start to follow him, but stop as he nears a narrow lane.

The buildings lean in close together, their eaves almost touching, casting deep shadows over the passage.

He waves a hand, beckoning me forward.

As I see it, I have two choices. Wait for the butcher shop to open and ask for directions inside... or follow this stranger.

My gaze flicks back to the sign on the door. **Closed Sundays.**

Damn it.

I guess that really only leaves me with one option.

My heart lodges itself in my throat, my gut screaming at me in warning.

Do I trust this stranger and follow him to God knows where—or do I tuck my tail between my legs, turn back and catch the next bus out of here?

But where would I go?

Anywhere, I suppose.

Just as long as I can keep running, as far and as fast as I can.

I tell myself—again and again—a silent mantra repeating on a loop.

I can run. I can run.

I. Can. Run.

But I didn't escape my shadow of a life in London—didn't risk everything to get to Verdon—just to falter at the first hurdle.

And aren't English men supposed to be gallant? Gentlemanly?

Swallowing down my fears, I cast one last glance at the sign on the door, foolishly hoping—just maybe—I had read it wrong. But there's no mistaking it.

Fate, I realize, has already made the decision for me.

Drawing in a deep breath, I tighten my grip on my bag and pull it closer to my chest.

Then, stepping forward...

I follow the stranger.

Chapter 3

The Bookshop

The lane, which is more of an alleyway I now realize, is cold and dark—despite the residents' best efforts to make it bright and inviting.

When I first stepped into the village, I was awestruck.

Compared to London, even compared to the town where I grew up in Connecticut, it felt untouched. The roads were clean, the air untainted by the smog that clings to the city like a second skin.

Peaceful, tranquil, even. The constant hum of sirens, traffic, music, bodies moving in an endless erratic rhythm—gone.

But here, in the alleyway, the illusion wavers. As if beneath the picture-perfect charm, something lingers, clawing at my already frayed nerves, making me wonder if maybe things aren't so different here after all.

The specter of his presence constantly looms at the edge of my vision, threatening to step out of every shadow. My attention snapping toward every strange sound in this *too-perfect* place.

I shake it off and pick up my pace to try to catch up to *'Blue Eyes'* as he strides ahead, confident, seemingly unbothered, leading me toward the river.

"You got a name?"

My mouth goes dry, my heart racing at the seemingly innocuous question.

He turns, flashing that brilliant smile. His pace slows and he tilts his head, lifting an eyebrow curiously beneath the loose fringe of his unstyled hair.

I suddenly realize I've left his question hanging too long in the air between us.

"Sorry, what?" I rasp, my voice is raw—still frayed, still unsteady from the tubes they'd forced down my throat.

"Your name?" he asks again, dipping his chin and smiling, a deep dimple pulling into the side of his cheek, amusement lacing his tone.

My mouth gapes at him, like a fish on dry land, my voice completely useless as I search for an answer.

"I mean, you do have one, don't you?" He teases, his gorgeous smile disarming me as his grin widens.

I take a breath, weighing his unknowingly loaded question.

I should have been ready for this. I can't believe I hadn't thought about how I might answer someone asking the simple question of my name. But, giving anyone my name might lead *him* to me and I can't let that happen.

"Er... it's Ni..." my mouth snaps shut, my gut screaming at me to lie. I glance down at the crumpled letter in my fist, my fingers tightening around it. The name inked onto its page. The relative I hope to find.

Thinking quickly, I clear my throat and start again.

"Cole... I'm... I'm Cole - Cole Baker."

Blue Eyes stops so suddenly I nearly collide into him.

"Cole?"

My chin dips in a shallow nod. He's silent for a beat, his icy eyes studying me. But then his smile is back and he shrugs a shoulder as he turns to start walking again.

"Unusual name. But then, I guess you're a Yank, so...

He lets the end of his statement hang between us.

My heart hammers as my mind races for a response, overthinking every possible meaning he might have loaded behind that comment.

I realize, a little too late, that he meant it as a joke when he stops again, turning back to face me. His smile drops when he sees the troubled look on my face.

"Hey now, don't be like that. I'm only joshing with ya."

He steps forward, his grin wide as he extends a big hand toward me and I feel his warmth bridging the space between us.

"I'm Zavier. Zavier Johnson."

He seems genuine enough, but throughout my life, my experience with men has shattered my ability to judge their intentions beyond repair and I really can't afford to take chances at all right now.

Maybe it's the stress of the last few days.

Hell, who am I kidding... the last several years.

To be honest, it's probably just being near someone who seems completely at ease in his own skin. Someone who simply, in his own way, is trying to help me feel at ease.

Steeling myself, I blow out a slow breath. Keeping my head low, I reach out to press my palm into his, watching my hand disappear as his huge, calloused one completely engulfs mine.

I feel a bit of tension leave me when his warm smile stays in place and he gives my hand a small, firm squeeze. But the longer he keeps my hand gripped in his, the more my nerves flood right back again. A nervous giggle bubbles out of me, the sound escaping before I can stop it.

Before I remember my laughter comes with consequences.

I rip my hand from his to cover my mouth, my sleeve slipping up my arm with the movement. His eyes land on the bandage wrapped around my wrist. The smile drops from his face when I yank it back down, wrapping my arms around myself and quickly step away from him. I fold into myself.

He hunches forward, his eyes scanning my face—seeing too much. They darken as he takes in the dark purple crescents under my eyes, the line of stitches running across my brow, the split lip, still swollen and raw.

"What the fuck...?"

His words are barely a breath as he takes a cautious step forward. His hand slowly reaches toward my chin to tip my face up to his, causing my hood to slip off my head.

I back up, stepping out of his reach and shake my head—my eyes pleading with him not to ask questions I'm not ready to answer. Silently begging him not to delve deeper into that particular black hole—the nightmare, still too fresh to relive the tale to someone new. Someone I don't even know.

Zavier exhales, long and slow, his pale brows drawing together, a deep line forming between them. His face hardens as his icy eyes darken further.

Something shifts between us. I don't understand it. I don't know him. But suddenly, the ground feels unsteady beneath my feet. I shake my head. Pinch my eyes closed.

Panic floods my veins as I wait for his reaction, the silence near deafening as the air grows heavy between us.

I should have been ready for this. Should have anticipated how someone might react to the way I look.

But I'm so tired. Tired from running—tired from everything that's led up to it.

Finally, with a quiet sigh, he stands back to his full height.

Sensing his movement, my eyes open and I take him in, cautiously watching... waiting—my breath held.

His face softens, his lips still pressed in a tight line, but he gestures me forward.

"Come on, Cole. We're nearly there."

He smiles, but his tone seems to have shifted, taking on a rougher edge.

But within moments, he's back—kind, chivalrous, the perfect English gentleman, guiding a stranger on her way.

His hand hovers just above the small of my back. I feel the heat of him—like waves, bridging the narrow space between us. An invisible force, gentle yet undeniable, urging me forward.

I suck in a deep breath in an effort to shake off the awkward exchange and the heaviness I imagine now hangs between us, letting him guide me to my destination.

Moments later, we emerge onto another lane, this one running alongside the most beautiful river I've ever seen.

Its waters glide smooth and clear, a quiet song against the hush of morning. Across its not-too-wide expanse, a dense forest rises—twin to the one behind the village. Shadowed, watching, as if holding hidden secrets within the darkened recesses of the trees.

A pub sits directly opposite, perched at the river's edge. A weathered jetty juts into the water, its flat-bottomed boat tethered by a cable hooked to a post on our side.

Zavier follows my stare.

"That's the Wye Inn, one of our locals. Greg, the landlord, usually sends one of his staff out to man the boat, ferrying the good folk of Verdon to and from his fine establishment. Best brews in the village, if you ask me."

I smile, a little bit of the weight lifting off my chest as I envision riding the boat across the river, the cool breeze lifting the hair from my face as it glides across the water.

Everything here feels so different from living in the city.

It's more similar to the gentle countryside around Greenwich, Connecticut, where we had lived before his work took us across the ocean to London.

The woods here exude an ancient presence, dark and foreboding to the unwary traveler. The dense canopy of regimented evergreens stands sentinel over the valley, punctuated by clusters of oak, beech, and chestnut, their cloud-like foliage softening the rigid ranks of pine. Below, the Wye river carves its way through the land, the village nestled against its banks like a secret kept by the trees.

The only broad sweep of grassland visible stretches toward the grand manor I'd noticed earlier. It sits perched halfway up the hill, gazing down over the village—larger than any building I've ever seen.

I even wonder if it could perhaps rival Buckingham Palace. Its two wings extend like arms, embracing the landscape, while sunlight gleams off countless windows speckling its façade. Even at this distance, the place commands attention.

As my gaze lingers, I imagine the owner standing at one of those windows, watching—his eyes meeting mine across the parkland.

A soft chill slides up my spine, feather-light, almost like the breath of a ghost. The sensation is fleeting but leaves an impression, a whisper of something unseen.

I wonder absently who might live in such a vast estate, but before I can dwell on it, Zavier speaks, his voice firm, pulling my attention back across the water.

"You're also looking into Wales," he points out.

I knew we were near the border, but I hadn't realized just how close. "Wow…" I whisper.

He beams at my reaction, his eyes alight with satisfaction that he's impressed me with that tidbit of information. Then, with easy confidence, he turns my attention back to the river, pointing out more features along its banks.

As his hand comes to rest lightly on my shoulder, something within me shifts—a quiet, subtle warmth that wasn't there before, and I feel my nerves truly settle for the first time since leaving the hospital that night.

He moves again, his hand dropping to the small of my back, guiding me and gently positioning me, until I'm facing a long, low building. I take it all in, its large window frames and door still bearing the scars of old, peeling green paint. The blue-gray sandstone of its walls looks weathered but strong—a silent keeper of history.

The grass in front has grown too long, wild as though the owner has run out of time or energy to tend to it. Several battered picnic benches dot the space, worn from years of use. Above the door, in faded lettering, I make out the name:

Allbright's Bookshop

All the nerves flood back and my eyes sting as relieved tears threaten to spill.
I've made it… I'm here.
Bracing myself, I exhale a long, shaky breath before finally taking another step forward.

The scream rips out of me before I can stop it, when a massive, gray-brown form bursts from the tall grass. I stumble backward—straight into Zavier's hard chest.

Everything crashes back into me at once. Panic as Zavier's large hands grip my shoulders causes my fear to overtake me and I scream again. Sheer terror grips me and I feel trapped until the sudden awareness of my body being pressed against his hits.

He pulls me tightly to him, the smell of freshly tilled earth warmed by sunlight fills my nose and his large arms hold me close as he lowers his head to my ear.

"Easy now... you don't want to get too close to old Hannah," he murmurs, the heat of his breath ghosting against my ear, causing a warm shiver to trail down my spine.

His voice is edged with warning, laced with a bit of amusement, his tone teasing as the tip of his nose trails along my cheek.

"She's a crafty old bugger and more likely to bite you than not."

I force myself to look away from Zavier to take in the braying beast before me.

The donkey stares back.

She shakes her short mane, stomps her front hoof and chuffs out a short breath, studying me–her gaze taking me in with a sharpness of something older than time.

I can't put my finger on it, but there's something familiar about her—the way she stands, the weight of her gaze, the stoic and quiet strength of her presence.

Like the horses at the farm where I grew up. Especially my sweet Sundance—forever my protector—keeping me safe as I hid in his stall, until I had no choice but to return home again.

The familiar comfort of her stare calls to me and, ignoring Zavier's warning, I move out of his hold and step toward her, slowly reaching out my hand.

Hannah sniffs at my palm, her warm breath curling against my skin. Her wise eyes hold mine—searching, understanding. A kindred spirit recognizing another who's been forgotten.

Her soft, warm muzzle draws me in further.

"I'm sorry I don't have anything for you to eat," I whisper as she roots around my hand.

Emboldened, I step closer, pressing my forehead against her cheek.

"Er... Cole..."

I had almost forgotten Zavier was still here. Had almost let myself be here. His voice, once confident, is hesitant now.

"She bites..."

"Oh, tosh!"

The new voice jolts me, startling Hannah too. She stomps, snapping her head back and letting out a braying protest. I force myself to channel the calm I felt only moments ago—sending it back to her as I grip her again to stroke a gentle hand between her eyes.

"Zavier Johnson, you know Hannah only nips the badduns!"

A melodic laugh dances after her words, blending with the river's song. Hannah instantly settles, her twitching muscles relaxing beneath my arm.

"Kya," Zavier mutters, shifting his feet as I curl my arm under Hannah's neck.

"This is Cole Baker. Found her wandering the High Street looking for Jesse's shop."

"And you just had to be the prince in shining armor to rescue the poor damsel in distress?" She drawls, rolling her eyes to the clouds.

She's a beautiful lady, her skin glowing golden—like rich Demerara sugar, the kind my mother used to spoon into her coffee, as we would sit on the patio, on the days when my father was away, quietly soaking up the peaceful morning sunshine.

A bright, billowing skirt swirls around her legs—blues and purples as deep as twilight, splashed with hints of bright pink. Her feet are clad in Grecian sandals, grounding her ethereal presence. She looks otherworldly, her long, gleaming brown hair cascading down her back like silky molten chocolate, framing a face illuminated by wide, vibrant amber eyes, that seem to hold a smile within them.

I feel all too aware of her eyes on me, knowing she's looking at my blackened eyes, the scrapes and bruises on my face. No longer hidden by my hood, they're now on full display in the bright light of the morning sun.

My clothing too...I realize I must look like an absolute mess—*He would never have let me leave the house like this*—dressed in two-day-old clothes, stained and worn. My face, bare of makeup, my auburn hair hanging limply in a loose ponytail over my shoulder.

I should care.

I just don't know what caring is supposed to feel like anymore. Nor do I have the energy to pretend.

Still, Jesse Allbright deserves better than this version of me.

Swallowing my nerves, I lift my eyes back to her face. I steel myself to ask if there's somewhere I might be able to freshen up before meeting my supposed relative.

But before I get the chance, she's already rummaging through her patch-work bag, fingers closing around a set of keys.

"You can bugger off now, Zavier," she says, striding toward the bookshop's doors. "I'll take it from here."

Zavier's hesitation is palpable, his mouth opening like he's about to argue her dismissal. But one sharp look from her has him snapping his mouth shut, silencing any further discussion on the subject.

"Come with me, *Cole,* is it?" she says, pushing open the door.

I gulp, swallowing down the fresh wave of nerves bubbling inside me.

"Er... yes, thanks."

I pat Hannah's nose once more, then turn back toward Zavier to thank him for his help in finding the bookshop.

His eyes are on Kya, his brows pinched, lips pressed into a thin line. I can see he really doesn't want to *'bugger off'* as she had so eloquently put it, but when he sees my attention is back on him, his kind smile returns.

"Thank you for your help, Zavier. It was very nice to meet you." I smile back, giving him a timid wave.

His replying grin is beaming, his dimples going deep on both sides. He winks, his blue eyes sparkling in the sun. My heart pounds as I feel a rush of heat to my cheeks, my face flushing. It's been years since any man has dared to show me any kindness, let alone... *is he flirting with me?*

My eyes quickly pull to the ground, heat rushing up my neck to pinken my cheeks, a shy smile tugging at the corners of my mouth but it drops quickly as I bat away the thought.

I know not all men are like *him.* I can't even bring myself to think about the past few days, or years for that matter—the pain, the hurt, is all still too raw. But there's no way this stranger is flirting with me... especially in my current state.

I lift my eyes just as Zavier turns back toward the alleyway, Hannah braying after him loudly.

I watch him walk away, admiring the way the muscles of his broad back shift under his shirt, his thick arms swinging loosely at his sides, before turning back toward the bookshop. Kya waits, patiently holding the door open with a smile.

My grandfather's bookshop.

I wonder what he'll think of me.

Will he like me?

Will I be enough?

Gathering up a final wave of courage, I draw in a deep breath and step past her into the darkened space.

Dim light filters through the shop, but the scent of dust and old books hits me full force.

The air carries the weight of something once treasured, something sacred—but left to ruin, like the temples of Athens or the palaces of long-dead kings. A large, dark wood desk looms to my left, an old cash register resting on its surface, paper ledgers stacked haphazardly beside it. Rows of bookshelves stretch ahead, half-empty, cobwebbed, forgotten.

A sunroom sits tucked at the back—a remnant of what was once a small café. China cups still rest in saucers. Metal display stands—now bare, once having held scones, cream, jelly, delicate cakes—all coated with a fine layer of dust.

I take it all in envisioning it as it may have once been. If I close my eyes, I can almost smell the Earl Grey tea, the rich scent of freshly brewed coffee and pastries, baked just that morning, rising like a memory. The fragrance lifting the spirits of those who had once stepped through these doors, welcoming them in to search for just the right book.

The rhythmic tapping of short, painted nails against wood shakes me from my daydream.

"*Cole Baker*, you say?"

Kya's voice is kind, but wary. She watches me as though she can see through me.

"And how is it that you know Jesse?"

Trying to still the tremor in my hands, I pull open my bag, fingers curling around the bundle of letters—the ones our maid hid from him. Then, from my pocket, I pull the last one. The letter asking me to visit. It's dated six months ago.

Six months ago, I was still a prisoner.

It took near death to finally give me the opportunity to be free—though Kya doesn't need to know that.

"I believe Jesse was my grandfather," I begin, cursing the timid shake in my voice. "My mother was Maryanne Allbright."

Kya sucks her teeth. Her fingers resume their tapping.

I slide the last letter toward her—the one with spidery handwriting barely visible now, the ink bleeding having been washed away by rain—or tears. I no longer know which.

"That's funny," Kya murmurs skeptically as her fingers smooth down the crumpled edges of the envelope.

"Just before he passed away, Jesse spoke about a granddaughter. An American."

I can see Kya's lips moving, her words forming shapes I can't decipher. The blood rushing in my ears drowns out everything else—a relentless roar that swallows the world whole.

My last hope—Jesse, my grandfather—*dead?* That's when I feel it—the tiny flicker, the spark that drove me across the country—extinguished, snuffed out, by her words.

How can this be?

My heart pounds—wild, erratic—like a drummer's sticks hammering out a relentless staccato, smashing against my ribs.

I grip numbly at the side of a nearby bookshelf, the edges of my vision blurring as my head swims. The sound of her voice becomes muted—turning to the sound of an ebbing echo.

Through the chaos, her final words hang in the air before me.

I see the shift in her face.

The way her brow lifts—curious at first—before her eyes narrow. Welcoming, then wary. Hope faltering, giving way to unease.

"And her name wasn't Cole Baker."

As the last words fall from her lips, the world tilts.

The floor rushes up to meet me moments before everything goes dark.

Chapter 4

Cole

"Nicole!"

Crouched inside the barn, I duck down behind a bale of hay, praying the sounds of the horses muffles my pounding heartbeat. I sit in wait, hoping that maybe—just maybe—this will be the time he'll stop looking. This time he'll give up his hunt for me.

"Nicole!"

I can always tell by the tone of his voice when he's been hitting the whiskey again. Irrational anger mixed with a slight slur—the slur always more pronounced the more liquor he's swallowed down—warning me that the beatings are coming... again.

This is why I hide.

For some reason, he always sets his sights on me, and he RARELY gives up the chase.

His bulking shadow stretches across the dust lined stalls in the fading afternoon sun, making his presence feel even larger as he rounds the corner. The smell of his tobacco hits me first, just before his staggering form comes into view.

I tuck myself back into the corner as far as I can, trying to make myself smaller... wishing I could be invisible—or maybe I could just disappear altogether...

Sundance lets out a loud whinny, chuffing and clamoring to the side as the stall door swings open, the earth kicking up around me as I scramble to get away. But his hand—big, unyielding—snatches the back of my t-shirt, the fabric tearing as he yanks me to my feet.

Spinning me to face him, he blows a large plume of thick cigar smoke into my face, the smell mixing with the acrid stench of the liquor.

"Gotcha you fucking brat! Thought you could hide from me huh? Wrong again, little slut..."

I open my mouth to scream but...

"Cole?"

My father's lips move, but a soft, female voice comes from his mouth.

Then there's the touch of a gentle hand, lightly tapping my cheek.

"Cole? Wake up, hun."

The stranger's voice cuts through the vacant scream that never quite leaves my throat in my dreams, shifting my awareness back to here... now.

"Cole?"

I flinch as the hand lightly pats my cheek again, my eyes fluttering open. I jolt as my hazy vision lands on wide, concerned amber eyes staring back at me.

"There you are."

Kya breathes out a sigh of relief. Her hand grips mine, her thumb softly stroking across my knuckles as she gently eases me back into reality.

Her brows pull tight as her eyes sweep over me, assessing me.

The weight of her stare feels heavy, lingering a bit too long on the marks on my face.

She gently squeezes my hand, before gracefully rising up. I watch her as she moves toward her bag on the desk.

I draw in a deep breath, the scent of old paper and aged wood filling my senses. I cringe, every muscle aching when I try to straighten. Kya kneels back down beside me, helping me sit up, easing me back against the counter. Once I'm settled, she presses a cool bottle into my hand.

"Here, drink this."

Her voice is a gentle, coaxing command.

Years of conditioning to do as I'm told without question, I take the bottle, tipping it up.

"When was the last time you ate anything?"

I blink dumbly up at her, unsure how to answer her unintentionally loaded question. I wonder if she'd count the single spoonful of soup I managed to swallow before my world almost ended?

Her brow furrows deeper and she scowls, her lips pulling into a tight, thin line when I don't answer her, offering her a small shrug instead.

"Right then." She says, pushing to her feet.

There's no question, Kya is a person of action.

"Drink some water, and we'll find you something to eat. Then we're going to have a talk."

She moves across the shop like a dancer, fluid, graceful, utterly at ease in this forgotten space, her colorful skirt swirling around her as she walks. I notice her natural curves, the strength in her posture, the richness of her dark skin—it only makes me more aware of my own frailty.

The memory of our conversation comes back to me then and the realization hits me like a punch to the stomach.

My gut twists forcefully when the reality of my situation floods me. The last hope I'd been clinging onto... the one person who I'd come here to find... *is dead.*

Which means I came all this way for nothing...

There's no one here...

Nothing left for me here.

No one is going to save me...

I curse my naivete for letting myself believe I would be welcomed with open arms. Curse myself for daring to hope there might be something for me here. Somewhere I would be safe... *somewhere he wouldn't find me.*

Seeing the way Kya watches me from the corner of her eye, untrusting, guarded, I curse my paranoia too. I've given her no reason to trust me, no reason to believe me having given a false name. But I couldn't take the chance... I had to do it.

Because if he finds me here, not only will he drag me back to London like he has so many times before, back to his idea of luxury—*back to my personal hell*—but this time, there's no question, it will be worse.

I grab my bag and pull it close, throwing the zipper open to check the small amount of cash I've been squirreling away for the past year, my fingers skimming over the reassuring edges of the bank card inside the pocket.

A flurry of thoughts whirl through my mind, a tornado of ideas brewing as I work to come up with a new plan.

Maybe there's enough left to get me somewhere else.

Enough to find room and board for a few weeks.

And then, maybe I can find a job.

And then maybe I can...

"Cole?"

Her voice cuts through my spiral, once again snapping me back to reality.

She's crouched in front of me, her amber eyes warmer now.

"Don't worry, they're right here, hun." She holds Jesse's letters out to me, assuming that's what I had been furiously hunting for in my bag.

I take them from her, but the envelopes tremble as they transfer to my grip. I cram them into my bag to try to hide the shake in my hands.

She lets out a soft sigh and stands again, her patchwork bag slung across her shoulder. Beside her is a bucket filled with some sort of animal feed.

I blink a few times, realizing how stupid I must look, sitting on the floor, staring dumbly up at her, my fingers clutching onto my bag in a death grip.

She smiles—light catching the ring in her nose, the corners of her eyes crinkling.

"Come on."

She reaches for me and I grasp her hands, letting her pull me up.

I wobble slightly, a fresh wave of dizziness washing over me as I stand and grip her a little tighter to try to hold myself upright.

"Steady," she coos, bracing me until I'm stable enough to move on. She watches me like I'm fragile.

I guess I am.

Cupping my elbow, she guides me out of the bookshop, locking up behind us before easing me onto one of the benches outside.

Hannah trots over, her nose quickly burrowing down into the bucket, greedily eating the feed Kya had carried out for her.

She laughs softly, stroking the donkey's coarse fur and, for whatever reason, watching her warms something in me. Something small. Something long frozen. Pushing gently against the shard wedged in my chest for so many years.

Hannah's long neck dips as Kya lowers the bucket, ruffling the short black hairs of her mane and patting her on the neck before turning back to me.

In the distance, church bells ring out, their peals stretching across the village, reverberating over the river before bouncing back toward us. I stare off into the distance, letting the peaceful swell of each toll wash over me, but then my chest squeezes.

I don't belong here. I have to figure out where to go next.

"You do that a lot, don't you?"

Her voice pulls me out of the thought, and there's a hint of amusement there. I look up at her soft smile and blink.

"Do what?"

"Sort of..." She waves a hand vaguely in front of her face. "Zone out. Like your mind seems to constantly be elsewhere."

Immediately, guilt creeps in—tight, familiar.

Yep... I've done it again.

"I'm sorry," I whisper, my eyes dropping, avoiding her gaze. My fingers absently trace the strap of my bag on my lap, studiously avoiding the reprimand I'm sure is coming.

"Someone sure did a number on you, didn't they, honey?"

I shudder as her fingers graze my shoulder.

She hesitates, her hand hovering just above me, then settles her fingers lightly there again before giving me a gentle squeeze. The warmth of her soft touch grounds me.

"Come on, hun. It's not far."

I let her lead me away, past Hannah, her tail swishing as she finishes her breakfast—heedless now of our departure.

We follow the lane beside the Wye toward the alleyway Zavier led me through earlier. Before long, we stop at one of the terraced houses at the mouth of the lane. Only now do I notice the sign hanging above it, *Lover's Lane.*

Adorable, quaint.

I feel the corner of my mouth lift and shake my head at myself for thinking it had seemed so daunting earlier.

Kya steps up a few stone stairs, plants in colorful pots decorating each one. Their summer blooms now faded, dulled by the creeping grasp of the encroaching fall season.

The front door is painted a bright, welcoming yellow and the earthy scent of patchouli wafts out as she pushes it open.

"Come on in."

Like its owner, the house is practical but vibrant. Color spills across every surface—mismatched furnishings, somehow working harmoniously together. Plants are everywhere—a towering cheese plant dominates one corner of the hall, guiding the eye up a long flight of stairs. Rainbowed sunlight plays on the wall through a stained-glass window overlooking the river, scattering jewel-toned reflections throughout the space.

Kya stops to hang up her bag and nods toward the back of the house, directing me toward the space behind the stairs, where another doorway opens into a rustic kitchen. Again, nothing matches—yet somehow everything fits.

I step toward the window behind the sink, my gaze drawn to the walled yard beyond. Plants sleep beneath autumn's chill, waiting for the return of spring. Water trickles constantly somewhere, a soft, soothing sound. I scan the area until I spot a raised pond, tucked beside a tiny greenhouse.

I'm so entranced, I don't notice the other inhabitant of the house until a cold, wet nose presses against my leg—followed swiftly by a heavy paw. I jump, startled at first, but then laugh, smiling down at the little face looking up at me.

"Grumbl!"

Kya rushes forward, looping her fingers through the collar of the puppy. He stares up at me, brown eyes wide beneath a soft, squishy face, his whole body wiggling with excitement.

I drop to my knees beside him and offer my fingers for him to sniff.

"It's okay," I giggle as the tiny whiskers on his lips tickle the palm of my hand. "I love dogs..."

Grumbl, ignoring Kya's hold, pushes closer, placing a golden-tipped paw on my arm, then rests heavily against me, groaning in bliss as I scratch the many wrinkles lining his chin.

"Well, I think you have an admirer!" Kya laughs, leaning back, watching her puppy succumb to my touch.

I giggle as he rolls to his side, allowing me better access to his round belly.

"I always wanted a dog, but...," I shrug, then pause.

Kya lets me trail off, but I can feel the weight of her curiosity as she watches me.

"Grumbl is three months old—so he's clearly still learning his manners." She chuckles, ruffling the folds of his head.

Where his paws are golden, his back and head are a deep, rich chocolate and his chin and belly are white as he rolls even further onto his side, begging for more scratches.

He groans loudly again, eyes fluttering shut, his tongue lolling out the side of his wide mouth. Like Hannah, his innocent presence does more to warm my heart than Kya could possibly know.

My chest tightens as my inner thoughts return to needle at me...

Don't get attached... You won't be staying.

"Would you like a cup of tea?"

My face must twist—my opinion of British tea well past redemption.

Taking one look at my face, she smirks. "I'll take that as a no."

She considers me for a minute, then her face brightens. "I could make you some fresh coffee, if you prefer?"

My lips pull into the first real smile I've felt in days. "That would be amazing! Yes, please... if it's not too much trouble. Milk, no sugar."

"Okay, hun." Her smile is soft, her tone gentle as she slides the bowl of sugar beside me. "I'll just leave this here for you—in case you change your mind." She taps her finger, pausing a moment, considering her next words.

"I know it's none of my business, but if I had to take a guess, it seems to me a spoonful of sugar might be exactly what you need right now." She gives me a wink before spinning back to the refrigerator.

"Now for some food. Would beans on toast be alright?"

Although I've heard of this British 'delicacy,' I've never tried it before.

Kya grins, amused by my attempts to school my features, unsure of how to respond.

But of course, that's when my stomach chooses to rumble loudly, earning me a genuine laugh from her.

"Yes, please..." I say with a guilty smile, my cheeks turning pink.

I give Grumbl one last scratch and follow her to the island, propping myself onto one of the colorful stools.

I sigh inwardly as I watch her pull out a french press and a bag of fresh coffee from the fridge. Coffee was the one bit of pleasure I gleaned from life every day. The one thing that brought me a modicum of warmth and comfort. The sight of it now, triggering a near Pavlovian response, my body responding of its own accord, relaxing into the fragrance instantly.

"What type of dog is Grumbl?" I ask, watching him waddle to his bed, circling three times before flopping down with a heavy sigh, eyes still fixed on us.

"English Bulldog."

Kya glances toward him, her gaze warming as a long pink tongue flashes out, licks his nose, then hangs there—neither fully inside nor out, making us both laugh.

"The absolute love of my life."

I accept the hot mug of coffee, stirring in a spoonful of sugar. She pops two thick slices of buttered toast onto a plate, just as the microwave pings. She pulls out a small container, steam wafting out as she lifts the lid. The smell of the hot food hits me and my mouth instantly waters.

I watch curiously as she tilts the container, sending glossy orange beans cascading over the toast, thick soupy liquid pooling at the edges.

I grip my knife and fork, not knowing quite what to expect, but my empty stomach growls, nonetheless.

"Wait! Wait!" Kya holds out a hand over my plate then rushes back to the fridge to pull out a large slab of yellow cheese before spinning to grab a small brown bottle from the cupboard.

"You gotta have some cheddar and Worcestershire sauce on it! Trust me—it completes the dish!"

I watch as she grates the cheese with quick, practiced strokes, then dabs a few drops of watery, brown sauce over the beans. She steps back, proudly admiring the plate before me.

"Tuck in, hun." She watches me, sipping from her milky mug of tea.

I lift a forkful, making sure to get a little bit of everything and tentatively take a bite.

The tangy flavor of the Worcestershire sauce bursts across my tongue first—sharp and bright, sending the tomato flavor of the sauce coating the beans into a deeper embrace with my tastebuds.

The beans themselves are unexpectedly perfect. Firm with just enough bite, when I had feared they would be mushy and soft.

Admittedly, I had always imagined it would be oddly textured, the flavor overall lifeless and bland. The bread is thick and fresh, toasted to perfection. Its soft center, balancing with the salt of the butter and cheese flawlessly.

If I had any idea this particular recipe could taste this good, I might have tried to smuggle cans of beans into the apartment in London years ago.

Kya smiles, seemingly pleased that I'm eating with such enthusiasm, clearing my plate faster than I'd even thought possible.

It's not until I lift the final bite to my mouth, shamelessly licking the last of the sauce from my knife and fork, that I feel her gaze on me, quietly waiting, her smile soft and satisfied at having her offered meal so well received.

"Feeling a bit better now?" She asks, reaching across the island to take my empty plate, moving it over to the sink to wash it off.

"Much, thank you!" I say, swiping my napkin across my lips.

I feel her eyes on me, assessing me as she returns to her seat, picking up her mug again to take another sip of her tea. It's clear she's trying to work out the truth of who I really am—why I have Jesse's letters addressed to someone she believes is not me and why I look the way I do.

"My name," I begin, sitting back in my seat a bit, bracing myself against how this is going to go, "is Nicole Allbright."

My stomach clenches, the lie tasting bitter on my tongue, but I'm too far in to stop now, so I continue to spin my web of deception.

"Maryanne Allbright was my mother. Tex Baker, my father."

Kya's eyes narrow, studying me. "So why did you tell Zavier your name was Cole Baker then?"

My throat tightens and my eyes sting—the truth still too painful, too new and far too dangerous to let loose into the world.

Don't cry, Cole. Keep it together and don't fucking cry.

But as hard as I fight against it, my chin wobbles and my vision blurs, unbidden tears threatening to spill against my best efforts.

Kya studies me, her eyes taking on a knowing look and shakes her head, seeming to understand the *something* that needs to remain unspoken between us. A silent acknowledgment that even though she's been kind, she's a stranger to me and trust isn't blindly given. It's earned.

Truthfully, I'm not sure I have enough left in me to offer to anyone anymore.

"Okay, a story for another time then," her tone is comforting, as she reaches across the island, placing her hand over my tight fist, giving it a reassuring squeeze.

I offer her a watery smile, grateful that she's letting the question drop.

"I was only now able to come visit Jesse—to find out if my mother was his daughter. To see if I really have family here. If I ever did." I blow out a slow breath. "But I guess that's all moot now, huh?"

"Maybe," she mutters. "Maybe not."

She pushes herself back from the bar, tapping her nails against the surface—just as she had done at the bookshop.

"Do you have any ID with your name on it?"

I nod. My bag contains the only tidbits of the real me. My birth certificate and passport, both of which still show my maiden name and, while I have my marriage certificate tucked away deep inside a hidden pocket in my backpack, I certainly don't plan on letting anyone see that. It's the one thing I took with me that reveals the name I've lived by for the past ten years.

"Good."

A loud rap sounds at the front door, followed by a deep voice calling Kya's name. A low chuckle follows as the puppy scrambles awkwardly from his bed and waddles out to greet him, his stumpy tail wagging hard enough to shake his entire backside.

The sudden intrusion into this brittle bit of trust Kya's managed to instill in me, shatters my calm.

I sit bolt upright, every muscle in my body coiled like a spring, taut and ready to snap, my fight or flight instinct set firmly to flight.

My sudden tension draws Kya's focus away from her puppy, away from the door leading to the hallway, and squarely back onto me.

Putting herself between me and the door, she raises her hands, slow, deliberate—like someone approaching a wild animal caught in a trap. Dangerous. Wounded. Likely to lash out.

"Oh God, Cole! Please don't be mad," her voice soft as she tries to calm me when she sees the color drain from my face. "but I called a friend. A solicitor... a lawyer, of sorts. He's someone who can explain things to you better than I ever could."

"Explain what? And when? When the hell did you call him?"

The barrage of questions spill out in a rush, my breathing ragged and wheezing, my throat growing too tight as panic sets in fully.

Kya cringes, her face twisted into a remorseful grimace.

"When you passed out in the bookshop." She keeps her tone low, careful and measured. Her eyes track me, noting my fraying nerves as I unravel in front of her.

"Please understand, Jesse and Margaret were very dear to me and were much-loved members of our community. When you told me your name and it wasn't who he had told me to expect... well, I just needed to make sure you weren't going to trample all over his and Margaret's memories..."

The front door shuts firmly behind the newcomer. The sound cracks through the house like a gunshot and panic detonates in my chest.

I lurch off the stool and grab my bag, sweeping the letters into it—my pulse pounding as I push past her and dart toward the door.

"Why would you do that?" Sharp and frantic, my words rip out of me.

All her prior kindness forgotten, I feel nothing but terror and betrayal.

My mind is spinning...

I can't think straight...

I have to leave.

Coming here was a mistake.

He'll find me now...

He always finds me.

But, moving fast, she steps in front of me again, blocking my path, her hands still raised.

"Whoa—Cole! Wait! Please, just calm down and wait just a minute!"

"I... I'm sorry... I can't! Please, you don't understand... I have to get out of here! I have to go!"

Tears spill down my cheeks as panic coils tightly in my chest, threatening to choke me. I shove past her, only to collide with a wall of solid muscle.

Huge hands brace my shoulders, steadying me on my feet, while I stand frozen in place, blinking up at the brick wall of a man I just slammed into.

He's so tall... easily six feet or more—his broad body taking up nearly the entire width of the entry way. My eyes track up his chest, over the corded muscles in his neck and land on a grin—brilliant and white, smiling down at me.

I stare dumbly up at him, my mouth going completely dry.

"Whoa! Steady on! You alright there, Red?" he says, his voice deep, rich and warm, his gentle smile lighting up his entire face.

Holy hell... he looks like he walked straight off the cover of GQ magazine.

"S-s-sorry..." I croak out, slipping my shoulders out of his grip.

"Brick!" Kya shouts from behind me. "Don't let her get by you! And for God sake, will ya tell her that you're not some mountain gorilla intent on harming her!"

Brick raises his hands—palms up in mock surrender.

Who is Kya kidding? There's literally no way I could get past him in this narrow hallway.

"I am not some mountain gorilla intent on harming you," he says flatly, rolling his eyes at Kya.

His accent is refined—none of the West Country inflections I've heard in Kya and Zavier's voices. Like he went to school with royalty or something.

Feeling like a cornered animal, I stumble backward, white-knuckling the strap on my bag, my heart hammering in my chest.

He takes a cautious step toward me, his hands still held up, a silent vow of submission.

"My name is Thaddeus Brickton, the Third, but you can call me Brick. That's what my friends call me."

He reaches a hand out, his eyes locked on mine, watching me... waiting.

When all I can do is pinball my eyes between his face and his hand, gripping the strap of my bag as if it's the only thing keeping me tethered to this spot, he pulls it back and tucks it into his pocket. His smile never wavers. Instead, he offers me a small nod.

I back up a few more steps until I'm standing beside Kya, studying him as he makes his way into the room.

He doesn't look like a lawyer, or a *solicitor*—whatever the hell Kya had called him.

He's dressed in jeans, a red and white sports shirt emblazoned with a logo that looks like a lion in a shield. The bold lettering is, what I can only assume is a team name—*Gloucester Rugby*. The fabric is worn, the colors faded, like it's been through a hundred matches and a thousand arguments. He's built like someone who might play the offensive line in football.

"You...umm...," I swallow hard against the lump in my throat, "Sorry, but you don't look like a lawyer."

His lips pull into a smooth, practiced smile.

"Well, I'm only a lawyer... *sometimes*. As a solicitor, I don't spend a lot of time in court, so I don't really need to dress the part. Which is nice because I *really* hate suits." He tips his head, giving me a wink. His chuckle is warm and a bit of my tension ebbs away at the sound.

"Mostly, I'm here as a friend and I just want to help."

Brick casually steps further into the room, comfortable in the space. He runs a big hand through his sandy brown hair, the locks falling perfectly back into place. A glint of sunlight catches on a watch—a sleek, expensive contrast to the battered sports shirt.

"And," he continues, "I have the last will and testament of Jesse and Margaret Allbright."

My breath catches.

"If you are, in fact, their granddaughter, then we have a lot to discuss."

Chapter 5

Rogan

Urrgh! I want to stretch so badly. After another night of very little sleep—albeit for mostly very enjoyable reasons—my eyes drift down the length of the body draped over me, her long, supple legs tangled with mine and the bedsheets.

If I could just get out from under her, I could sneak to the shower without waking *Betty? No... Belinda...? or was it Beatrix? Bloody hell, I swear it was something beginning with B!*

Or maybe it was P?

Brick would be laughing his arse off right now if he knew the predicament I'd landed myself in... *again.*

Then again, even he—with that infuriating eidetic memory—might struggle to recall the name of whichever model had been draped over his arm at last night's soirée, considering the number of shots he sent down his throat.

Brittany—*or maybe it was Penelope*—moans softly, shifting in her sleep. She moves just enough to give me space to maneuver out from under her.

I watch her as I slowly, carefully slip out of the bed, praying she doesn't wake up. She may have been appealing last night—her skin tight red dress clinging to every curve of her overly curated body, her oversized, fake breasts barely concealed behind the thin fabric.

But now that I've fucked her out of my system, I'm just not interested anymore. All I really want now is for her to leave, so I can *try* and get some sleep before I have to return to tackling the affairs of the village below me.

Not wanting to chance making too much noise, I don't bother to dress as I stride to one of the large floor-to-ceiling windows and gaze out across the property.

Verdon Manor—once the country home of a long-dead ancestor and now our family's main residence—is nestled into the side of the hill. Below, like a silver snake, the River Wye meanders—or rages when the rains are heavy in the Welsh mountains.

The village, named after that very ancestor, lies alongside it.

Across the parkland, where the estate sheep are scattered like little clouds, I can just make out the pub on the far bank, the small ferry docked there, set to shuttle people back and forth throughout the day, and the blasted bookshop.

My hands planted on either side of the window frame, unashamed of my nakedness, my gaze zeros in on the scene below.

Old Allbright was never going to relinquish his lease on the bookshop to me—no matter how much money I threw at him or how many times I promised him a comfortable life in the retirement home, all expenses paid. That bookshop is an untapped goldmine if used for the right purpose—the perfect place for intrepid adventurers to hire a canoe or even to rent or purchase equipment for rock climbing or camping.

As a mere bookshop, it's wasted. As a business that genuinely utilized the resources around it, it would surely bring in a flood of adrenaline junkies, catering to people who would be rich enough—*or stupid enough*—to part with their money in search of the ultimate rush.

I have less than a week to wait. If the will isn't contested, then I'll finally be able to stake my claim.

Just a handful of days—victory is so close, I can almost taste it, feel it settling on my tongue like rich wine, intoxicating with possibility.

Brick, acting as solicitor for the Allbrights, has assured me it will be smooth sailing. And I believe him. He's been like a brother to me for so long, I completely trust him.

He always has my back—since our Eton days, through the summers he spent with me here at the Manor. His presence here helped me to sidestep more than a few of the punishments my father so eagerly doled out after my older brother was killed in action.

Then came our own stint in the Army—Brick at my side, a Lieutenant to my Captain. Always there, pulling me out of trouble.

Or, more likely, throwing himself straight into it with me.

It's as I'm considering all this that I see a tall man, dressed in denim and plaid, a mop of shaggy blond hair, walking toward the shop.

Zavier—*the piece of shite. A constant thorn in my side.*

Anger and frustration churn deep within me and my fists clench. The world would be a far better place without the blight of this smarmy git and his constant, incessant interfering.

The familiar pain of yet another tension headache stabs at the back of my eyes when my jaw pops from how hard I'm grinding my teeth.

As he approaches the bookshop, I realize he's not alone when another figure captures my attention. Squinting, I see there's a diminutive figure trailing a few paces behind him. I step closer to the window, my breath blooming against the glass, momentarily clouding my view.

When the mist from my breath clears, I refocus my attention fully on her, noting the way she holds herself—arms locked tightly across her body, as if bracing against the world. Head held low, her bag clutched tightly to her side. Bright auburn hair catches the sunlight like a burning ember, setting her apart.

No one in the village has hair like that.

Zavier looks to be giving her a tour of the area, his arm raised as he points to the features of the landscape. She turns as he points, surveying the scene—the river, the bookshop, the pub. But when her gaze lands on the Manor, her attention freezes, her head tilting upward toward the window where I'm standing.

A chill creeps along my spine. There's no way she can see me—not through the glare of the autumn sun streaking across the window panes. Not from this distance.

But I swear I feel her eyes on me and my breath catches in my throat.

A powerful sense of curiosity overtakes me and I begin to wonder about this woman.

What color her eyes might be...

What her hair might feel like, gripped in my fist...

How her lips might taste as I suck them between my teeth...

I have a sudden urge to tug her arms away from her own cautious embrace, ease them over my shoulders, then press the warmth of my body against her instead.

My pulse kicks at the thought of our eyes locking, even though I know—*I know*—she can't see me.

As unbidden, salacious thoughts begin to roll through my mind, I move even closer to the window, my attention fully locked on this newcomer... this woman who I can barely see from this distance and my cock twitches.

Long fingers slide around my waist and trace their way up my abs, effectively pulling me away from the mesmerizing stranger's gaze.

I feel my muscles clench involuntarily as she follows the patterns of the tattoos that cover my chest and shoulders. Geometric shapes and Celtic symbols, concealing the worst of the scars my body has borne. Her nails, painted a deep scarlet, ending in vicious tips, rake along my skin as her full lips trace kisses across my back, along the scars that lie hidden there.

Last night, her touch was a turn on, but now that I've fucked her... now that I can clearly see the plasticity of her body in the cold light of day—her lips injected with fillers, her fake, oversized breasts, her facial features near unmoving from all the Botox treatments—have the opposite effect.

Her fingers trace down my body and I want to push her away, my body and mind both so goddamn tired.

My eyes flick back to the movement of the donkey recapturing my attention. My cock twitches again as the woman strokes her hand down the beast's face.

What would that hand feel like stroking me?

I blink as Kya appears, swiftly whisking the woman into the bookshop.

Zavier lingers at the closed door for what feels like an eternity. My jaw tightens painfully as I glare down at the idiot below, willing the fucker to just bugger off already. It's not until the donkey charges toward him, that he quickly turns, finally heading back in the direction of his farm.

That wanker's never been Hannah's biggest fan.

I exhale through my nose—long, slow, controlled—when the press of warmth behind me reminds me I'm not alone. She moves her hands further down, gripping my dick in her long fingers. She sighs loudly when my cock fails to respond to her touch.

Determined, she slithers around me, repositioning herself under my arms, pressing her too large breasts against my torso, rolling her hips into me. She pouts and lets out a breathy huff of annoyance when I stare blankly down at her.

Clearly not willing to give up on what she wants, she drops down my legs, settling onto her knees and cups me, squeezing my balls with an artful deftness, smiling as my body begins to betray me.

My hands open, fingers flexing, digging into the wood of the window frame as she slides my half-hardened cock into her mouth.

I close my eyes when my dick starts to respond to the wet heat of her mouth as it glides along my skin. She flicks the tip of her tongue along the slit of my now hardened cock, then licks along the thick veins of my shaft as she swallows me whole.

Moving in a long, slow, deliberate lick back to the crown, swirling her tongue only to take me deep down her throat once again. I can feel myself harden further as she works my length, her blue eyes watching me, pleased that she can tempt me, little knowing that it's not her I'm imagining, it isn't her lips I'm seeing wrapped around me.

I thread my fingers through her platinum hair, gripping it roughly and begin to thrust harder, the crown of my cock hitting the back of her throat, again and again. Tears roll down her cheeks as my pace turns punishing. Crushing my eyes shut and gritting my teeth, I tilt my head back—it's not her face I want to see. It's a fleeting glimpse, even from a distance, of the stranger entering the bookshop. It's auburn hair I see moving up and down as her mouth molds around me.

The vision sends a warm tingle across my spine and my balls tighten, my cock pulsing as I explode down her throat.

I grip her head tight and groan when I feel her throat working as she swallows every drop. The muscles of my ass clench tight and I shudder, the last waves of my climax rolling through me.

"Well, that's certainly one way to get her to stop fucking yapping." My bedroom door opens, Brick strolling in—clearly too comfortable in my space—laughing at the sight of my tense backside framed by the woman's clawed embrace.

"Thought you'd have been done by now, mate!" He continues laughing, his hands held up as if to shield his eyes from the sight.

I push the woman off and turn to face my oldest friend. I regard him with feigned annoyance raising a thick, dark eyebrow in a questioning arch.

Ignoring me completely, he saunters in, settling himself into one of the antique wingback armchairs flanking the fireplace. He helps himself to the bowl of fruit that sits on the coffee table, popping a couple of grapes into his mouth, his wicked smile taking in every detail.

"Are you going to put something on, or do I have to share my news with you stark bollock naked?" He laughs again, popping more grapes into his mouth.

"Dick head," I mutter as I retrieve the pants I'd worn the night before from the floor, pulling them on.

Berenice, *I think,* sighs again and moves back to the bed, tugging the sheet up and over her body, pouting in what I can only assume she considers an attractive pose. I move to the opposite chair, propping a bare foot up on the table, knocking the bowl of fruit aside as he reaches for more.

"Well?" I say, aware of my tone—I have no tolerance for my time being wasted, especially when I've had zero sleep for the past couple of days.

Brick's playful smirk stays in place but, accustomed to my moods, he gets on to his point, clearly able to tell my patience is nearing its limit.

"So, the divine Kya just called me."

He's harbored a quiet, lingering crush on her for years—ever since we shoved her into the Wye when we were teenagers. We were the *posh boys* from the big house, full of careless arrogance, tormenting the village kids because that's what was expected of us.

But in true Kya fashion, she hadn't played victim that day, nor a day in her life. She'd clambered out of the water in seconds—dripping wet and absolutely furious—and shoved him in with an almighty splash. The river had swallowed him, his gasp lost beneath the rippling current. But when he resurfaced, sputtering, wiping water from his eyes, he was already looking at her differently.

I don't think she knows the effect she has on him. Or on most men, for that matter. She moves through life unbothered, chatting to everyone and anyone, disarming them, charming them before moving on to the next visitor, the next group. Her new puppy trundling along in her wake, adding to her indefinable, pleasantly elusive charisma.

"And?" swirling my hand in a 'get on with it' motion, my tolerance fraying. Right now all I want is some peace and quiet. I need both Brick and this woman out of my room. Preferably out of my house.

"Annndddd...," he drags out, "someone has just turned up claiming to be the granddaughter of the Allbright's."

Heat flares in my chest, my temper rising before I can suppress it. The shock of his words must be etched across my face—plain, undeniable.

I lower my foot to the floor, straightening in my chair. Every muscle coils, rolling beneath my skin as I grind my molars.

I draw in a slow, deliberate breath, close my eyes, then exhale... long, slow, controlled. A low growl rolls through my chest. My breath brushes over my hands as I lean forward, twisting my neck until it cracks with an audible pop.

My eyes snap open, locking on to the coffee table.

The redhead I saw with the donkey—it must be her.

My eyes narrow as I consider what this might mean for my plans.

"But," Brick's calm interjection pulls me out of my spiraling thoughts. "She gave Kya a different name than what's listed on the will."

He shrugs, his confidence always at the forefront.

"Probably nothing to worry about, but I'll look into it further. It's entirely possible she's not related to them at all and this is just some big mix up."

He winks, his cocky smile returning as he reaches for the grapes again, plucking one from its stem then tossing it into his mouth with practiced ease.

But his eyes—the color of melting chocolate, eyes that can both disarm most women, and instill fear into the souls of the evilest of men—hold steady on me. Watching me. Reading me. Tracking whether I'm settled by his reassurance or if I'm about to erupt.

"Okay," I murmur, leaning back in the chair, a thumb absently dragging across my lower lip as I consider all the ways this could unfold.

I trust that he'll uncover the truth—he always does—and together we'll remove this nuisance before she can get in my way.

"When are you going to meet her?"

"Right now." He slips another grape between his teeth, biting down on it with a pop.

"Good. The sooner she's moved on, the better. Less than a week—that's all I bloody needed. We need to make this go away."

Brick rises from his chair, the muscles across his shoulders and arms testing the limits of that old rugby shirt he's constantly wearing. *He always was a bulky bastard.*

"I'll fill you in when I get back." Pausing, he casts a glance at my guest in the bed.

"Want me to show Bethany out?"

She's still pouting, but her eyes heat when she sees my attention shift back onto her. She lets the sheet slip from her fingers, the material sliding down her body to expose her bare breasts.

There's more than one way to relieve the excess tension coiling itself like a viper in my muscles from the gut punch of Brick's news.

I already know *Bethany* is more than willing to help work it out of my system.

Not breaking her gaze, I shake my head.

"Right, then! I'll leave you to it." Louder than necessary, Brick rises from his seat. He knows me well enough to predict exactly where my thoughts have gone. He strides out the door, closing it gently behind him.

I push myself up, stalking over to her like a predator. I keep my voice low, giving it a dangerous edge.

"Do you want to show me that you've been a good girl, Bethany?" I purr and her eyes heat further—a slow, devious smile spreading across her lips.

She nods, teasing the tip of her tongue along the sharp point of one long nail.

I step closer, unfastening my button and sliding down my zipper. I tug the sheet off her, exposing her fully. My eyes track down her naked form, taking in every inch of her bared to me. She spreads her legs wide, her pussy already wet and glistening—ready and waiting to be fucked.

"Lie back." I keep the tone of my voice low as I deepen it further, my intentions clear—I will be obeyed. She's quick to follow my commands.

I'll have her screaming my name before she leaves. Ruin her so no other man could ever satisfy her the way I can.

"Arms above your head." Again, she complies.

I reach in my pants and grip my cock, sliding my hand up and down my shaft, squeezing and stroking myself. She licks her lips and lets out a needy moan as she squirms on the bed and whimpers, watching as my dick stiffens in my hand, once more witnessing my size when I am fully erect. I smile wickedly.

She moves to sit up, reaching for me, but I step back and give her a warning look.

"Lie back." I repeat myself, "hands above your head."

She bites her lip, resuming the position as her legs squeeze together, hunting for the friction I know she needs.

As a reward, I push my pants down and let them drop to the floor. I step out of them, before straddling her. She lifts her hands, reaching for me again. I stop my approach, leaning back out of her reach, giving her a disapproving stare. She drops her hands back above her head, quickly catching onto my rules.

"Am I going to have to restrain you, Bethany?" I ask darkly, my hand working my cock again. I feel it pulsate, growing thick as it strains for release.

My brows lift in surprise when she nods, her eyes mesmerized by the way I grip myself. I scan the floor, spotting my belt mercifully close to the side of the bed.

I lie across her, one long arm reaching down for the belt.

She grinds her hips against me and I can feel how soaked she is already. Grasping her hands, I wrap them securely together before letting them drop above her head again. I look at her once more, her breaths coming in quick pants as her excitement builds.

"Pineapple, you remember?" I say, reminding her of the safe word I had told her to use last night. "Repeat it back to me."

She does.

"Say it if you want to stop."

She nods, eager for me to begin, licking her lips as though remembering the taste of something sweet. Remembering the taste of me on her tongue.

I laugh low in my throat, "Mmmm, good girl." I purr as I move down her body, my tongue dipping into the valley between her breasts, down to her navel, down further, until my tongue teases along her soaking center.

The touch, barely a whisper against her over sensitized skin makes her buck and she lets out a sharp cry, her legs tightening around my head. I grip her hips, pressing her thighs wide as I hold her in place, taking my time. She whimpers and wiggles, but I hold her firm just grazing her cunt with my tongue and teeth. She pants and whines, writhing as she tries to buck her hips up to my mouth again, needing more pressure, more of my touch.

"Rogan... please!" She begs, breathing hard as she struggles to get her pussy closer to my mouth. A wicked grin spreads across my face when I finally drive two thick fingers into her weeping cunt, then drop my mouth onto her clit, sucking hard.

She throws her head back, letting out a long low moan that echoes in the large room. Thrusting my fingers in and out of her, I swirl the tip of my tongue around her clit in small, tight circles. Her pussy pulses, tightening around my fingers with each stroke.

Just as she's about to tip over the edge, I slip my fingers out of her, my mouth lifting off her as my eyes lock onto hers.

She gasps, glaring down at me with venom in her eyes, letting out a loud angry growl of protest.

I smirk, loving this part of the game.

"Shhh, quiet now... don't make me punish you..."

Her eyes sparkle with wicked delight, her chest rising and falling heavily as she pants. I can see her internal debate over whether or not she should push the boundaries. Whether she should seek my punishment.

"Do exactly as I say and *maybe*... I'll let you finish. But you'll only come when I say you can."

My house. My bed. My rules.

"Now... you're going to be quiet. I don't want you to make a sound. If you do, you'll be punished. Is that clear?"

She whimpers softly again, but nods.

My eyes stay locked on hers as I dip my fingers back inside her, curling them to find the spot that will send her reeling uncontrollably. She tenses around me, her thighs shaking in anticipation and she lets out a low moan. I tip my head, my eyes admonishing and pull my fingers back out of her at the sound.

She clamps her lips together and stills, her eyes pleading as she looks into mine.

The corner of my mouth lifts into an approving smile and I slide them back into her, starting a slow, steady thrusting rhythm. Her inner walls begin to quiver, her chest heaving as she takes in gasping breaths with her efforts to keep quiet.

Just as she's about to come, I halt the thrusts of my hand, causing her to cry out in frustration.

Smirking, I reach into the partially open drawer beside the bed, pull out a condom and tear the packet open with my teeth, then deftly roll it on with one hand, the fingers of my other hand lightly fucking in and out of her.

Slowly, torturously, I pull my hand out of her, and grip her hips, pulling her pussy toward me, dragging the underside of my hard cock through her wet folds.

She's panting hard now, her chest quickly rising and falling, as she writhes between my hands. Her eyes wild with lust, I can see how much she wants to reach for me, to touch me, her fingers twitching in their constraints.

But she knows my rules, wants to come... so being a good girl for me, they remain above her head.

With one quick move, I flip her over and she squeaks at the sudden movement. Her round arse, presented so beautifully to me—ripe and ready like a peach.

I slap her right cheek, the palm of my hand stinging, before caressing my fingers over the reddening flesh. She jumps at the unexpectedness of it, but then releases a long, low mewl. She wiggles back into my palm, begging for another smack. I reward her, giving her what she wants, then lower my lips to her skin, my tongue dipping out to lick along her thick flesh before I nip at her, pinching her skin between my teeth.

She moans, the sound swallowed by the mattress when she buries her face into it. Her fingers dig into the sheets, her bound hands seeking purchase as she reaches for something to grip on to.

I knock her legs further apart with my knee, spreading her wide for me and line up the head of my straining cock with her entrance before plunging into her in one firm thrust.

With a deep, guttural groan she rocks back into me, encouraging me as I drive into her harder, faster.

I grip her hips pulling her onto me as I drive my own forward, sinking into her again and again. Our bodies slap together loudly as I fuck into her at a punishing pace, working out my frustrations, getting the most from her before she becomes just another hazy memory in a sea of forgotten trysts.

I feel her cunt tighten around me, and I grip her hips harder, feeling my fingers dig into her skin hard enough to leave marks.

"Come for me." I growl, gritting my teeth as her pussy starts to pulse, her orgasm exploding through her.

Her body quakes, her pussy clamping down hard on me. She grinds herself back against me, screaming my name so loud I'm all but certain it can be heard all the way down to the village.

I continue to drive into her, my thrusts becoming erratic, until I finally find my own release. I slam into her one last time and still—my cock pulsing deep inside her as I erupt, emptying myself into the condom.

Only then, in that moment of ecstasy, caught in the euphoric high of the orgasm, can my body take over for my mind. Only then can I disengage from my near constant mental torment and feel a fleeting moment of peace. The briefest respite before my inner demons return to haunt me, the ghosts of my past ever present at the edges of my tortured mind.

I slide my softening cock out of her, panting hard, sweat coating both of us and drop down on the bed beside her, my heart rate slowly returning to a normal rhythm.

Bethany snuggles into my side, draping an arm and a leg over me. I instantly feel claustrophobic, a wave of disgust washing over me as reality begins to settle back in and I have to fight the urge to push her off of me.

Instead, I blow out a slow breath, force myself to close my eyes, and try to re-capture the brief feeling of bliss I had felt just moments ago—until the unbidden memory of auburn hair, shining in the sunlight creeps back to the forefront of my mind.

Chapter 6

Cole

Brick's brows furrow as he carefully checks my ID, my birth certificate and scrutinizes my passport—fortunately all still in my maiden name. Then he scans the pages of the document laid out on the breakfast bar.

I wince as my teeth tear the tattered skin along my fingernail—a nervous habit I've never been able to stop, despite the fact it would have earned me a punishment before. I brace for a comment, a snide remark, a barking command... but it never comes. Instead, they don't even seem to notice.

My knee starts to bounce, anxiety rocketing through me, until I feel a solid, warm mass lean against my shin. Grumbl, positioning himself next to me, offers me silent comfort. It's an act not lost on his mistress, who smiles at her pup.

"This all seems to be legit," he finally remarks.

But his tone and expression seem conflicted and I can't quite tell if he's pleased with this or not. He takes a deep breath, blowing it out slowly before looking me square in the face.

That's when I really see it... the immense intelligence he possesses. A weapon he keeps hidden behind his initial humor and charm, only unleashing it upon his unwitting opponents when it best suits his needs.

He turns the will around and points to a paragraph.

"This states the entire bookshop—along with the land it stands on, the attached cottage, and even Hannah the donkey—has been left to the only surviving child of Jesse Allbright. His daughter, Maryanne Allbright. It further stipulates that, should Maryanne Allbright be unable to claim this inheritance, the rights to claim it shall be transferred to her daughter..."

He pauses, studying my face before continuing.

"One Nicole Allbright."

I swallow hard, the lump in my throat tightening like a vice.

He draws another breath, sliding his finger further down the page before me.

"He also left a sum of money," he adds, and my gaze follows his finger as it settles next to the figure printed on the page.

My eyes widen so much I swear they might pop right out of my head.

It's more money than I've ever seen—at least, in my own name.

Everything I needed, everything I did... he'd made sure I'd been wholly reliant on him. Not allowing me so much as an inch of breathing space to be my own person or do my own thing.

I had no idea how I was going to get away from him, until Maria, our maid, had offered to help. She was the only one who knew what happened behind the closed doors of our *picture-perfect* life. She saw it all—helped me cover up the bruises, bandaged my wounds and nursed me back to health whenever the beatings took me out for more than a couple days.

There wasn't much she could do to help, other than that. He's got something that he's holding over her too. He always seems to have something on everyone, keeping them under his thumb... keeping them loyal to him—*keeping them silent.*

She finally came up with the idea to take small amounts of cash out from any transactions I made each time I used the credit card he allowed me to have. The one I was to use whenever I got my hair or nails done, or did any shopping—*the one he could monitor.*

Taking out small amounts during each transaction allowed me to get the money past him, without him noticing. Maria would then take the cash and deposit it into the account she opened for me under my maiden name, using her home address—making sure it would remain untouched by my husband's influence.

She was the one who'd packed my backpack, the very one I've been clutching on to for dear life all this time. Had she not retrieved that money, rushed to the hospital, arranged for him to be distracted just long enough for me to slip past him...

My thoughts drift back to that night... the night she gave me a chance to escape...

"Vamos, Miss Nicole. We have to hurry. I do not know how long Juan Carlos will be able to distract Mr. Cain."

She glances over her shoulder as she settles the strap of the bag into my trembling hands, before rushing me into the open hospital elevator.

"Go, Mija! You need to leave now!" she whispers, frantic, shaking. "Before he really does kill you."

She places a hurried kiss on my cheek, tears welling in her eyes before stepping out and reaching around to push the button that would close the doors, sending me on my way.

As the elevator doors slide shut in my memory, I blink, looking up to see Brick and Kya both watching me with similar expressions of concern.

My breath catches, my heart hammering against my ribs. Slowly, I stretch out my hand, my finger trembling as it traces the number.

£100,000.

"Now, I do need to let you know..." Brick speaks again, pausing gauging me. "There are stipulations to gaining the full inheritance."

His voice is heavy with measured seriousness.

My heart sinks. *I knew it had to be too good to be true.*

I inhale deeply and meet Brick's gaze, grounding myself in Grumbl's steady warmth as he leans his weight against my leg.

"You have two choices. First, you have the option to receive half the money now, to spend as you choose—no strings attached. If you wish to leave, you may. But the business, the land, and the cottage will then be auctioned off to the highest bidder. The remainder of the money will go toward solicitor fees, inheritance taxes—that sort of thing."

Sitting up straighter, I zero in on what he hasn't said.

"And Hannah?" The strength in my voice surprises me, shocking myself when I hear the sharp biting edge to it that cuts through the formal weight of his words. "If I choose this option, what will happen to her?"

Brick casts a sheepish glance at Kya, toying with the pen he's holding.

"If you choose to forfeit the properties attached to the will—and a new home can't be found for her—considering her age and her proclivity to bite—"

"Only those people she doesn't like!" Kya interjects indignantly, her posture bristling, anticipating his next words.

Brick lets out a long, regretful sigh, shifting his attention fully to her.

"I'm sorry, Kya. Truly, I am. But if no suitable home can be found for her, the only alternative is...," he lets out a heavy breath, his chocolate brown eyes sincerely apologetic, "she'll have to be put to sleep."

The words land like a blow. My throat tightens, a single unbidden tear spilling over my lower lashes. Finding my voice, I square my shoulders.

"No."

Both Brick and Kya turn their eyes to me.

"That can't happen. I'm not going to let an innocent animal suffer—not when I have the power to stop it!" I clench my fists so hard my nails dig into the skin of my palms.

"You said choices—plural. What's the other option?"

Brick lifts a shoulder, his gaze turning matter-of-fact.

"The second choice is that you stay—but for a minimum of six months. This isn't just signing a contract, Cole. It's a commitment—to the bookshop, to the land, to everything tied to it. You'll need to spend those six months with the sole purpose of bringing it back to life. Not just keeping it afloat, but giving it a real chance to be what it once was."

He pauses, watching me, eyes assessing me—sharp, searching, waiting as I weigh the two possible paths I could take. Each one leading me in a whole new direction.

"The first half of the money will be deposited into your account in monthly installments of roughly £8,000—which should be enough to care for Hannah, to begin shaping the bookshop and cottage into something sustainable. Maybe even something profitable."

"At the end of six months, if you choose to stay, the final sum of £50,000 will be transferred into your account. If you decide to leave at that time, the bookshop, land, and cottage can be sold, but the money will all still be yours."

Kya beams hopefully at me, gripping my hands in hers.

Brick's fingers fidget with his pen, waiting for me to make my decision, but I'm frozen. My uncertainty feels like a lead weight hanging around my neck, making the added weight of his expectant gaze feel like it's pressing down on me all the more.

When I don't answer, time seems to slow to a crawl and the air hangs heavy in the space between us.

He clears his throat and taps his pen on the document again, his face tense, his brows furrowed.

"So, Cole… now you need to decide. You can take the £50,000 now and leave, relinquishing the bookshop, cottage and land and go on about your life. Or stay, and try to rebuild the bookshop back to its former glory and make a life here."

My eyes flick back and forth between Brick and Kya. Between the looks of doubtful concern on this man sitting across from me, and then to the bright, hopeful smile on Kya's. Her wide, shining eyes seem to be telling me the choice is a clear and simple one.

I wish I could share in her excitement. But the thought of it—*this permanence*—is overwhelming. Six months is a long time to stay in one place. A long time to trust people I barely know to protect my name. A long time to risk him finding me… *again*.

My eyes shutter closed as more thoughts snap back to the forefront. If I take the £50,000, I could run, try to disappear. Maybe start again in another country. Take on a new identity to ensure I am truly, irrevocably hidden.

Safe.

But I would be alone—*lonely*. Always watching my back, never trusting anyone. Not to mention, I'd basically be sentencing poor Hannah to her death…

Grumbl shifts, pushing his soft wrinkles more firmly against my leg, bringing me back out of my spiraling thoughts. I smile and reach down to rub between his neck and cheek. He lets out an adorable groan as he snuggles the weight of his chin into my hand.

Then I picture someone coming for Hannah, taking her away to meet an untimely end, all because no one cared enough to see past her faults.

No—*I can't let that happen.*

If I stay, at least I'll have time to find her a home, somewhere she can live without the threat of an uncertain fate looming over her.

I know all too well how that feels, never knowing what threat may be lying in wait from day to day.

That dark specter hovering, whispering in the shadows...

"Let me be your escape..."

The room is silent. I've been quiet for too long. Kya's exuberance fades, anxiety pooling in the space between her and Brick.

I open my mouth to answer, but the words catch in my throat, no sound escaping as my thoughts pinball between my choices and the faces staring expectantly back at me.

He leans forward, about to speak, but Kya snaps before he can even get a word out.

"Brick, you idiot!" Her words startle him and he sits back, snapping his mouth shut and dropping his eyes from mine, turning to face her instead. He blinks dumbly at her, eyes wide and his cheeks pinken at her harder than necessary tone.

"She needs time to process what you've just dumped on her, you great buffoon! More than a flipping minute!" She lets out a long, exaggerated sigh, clearly frustrated by her friend's eagerness to rush things.

"You don't understand, Kya," he begins, his tone a bit sheepish as he tries to appeal to her. I watch as they verbally spar, their words clashing in the space between them.

"There's a time limit to this. If Cole doesn't sign the papers before Wednesday, the will and everything attached to it becomes *bona vacantia*—ownerless goods. Everything reverts to the Crown."

"And just what the bloody hell does that mean?" Kya folds her arms, an eyebrow arching, unimpressed by Brick's choice of words.

"What it means, Sunshine," —she stiffens slightly, one long leg folding over the other, her sandaled foot tapping against the air— "is that if Cole doesn't claim it, everything will go to the highest bidder. And your new friend here," his eyes flicker toward me, as if only now remembering my presence, "will get nothing."

Kya pauses. The air is thick with her unspoken thoughts.

"Okay, give her a day, then. A bit of time to decide."

"I know it's a lot..." Brick starts to say, turning his attention back to me.

"Damn straight it's a lot!" Kya snips.

She turns her attention fully back to me, taking both my hands into hers and begins talking over Brick's next words, her eyes alight.

"Tell you what," her tone notably changing from irritation to a more gentle, calming one, smiling brightly as she gently squeezes my hands in hers. "Let me give you a tour of the village. We can grab a bite at the pub, give you some time to clear your head," she gives Brick an annoyed glare before adding; "have some time to properly think about this massive decision that's just been dumped in your lap."

I look up at her wide, waiting eyes and blow out a breath, then nod. Maybe some fresh air—without Brick's expectant gaze—will help.

Glancing down at my disheveled clothing, I cringe.

"Would it be okay if I got cleaned up a bit first?" I ask, pulling a hand from hers to toy with the dry ends of my mangled mop of hair—the majority of my ponytail hanging loose, having slipped out of the hair tie. "I must look like an absolute slob!"

"Of course you can!" she says, patting my hand before gesturing toward the stairs. "I'll show you."

She moves gracefully from her barstool, leading me out of the kitchen. Behind us, Grumbl yaps excitedly, his nub of a tail wriggling furiously as Brick, half-distracted, pulls his phone from his pocket, fingers tapping out a message.

"Brick!" Her voice snaps through the air, and I swear I see him jump, pocketing his phone like a kid caught sneaking cookies.

"Make yourself useful and keep the pup entertained while I help Cole get sorted."

Brick grins widely at her, his whole face lighting up in an instant. Shooting her a quick salute and a wink, he slips off the barstool, crouching down as Grumbl barrels into him, smooshing his face into Brick's hands, the pup's tongue licking out in every direction. Behind us, Brick's laughter fills the room, warm and unrestrained, as the pup's enthusiasm takes over.

I can't help but smile taking in the sight of this huge man on all fours, tussling with such a small and cuddly creature. I blink, and turn my attention back to Kya as we head toward the stairs.

"There are fresh towels in the cupboard, and soap if you want to wash up a bit." Kya informs me as I follow her up the stairs. When she reaches the landing, she pauses, her fingers tapping the newel post, once, twice... then turns, her skirt swishing as she faces me.

"I just hope you think seriously about what Brick's said—really consider the offer to stay. I don't know what it is," she murmurs, amber eyes locking onto mine, "but I think we could be great friends. And I've learned to trust my gut over the years, because it's never steered me wrong." She winks, a knowing smile dancing across her lips.

Her eyes drop to the stains on my top and she sighs. "I'll grab you a warmer jumper as well."

She disappears into the master bedroom and returns with a bright pink sweater.

"It's going to clash awfully with your hair," she teases, holding the material against me, "but it'll be a hell of a lot warmer than your hoodie."

Her grin drops from her lips when her gaze returns to my face. A soft sadness comes into her eyes and her fingers lightly graze my chin as she studies me, her voice quiet and gentle with her next words.

"There's a drawer to the right of the sink with some makeup in it. You're welcome to anything in there, hun." She gives me a sad, knowing smile and gestures toward the bathroom door.

From downstairs, Brick chuckles, tossing something across the floor for Grumbl to chase. The little puppy's joyful yaps fill the home, warm and alive, seeping into the quiet edges of the space—something soft, something comfortable.

Gratefully, I take the jumper, running my hands across the cashmere, feeling the weight of its softness, the unspoken kindness wrapped up in the gesture.

As Kya turns to head back downstairs, her hand trailing lightly along the banister, I call after her.

"Kya?"

Her sparkling amber eyes turn back to me.

"Thank you for... well, for everything."

My voice falters, words shrinking under the enormity of the sentiment.

She just smiles, winking again before disappearing down the stairs to rejoin Brick and Grumbl.

I step inside the small bathroom and take a breath as the door clicks shut behind me, letting the solitude settle around me. I relieve myself quickly, then wash my hands.

As my eyes lift to the mirror... I freeze.

The reflection staring back at me is unfamiliar.

Reddish hair, limp from neglect, a mockery of its former vibrance after two days untouched by water or care. Shadows cling to my skin—too pale, too thin—formerly purple bruises now blooming into yellow ghosts.

But my eyes... *my eyes strike me to my core.*

The green of my irises—too sharp against my hollowed skin. Like jade on brittle porcelain. Pupils—pinpricks. The shape of my eyes, wide—lost and shadowed.

I don't recognize the person looking back at me.

I don't know who she is.

Who is this stranger?

This 'Cole Allbright'.

My eyes burn as a single tear spills over my lower lashes, tracing a path down my cheek. I suck in a deep breath, my cheeks hollow—pulling inward. Brushing it away with a swift, determined movement, I curl my fingers around the rim of the sink, glaring at the stranger looking back at me.

I can do this, I tell myself, grasping at the remnants of the courage buried deep inside me.

I can become Cole Allbright—whoever she may be.

Chapter 7

Cole

The warm, soapy water cascades over my skin and I sigh at the feeling of near bliss after going so long without it—finally cleansing the sins of the past several days from my battered body.

I towel off and run a comb through my hair, gradually working it through the many tangles and knots that had formed there, then fasten it back into a low ponytail.

I can't help but groan as I pull the tattered material of my battered leggings on, wishing again I'd had something else to change into, then slide the fluffy pink sweater over my head.

Kya was right, the color is atrocious, but the feeling of having something so warm and soft to wear for a change, brings me more comfort than I could have even imagined.

I can hear them talking in the hallway downstairs, their voices muffled by the closed door of the bathroom. I open it as quietly as I can and step softly onto the landing.

"He's not going to be happy," Brick's hushed baritone rumbles up the stairs.

"I don't give a flying fuck what the *Duke* says or thinks," Kya snaps. The way she stresses his title makes it clear—her opinion of this man is apparently less than stellar. "The fact is, she's here now, and she's entitled to her inheritance. Now... if I have anything to say about it, and you know *I* most certainly do... she'll give it a fair chance. Surely someone as all-powerful as he is can afford to wait a few more months."

Brick lets out an exasperated breath, as if he's explained this a dozen times before. "You know he's not a patient man, Kya. He's not going to be happy and he won't want to wait."

Kya harrumphs loudly. "Well, tough shit! That's no longer up to him, now is it?"

I don't want to hear any more. Whoever this *'Duke'* is, he sounds like an absolute asshole. And if he's got it out for me, then I really don't need the thought of him lodged any deeper in my mind.

I make a point of making my steps heavy as I descend the stairs, the conversation dying instantly at my approach. Two pairs of eyes snap in my direction.

"Shall we go?" Smiling at them, I try to make my voice sound steady, and hopefully, confident. I'd prefer they didn't know I'd been eavesdropping on their conversation.

Kya recovers first, her smile effortlessly flickering back into place. She elbows Brick in the ribs and his reassuring smile pops back into place as well.

"Come on then. Time to go, you big oaf!" She's got him by the sleeve, leading him toward the door. She gives him a little shove on the shoulder as he ducks out through the doorway, chuckling as he lets her move him along.

"You can tell *His Grace* Kya says he can hold his hand on his aristocratic arse!" She barks after him, giving him a dazzling cocky grin.

He walks backward down the lane, offering her a returning grin, somehow even more dazzling than hers and I'm once again taken aback by how handsome he is. He gives her a mock salute and winks at her before he turns forward again.

When the door clicks shut she moves to the window, watching him walk away. Her eyes follow him until he's out of sight. Exhaling a long sigh she turns back to me.

"Right then!" she chirps, slapping her thigh a few times to call Grumbl to her side. She grabs his lead and harness from the hooks, fastening them with swift, practiced movements.

"Let's go."

Kya leads me and Grumbl back down the narrow lane I'd followed Zavier through earlier that morning. The terraced houses on either side are packed so tightly together that barely a sliver of sky is visible above.

Again, I notice the sign, *Lover's Lane.*

It's still early in the season, and the trees lining the street ahead are just beginning to turn gold and crimson. Their leaves shiver in the soft breeze drifting along the road. By British standards, I suppose the weather is warm. But I feel the damp creeping into my bones, the chill clinging to me like a second skin and I tighten my arms around myself.

But then again, maybe that's yet another reason to stay. A place where I can keep my shame hidden, the marks on my body covered by layers of clothing without anyone questioning it, wearing my own embrace like armor.

At the end of Lover's Lane, Kya pauses.

"Over there," she gestures, "is the shop—your go-to for bread, milk, magazines… all the essentials. The post office is inside as well."

She pauses, then adds, "Clive, the shop owner and postmaster, handles banking on Tuesdays and Thursdays when the mobile bank comes through the village." I nod, a bit shocked that one location offers all of these services.

"The shop itself is open daily, except Sundays and Wednesday afternoons. It's fairly well-stocked—you'll find most things there, but you'll need to make a trip to Coleford or Monmouth for a larger supermarket. Or, there's always the option to get a delivery from Tesco. You can order groceries right on your phone."

I fidget, running a hand absently up and down my arm. The movement catches her eye and she scans me, appraising.

"You don't have a phone, do you?" she asks pointedly, her eyebrows dipping slightly.

I drop my eyes and shake my head.

No. He never let me have one.

Like an unbroken drone in my mind, his voice slithers through the silence. Cold. Hard. Unrelenting.

"Why would you even need a phone, Nicole? You have no friends. No family. No one who wants you. It would just be wasted on you."

The words coil around me like a constricting snake, tightening with every repetition. Each memory, like a breath released, only pulls the grip tighter—preventing me from fully drawing it back in.

Kya studies me, then clicks her tongue, somehow picking up the fragments of me without me having to say a word. Yet another piece of the puzzle—this strange, fractured version of Cole Allbright—slotting into place in her mind.

With a gentle squeeze of my hand, effortlessly she pulls me back to reality, moving seamlessly back to our former conversation and points again.

"That's the chippy."

"Chippy?" I blink, raise a brow and smile at her. All these funny British terms make me laugh.

Her laugh is light. "Oh, honey, you haven't lived until you've had Meredith's fish and chips! Maybe later this week, you can try some."

She seems to be under the impression that me staying here is inevitable. As if I've already agreed to take on the bookshop, the cottage, the donkey, and every responsibility they carry.

The sound of voices drifts through an old, dark wooden gate—its frame thick with age, the beams heavy and weathered. A sloping tiled roof shelters it, an odd combination for an entranceway. It stands like a quiet sentinel before the churchyard, neither fully open nor closed, as if guarding something beyond.

Kya sucks her teeth and rolls her eyes as she steers me away from the parishioners spilling out of the church, the elderly vicar lingering at the entrance, shaking each person's hand with practiced solemnity.

"You'll find the majority of Verdon-on-Wye to be..." She taps a finger against her lip, pretending to ponder, then crinkles her nose. "A bit... fuddy-duddy."

My eyes widen, brows lifted as I smirk at her. Grumbl, apparently uninterested in our conversation, lifts his leg to pee on a road sign.

"Stuck in their ways. Old school. You know..." she grins wickedly at me, "a bunch of old farts."

Her grin turns conspiratorial as she flicks a finger between the two of us and leans in, keeping her voice low. "Not free spirits, like you and me!" With a theatrical flick of her hair, she dramatically throws one shoulder back in mock flamboyance, then turns to me waggling her eyebrows.

She's so animated, I can't help but burst out laughing, my hand quickly clamping down over my mouth, the sudden sound startling me.

I haven't laughed freely like that in... *God, I must have just been a little girl...*

Kya's grin widens even more comically at my laughter and when I snort, it sends us both spiraling, laughing even harder.

A group of the aforementioned 'fuddy-duddies' drift past, eyeing us with disapproving glances, muttering under their breath. One voice—sharp and clipped—grumbles something about *"that Stone girl has always been trouble."*

Kya practically sings after them, cheerful and unapologetic. "You're absolutely right, Miss Braithwaite! Trouble with a capital T!"

The woman spins back to face her, her lips turned down into a scowl. She huffs loudly, then turns back in the direction she had been heading, stomping off with a purposeful swing to her wide hips.

Kya waits long enough for the woman to be just out of earshot before turning and giving me a conspiratorial smirk.

"She was my old teacher," she whispers behind her hand. "A right old battleaxe!" She says, turning to stick her tongue out in the direction of the woman's back as she sashays around the corner.

We continue walking, laughter threading between us, light and effortless. With each step, I feel the tension unspool from my shoulders, the weight I've carried for so long loosening, if only for a few moments.

I feel giddy. Lighter somehow—just from being in Kya's presence, from the warmth she radiates so naturally, so freely.

She gestures as she talks, pointing out the quaint features of the quintessential English village, weaving descriptions into the air like a tour guide with no script, only instinct. I let her words wash over me as I take it all in, storing away questions in the back of my mind—notes for later, to be asked at another time.

But right now, I don't need explanations.

Right now, I am happy to simply bask in her glow.

We make our way down the road, the sidewalk quickly vanishing as the lane tightens into one of those impossibly narrow roads. A single car should be all it allows, yet the locals navigate it with a kind of kamikaze certainty, a reckless confidence I can only assume they're born with—part of their DNA, passed down through generations of near misses and blind corners.

Following a sweeping bend, I stop dead in my tracks. The sight before me is unlike anything I could have expected. Rising from the earth like a miniature fortress, two square towers, hewn from local stone, stand sentinel across a wide driveway that disappears into the hillside beyond.

Between them, a covered stone bridge spans the gap. A long window stretches horizontally across it, reflecting streaks of muted autumn light, while smaller, square windows puncture the towers like watchful eyes. Below it all are two oaken doors, heavy and weathered, set deep into the stone.

"What's that?" I ask, the words slipping out before my mind can catch up.

I've seen palaces. Castles. The grand landmarks of London, rising with history etched into their stone. He even walked me through some of the older Victorian streets once when we had first arrived in London, pointing out buildings worn by time.

But I was never allowed to linger. Never allowed to run my fingers across ancient walls, tracing the lives they had once housed. Never allowed the time to imagine—to picture the streets crowded with merchants and poets in Elizabethan England. To imagine the echoing footsteps from Dickensian London, the hum of carriages, the voices of people who belonged to the past but had once been alive, vibrant, real.

Kya's voice pulls me back.

"That's the Gatehouse for Verdon Manor."

She gestures toward the drive, and I follow the movement, my gaze settling on the house I had glimpsed from the riverbank. The sun glints off its windows, spilling golden light over the manicured lawn. And in front, like jewels scattered across the estate, is a fleet of gleaming cars—polished, pristine, belonging to a world that feels entirely separate from my own.

"Who lives there?"

"The Duke," she wrinkles her nose.

Is this the same 'Duke' she was so dismissive of when she was talking to Brick?

I imagine him to be a grouchy old man with flushed, reddened cheeks and bloodshot eyes from drinking too much expensive whiskey, a pot belly from indulging in too much fine food with a disagreeable nature. It makes me shiver when it reminds me far too much of my father.

"I don't think I want to meet him," I mutter under my breath.

Kya shrugs, her eyes lazily scanning the vast lawns of the manor, "While he certainly can be a bit of a bastard, Brick respects the hell out of him, and we've all been friends since we were kids. Plus, now that he's Duke, I suppose we all have to put up with his sometimes-mercurial ways if we want to have a happy village."

I tip my head, studying her, more confused than ever. I can't determine if she hates this man or if she has some level of friendship with him.

Changing the subject, I ask, "Does anyone live in the Gatehouse?"

Kya nods. "That's where Brick stays most of the time. Unless he's staying in the main house with his *'Lord and Master'* at the Manor." Miming air quotes with her fingers and rolling her eyes theatrically. Her expressive eyebrows knit together when she sees the way I'm looking at her.

"So wait... I'm a little confused. I thought you hated him, but you say you were friends as kids?" I ask, meeting her gaze. "The Duke, I mean."

She shrugs, the corner of her mouth quirking up as she tries to come up with a way to describe the way she feels about him.

She blows out a long, slow breath.

"It's not that I dislike him. It's just..." She hesitates, searching for the right words. "I've seen how he can be when he sets his sights on something. When he wants something bad enough, he'll do whatever it takes to get it."

She looks thoughtfully up at the Manor. The wind picks up, blowing a strand of her chocolate-colored hair across her face. She tucks it back behind her ear and then wraps her arms around herself, shivering as the chilly gust whips dry leaves around our feet.

"Believe it or not, when he's not consumed by business or chasing his next conquest, he can be... sweet. Charming, even."

She shakes her head, chuffing a laugh, "He just does a bloody good job of hiding it most of the time."

I stiffen, my throat tightening at the thought. He sounds too much like *him*... calculating, cold, selfish. Dangerous.

I force myself to turn away from the Gatehouse, away from the Manor, dragging my gaze back to the lane. At my feet, Grumbl snuffles at the ground before plopping himself down with a huff, pressing his weight against me.

"He's really taken to you!" Kya beams, reaching down to ruffle his velvety ears. "You've gotta stay now—my pup's going to be heartbroken if you leave!"

Reaching down to scratch behind his other ear, causes him to groan as he turns into my hand, the sound making me smile. I have to admit, it feels good to be wanted.

The thought that this adorable creature might actually miss me, that I might linger long enough in his memory to matter, sends a quiet warmth through me.

"Where to now?" I ask.

Kya pushes herself upright, brushing dust from her skirt before pointing toward a narrow path threaded through a dense copse of trees. I wouldn't have noticed it if she hadn't shown me—hidden, waiting, barely a gap in the foliage.

We cross the lane quickly and step into the cool embrace of the trees, walking single file through shifting shadows. Brambles snatch at my leggings, tugging like mischievous hands. Ferns tickle my fingers as I brush past them, their fronds feather soft against my skin. Overhead, birds weave their melodies into the canopy, their songs punctuated by the rustling of leaves in the autumn breeze. Sunlight spills through the branches, dappling the path, painting Kya and Grumbl ahead of me in a flickering kaleidoscope of vibrant shades of gold.

I inhale deeply.

Here, in the hush beneath the trees, surrounded by earth, movement and life, I feel like I can finally breathe.

The city had never suited me. A part of me—one I had buried beneath concrete and streetlights and the relentless press of people—had always longed to be back in the countryside. To stretch out in the pastures, arms and legs spread wide, shaping a star against the land. To watch birds carve their paths through the sky, through streaks of sunlight, dancing amongst the clouds—untethered and free.

I'm lost in my daydream, head tipped up to take in the branches and leaves of the trees swaying above me. So lost, I don't see Kya halt in front of me until I collide into her.

"Steady, hun," she says, lightly gripping my arm and giggling as she steps aside and gestures outward, her arm sweeping over the scene like an artist unveiling a masterpiece.

Stepping back with an embarrassed chuckle, I lift my eyes to follow her gaze. "I'm sorr..." my breath catches, stopping the words from forming.

Before us, the apple orchard spills across the land, trees heavy with fruit, their fallen bounty surrendered to worms and insects—returning to the earth in silent offering. The long fronds of unmown grass ripple in the breeze, bending just enough to reveal a winding path, a quiet invitation leading toward a thatched cottage.

For a moment, I'm pulled back—back to an orchard that was once my sanctuary, back to a time when the scent of apples meant comfort.

Until the day my father found me... and it wasn't.

I draw a deep breath and force myself to notice the differences.

This orchard was loved—its trees supported, full of life, their branches hanging heavy with fruit. It's only recently been left untended. Sunlight cuts through the shadowed places, and the air hums with the gentle buzzing of insects and the song of birds.

It feels ancient, forgiving.

It can be brought back to life—given a second chance.

Maybe there's a second chance here for me too.

I turn to the cottage, nestled within the orchard like its keeper. Its lower walls are whitewashed, glowing softly in the afternoon light, as if time itself has settled here—unbothered, unchanged. It looks like something lifted from a Christmas card—quaint, untouched, steeped in nostalgia.

A familiar braying fills the air, bright and unabashed. Hannah rounds the cottage, trotting straight toward us, her soft nose pressing eagerly into my hands, seeking the touch she already seems to remember. I laugh, scratching her behind the ears, running my fingers through her mane.

She stretches her long neck down toward Grumbl, bestowing him with a broad, wet lick—sending him stumbling sideways and he yaps in indignation at her.

Kya chuckles. "Welcome to Haven Cottage," she says. "Once home to Jesse and Margaret Allbright. But now...it could be yours—*if* you choose to stay."

I stare at the cottage and feel the corners of my lips lift as something about it tugs at me, whispers to the part of me I had buried, the part I had dampened down for survival.

Hope?

I turn in a slow circle, taking in all the life, the potential around me. I envision the spring—the apple trees in full bloom, Hannah wandering lazily beneath their blossoms while I tend the garden. The clean smell of fresh air as I throw open the small windows, letting the breath of the countryside drift inside. Peaceful, warm... reminding me of a time when I was happy.

In this place, a spark of warmth flickers inside me—a faint glimmer of something akin to hope.

A quiet voice whispers...

I think I could be happy here... Maybe I could stay.

Kya gestures to the path behind the cottage. "The bookshop is just down there, so you wouldn't have far to go for work," she laughs.

I follow the direction of her hand, catching sight of the sunroom, the sun glinting off the windows at the back of the turquoise building.

I inhale deeply, unsure how to answer her. So I just smile, my hands moving absently across Hannah's neck.

"Hungry?" Kya asks.

As if in response, my stomach growls—loudly, making Kya and I both grin widely.

"Famished," I admit, and once more, arm in arm, we walk together—past the cottage, past the bookshop, and toward the banks of the River Wye.

Chapter 8

Cole

"Hello again," a deep voice greets us as we walk toward the small jetty. I spin with a start, my heart rate ticking up several notches, before I recognize the owner of the voice.

"Oh, hello Zavier." I reply, smiling up at him.

He's changed out of his work clothes, and is now wearing fresh, clean jeans, a new flannel shirt, buttoned but open just enough to show his tanned chest and a hint of the soft, golden hairs over very well-defined muscles.

He nods across the water to where a teenager is struggling with the flat-bottomed boat attached to a wire that spans the width of the river.

"Off to the pub?" he asks.

I nod, my arm still firmly hooked with Kya's, anchoring her as she tries to keep Grumbl away from a flock of ducks that have decided to waddle up from the water.

"Mind if I join you?" he asks, his smile wide and guileless.

"Not at all!" I reply, my voice light with warmth. "In fact, would it be alright if I buy you a drink?" I shrug, suddenly self-conscious. "You know, as a thank you for helping me out this morning."

That earns me another radiant smile and he nods, the brilliant blue of his eyes sparkling in the afternoon sun. He takes a few steps closer to me, the light wind carrying the scent of his cologne. It's earthy and warm, mixed with the bright notes of freshly cut grass. Standing beside him, caught in the glow of his charm, I feel the tug of something familiar, something unsettling in its intensity.

We wait in a loose line as the boy hauls the boat toward us, his face flushing from exertion. Zavier's eyes lift to the boy, a look of frustration hardening his features.

"Oi, Billy! Hurry up, mate, or we're gonna die from thirst!"

Zavier's sudden clipped tone startles me and I take a quick step back, knocking into Kya. She wraps a protective arm over my shoulders and scowls at Zavier.

"Is all that really necessary?"

He stuffs one big hand into his pocket and rakes the other through his hair, dropping his eyes, sheepishly shrugging his shoulder.

"Sorry, ladies," he mutters. "Just trying to move things along."

Kya glares at him a moment longer, then turns a concerned look to me. "Okay?"

I nod, straightening my shoulders, giving her a tight-lipped smile. I'm grateful for her quiet reassurance, but damn it! I wish I could stop being so jumpy!

If I'm thinking about staying here, I'm going to have to figure out a way past this fear, this constant paranoia. I can't keep letting the instinct to flinch at every loud or sudden sound get under my skin.

I have to believe not all men are cruel.

Jesus, I hope that's true, at least.

The boat bumps the jetty and Billy carefully ties it off.

Zavier holds out his hand to help us aboard and I smile, forcing myself to meet his eyes. The craft wobbles beneath my feet, and I stagger back, but he lightly grips my shoulders, steadying me. I feel the warmth of his hands through my sweater. I glance up to see icy blue eyes smiling down at me and tingles race up my spine.

"Thanks." I smile at him awkwardly and feel my cheeks heat.

He takes my hand, keeping a gentle hold on my shoulder and guides me toward one of the benches. Once I'm seated, he turns his attention back to Kya, who's struggling to get herself and a squirming puppy over the lip of the boat and hurries over to help her.

Once Kya and the pup are safely aboard and settled into the seat beside me—Grumbl panting heavily in her lap, she smiles at me, blowing a long lock of hair off her face.

Billy struggles to dislodge the tether that's now jammed. Zavier lets out a sigh and makes his way over to him. As he patiently helps him unjam the tether and walks him through a simple technique of maneuvering the boat from shore to shore, I can't seem to take my eyes off him.

The way he teaches—effortlessly confident, his warmth softening the sharp edges of his presence. Billy listens intently, watching his every move closely as he absorbs every instruction.

After he makes a few quick adjustments, the boat glides seamlessly across the water and we all cheer, making the teenager beam with pride. His cheeks, already flushed from exertion, deepen to a vivid crimson and a broad grin deepens his dimples. Zavier claps him on the back, knocking the skinny boy a bit off-kilter and we laugh, sharing in his triumph.

This feels... *right*. To be here—with these people who could possibly be friends. In this place that somehow seems to promise comfort and hope.

And to think... a bookshop.

My very own bookshop.

I've always loved books and reading. Books equaled an escape from reality. A place where I could lose myself in the pages. Live in a magical land, go on an adventure, become the hero... the strong warrior, choosing my own path, fighting the demons and winning the battles. Creating a world where I could be anyone I want to be... even if it's only for a short time. The thought of being surrounded by books, only deepens the sense that this is exactly where I should be.

We arrive at the jetty of the Wye Inn and Zavier heads to the dock. His long legs have him stepping off the boat even before it quite reaches the shore. He guides it the rest of the way to the jetty, helping Billy to tie off the tether, then turns to offer his hand to help us step off. Heat rushes to my cheeks as his warm fingers wrap around mine, lingering for just a moment. His blue eyes lock onto mine as his thumb strokes gently over my knuckles just once before releasing my hand and my pulse flickers beneath my skin.

I turn to follow Kya and Grumbl up the path toward the inn. From the look of the outside of the pub, it feels like it should be dark—heavy wooden beams and cramped tables, everything seemingly steeped in time.

But once we step through the doors, it's something entirely different than I'd expected.

The space opens around us, the bar set at the heart of the room, with tables and booths lining the edges. There's a large, deep fireplace along one wall, logs stacked carefully, ready to be lit when the weather turns colder. Both sets of doors—one leading to the jetty, and one I assume leads to a parking lot—stand open, allowing the crisp river breeze to filter through. Instead of heavy and dim, the air is fresh, bright and welcoming.

The barrel-chested man at the bar, his cheeks rosy above a thick brown beard greets Kya warmly before reaching across the bar to shake Zavier's hand.

"The usual?" he asks him, already placing a pint glass under one of the taps labeled Butty Bach, then shifts his kind eyes to me.

"And who might this be?" he asks, his beard breaking to show a wide, welcoming smile.

I meet his smile with my own, opening my mouth to reply.

"This here is Cole." Zavier announces, his hand dropping to the small of my back, moving in close beside me. I feel my cheeks flush at his unexpected closeness.

The barman shifts his warm gaze back to me and reaches across the bar, his two massive mitts completely swallowing my hand in greeting.

"Well then, Cole, you are very welcome here at the Wye Inn. What might I offer you to drink?"

"A couple of lager shandies for the ladies, Greg—and you can go ahead and put that on my tab." Zavier tips his head toward him, smiling broadly down at me as he orders for us.

I cringe inwardly. I hate lager, but I don't want to seem ungrateful when he's offering to buy our drinks. I smile politely at him, then drop my eyes.

You'll take what you're given, Nicole. Just be grateful you're out with me tonight..." his voice echoes in my mind.

"Hold on, Zavier. Did it ever occur to you that she might not want a bloody shandy? I know I certainly don't! No offense, Greg, but the lager shandy straight up tastes like piss!" Kya quips.

"Sorry Cole, force of habit I guess…" Zavier shrugs, running a hand through his hair looking a bit sheepish.

"It's okay." I give him a small, reassuring smile, then turn back to Greg, "May I have a Diet Coke, please?"

"Ahh! She's got manners too! I like her already!" Greg's deep voice booms as he beams at me.

Kya orders a glass of sauvignon blanc then hands Grumbl's leash to me so she can go behind the bar to talk to Greg about picking up some extra shifts in the week.

Zavier grabs our drinks and leads me over to a table overlooking the Wye and my bookshop.

My bookshop.

Once again, warmth spreads through me. Followed very quickly by trepidation and nerves and a flurry of fretted fears rush into my mind.

If I stay, will I do my grandparents' memory justice?

Can I truly run a bookshop?

Can I survive on my own, away from the superficial beauty of my gilded cage?

Without the rigid, regimented rules—the routines that have shaped my existence for so many years—will I still know who I am?

Can I really, truly be free?

I stare out the window, lost in thought as we sit in companionable silence. Turning my attention back to the room, Zavier's eyes are on me as he tips up his glass, taking a large sip of his ale. He lowers the glass, smiling widely at me and I giggle when a bit of froth clings to his upper lip. He looks a bit confused and I shake my head, still smiling as I reach across, wiping it off with my thumb.

His eyes lock onto mine, darkening. My smile drops and I pull my hand back, quickly dropping it into my lap.

"Sorry." I apologize, my cheeks growing hot.

He tugs his top lip in with his bottom before slowly releasing it. Then he winks, smiling coyly at me before tipping his glass back to his lips, his glacial gaze never leaving me. My heart races and my skin prickles under his stare.

My pulse is still hammering when Kya rejoins us. I breathe out a sigh of relief when she sits down and we fall into easy conversation.

I offer little bits of my life to them, telling them about my hometown in Connecticut, how I had lived in London before traveling here to meet my grandfather. Just enough to be social, but not enough that they might guess too much about the truth behind why I'm really here.

As one of the barmaids makes her way over to us to take our lunch orders, the roar of a powerful engine pulling into the parking lot takes over the din of the pub. I just catch a glimpse of the hood of the shining black sports car as it pulls up to the pub's main entrance.

I feel an instant dislike toward the owner of such a loud, obnoxious vehicle.

Kya turns in her seat, casting a quick, concerned glance at Zavier, then to me, but my gaze is locked on the figures striding through the door, their outlines stark against the noon sunlight, nothing more than silhouettes as they step into the dimness of the pub. They stroll confidently in, making their way to the bar and I recognize the first man—Brick. He spots us, smiling a brilliant smile, lifts two fingers in a quick salute, then turns to talk to Greg.

But it is the man behind him who captures my stare. He's taller than Brick by a good few inches, having to duck under a beam that's got to be at least six feet off the floor. His dark brown hair is styled with careful precision, accentuating the sharp lines of his chiseled jaw, the expertly sculpted stubble adding just enough edge to intentionally soften the perfection. His broad shoulders and toned frame strain against his shirt, the top few buttons undone, offering a glimpse of dark tattoos that curl over his chest—shadows of ink against skin. My gaze tracks down his body, taking in his overall presence, noting how his jeans mold to his legs just right, leaving little to imagination.

My mouth suddenly goes dry and I absently reach for my glass to take a sip. But when he turns toward the room, sliding his sunglasses down the bridge of his nose, it's his eyes that arrest me.

Sharp. Calculating. Steel gray. They drag over the room, taking everything in, landing—finally—on me.

In that moment, everyone and everything else disappears—Kya, Zavier, the hum of conversation, the clatter of plates and silverware—it all just fades. I'm caught in the vortex of his gaze, locked in place—helpless against its pull.

The snap of fingers beneath my nose pulls me back abruptly, the sounds of the room rushing back in around me. I feel the gentle pressure of a finger beneath my chin and the stranger's attention immediately shifts, zeroing in on the point where Zavier's skin meets mine. I see a flare of something sharp, hardening in those steely eyes before I blink, finally able to tear my gaze away from his, returning my attention to Zavier, Kya and the waitress.

"I'm sorry, what?" I stammer, blinking at the waitress.

"I said, what would you like to eat, love?"

I hurriedly drop my eyes down to the menu, the words jumbling in my rush to answer her. I feel undone. Like the earth beneath me has turned to sand, shifting away as I try to regain my footing, only to slip away again before I can recover my balance.

"I, umm... I'll just have what Kya's having." I stutter out my order, my voice barely a whisper, as I try to figure out what the hell just happened.

"Right then! You've got it dear!" the waitress quickly jots down my order with a smile and a wink, then briskly walks off.

I glance at Zavier, the muscle in his jaw rippling, tension hardening his expression as he stares at the backs of the men at the bar. While his attention is focused on the bar, I lean toward Kya.

"Who is that?" I whisper, my eyes darting back to the stranger.

Kya's gaze follows my own and she angles into me, dipping her chin, her brows raised matter-of-factly.

"That, my friend, is our very own Duke of Wyeholme." With a quirk of her lip, she raises her glass up...

"Rogan Cavendish."

Chapter 9

Rogan

Green eyes.

Wide, fathomless. Innocent.

Like the tender leaves on spring flowers. Eyes that draw me in, whispering intoxicating secrets of the heart I'd never dared to consider before.

Those eyes, framed by a pale face, with the faintest dusting of freckles dappled across the bridge of her nose, hold me captive. The auburn of her hair, far deeper, richer than I had imagined when I first spotted her from my room. Even from that distance, I'd wanted to touch it, to feel those silky locks slide through my fingers.

Full lips, her face stunning, with barely a hint of makeup.

But when I see the slight purplish hue, the outer edges now fading to yellow, beneath those eyes—healing bruises—something primal awakens within me. A fierce, unrelenting urge to hunt down whoever hurt her and tear them apart with my bare hands.

Time all but stops as I take her in.

She's nearly swallowed up by the garish pink jumper she's wearing. She's a tiny little thing, making herself even smaller as she curls in on herself in the booth.

Her breath catches as those hypnotic eyes lock onto mine.

For just a moment, the rest of the room disappears. Hell, the pub could be on fire right now, and all I would see is her.

I'm hit with a sudden, enigmatic urge to hear her voice. A perplexingly magnetic pull, demanding I move closer—to answer that nagging tug. An unbidden desire to stoke the ember threatening to catch fire inside me.

I want her.

Zavier grips her chin, a single finger tipping her face to his, pulling her gaze from mine, breaking the strange spell she's somehow cast on me. He speaks to her, his words lost to the noise of the room, but my eyes fuse to the spot where he touches her—touching skin that, for reasons I can't fathom, I want to claim.

The tips of my fingers tingle with an inexplicable need to touch her. To caress her cheek and smooth away the pain etched so clearly across her face.

My jaw clenches, my hands curling into fists when I catch the hint of the fleeting upturn of those damnable lips as she returns her attention to him.

Taking a deep breath, I force myself to pull my focus back to Greg to order my Diet Coke. Brick orders a double Scotch on the rocks, chuffing a laugh when he sees my face.

"Might want to try to get your expressions under control a little better than that when you meet her." He teases, sipping from his glass.

"What the fuck makes you think I'm going to meet her?" I snap incredulously, scowling at him as I lift my glass. The pungent smell of his Scotch churns my stomach. I can't stand that shit after living with my father's proclivity for it.

He swirls his drink, the ice clinking against the glass as he chuffs a laugh, the side of his mouth lifting in a cocky grin and shakes his head.

"What are you on about?" I snap, losing my patience with his insistence on being deliberately obtuse.

Leaning his shoulder against mine, his eyes tracking to the table where she sits, he nods in her direction. "That, my friend, is Cole Allbright. Granddaughter of Jesse and Margaret Allbright."

He sits back, taking another sip from his glass, his eyes shifting to where Kya is bent over giving her pup a chip—biting his lip while his appreciative gaze lingers a moment too long on her backside.

"She's the one you'll have to convince to leave if you want any chance of claiming that property for yourself."

Well, shit... Fuck my life.

I settle at the bar as they eat, chatting as if they've known each other for years rather than hours.

I watch them discreetly, feigning focus elsewhere while my mind wrestles with its relentless pull toward her—clashing frustratingly with the realization that she's the sole obstacle blocking my path. It hits like ice-cold water poured over my head. Sudden, conflicting emotions surge within me.

A primal part of me wants her to stay, just to see whether she'll live up to the fantasies I've already begun to craft—to indulge in the temptations of my mind.

But the part of me that's been honed to be nothing but a calculated business-man, ruled by ambition—*the Duke*—wants her gone. Erased. Removed. So my plans can proceed, unhindered.

The waitress moves in, collecting their plates. I notice Cole has barely touched the food on her plate. Her eyes flick back to mine, and once again, that electric tension courses through me.

"Ready?" Brick claps me on the shoulder, snapping my attention back to him. I tap my fingers against the bar, stealing a moment's reprieve before stepping into the inevitable. Nodding once, I join him as we push off the barstools and head over toward their table. I let Brick lead. From many past business endeavors together, I rely on his natural affability to disarm them.

"Kya!" he bellows, planting his hands on her shoulders and leaning down, pressing a quick kiss to her cheek.

"Get off, you oaf!" she giggles, pushing playfully at him.

"Good to see you again, Cole." He nods at the redhead, then stretches a hand across the table. "Zavier."

Zavier's eyes narrow as he stares up at Brick, offering him a tight-lipped smile before his gaze flicks to me, his already sullen smile dropping entirely.

Zavier cringes when he takes Brick's offered hand, and I can't stop the satisfied smirk that creeps across my lips when my friend clamps his massive paw down with a bit more force than necessary.

Brick holds him there for a few seconds longer, Zavier's hand pinned in his iron grip, then lets it drop. Zavier sits back hard, hitting Brick with an indigent glare. He flexes his fingers, then grabs his beer before turning his attention to me.

"Rogan..." he says, coldly.

Zavier and I share a long history. The Johnsons had once managed our estate and the surrounding farmland—trusted workers for generations. That is, until everything went to hell.

My father had just passed away the week before, leaving me as the Duke—the new master of the estate. After what happened that day... I did what needed to be done. I told no one about what I saw—except for Brick, who handled the legalities of it all.

"Mind if we join you?" Brick asks, pulling me from my thoughts—already dragging a chair from a nearby table. He wedges himself between Kya and Zavier, reaching down to ruffle the ears of Kya's roly-poly puppy.

I grab my own chair, placing it in the only remaining space at the table—right between Kya and Cole. I curse inwardly as my knee brushes against Cole's thigh, sending a tingle through me, straight to my groin. I tense, clenching my jaw and exhale slowly, forcing myself to turn toward her. The second her eyes meet mine, every thought leaves my head, every word in my vocabulary seeming to leave me all at once.

"Hi."

I cringe as I hear the lackluster greeting fall from my lips.

Hi?

What the actual fuck!?

Could I possibly sound more ridiculous?

More juvenile?

Where the fuck is my charm?

Where are the words I should be using to captivate her—my usual ability to ensnare my potential targets into my web?

For fuck's sake! What the hell is she doing to me?

"Hello," she replies, a soft smile lifting the corners of those plush lips. She keeps her chin dipped slightly, her eyes not quite meeting mine. Even with that one word, I catch the faintest trace of her accent, and like a drug, I crave more.

"I'm Rogan," I say, offering her my hand. "Rogan Cavendish." She looks up at me, her green eyes even more mesmerizing up close. Flecks of brown and gold shimmer within the leafy green, with threads of deep blue woven through.

"Cole," she says, then, casting a nervous glance in Zavier's direction she adds, "Cole Allbright."

She places her small hand in mine and time stands still. The surge of energy I'd felt when our legs touched was nothing compared to the electricity of her skin directly touching mine now.

Kya, Brick and Zavier disappear from my periphery and in this moment, there's just us. There's no pub. No bookshop. No need for anyone or anything else. As though the world just doesn't exist.

My mouth goes dry and I swallow thickly while trying to come up with something... anything to say. Literally *anything* besides asking her to come back to my house... *to my bed*.

"I was just telling Rogan that Cole here might stay on for a bit." Brick's voice pulls me back, the sounds of the room, muffled by the storm raging inside me, now slowly coming back into focus.

Blinking back to reality, I realize I still have her hand clasped in mine and her eyes are locked onto me. I clear my throat, forcing myself to let her go, compelling myself to look back at Brick, who smirks knowingly at me from across the table.

"I hear you might take on the old Allbright Bookshop?" I say conversationally, finally finding my words.

She rubs her hands together nervously, then tucks them between her thighs, hunching forward, curling in on herself again, like she had been before we came over and sat down, making herself smaller.

"Maybe," she says softly, a slight shrug lifting her shoulders. "Kya and Zavier are still trying to convince me to stay." She shrugs again, dropping her eyes, causing something to clench inside my chest—the uncertainty in her voice matching the conflict in my own thoughts, "I guess I'm still not really sure yet."

I inhale, and her scent hits me like a force.

A perfume unlike any I've smelled before—the crisp sweetness of apples and patchouli tangled with the fresh bite of air rolling down the river from the mountains. Earthy. Pure. Untouched. As if she'd bloomed that very morning, ripe and ready to be plucked.

It's intoxicating. Powerful. Rocking me to my core, addling my brain even further.

"Well, Cole, before you make up your mind, Rogan has a proposal for you." Brick interjects, still smiling, his teeth flashing as he delights in the tableau I am putting on.

I straighten in my seat, clearing my throat. Remembering the target I have my sights set on. Remembering who I am and why I'm here.

It's time to stop this nonsense and let my head rule, rather than my dick. Nothing can make me waiver. Not this petite beauty sitting next to me. Not her scent. *(My God, will I ever get enough of her scent?)* Not her eyes, the way they make me want to dive into them and never resurface. Not the way her teeth sink into that full bottom lip, just begging for me to run my thumb across it...

I clench my fists, digging my nails into my palms, hoping the pain will help return me to my senses and snap me out of this fantasy.

I continue, trying to keep my tone firm, steady. "I understand you have two options, to stay or to go?" I ask curtly.

She nods, her eyes looking everywhere except at me.

"And that you'll be compensated, regardless of which option you choose?" She nods again.

I breathe in again, and immediately regret it as her scent hits me full force again. I force my nails deeper into the flesh of my palms, wincing when I feel the skin break.

Determined to get my point out, I push forward.

"I'm going to shoot straight with you here, Cole. As I'm sure Brick has probably told you by now, I've wanted the Allbright's property for a long time. I offered to take it off Jesse's hands several times. So, now I'll make my offer available to you. If you agree to relinquish your inheritance, I'll double the money Jesse left you. Hell, I'll even pay to help you get back home, if you want?"

At that, her head snaps up, her eyes flaring wide with a look of something akin to terror. She shakes her head vehemently, her pleading stare locking on mine. The look in her eyes threatens to knock me off balance yet again, forcing me to pause mid-sentence, my mouth snapping shut before I can continue.

I shake off the staggering surge of concern sparked by her piercing stare. I drop my chin and hold up a hand, silently waiving off my previous suggestion and press on.

"But either way, you leave the business—give up your claim to the land and the cottage. Sign it all over to me, and then..."

I hesitate, taking in a deep breath. My heart hammers as her intoxicating scent refills my lungs, begging my mouth to stop, knowing if she goes, I'll never find out what those lips taste like. I'll never have the chance to wrap that auburn hair around my fist, never know what it feels like to have her beneath me while I sink my cock between her creamy thighs. Knowing deep down, I truly want to ruin her in ways beyond just the business.

I swallow back those thoughts and force the words out with as much finality as I can muster.

"You go. You leave Verdon-on-Wye. And that will be the end of it."

At my last words, it feels like the entire pub goes silent.

I feel everyone's eyes on me—Brick, steady in his support. Zavier, burning with resentment. And Kya? Well, let's face it. She looks like she's just about ready to scratch my eyes out.

Forcing myself to ignore them all and focus on the only one who really matters right now, I need her to make the right decision. I need her to accept what I'm offering and agree to leave. But my gut twists, tightening, knotting itself up. What is it about this quiet little fawn that keeps throwing me off center?

She turns her attention to the window, looking past the river to the bookshop. To where Hannah is cropping the grass, a small cat perched on a bench nearby, licking its paws.

"Cole should stay," Zavier pipes up. "God knows Verdon needs some new blood." He tips his glass up, emptying its contents.

The way he looks at her, his eyes sweeping over her like she is already his, makes my fingers twitch—my jaw tightening, clenching, my patience threatening to snap. One word stuck on a persistent loop in my mind... *MINE!*

I suddenly have an insatiable urge to reach over, grab him by the collar, and drag him out to the car park to beat the bloody hell out of him.

My fists tighten, clenching so hard my knuckles turn white. Brick, ever observant, catches the movement—his sharp gaze flicking to my hands when the joints pop. He shifts, positioning himself between us just enough to intervene, to stop me from doing something I might regret should Zavier push me too far.

"That's Cole's decision to make, Zavier. It's not up to anyone but her and she'll be the one to decide what she wants to do." Saint Kya—savior of all strays—interjects, always at the ready to defend the next lost soul. She leans forward, passion fueling her words, as though the conundrum of Cole Allbright is up for debate.

I tune them out. Their voices fade into the distance and my eyes remain fixed on her. She's turned just enough to be able to see the view below the pub, her gaze distant. Her fingers lightly trace her full bottom lip, completely lost in her thoughts, almost as if the bickering at the table isn't going on around her. I watch her, unable to read her, but her entire body screams stress—but there's something else there too.

The realization strikes like a bolt of lightning.

Fear.

My Little Fawn is afraid.

My mind spirals, and I feel my walls collapsing around me as I begin to lose my resolve. Maybe she'll be more willing to accept my deal if I share my vision with her. Make her see what I see when I look at the bookshop—show her the potential I envision it could have—then maybe she'll understand. Understand and go. Maybe then that tortured look in her eyes won't haunt me as much.

Brick's voice—calm, steady—cuts through the background noise, weaving into Kya and Zavier's ongoing discussion, trying to interject a level of calm into their incessant back and forth, as though Cole isn't even sitting at the table. As if she's some puzzle to be solved, some possession to be claimed in some childish tug-of-war.

What is it about this woman—here for only half a day—and already people are fighting over her? What is it about her that makes them think they can control her, have her—*keep her*?

Again, that inner voice flairs in my head... *Mine*.

"Cole..." I pitch my voice just enough to cut through the others, turning toward her, leaning my forearms on the table between us, bringing my face level with hers.

"No."

I blink, sitting back again. "Sorry?" Her voice is so quiet, I'm not sure I heard her right.

"She said no, Rogan." Zavier leans back in his chair, one arm lazily draped along the backrest, his cocky grin splitting his face like he's just won a prize.

"She wants to stay." The smirk in Zavier's voice grates against me. "I'll even help her turn that orchard into more farmland, maybe tear down that old bookshop and—"

"No."

Again, her small voice—stronger this time, cuts over him.

She turns her attention back from the window and sits up straighter, her fists clenched together on the table in front of her. Her eyes immediately land on Kya, who dips her chin, encouraging her to say her piece.

I swallow, my dry mouth turning to sand as she shifts her mesmerizing gaze back to me. But now there's a new resolve, a new strength glowing in those green eyes, her new friend's silent reassurance bolstering her confidence.

"Thank you very much for your offer, Mr. Cavendish."

I balk at the formality, but I can certainly appreciate her level of professionalism.

"But something tells me that if grandpa Jesse didn't want to sell to you, he must have had a good reason for it. No offense, but I think if I were to take you up on your offer, I would be dishonoring his memory. I think I need to stay. I have to believe it's what he wanted or he wouldn't have gone to so much trouble to create the will the way he did." Her voice carries more strength with each word she breathes, her confidence growing the more she commits to her truths.

"So, I'm very sorry to disappoint you, Mr. Cavendish..."

I hold up a hand, interrupting her.

"Rogan, please just call me Rogan."

"Sorry... Rogan," she corrects, "I know you had your heart set on his property, but I think I am going to try and give this opportunity he left me, a chance."

She shifts her attention to Zavier. "And, Zavier, please understand, it's not because of what you're suggesting either. I appreciate everything you've done to help me, but I couldn't possibly let you tear it down. If grandpa Jesse didn't want the bookshop sold, I certainly can't imagine he would have wanted it torn down and made into more farmland."

Chancing a brief glance in his direction, my lips quirk, savoring the flicker of irritation on his face.

"I want to try to turn it into something that would have made them proud. To do something on my own. Make it into something that's mine."

Her eyes shine, silver pooling along her lower lashes, not quite spilling over—clearly this decision means more to her than anyone at this table could have possibly guessed.

"He said I have six months. So I'm going to take a chance on *me* for once."

Her eyes scan the table, stopping pointedly on each man sitting around it. When she speaks again, the meekness has completely dissolved from her tone, and a fire replaces the fear that formerly dwelled in those vapid, emerald pools of green. Her next words hold an unwavering strength I wasn't expecting—

"And I won't be bullied anymore."

The knot in my stomach plummets, leaving me cold.

Anymore.

That one word, spoken with such sudden, unexpected fire, hangs in the empty space between us. I blink as I feel it slam into me like a freight train, decimating me.

The jewel of a tear clings to her lashes as her eyes drift back to her new friend, who beams, pride rolling off her in waves.

"I assume it would be okay for me to live in the cottage right away?" I see her hope fade and she instantly deflates when Kya grimaces.

"I've been keeping an eye on things since Jesse passed, caring for Hannah," she tells her gently in an attempt to brace Cole for the bad news she's about to give her. "I'm sorry, hun, but it's in a terrible state. No electricity, damp patches everywhere, and I don't know when Jesse last had the roof rethatched. It's furnished, but pretty much everything's been ruined by time and moisture."

Cole sinks back in her chair and she turns away, clearly warring with her emotions, her worst fears being realized as her mind scrambles furiously with indecision over what she might do—where she'll stay.

"But," Kya leans over me and tugs on her hand gently, coaxing her to turn back. Her eyes are red-rimmed, her already pale face turning ashen, exhaustion evident in her tired eyes. "You're more than welcome to stay with me until the cottage is livable again. For as long as you need."

Cole's eyes widen—shock, gratitude, or something in between, warring openly on her face. My gut whispers this woman hasn't known much kindness in her life, and likely hasn't learned how to accept it when it's offered freely.

My gaze drops to her mouth as her tongue slides along her lower lip, catching the corner between her teeth.

My eyes lock on that spot until she releases it, finding her voice again.

"R-really? You... you would really do that? For me?" She pauses, her puzzled expression deepening. "But you hardly even know me..." The last part is barely a whisper, her voice trembling as this time, tears spill over her lower lashes.

Something clenches in my chest, tight and unfamiliar. My throat works as I swallow down the emotion rising at the sight of those tears.

Why can't I stop staring?

Her delicate fingers tug at the pink cuffs of her jumper, searching for something to anchor her trembling voice.

Kya stands abruptly, reaching over to pull Cole to her feet, tugging her into a tight embrace.

"I'm absolutely certain, hun," Kya says softly, her voice steady and sure.

With Cole standing between my thighs, I'm suddenly hyper-aware of her slight weight pressing lightly against me as she leans in to return Kya's embrace.

I inhale sharply and instantly regret it, as the sweet scent of her overwhelms me.

I close my eyes, forcing my mind to focus on anything

—anything—

other than the press of her body between my legs and the tightness of my groin.

After what feels like an eternity, Kya lets go, releasing Cole from her bear-like hug and they settle back into their seats. I close my eyes, drawing in a slow, steadying breath before slowly exhaling, trying desperately to regain my center. When I reopen them, my gaze sweeps across the table.

The only one who seems to notice my tension—*thankfully*—is Brick. He leans back, legs spread in effortless confidence, the picture of someone completely at ease. One eyebrow quirked, a small, knowing smile curling his lips as he raises his Scotch and takes a slow sip.

He's got an uncanny ability to put you at ease—until you remember he sees everything. He's someone who watches, waiting patiently for the perfect moment to strike, whether with words or fists, depending on what's needed in the moment. His smile is easy, convincing. But his eyes—they linger. Calculating, knowing full well this isn't the outcome I'd wanted.

I nod, giving him the go ahead to move forward.

"Right then," he claps, sitting forward in his seat. "I'll come by tomorrow morning with the paperwork." His performance is flawless—the perfect balance of warmth and effortless charm.

The rest of the table thankfully remains oblivious, as he seamlessly guides them into less formal conversation. They see his charisma; I see his strategy. He has the ability to read me, dissecting every flicker of my eyes, every minute shift in my expression. And I play along, expression smooth, posture steady. But inside, something twists—a quiet frustration, a recognition of the game I'm losing even before it begins.

Cole stifles a yawn. Kya takes it as her cue to bid us farewell and stands. She scoops up her dog's leash, pecks Brick on the cheek, and leads Cole out the door, back toward the boat.

Zavier takes his time standing up from his chair, watching as the women make their way across the lawn.

"You lost that one, mate," Zavier mutters as he passes me, his tone dripping with smugness.

My jaw tightens and I grip his arm before he gets by me.

"If you lay one finger on her..." I hiss through gritted teeth, keeping my voice low, my fingers digging into his flesh.

"You'll do what, Rogan? Sack me? Too late." He scoffs, leaning in close, his breath hot against my ear, lowered so only I hear him.

"And she's not yours to make threats over. If she wants me to touch her," his voice drops, venomous like the snake he is, "and, believe me, she'll want me to...," a small laugh, "then you better believe I'll make her scream."

A low growl rumbles through my chest as I rise to my full height, towering over him, making my point without words. Zavier doesn't break our stare, but I'd have to be blind to miss how his Adam's apple bobs with his slow swallow as he moves to square up with me.

Brick's hand clamps down on the back of Zavier's neck, pulling him away.

"Come on, princess," Brick moves forward, his tone unyielding, his hurried pace causing Zavier to trip over his own feet as he steers him toward the door. With a firm shove, he sends him out. Brick stands in the doorway, arms crossed firmly across his chest, effectively blocking the entrance. Once Zavier is well on his way back to the boat, he returns to the table, settling himself into Cole's vacated chair. I drum my fingers on the rim of my empty glass as I think.

He stares at me, those observant eyes ever watchful, waiting for me to get my head around my recent loss, gauging what I might need from him next.

"Give her the papers. Put together an estimate for the monthly costs—renovating the bookshop, the cottage, the land. Caring for the donkey. Let her see just how quickly it will eat away at her allowance."

Brick nods, his sharp mind already calculating.

"Paint the darker side of small business ownership," I continue, "in a country that isn't hers, in a village so steeped in tradition that any outsider is treated like an alien. After a month or two of barely scraping by, she'll have to come running to me. I'll just bide my time. Sooner or later, she'll accept my offer."

Brick watches me, silently accepting my feigned confidence, the conflict warring within me.

"And?" he asks, his tone loaded.

"And what?" I sigh, pinching the bridge of my nose, my patience completely shot after the storm of emotions from the last half hour.

"Hmmm... how about the fact that you were pretty much undressing her with your eyes the entire time we've been here?" He grins wickedly, waggling his eyebrows, reminding me of the boyish humor he's always used to help get me through the pain of the beatings I'd had to endure at my father's hand.

He's always been there for me, no matter what we've been through, ever since we were boys at boarding school. I shake my head and chuff a laugh, relieved he seems to believe my interest in her is nothing more than the usual lust, coupled with the turmoil of having to try to drive her away, being what's got me so off kilter.

"Fuck off," is all I can muster, returning my gaze to the window as I watch them disembark from the boat. Cole rushes away, disappearing into the orchard, her footsteps quick, shoulders tense as she vanishes between the trees.

I watch her go, my brow furrowing at the tense feeling of unease I have in the pit of my stomach. Kya hurries to get off the boat, struggling to get the puppy over the side. As soon as her feet hit solid ground, she heads in the same direction Cole had run, turning to say something to Zavier before slipping down the path.

Zavier runs a hand through his hair, backing up a step too close to the donkey. A sharp bray erupts—loud, indignant, carrying across the water, loud enough to turn a few heads. He jolts away from her as she nips at his arm. He heads toward the orchard, muttering under his breath, as the donkey, satisfied, swishes her tail in judgment. I smirk, glad to have been able to witness Hannah try to take a bite out of the dickhead.

Kya reemerges from the orchard a few moments later, running head first into Zavier. He grips her shoulders as her hands flail, her head whipping from side to side. The smile slips from my lips when my momentary mirth is replaced by something colder, sharper.

Something is wrong.

Brick taps his toe against the leg of my chair, snapping my attention back. "So, what do you feel like doing now?"

I lean back and exhale, slowly, watching as Zavier follows Kya back to the orchard. I'm fucking exhausted from lack of sleep, but who am I kidding? It's not like I'll be getting any sleep right now anyway.

"Let's see if Brittany is free again tonight."

He grins at me then. "Bethany," he corrects, "and maybe she can bring a couple of friends as well," he adds.

Maybe he's right. Maybe what I need to get out from under Cole Allbright is to get somebody under me—or maybe *multiple somebodies*.

Chapter 10

Cole

As if wading through a dense fog, my mind clouds, the world dulling around me.

I barely sense the people near me—Kya, steady at my elbow, guiding me onto the boat. Zavier, arriving moments later, his body uncomfortably close, his thigh pressing against mine.

The beauty of the river is lost, the conversation around me muted, as strangers discuss my fate.

As the boat makes its way across the river, I watch Hannah—her tail swishing, her head dipped as she grazes. The cat, surely the same one I'd seen this morning, watches her perched on one of the nearby picnic tables—a kindred spirit.

I attempt to envision the bookshop as it could be.

Fresh turquoise paint framing the doors and windows. Umbrellas unfurled over freshly renovated benches. Couples and families sipping tea and coffee and children nibbling scones with books purchased from within, laid out in front of them.

I see happiness. The community that could bloom here.

There's even a glimmer of me. An impossible image of myself—whole, unburdened.

I picture myself stepping out of the bookshop, chatting with customers. Smiling. Laughing.

I see Kya—Grumbl at her side—laughing at Brick as Hannah steals a cookie right off his plate.

But then I'm lost in the memory of depthless steel-gray eyes, locked onto mine. His words haunt me as his low, sonorous voice reverberates through my mind...

"...you give up your claim to the bookshop..."

"You go... leave Verdon-on-Wye."

"...I'll even pay to help you get back home..."

"back home..."

Those words unmake me and I shiver as the dream decays, the nightmare crawling in, darkening its edges with rot, swallowing it whole.

He's coming for me, his voice sharp, biting—calling my name. Furious with me for daring to leave. Reminding me how badly I've fucked up. Of the price he'll make me pay for running. For believing I was worthy of a life without him. Proving, once again, as he has so many times before...

I am no one...

I am nothing...

And I've failed.

The ghost of his hands skirt over my skin—fingers tightening as they wrap around my throat. Shoving me backward, into the shadows. Back into the pain. The pool of blood growing beneath me, swallowing me into its depths, consuming me until there's nothing left.

The dream of warmth and friendship fading into oblivion.

What have I done?

"Oh dear God... what have I done?"

I must say it aloud, because Kya's arm wraps around my shoulders, pulling me into her, holding me close. The earthy scent of patchouli envelops me and her soothing murmured words and comforting touch begin to ground me.

But then the weight of another hand threads around my waist.

Strong. Heavy. Hot.

Zavier's hand.

The weight of his arm presses firmly against my spine.

All I want to do is scream as panic resurges. My chest squeezes as claustrophobia sets in.

I claw at my throat.

I need space.

Air.

Escape.

The urge to run swallows me—becoming all consuming.

My heart races and all I can think is...

Run—farther, faster.

Run until breath is a forgotten thing and all that remains are the splinters of shattered hopes and the shards of broken dreams...

The boat slams hard against the shore, the impact freeing me from the prison of his hand.

I push away from them both, breaking completely out of his grasp, leap over the side of the boat—*and run.*

Past Hannah, past the tortoiseshell cat, skirting the bookshop and into the orchard.

I feel the vacant windows of Haven watching me like eyes, tracking me as I vanish into the trees. From somewhere in the distance, faint voices call my name.

No, no, no!

Not again!

I can't let him find me!

Not again!

I stumble beneath the sprawling boughs of an old apple tree, its gnarled roots rippling across the ground like ancient fingers, tripping me. My legs give way and I drop to my knees. My chest heaves as I gasp for air but no matter how much I try, I can't seem to fill my lungs. Little sparks of light dance before my eyes and my vision begins to tunnel.

Shit, I'm going to pass out...

I can't let him find me. I have to hide.

Make myself small.

Disappear.

Tucking my knees to my chin, I curl into myself—my body shrouded by the tall grass.

My wrists throb, the wounds a cruel reminder of how close I came to losing my ability to choose ever again.

The world around me dims as I begin to lose myself, wishing I could just stay right here, become part of the roots, be pulled into the soil, hidden in the earth's quiet embrace forever.

Where no one will find me.

Where *HE* can't ever find me again.

Where no one can force me to continue to exist in this miserable world where my choice is nothing more than a fragile illusion, ripped away as easily as a breath.

I squeeze my eyes shut, the world around me fading as the ever present thought quietly creeps back in—a dark specter whispering...

"Let me be your escape..."

Chapter 11

Cole

"She's here!"

A deep voice bellows as a large presence crouches in front of me. Gentle fingers sweep the hair from my face and a strong hand gently grips my shoulder.

A slightly calloused thumb softly brushes along my cheek, tracing skin chilled with exhaustion.

"Cole?"

I cringe, a soft whimper escaping my throat before I can catch it. I cast an unseeing glance toward the voice and blink blearily at the gray eyes looking down at me.

"Cole? Can you hear me?"

His lips move, but the ghosts of my past hold me hostage, haunting me, trapping me in my mind.

No, no, no, no, no!

Not again.

I don't want to be found.

I want to stay here.

Let the earth swallow me whole.

Hide me.

Keep me buried in its depths where no one can find me.

Where he can't hurt me again.

The sudden realization that I've been found sends a flash of terror racing through me and I lash out—wild, desperate—a pitiful scream ripping from somewhere deep inside me.

He reaches for me and I slam my fists against a solid wall of muscle, refusing to be taken without a fight. He doesn't flinch when I slap and scratch at his face and neck. Doesn't let go when I buck and kick as he lifts me off the ground. He sweeps my legs over the crook of his elbow, cradling me firmly against his chest with one strong arm wrapped tightly around my shoulders.

"Please..." I beg, sobbing as my tears soak the material of his shirt.

The heat of his breath presses softly against the top of my head as his deep voice hushes me, a murmur so low I feel it, more than hear it.

It calms me and I feel boneless in his arms as the tension in me slowly begins to ebb away. I tuck my head under his chin, the soft vibrations of his voice soothing me. I'm suddenly cocooned in a feeling I realize I have no idea how to accept.

The world tilts, the ground slipping away beneath me, yet his hold is steady, unwavering. I should resist. I should fight, push away the unexpected warmth threading around me—but something inside me falters, caught between the instinct to flee and the unfamiliar pull of safety.

I drag in a ragged breath, expecting the sharp sting of expensive cologne and cigars, or the acrid scent of whiskey and cigarettes. But instead I'm met with the clean scent of bergamot—bright citrus, laced with something richer beneath it. Something untamed, earthy, calming. Like the crisp air on a summer morning.

Peaceful.

I bury my face against him, my numb fingers grasping blindly at the fabric of his shirt. The material is solid beneath my touch, something real, something warm. Shadows swirl at the edges of my vision—thick, heavy—my grip slackens, my breath catching as my consciousness threatens to slip away.

I slump against his chest, the last of the fight finally leaving my tired body. The last thing I hear is the steady, soothing beat of a heart, the gentle rhythm lulling me into oblivion.

I feel myself sink—into the looming exhaustion, finally succumbing into the darkness as it drags me under.

"Nicole! Get your fucking whore ass back in this house! Where are you, you rotten little bitch?! You know you can't hide from me!"

My father's rage is palpable, his voice getting uncomfortably close to where I'm hiding... again.

The Miller's orchard sits at the edge of our property, just beyond the rickety barn that once held the cider press. The scent of fermenting fruit lingers, seeping into my pores.

I duck down beside the largest one, its gnarled trunk twisted and warped, its roots clawing up through the ground like witches' fingers. It's here I'm hoping to find solace, nestled among the red leaves blanketing the ground, the air thick with the tang of rotting apples—fallen, forgotten, left to sink into the earth as the orchard grows wild after years of neglect.

I bury myself beneath them, the damp press of leaves and ruined fruit clinging to my skin. I try to make myself small, pressing my body into the earth, willing it to swallow me whole.

Pain throbs, both from where he struck me and from the fresh burns searing my arms.

"Please, God. Don't let him find me..."

A flicker of gray eyes. The steady beat of a heart. Soothing words whispered against my skin. Twigs breaking beneath booted feet...

The heavy stomps of his booted feet stumbling down the pathway are closer now. I'm hit first with the smell of whiskey and cigars, the putrid scent mingling with the sickly smell of the apples.

"Ahhh, there you are..." he slurs. "I told you; you couldn't hide from me!" I yelp as his calloused hands reach for me, pulling me from the bed of leaves. The back of his hand cracks across my cheek, and the taste of hot copper fills my mouth, blood

splattering the leaves. My head rocks back as he lands another blow and my vision dims.

Soft fabric locked between my fingers, the clean scent of citrus surrounding me, the curl of a strong, warm arm around my shoulders.

I'm thrown to the ground and his thick hand grips the back of my neck, pressing my face into the mulch, filling my nose with the acrid stench of the apples and his massive weight pins me down as he straddles my legs.

A deep, gentle tone humming in my ear...

"Shh, you're alright Cole. I've got you, Little Fawn."

"So you want to whore yourself out by kissing the Sullivan boys, huh?"

There's a clang of metal as he undoes his belt. I brace myself for the lashings, hoping he'll only use the leather end and not the buckle this time.

The heat of his clammy hand reaches beneath my dress exposing my backside as he throws my skirt up around my shoulders.

"You're dumber than I thought if you think they only want a kiss, you stupid bitch?"

He drops to his knees behind me and digs his fingers into my hips, lifting my rear up, knocking my legs apart with his knee.

"I'll show you what they want, Nicole!"

My heart thunders in my chest like a caged bird—pounding, frantic, fluttering like wings beating against the bars, the ache of escape pressing desperately against my ribs.

Warmth against my cheek, the gentle thrum of a steady heartbeat, a strong embrace holding me tight.

"You're nothing but a dirty little whore! Just like your worthless fucking mother!"

His breath is hot as he presses his mouth against the shell of my ear. I have to fight the retch as the putrid stench of sour whiskey and smoke invade my senses. His blackened spittle rolls down my cheek as the heat of his chest presses against my back. His meaty fingers claw at my thigh, ripping my panties from me and I squirm, clawing at the damp earth, trying to scramble out of his grip. This is different from the usual beatings. Something is wrong.

*"A dirty," a sudden, ripping pain like I've never felt before erupts through me and a silent scream sticks in my throat, "fucking," his hips slam forward and he thrusts into me, the pain tearing me apart, "bitch," I scream—the sound lost as he buries my face into the rotting leaves and fruit, forcing himself into me again "**whore!**" His voice echoes through the orchard as he bellows his last word, then lets out a loud, low groan—his hips stilling as I feel him pulse deep inside me.*

He collapses on top of me, driving the last bit of air from my lungs. I can't move. I can't breathe.

The branches in the tree above me creak softly. It's the only sound I can hear over his panting, his fetid breath pouring across my face.

Finally, he pushes himself up. I wince and bile rises, burning my throat at the sickening feeling of his now flaccid dick slipping out of me. I draw in a deep breath, trembling as I try to remain still—afraid that if I move or make a sound, he'll be on me again.

His shadow looms over me and the buckle on his belt jangles as he pulls his pants up, breathing heavily with the effort it takes him to refasten them.

"They don't want you, Nicole. Those boys just want to get their dicks wet. So what do you think? Did you like that, you little slut?"

He spits, the moisture tangling in my hair before dripping across my nose, mixing into my blood and tears as it slides across my face.

He kicks at a pile of leaves, his boot digging deep enough to churn up the wet dirt, scattering it over me.

"Cover yourself up, whore."

Finally he turns, stumbling back toward the house, back to his whiskey and cigars.

Only when I am certain he's far enough away, do I give in to the silent scream I've been holding in. Only then do I allow myself to move, pulling my legs up under me as I lie in a broken, battered heap. Curled into myself, my tears and my blood soaking the ground around me.

It's then that I finally understand—safety is only an illusion. It's never been anything more than a fleeting dream. There's no where I can hide. No where I'll ever truly be safe.

Because the truth is, he will always find me.

Chapter 12

I shift onto my side, soft warmth billowing around me, followed by the faint creak of wooden furniture settling in the quiet.

Hazy fragments of the dream linger, slowly lifting from my mind like mist. My heart pounds rapidly in my chest and I have to remind myself it was just another nightmare.

I'm not there... curled under that tree, hiding in the orchard, suffocating under fear as the vestiges of my father roaring for me echo around my head.

My eyes feel swollen and raw and I blink several times trying to focus.

My whole body feels stiff, my muscles groaning as I move to sit up. My mind grapples with the tattered memories of the afternoon, trying to make sense of it, but the last thing I can seem to remember is the smell of apples, and...

Citrus?

What in the hell happened and where the fuck am I?

I scan the room, taking in my surroundings. I'm in a strange bed, in a room brightly painted with pops of color. Mismatched furniture decorates the space, somehow fitting together in perfect harmony.

The scent of patchouli laced with the faintest hint of apple mingles with the warm scent of something cooking in another room and the soft sound of music carries from the floor below.

I lift the blankets, and my stomach drops when I realize I'm not in my own clothes. The pink sweater is gone, replaced by a long t-shirt that drapes nearly to my knees, my bare legs peeking out below the hem. My hands fly over my body and a glimmer of relief washes over me as I realize my bra and underwear are still in place.

But then I remember my arms...

My gut churns at the thought of whoever undressed me having seen them—knowing there will be questions I don't think I'm ready to answer.

My stomach sinks further when I see the bandages the nurse at the hospital had wrapped around them, have been replaced. The deep purple bruises where the catheter transfused the blood I had lost, now unequivocally visible.

The small, circular scars—some old and fully healed, others painfully fresh, still red and angry—an assortment left by cigars, and cigarettes, all on prominent display. There's no way whoever dressed me missed them...

"You keep those covered up now, Nicole. You'll only make it worse if you try to drag anybody else into our business."

The ghost of his voice chastises me. Admonishing me for yet another failed attempt to hide my perpetual shame.

Tears burn my eyes—tears I've been holding back for days. They crest my lower lids, finally spilling down my cheeks and I drop my head into my hands—and sob.

There's a gentle tapping on the door, followed by a slow creak as it pushes open.

"Cole?"

Long fingers curl around the edge and soft, concerned amber eyes peek through the opening.

"Oh, honey!"

Kya steps in, her voice full of compassion and rushes to the bed. She sets a mug on the bedside table, then gathers me into her arms, holding me close, rocking me gently.

I fold into her, needing the warmth of a kind embrace more than I realized and like the force of a dam breaking, I let myself cry uncontrollably on her shoulder.

Chapter 13

Cole

"I'm sorry," I say for the hundredth time, sipping the coffee Kya brought me. The sweetness of the sugar and cream she's added is soothing and somehow grounding.

We sit beside one another on the bed in Kya's spare room. Grumbl, having made his way onto the bed, with a little help from Kya, plops his solid weight between us. The warmth of his little body snuggled into me as he snores softly, anchors me, calming my nerves.

Through the window, I see her garden, the backs of the terraces lining Lover's Lane. The early evening sun filters through the branches of a neighboring tree, scattering a filigree of golden light across the floorboards.

"Cole..."

Kya's voice is tentative as she plucks absently at the blanket. Her long legs stretch out in front of her, mirroring mine, though mine are still tucked beneath the covers.

I grip the mug tighter, bracing myself.

She's going to ask about my scars.

I think furiously, scrambling to prepare a half-truth, something carefully constructed, palatable. He had me conditioned to lie. To always have an excuse at the ready. Something that sounds believable and hopefully not raise too many follow up questions.

But these wounds are new. I haven't had time to craft my lies yet. Haven't come up with a *plausible reason* as to why my arms look the way they do. She must already think I'm crazy, running off the way I had. What will she think when she sees how deep that madness truly runs?

"I want to tell you something."

And just like that, the dark cloud is looming over me again. I'm about to lose yet another someone, who could have been a friend.

"I want you to know that you can stay here—with me and Grumbl—for as long as you want. I can help you out with Hannah, take you to Gloucester or Monmouth to get you some clothes—you know, things to help you feel comfortable."

She breaks out into a wide grin and rolls her eyes, "I can even help you navigate the whirlwind that is Thaddeus Brickton the Third, and the minefield that is the Duke..."

My mouth gapes as I turn to face her.

She drops her eyes to the warm pile of wrinkles snoring softly between us, reaching down to stroke her fingers through his soft fur.

"And well..." her voice softens, a tenderness lacing her tone, "he loves you. And, like I said before, my gut says you're a good person. So..."

I set the mug down, turning back to face her—my eyes wet as I fight back more tears and take her hand in mine.

"I'll stay."

Warmth unfurls in my chest as I manage to accept her offer with unexpected ease.

"That would be so wonderful, Kya! Thank you so, so much!"

She tugs me into a bone-crushing hug and squeals loudly, waking up the snoring pup, who immediately hops up, bouncing and yapping happily.

"You'll love it here, I promise you!"

And for the first time since we've met—I think I might be starting to believe her.

Chapter 14

Rogan

I pace in front of my bedroom window, practically wearing a path into the carpet, unable to pull my thoughts away from the apple orchard below.

A ghostly silhouette forms around my fingers as I rest my hand against the glass—the cool pane a haunting echo of the memory of her chilled skin when I swept the hair off her cheek.

The cloying scent of crushed apples had seeped a fermented sweetness into the air, mixing with the weighted silence as I crouched before her—the fragrance nearly choking me with its pungent perfume.

She looks so small, with her body curled into a tight ball, tucked tightly against the base of an old tree, her tiny form almost completely swallowed by the long grass. Those emerald eyes, pinched shut. Her long lashes fanning over bruising, now far clearer where her tears had washed away the concealer she'd applied to hide them.

Fire burns in my gut at the memory of those marks, my hands scraping down my face as I continue my relentless pacing.

I can still feel the battery of her fists as they slammed against my chest, each hit waning in strength as she struggled, fighting me off—the last dregs of desperation, the only thing fueling her spirit.

I held her tightly, keeping my grip as gentle as I could manage, whispering calming words into her hair. The soft scent of her shampoo, stirred by the warmth of my breath, flooding my senses.

There was a notable shift in her the moment my words caught, as she relaxed in my arms, settling against my chest, her body still shaking, her breath hitching through broken sobs.

But when her fingers curled into the fabric of my shirt, grasping, clawing for something... anything to help keep her afloat on this side of sanity, it was as if a switch flipped inside me, causing my heart to hammer against my ribs—a gripping tightness within the walls of my chest. Something foreign demanding I lash out against anything that might hurt her.

Hold her.

Keep her.

Claim her.

A roaring voice screaming into the void... *MINE!*

This same woman who threatens to derail my plans, is somehow tipping me precariously close to going over the edge, into a place I've never dared to venture.

"I won't be bullied anymore..."

Her words said with such fire—such defiance. A strength I hadn't expected.

But I also witnessed the cost of that moment of bravery. That same fire snuffed out, vanishing as she folded in on herself, trying desperately to disappear, to lose herself in the fallen leaves and rotten fruit piled amongst the roots of the tree. Her mind shackled in the grip of an invisible ghost, trapping her in some haunting memory.

The thrumming bass of music woven with the sound of women's laughter, Brick's deep voice filtering between them—pulls me away from the thoughts rampaging through my mind.

He'd invited them before everything shifted. Before my conscience wouldn't let me just drive by as Kya paced frantically along the lane between the orchard and the Gatehouse, her body screaming worry long before she even spoke a word to us.

"It's Cole!"

Those two words had me gripping the steering wheel so tightly my knuckles popped, the hum of the car's engine beneath my hands fading into irrelevance.

The weight of her words blindsided me, settling in the pit of my stomach like small sharp stones as they sank in, my gut wrenching painfully.

I don't even think the car was at a full stop when Brick had leapt out, rushing to Kya and pulling her against his chest—stroking her hair, whispering words I couldn't hear, calming her. She burrowed into him, her fingers curled tightly into the fabric of his shirt as he absently took the puppy's leash from her hand, looping it around his knuckles, his eyes scanning the path to the orchard. As I stepped out of the car, he said something else to her and she nodded again, straightening and wiping at her eyes, a look of resolve replacing her fear.

He walked her and the pup over to the car where I stood, locked stupidly in place, my knuckles deathly white as I clutched the door frame, unable to break my hold. Her unspoken concerns about what may have happened to Cole, paralyzing me.

Kya's wide, wet eyes flit from place to place, never stopping, frantically searching. The look of panic etched in her features only added to my own concerns, my imagination now running rampant.

What the fuck could have happened to her since they left the pub?

All I could think was, that cunt Zavier had been with them and my pulse raged, praying he hadn't done something to her.

Brick kept Kya tucked close to his side, gently smoothing his palm down her back as he spoke softly, his lips pressed into her hair.

His gentler side—the side others rarely get to see, coming out only for her.

"Hush now, Sunshine." his words having an immediate effect on her, she settled into him.

"We're here now. Everything's going to be alright. Now, tell us what happened with Cole?"

His reassurance the permission she needed, her words came out in a rush as she exploded under the weight of her worries, the dam she had them locked behind, finally breaking free under their weight.

"I really don't know what happened! She seemed a little distant when we first got back on the boat. Like she was lost in thought... you know, off in her head somewhere." She shakes her head, lifting her shoulders in a small shrug.

"She had so many things come at her all at once today, so I figured she was just processing it all. I didn't want to push, so I just kept quiet and let her be." She sniffed loudly and wiped her sleeve under her eyes, before curling herself back into Brick's side, wrapping her arms around his chest.

"She just bolted off the boat the second we got to shore and before Zavier and I could get off... before we even realized what was going on, she had disappeared. Brick..." she whimpered, her voice filled with desperation as she turned to look up to him, chin wobbling, fresh tears spilling from her red-rimmed eyes, his shirt tightly gripped in her fists.

"I've looked everywhere and I can't find her! She doesn't know the area. What if she got into the forest and couldn't find her way back out? What if..." she shivered, her breath catching in her throat on a sob, "What if something's happened to her?" She dropped her forehead to his chest, her shoulders shaking as she cried against him, "I should have been there. I should have been faster, gone after her sooner. This is all my fault..." she started to ramble, her words muffled into Brick's shirt.

He hugged her tighter, shushing against her hair, but his eyes found mine, his brows pulled together with a look of knowing concern.

Whatever that *something* is that Cole had somehow awoken within me clenched, making my heart jolt. Ice flooded my veins and my face hardened as I met his eyes, my lips pressing into a tight line.

"We'll find her." I finally spoke up, snapping out of my stupor, my stare locking onto his.

In the Army, they always called us *'The Telepaths'*, for our uncanny ability to communicate without words. Instinctively, we always seemed to know what the other was thinking. The down side was we were perpetually sent on missions deemed impossible by everyone else.

It never stopped us though. No matter what the task, we always knew we would have each other's backs. We'd head into the unknown, an unspoken plan forming between us with nothing more than a series of facial expressions and hand signals, so that even without words, we each knew the other's intentions.

Understanding his silent marching orders, Brick nudged Kya back, holding her gently by the shoulders. He dipped his chin to meet her gaze—his eyes connecting with hers, reassuring her. She nodded at him, trusting him fully, then buried herself against him again, letting him lead her back toward the village, Grumbl plodding alongside them.

I clicked the button on the key fob—the chirp of the car's lock activating, seeming loud in the silence. I stepped into the path, remembering there had once been a time this space had been my sanctuary. A place where I could lose myself to the quiet of the trees, where, if only for a short time, I could find a sliver of peace after my father's 'lessons'.

I felt frozen as my eyes scanned the tall grass covering the overgrown path beyond, spotting the thin trail, broken down by her footsteps, giving away her hiding place. I drew in a deep breath and followed it into the trees.

The delicate chirping of birds and the low hum of insects were the only sounds—besides the near-deafening rush of blood in my ears as my heart beat frantically. An unbidden sense of worry coursed through me, cloying and heavy as I searched the area for more evidence as to which way she may have gone.

Jesse had been proud of this orchard once—selling apples to the local cider mill and bakery, then using the drinks and pastries they'd crafted from them to tempt customers into his failing bookshop. A business set too far away from any major town in the forest. Located on a dead-end road, forgotten half the time and surviving only on occasional locals and curious visitors looking for the back way to the pub across the water.

Profits had been falling for years, even more so after Margaret had passed a few years back. Jesse seemed to lose more and more interest with each passing year he'd had to run it alone, but he still refused to give it up, convinced it had some hidden value.

Cole didn't stand a chance—she'd inherited a dying dream.

But they'd been smart, saving everything they could over the years—a bit naive perhaps—leaving their legacy to their daughter, who'd moved to the states years ago, then extending that legacy to a granddaughter they'd never even met, banking all their hopes on them being the miracle that would someday bring their little bookshop back to its former glory.

If only he'd sold it to me. I could have turned it around, made it thrive—books and pastries be damned. But that had been where Jesse and I had always clashed. He couldn't see it the way I did, couldn't recognize the potential of my vision for it—the right inventory, a new purpose, marketed to the right people.

To him, that had been blasphemous. His little shop wasn't just a business for him. It had been a place of peace. A place of learning. His precious books within, representing an escape from reality. The idea of tearing it apart, flooding it with the pulse of high-octane thrill seekers and arrogant tourists, hell bent on adventure, had been unthinkable to him.

It had been his haven. And maybe, just maybe, I was beginning to see it through Jesse's eyes. Because here—this very spot—this had been where she had run. To the very same spot I would run to, to escape the horrors of my own life when I was a boy.

I waded through the sea of tall, wavy grass, making my way through the trees, my boots crushing fallen apples into the soil. My gut, gnawing at me relentlessly, had guided me—pulling me toward where she must have been.

As I neared the edge of the orchard, I stopped, turning in a circle to take one last look around before moving on to look elsewhere.

But the moment I moved to turn away, I heard a shuddering cry, so small it had barely been audible, the sound immediately swallowed again by the silence. I zeroed in on where it had come from—there... at the shrouded base of what had to be the oldest, largest tree in the orchard.

A soft breeze caressed the blades of tall grass, parting them just enough for the last flicker of evening light to catch on her fiery auburn hair.

The relief that flooded me was instant and my heartbeat stuttered. I tried to ignore the feeling in my chest as I rushed to her, dropping down beside her tiny form, curled in on herself, shivering against the invisible demons holding her hostage in her mind.

My heart clenched as I'd recognized her state, knowing exactly how that feels... what it's like to be held prisoner within the horrifying memories of past terrors. I may not know what this poor girl has been through, but whatever it is, has her scared out of her mind.

Kya's broken cry of relief as I'd carried her new friend through her door, Brick holding it open, clearing a path for me to carry Cole through the house, up the stairs then finally lying her down on the mattress of the small bed.

I can still hear Kya's weeping gratitude, as she clung to Brick's side. Cole had stirred then, Kya pulling away from him to rush to her side.

"You better go..." she'd said, her eyes pleading, concerned our presence might trigger Cole again, should she see Brick and I looming over her in the tiny room.

Our jobs done, we made our way back down the stairs and let ourselves out, heading back to the Manor.

But why was it so hard to leave?

Once again, the sound of laughter snaps me back to the present. *Bethany and her friends*—former temptations that once seemed enticing—now feel hollow and unappealing.

Brick can have them.

The desire to try and dull my anxiety, my frustrations, by losing myself in the erotic touches of strangers seems to have evaporated, replaced instead by this strange, insistent pulse rising in my chest, the feeling foreign and unsettling.

I jolt, trying to shake it off and chastise myself.

Bloody fool! What the fuck is happening to me?

The grating cackle of one of the women echoes down the hall and I'm hit with a blinding surge of claustrophobia—a sudden urge to leave the choking space of my rooms, to get out of the range of their voices. I need something to distract me from my thoughts, something to free me from this onslaught of aberrant emotions—something punishing.

I need to run.

I strip out of my shirt and jeans and pull on shorts and a tank top, then tie my running shoes with sharp, deliberate movements.

I pass the living room, barely sparing a glance at the woman grinding herself on Brick's lap, while the other two paw at him, their drinks sloshing drunkenly over the rims of their glasses.

I hurry my steps, hoping they won't notice me as I sprint past. I cringe, bile climbing my throat, disgusted with a sight that just mere hours earlier, I would have been more than happy to indulge in myself.

My sights seem to be locked on a new path. One I need to get out of my head if I'm going to regain any semblance of normalcy.

Shoving in my earbuds, I crank the volume. Hoping the loud, thumping heavy metal, the relentless drums and screaming guitars will somehow drown out my racing thoughts.

As my feet hit the drive, my toes dig into the gravel and I don't waste another second.

I run.

As hard and as fast as I can. Each pounding footstep pulsing through me, a punishing rhythm of exertion and escape. I push harder, ignoring the burn in my lungs, the fiery ache in my muscles, sprinting up hills, back toward the river and through the forest.

I run.

With every fall of my foot on the trail, I try to run Cole Allbright out of my mind, out of my head. Try to run her clean out of my system. But the harder I run, the more my muscles burn, the more my thoughts circle—all I see is her...

My pace slows as I approach Lover's Lane, and I realize my efforts have been futile.

I stop when I get to Kya's house, my heart thundering, whether from the punishing run or from the potential of catching a glimpse of Cole, I'm not sure anymore.

Like an addict circling the source of their next fix, I take a few tentative steps closer, my eyes locked on the upstairs window—the room where I had placed Cole in the small bed not long ago. A soft glow from a bedroom lamp lets me know she's in there and something in my chest squeezes at the thought.

Breathing hard, I pace absently in front of the little cottage, disgusted with the fact that the run had failed to burn her from my mind the way I'd intended.

Furious with myself for giving in to these strange feelings, for letting myself linger where I don't belong, I force myself to turn away.

And I run.

Past my endurance, into the darkness. Pushing harder, faster. Leaning into the shadows as the night stretches out ahead of me, feeling limitless, praying for it to swallow me whole.

The burn in my legs. The fire in my lungs.

They've done nothing to burn the thoughts of her from my mind.

She's still there...

So I run.

Chapter 15

Cole

Six months...

I only have six months to make this work. To turn this mess into a miracle. It feels like both an eternity and a heartbeat. The days begin to blur together, carried more by momentum than intention and before I know it, a week has passed.

The events of what happened after my frantic departure from the boat are lost to me. When I ask Kya, I get the feeling she's trying to protect me by glossing over the details between when they found me beneath the old apple tree, hidden between its ancient gnarled roots and overgrown grass, as if I had wanted to disappear—and when I was carried back to her house.

But she breezes past the gap of time between my fading consciousness and waking in her home. She seems to be dancing around anything that might stir a relapse—like the wounds she carefully tended, the hands carrying me here—leaving the finer details to the shadows.

But each night, my dreams are haunted by gray eyes—*or were they ice blue?* They watch me from the hazy edges, blinking away the moment before I wake—torn from yet another echo of the punishments doled out by the men who were meant to protect me.

She'd cleaned me up as much as she could and changed me into a t-shirt before tucking me into the bed that I guess, since I'll be staying with her now, will be mine.

She never asks about my wrists. Never mentions the bandages. But every so often, I catch her glancing at my arms—a flicker of concern flashing in her eyes before she slides back to her perpetually sunny disposition.

The first few days are filled with mountains of paperwork Brick brings to me, all needing my signature.

Kya loans me clothes consisting of everything from thick, brightly colored wool sweaters to delicate lace panties, still brand new in the packaging.

I can't help but feel like I'm taking things that don't belong to me. Things she'd intended for herself. But the woman is like a bull in a china shop when it comes to getting her way, and there's certainly no dissuading her. So, I gratefully accept her offerings even though most of the items are too big for me.

Brick runs through the projected costs of renovating not just the bookshop, but the cottage and the land around it. He reassures me he has good contacts—men and women who've already been vetted and brought in shortly after my grandfather had passed. They'd reviewed the necessary updates, and supplied prices before I even arrived, while he and the solicitors worked to put the properties on the market. It's a quiet reminder of how close I came to missing my chance at claiming my inheritance.

"You were lucky you showed up when you did," he says, absently, eyes scanning through legal jargon I can't even begin to decipher. "Left it a few more days, and everything would have gone to the highest bidder. You would have had nothing."

Kya elbows him firmly in the ribs at his last remark, scowling at him before shifting her eyes to where I'm sitting.

"Sorry," he apologizes, sheepishly.

Once that paperwork has all been signed and everything is in order with my inheritance, he moves on to the projected monthly expenses I should expect now that I've agreed to the terms of the will.

He shuffles through his briefcase and pulls out another large stack of papers, laying each section methodically out in front of me.

Each neat stack has a total clearly circled in red at the bottom. My eyes nearly pop out of my head at the seemingly astronomical numbers.

I flop back in my chair, my face falling as all hope vanishes. Self-doubt once more swallows it whole.

It feels impossible.

After dinner, Kya and I sit on her back porch sipping chilled white wine from a local vineyard as I mull over the barrage of expenses he warned me to expect.

"Do you think I can trust Brick?"

Her glass pauses, hovering mid-air before reaching her lips.

"Brick is one of the best men I know…" her voice trails off, clearly not saying the rest of her thoughts as she goes back to sipping her wine.

"But?"

"But, he's fiercely loyal to Rogan. I don't know their full history, but from what I've heard, they've supported each other through some very dark times. Since childhood. There's no one Rogan trusts more. And Brick would do literally anything for him."

"Like what?" I ask, my intrigue peaking.

She cocks a brow and swirls the wine in her glass.

"Anything really. From acting as a pseudo-bodyguard—not that either of them needs one," she chuffs, rolling her eyes while taking another sip from her glass. "They can both hold their own when it comes to a fight.

"But he also has a knack for lining up business opportunities and finding the weak points of anyone who might get in the way—then fleshing out the details to make those deals all work out in Rogan's favor."

She tilts her head, eyes gleaming mischievously.

"You wouldn't necessarily think it when you first meet him. I mean, he's a six-foot-two rugby playing, brick shithouse and has the looks and swagger that could charm the pants off almost anyone. Women and men included."

Her cheeks flush to a deep shade of pink at her words and we both burst into laughter.

She tips up her glass, finishing its contents, then reaches for the bottle, refilling both our glasses before continuing.

"But he's bloody smart. His IQ is genius level, and annoyingly, he never forgets a damn thing."

I believe her. I noticed it when he was working through the paperwork with me. Half the things he was talking about, I didn't see anywhere on the pages, as if he was reciting it all from memory.

I take another sip from my glass and shift in my seat, tucking my feet under me as I turn to look directly at her.

I needed to know the truth.

"But... do you think I can trust him?"

She blows out a long breath.

"Yes and no... He's an honest man—a good man. But keep in mind he's working for Rogan, and if your plans don't align with the Duke's, Brick will likely make it his mission to ensure you fail."

The weight in my stomach plummets further.

I have to keep both men agreeable if I'm to have any chance of making this work. And after factoring in the projected renovation costs, inventory, vet bills, food and shelter for Hannah—I'm left with surprisingly little.

Still more than I've ever had of my own before. But little nonetheless.

Would it even be enough to live on?

I either mutter this out loud, or Kya can read me better than any book, when she rests her hand lightly on my arm.

"Don't worry, hun," her gentle smile eases my spiraling thoughts.

"Tell you what... I can ask Greg if you can pick up some shifts with me at the pub. That way, you can meet the locals, get a feel for Verdon, and start to network. This way you can learn how to run a profitable business—and make a little extra money too."

The thought sends a surge of excitement bubbling up inside me.

I haven't had a job since I got married. *He* insisted I leave my job at the stables nearly ten years ago. Before that, my father had forced me to work, my wages vanishing into his pocket, funding his addiction to whiskey and cigarettes.

My grandfather certainly did have all his affairs in order because it took less than a week for the first installment of my inheritance to hit my account.

Kya insists I use some of the money on myself. She drives me to Gloucester in her tiny, bright blue Mini Cooper, to a place called The Quays.

I gasp in delight at the renovated warehouses turned into sleek, modern apartments. The open spaces around the docks, brightly painted canal boats moored, and a tall ship sitting in wait, its sails furled, ready for adventure.

She takes me to the outlet center, where we replenish my feeble wardrobe—underwear, jeans, t-shirts, sweaters, a thick winter coat, and various sneakers and walking shoes.

It feels strange.

I haven't shopped for myself in years—haven't had the freedom to choose. It's overwhelming—the sensation of soft, comfortable fabric surrounding me. Shoes that don't pinch my toes or make my arches ache. The reassuring weight of a coat meant to protect rather than to decorate.

I run my hands across the thick wool of the winter coat, testing its warmth, the way it settles around my shoulders.

Mine. It feels unfamiliar, but in the best way possible.

The sneakers feel comfortable and solid beneath me. They aren't the stilettos he insisted I wear because I needed to be taller, sleeker, sexier.

These aren't for show, for fashion or for someone else's expectations. They're mine. Selected for function and comfort.

For the first time, my steps feel solid and secure.

Kya's grin is huge as she leads us to checkout, her own arms full of brightly colored fabrics.

I step up beside her, meeting her grin with my own, but I'm suddenly hit with a dizzying wave of... *God, I don't even know.*

My heart hammers in my chest as I look down at the clothing I have slung over my arms.

Buying clothes.

Choosing for myself without expectation or consequence.

It's new.

It's exciting.

It's terrifying.

I feel Kya's eyes on me, patiently waiting. A soft smile on her lips and a slight gloss to her eyes as she watches me come to terms with my new found independence.

I blink, quickly shaking off the feeling, as the sudden, undeniable revelation hits me.

That's what it is... freedom.

Raw, unshackled freedom, coursing through me like the first gasp of air after staying underwater for too long.

Buying something—*anything*—just for me without fear of judgement, ridicule or punishment. No ulterior motives. No second-guessing whether *he* would disapprove of my choices.

I smile, meeting Kya's ceaselessly encouraging gaze—her smile is warm, her eyes bright as she stands quietly beside the register.

Lifting my head high, I step forward and purchase my new clothes.

Our next stop is a shop called 'The Works.' Kya is absolutely beaming with anticipation.

My mouth falls open as we walk through the doors.

The shelves are practically bursting, spilling over with art supplies, kids' toys, and wall after wall of shelves positively packed with books. The air smells of ink and paper, mixed with something warm and inviting. I scan the book titles trailing my fingers along their spines, savoring the solid edges and textures of each one.

Books have always been one of my favorite things.

They gave me the ability to escape my life. To lose myself in a fantastical world, and leave reality behind, even if only for a short time.

Precious time spent with my mother, reading together beneath the apple trees on warm summer afternoons, as dragonflies danced among the tall blades of grass and wildflowers. Or cuddled up under a thick blanket by the fire on cold winter nights, a cup of hot chocolate warming my hands as the crackle of the flames warmed the room.

I can still hear her rich English accent as she read aloud, bringing each character to life. Those moments will always be some of my most cherished memories.

"Buy a couple, why don't ya?" Kya says through a grin, several books already stacked haphazardly in her arms.

I blink the mist from my eyes and can't help but smile back at her giddy expression.

When the heck did she even have time to gather such a huge stack of books?

I turn back to the shelves and scan the signs.

Three for £10

OR

Buy One, Get One Free

Well, that explains why she's got so many.

I smile and sigh, scanning the shelves again.

"There's so many... where should I start? I'm not even sure what genre I like. Or which authors. Or series..."

I'm aware I'm starting to ramble. The familiar flare of panic coils in my chest. My mind starts to spiral when the realization hits me...

If I can't even choose books for myself, how am I supposed to run a bookshop?

Never missing a thing, Kya effortlessly steps in to rescue me again, holding out one of the books she had in her stack.

"Why not try one of these?" she suggests, a wicked glint in her eyes. "They're a bit spicy, but I guarantee you'll love them!"

I blink. *Spicy?*

I don't know what she means, but I'm learning to trust her.

She tips her head toward a section, indicating I should follow her.

My eyes widen as I scan the titles. There seems to be 'spicy' books available in every genre. From dragons, fae and vampires, to ice hockey players and mafia bosses. She plops one on top of my stack with a cover featuring a vivid blue skull against a black back drop and winks conspiratorially at me.

As we leave The Works, giggling about our purchases, she leads me to a salon. She has apparently taken the liberty of pre-booking hair and nail appointments for us both.

A couple hours later as we step out of the salon, I take in a deep breath, letting it out slowly and smile as I look around at the surrounding streets and shops, feeling like a brand-new woman.

Hair trimmed, feeling soft and fresh as it falls down my back in gentle waves. My natural nails, rounded and smooth, painted a soft pink—not the long, fake nails *he* had always demanded I have painted a garish blood red.

I smile when I think about how much he would have hated these.

And because of that, I love them even more.

Our final stop is the cell phone store—Kya insisting it's a necessity—not just for working with the building contractors, but as a way for us to stay in touch whenever we're apart.

By the time we leave, I'm happily exhausted.

We drive home, her poor little Mini Cooper practically bursting with the spoils of our day. A sense of calm settles over me.

The last bits of the afternoon sun glitter on the waters of the River Severn as we follow its banks, heading back toward the smaller, gentler Wye.

I smile as I realize this really is starting to feel like...

Home.

Chapter 16

Cole

The next afternoon, as I step out the door to lock up the bookshop, Hannah starts to carry on, chuffing, stomping and letting out a series of discontented brays. I go to her, shushing her and stroking my hand down her course mane in an attempt to calm her, but she won't settle.

"What's wrong girl? What's got you so upset, huh?" I ask, starting to worry something might be wrong with her when she still won't calm down. I bend down to check her hooves, but she stomps them hard, rearing up, then quickly takes several steps back. It's when I straighten back up I understand what's got her so bothered.

Zavier is standing so closely behind me I can feel the heat of his body against my back. His sudden, close presence startles me so much that I let out a scream, sending Hannah into another bucking, braying spiral, knocking me back into him.

"Whoa, whoa! Alright then? I've gotcha! Stupid bloody beast! Go on now! Get on out of here!" He yells, swinging a fist at her, while wrapping a big arm around me, pulling me protectively against his chest.

I push him away, wriggling out of his hold and hurry to her side.

"Don't hit her! It's my fault." I say, grabbing her harness and trying to calm her down.

Once I get her settled, I whirl around and pin Zavier with a furious glare. He's at least got the decency to look ashamed as he apologizes.

"Sorry, Cole. I just thought she was gonna hurt you, is all."

He seems so genuinely abashed as he toes a small rock in the lane, running a big hand through his disheveled locks.

"I just wanted to surprise you...," he huffs out an embarrassed chuckle, crinkling his nose awkwardly. "Guess I kinda mucked that up, didn't I?"

I feel my anger soften, and my shoulders drop when I take in his humiliated state.

How can I be angry with him for trying to protect me?

The next thing I know, he's escorting me home and I've invited him to join us for dinner.

Over the next few days, Zavier starts showing up in the evenings after he finishes up his work on the farm.

I feel him watching me, no matter where I move, his gaze tracking my every step.

It's been a particularly long day of salvaging what I can from the bookshop and café, sorting what's worth keeping from what's a total loss. All I really wanted to do tonight was to curl up with Grumbl and lose myself between the pages of one of my new books, but Zavier has joined us again. So instead of relaxing, I'm sitting on the porch with him while Kya finishes up the dishes.

It's a chilly night and Grumbl's weight against me is so warm and comforting, I feel the stress of the day leaving me, as he quietly snores in my lap. I yawn as I run my fingers gently over his fur.

The rattle of ice at the bottom of Zavier's empty glass shakes me from my contented state—the sound reminding me so much of my father and husband, it sends a chill of foul memories rushing to the forefront of my thoughts.

I sit forward, taking my cue that he's expecting a prompt refill and move to gently lift Grumbl's heavy, sleepy head from my lap.

"No need, hun," Kya says, briskly stepping over to swipe the glass from his hand, her eyes softening at the sight of her puppy sleeping so peacefully.

"I'll get this."

She winks at me before strolling back into the kitchen, humming softly, her colorful skirt swaying with each swing of her hips.

I run the tip of my finger along the soft rope of wrinkled skin that lines the ridge of Grumbl's nose. He stirs at my touch, blinking sleepily up at me, then lets out a snort, sighs loudly, and stretches his entire body across my lap. Within seconds he's snoring again, his slow, rhythmic breathing grounding me.

I let out a long breath, gearing myself up to say what I've been thinking.

"I've been meaning to thank you."

I rush out the words, but don't lift my eyes to meet his.

He doesn't say a word, but I can feel the weight of his stare. After what feels like an eternity of loaded silence, I finally give in and look up—to find his glacial eyes locked onto mine, making my heart stutter.

"You have, huh?" His voice is low, measured. "And just what exactly is it you're thanking me for?"

I drop my eyes again and resume stroking Grumbl's fur, using him as a buffer to give me the courage I need to talk about this.

"For finding me that day in the orchard, you know... after I ran off the boat. And for helping me get back to Kya's."

I feel a bit braver after I've said my peace and chance a look up at him. He leans back in his chair, drumming his fingers against the wicker, his eyes studying me.

"That's okay, Cole," he says, a sweet smile coming to his lips, his eyes sparkling in the fading light of the evening.

He's quiet for a beat, his gaze sweeping over me before he leans forward, reaching out to lift my hand from Grumbl's head, curling his fingers around mine, giving them a gentle squeeze.

"I'll always find you." His voice is low, his tone serene.

It should be comforting. I should feel at ease, reassured by this man who treated me with such tenderness and so much care that day in the orchard. When I was so broken, so locked in the grasp of the demons in my mind, I didn't even know what I was doing.

But instead, an icy chill slips down my spine.

Forcing a smile, I try to tug my fingers from his grip. But he holds firm. I glance up from our hands to his face.

"Zavier?"

Dread creeps at the edges of my thoughts, but when I tug again, he lets go—just like that. As if he hadn't just been holding my fingers hostage.

Did I imagine that?

I chuff a nervous laugh, sitting back for a second before gently shifting Grumbl from my lap to stand.

"I'll umm... I'll just be a minute." I rub my arms. "I'm a little chilly. I'm just gonna go grab a sweater."

He gives a single slow nod as I leave the room, passing Kya in the doorway as she returns with Zavier's refilled glass. I keep my pace measured and my face calm as I step into the kitchen, and even though I can hear them speaking to each other, I can still feel his eyes on me as I walk away.

Once I'm inside, I rush up the stairs and close myself in the bathroom, bracing my hands against the vanity.

I just need space.

A moment to gather myself.

A bit of time not under his watchful gaze.

Shaking off his words, and the claustrophobic feeling of his hand tightly gripping my fingers, I take a slow breath—then another—as if relearning how to breathe.

Once I feel a little more centered, I lift my head, finding my own eyes staring back at me in the mirror and I remind myself...

Zavier isn't *him*.

I'm still okay.

He's not here.

Chapter 17

Cole

Days shift from what, at first, had seemed like a chaotic whirlwind, to more of a rhythmic cadence instead. Breakfast together, followed by a walk along the river with Grumbl. Then to the bookshop, to work on getting it cleaned up and to visit Hannah.

The more time I spend with the donkey, the more I fall in love with her. Every day, she happily trots out to greet me, her nose hungrily seeking my palm, nuzzling into me with her welcoming warmth.

The little tortoiseshell cat seems to be making her visits a daily occurrence too.

"It's a stray, I think," Kya comments one day, as the thin creature wraps itself around my legs, purring insistently.

From that moment on, every time I go to the shop, I bring a can of tuna to feed it.

On the day the vet comes to give Hannah a health check, I ask if she'd mind checking out the little cat too.

She's a kind woman, practical, with ruddy cheeks and a no-nonsense air about her. She keeps calling me *'ol' butt'*—making my nose scrunch each time she says it.

Kya, noticing my dismay, grins as she leans in when the vet is distracted with Hannah's hoof inspection, and whispers, "She's not being rude, hun. That's just a term common among Foresters, used for friends or when someone's name escapes them."

"This poor mite's been homeless for a while, I should think," the vet says, running her hands deftly down the cat's flanks, wincing as she feels its ribs. "She'll need treatment for fleas and," a quick check in its ears, "mites. Plus some good meals and somewhere warm to sleep. But she's a warrior, this one, and she'll be good as new in no time." She adds, scratching beneath the purring cat's ears affectionately.

The warmth of her smile is infectious as she shifts her kind gaze to me. "Looks like you've got yourself a new pet, ol' butt."

I smile happily back at her, no longer offended, understanding her unusual nickname for me, as I reach over to stroke my pretty new kitty from head to tail. Her purr grows impossibly louder as she pushes herself firmly against my hand.

A Warrior.

The vet's words ring in my mind.

I'm reminded of my favorite Greek Goddess, Athena—goddess of war and wisdom.

With a nod, it's decided. This little creature, determined to survive regardless of what this cruel world throws at her—her name will be Athena too. I scoop my little warrior up into my arms and snuggle into her warm fur. She settles against me, her purr rumbling against my chest—another comfort I never realized I needed.

Grumbl welcomes her without hesitation, and soon the two of them are curled up together by the fireplace at home, a picture of contentment.

I decide to take my break out at one of the picnic tables on one unseasonably warm afternoon when Zavier rolls up unexpectedly. The loud engine of his small tractor, the trailer rattling behind him, shattering the tranquility of where I had been reading in front of the bookshop.

"I've come to cut down some of those trees out back, open that wasted space up a bit," he announces, shutting off the engine and hopping off to unload a chainsaw from the trailer.

An unexpected torrent of protective rage floods me and I leap up, darting over to stand between him and the path leading to the orchard.

"Don't you dare, Zavier Johnson!" My voice shakes, but I stand my ground. "I meant what I said when I told you, you're not cutting down any trees in this orchard!"

It's become my sanctuary. A place where I can sit with my coffee, Athena curled up in my lap, Hannah grazing nearby while I lose myself in one of my spicy books.

Kya was right—I'm loving them!

"Cole," he sighs, sounding annoyed as he crouches down to check the teeth on the saw, his tone placating. "There's a lot of dead wood back there, trees that need tending to or clearing out. Just let me handle it so it's one less thing for you to worry about."

Drawing in a shuddering breath, my voice waivers, but I stand my ground. "If... if you step one foot in my orchard, then...," I struggle to think of a consequence, "then I'll have Greg ban you from the pub for the first three shifts that I'm working there!" I threaten, folding my arms across my chest and forcing my voice to sound as stern as possible.

Zavier's face shifts—looking perplexed as he studies me, as if struggling to piece together what I've just said.

I don't know whether I've shocked him with my threat—or if I've simply stunned him by making it at all.

His gaze drifts across the river, focusing briefly on the Wye Inn. His lips press into a thin line and the muscles lining his jaw ripple. When he turns back to me, there's a clouded darkness in his icy blue eyes, that wasn't there before.

He releases his hold on the saw and slowly rises up to stand.

"The pub?" His brows pinch, his upper lip curling in disgust as he steps closer.

Wait... Is he angry?

"You're going to be *working* there?" His incredulous tone seems to suggest my sanity must be in question. He takes another step closer and I reflexively step back, instinctively trying to keep the space between us.

"Surely there are better places. Have you ever even worked in a pub before, Cole?"

Now I definitely catch the note of condescension in his voice and my stomach plummets, nerves taking the place of my anger.

He looks from me to the pub again, his jaw ticking, his thoughts brewing in the silence between us. I watch him, my eyes locked on his features, reading every single cue I've learned to look for that would indicate danger—every nerve in my body, on edge, primed and ready to run.

I take another step backward, feeling my back hit the sidewall of the bookshop.

My fear ratchets up and my heart pounds in my chest.

I have nowhere left to run...

Then, his eyes brighten, that easy, familiar smile returning as if the darkness had never been there at all.

"Tell you what," he snaps his fingers, making me jump. He moves in closer, closing the distance between us, his big hands closing around my shoulders as his large form dwarfs me, trapping me between the solid wall of the building and his body.

His voice is warm, his honeyed tone persuasive. He keeps his grip on me gentle, but firm as he dips his chin to meet my eyes.

"If it's a job you need, why don't you just come work for me on my farm? You could help me out, make some extra money..." he smiles, and I flinch as he runs a finger tenderly along my brow, sweeping back a stray strand of hair that had fallen across my face. "And that way, I can keep an eye on you. Make sure you're okay."

He slides his finger along my jaw, applying a bit of pressure to lift my chin, leaning in so close I can feel his breath on my skin.

Out of the corner of my eye, I catch a bit of movement. Hannah ambles toward us, her long ears flicking, her gaze fixed on him.

He follows my gaze, seeing her approach, his smile widening as he shifts his focus to my mouth, his thumb stroking along my bottom lip.

"I can see how fond you are of animals," he says, shifting his eyes quickly to her then back to me again. But as she gets closer, he drops his hand from my chin, loosening his grip on my arm.

She stamps her foot, chuffing loudly. She moves closer and he steps back, releasing his hold on me.

It takes me a moment to find my voice, but when I do, I speak as boldly as I can, "No, thank you."

I wrap my arms around myself—pressing my back against the bookshop wall to keep from visibly shaking.

"The pub will be just fine."

His eyes narrow and my heart nearly stops when he moves back into me, his long legs quickly closing the distance between us again, his height forcing me to tip my head back to meet his stare.

I gasp as he slips his hand around the back of my neck, holding me in place as his thumb moves in firm strokes against my pulse. He leans in close, the hush of his breath coasting against the shell of my ear, his tone glazed with a dark edge, as he drags the tip of his nose through my hair.

"Are you sure, Cole? Pubs can be..."

Icy fear splinters through my veins and I feel paralyzed, caught in the spider's web, waiting for the moment he strikes.

"Dangerous."

The ghost of his breath against my neck with his last word sends a shiver snaking down my neck.

I swallow thickly, my mind spiraling as raging panic sinks its claws into my racing heart.

He won't hurt me. He's a good man... my mind insists. *He helped me... carried me out of the orchard. He made me feel safe when the memories overwhelmed me... He's only looking out for me...Maybe I should listen to him...*

The air grows heavy in my lungs, as panic coils tight around me, my chest squeezing, my vision blackening at the edges. Zavier's unrelenting grip holds me locked in place—trapped between his body and the building and time distorts—seconds stretching impossibly, feeling more like minutes... *hours.*

I'm consumed by my heart hammering against my ribs, the creeping edges of panic tightening around me.

Hannah forces herself between us, using her body as a shield and snapping me out of my spiraling thoughts. Her teeth flash as she nips at his arm.

"Ow! Shit! Okay, okay!" he says, laughing and backing up quickly, hands raised in mock surrender. The tension lingers, but he makes a show of easing it.

"Just let me know when you're ready for me to take down those trees," he adds, heading back toward his tractor.

As he loads his equipment back into the trailer, his voice carries across the space between us.

"And Cole," he calls out, an underlying insistence in his tone, "when you're ready to take me up on that job offer—you know where to find me."

He climbs back onto the seat of the tractor, the engine rumbling to life, a splutter of black smoke hanging heavily in the air between us that chokes my lungs and makes my eyes water.

After what feels like an eternity, he turns it around and heads back down the lane.

Fanning the last wisps of smog from my face, I gently stroke Hannah's shoulder.

"Thank you, sweet girl." I whisper.

She turns her head, warm ocher eyes meeting mine—silent confirmation she's heard me and I rest my head against the side of her neck, soaking in her warmth and comforting presence.

Movement by the fence catches my eye and that's when I see him...

The Duke.

Gravel crunches beneath his running shoes as he jogs past, the tinny sound of bass notes leaking from his earbuds.

His bare arms, tanned and gleaming with a thin sheen of sweat, pump rhythmically at his sides, a phone strapped to the defined muscles of his bicep. The intricate patterns of tattoos curl over his shoulders, disappearing beneath the fabric of his shirt to where they must continue across his chest, more ink trailing down and around each arm, his black tank clinging to his torso.

My gaze drifts lower—to the running shorts hugging his powerful legs, even more tattoos wrapping around his thighs and calves. The snug fabric leaves nothing to the imagination, my eyes traveling of their own accord, zeroing in on the large bulge at the front of them when suddenly, I feel, rather than see, his eyes on me.

I lift my gaze to find his stare locked on mine...

Gray. Piercing. Haunting.

My cheeks flame, realizing I've been caught staring and I offer an awkward smile.

He doesn't return it. Instead, his dark brows furrow, his jaw clenching tight—every muscle in his face rigid, as if barely containing his fury. He shifts his eyes back to the path in front of him and continues past without slowing.

He keeps his pace steady, and my eyes follow his departure, dropping to his backside. I can't help but notice how well defined it is as he disappears into the shadows of the woods.

I swallow involuntarily, my heart hammering in my chest in a whole new rhythm when the sound of the fluttering pages of my book pulls my attention back to where I'd left it on the bench, next to my now, very cold cup of coffee.

I blow out a slow breath, pulling my bottom lip between my teeth and laugh at myself, dropping my forehead back against Hannah.

I think these damn 'spicy' books that Kya's gotten me into are starting to get to me.

Chapter 18

Cole

Before long, each day gets easier, my new routines gradually becoming second nature. I have no doubt Kya's curious about my arms and the story behind the cuts and bruises I had on my face the day we met, but she never pries.

She's just there. A listening ear, should I need one—but more than that, a true friend. Her ceaseless support, always ready to catch me if I fall, randomly offering me bits of wisdom that seem well beyond her thirty-one years.

Every morning, I wake to fresh bandages and pain meds on my bedside table. A quiet acknowledgement. Never asking, but caring just the same.

My heart squeezes when I think about the treasure I've found in her friendship alone.

After a blissfully hot shower, I dress, pulling on jeans and a soft sweater—subtle comforts I'd never been allowed before. We have breakfast together, then walk Grumbl to the bookshop, Athena padding along in our wake.

I've slipped easily back into the skills I'd learned back at the stables in Connecticut to now tend to Hannah—getting her fed, brushing her coat, checking her hooves—muscle memory taking over with ease, the familiar motions returning as though I'd never stopped. Before long, Hannah's coat is shining, her eyes bright and content.

Occasionally, Kya will take Grumbl with her when she leaves for one of her part-time jobs, but more often than not, he stays with me at the bookshop. I spend the mornings tending to the flower boxes and garden in front of the shop—weeding, planting fall bulbs, imagining the beautiful blooms they'll become when spring arrives.

Zavier is relentless, nagging me about needing to remove the dead wood from the orchard. His grating insistence that I can't do it all on my own, finally wears me down and I agree to let him remove only the sections that are absolutely necessary for the health of the orchard.

I allow him in, but with strict instructions—no healthy trees are to be touched other than to remove any dead branches and to harvest the fruit.

I let him mow a path between the trees, but insist he leaves the long meadow-like grass around the base of each one. There's something magical about the tall blades. Each throng its own hidden sanctuary, humming with life as insects dart between the tangled greenery—like another whole world unto itself.

There's a part of me that remembers the peace that came from the ability to disappear into it—curled beneath the branches of the old trees, where no one could find me for long hours at a time.

Where I could recenter myself when the evils of the world overwhelmed me, giving me a place of solace, if only for a short time.

One quiet morning, while I wait for a group of contractors to arrive—my nose buried in a book, the loud snap of a twig draws my attention. A small thrill runs through me when I look up to see a deer just a few yards away, making its way through the fronds of tall grass with a quiet grace. The autumn sunlight turns its copper fur to a light auburn. I run my fingers through the end of my ponytail, noting how close the color is to that of my own hair.

She moves forward, bending to nibble an apple on the ground at her feet, when a little fawn steps out of the grass behind her. I smile at its tiny, innocent face, its bright blue eyes striking against its copper fur, its tiny body dappled with patches of white. It can't be more than a few weeks old at most.

The wind shifts, causing the dried leaves at my feet to swirl.

They lift their heads at the sound, turning in my direction. For a moment, we stare at one another, suspended in a wordless gaze. An unspoken secret shared between us, carried away by the whisper of leaves.

The sound of gravel crunching beneath tires as the first of the contractors arrives, breaks the tranquility of the moment, and they move again, vanishing between the trees into the denser forest beyond.

Throughout the day, contractors come and go, tossing prices and time frames at me, each one insisting their job should be done first. Disagreeing, delaying, a whirlwind of numbers and decisions making my head spin.

As each day hurries past and winter approaches, it starts to feel like time is slipping away faster and faster.

September melts into October and, with Kya's help, together we decide the bookshop should be renovated first. Mainly because the revival of the bookshop is the primary caveat of my grandfather's will, but since Haven Cottage needs so much work, and with Kya's firm insistence I stay with her indefinitely, we agree to postpone the repairs on the cottage until spring.

Cringing inwardly, I try not to balk at the cost of each job. But with every new contractor, every quote handed to me, all I see is my grandfather's inheritance bleeding away.

Late in the afternoons, before returning to Kya's, I find myself checking the clock, then finding some reason to linger outside the bookshop. Fussing with the plants in the window boxes, polishing the windows... all the things I've done many times over already.

But truthfully, I'm waiting...

Almost every day, without fail, he'll run past.

The steady rhythm of his steps against the lane, the metronomic beat, unyielding, controlled. Each footfall measured, a tempo exclusive to him—carry on the wind, arriving a few moments before he comes into view.

His approach causes my heart to stutter inexplicably.

My cheeks heat as I subconsciously make myself small and hold my breath.

A flurry of thoughts chant in my head... warring with my common sense, telling me to take my ass back inside. To stay away.

Will he notice me today?

Will he stop and talk to me today?

Will today be the day... everything changes?

But every day, he runs past, barely lifting his eyes to glance at me, before quickly shifting his focus back on the road ahead.

I shake my head, chastising myself as he disappears into the woods.

Why the hell does it matter, Cole? Someone like him could never want someone like you.

The beginning of October marks my first full shift at the pub across the river. I've shadowed Kya all week, learning the ropes, but so far, I've yet to be let loose on the public by myself.

Kya is positively giddy with excitement while we dress, helping me debate which shirt to wear as I slip on tights and some sensible black shoes. Taking me in, she beams as she straightens my name badge, proudly pinned to my chest.

"Now," she says matter-of-factly, brushing imaginary lint from my shoulders. "What do you say when a punter asks for a drink and looks too young?"

Earlier in the week, my quizzically cocked eyebrow earned me a laugh and a crash course in British slang—apparently a 'punter' is a customer.

"Show me some ID." I say, with mock sternness.

"Good." she says, smiling like I just aced an exam. "And if they refuse?"

"I point to one of the signs behind the bar and kindly inform them, if they look under twenty-five and have no ID, I won't be able to serve them."

"And if they still refuse?" she asks, tipping her head, a brow cocked... *she thinks she's got me now.*

"I get Greg." I say, crossing my arms across my chest, tip my chin up and give her a firm, no nonsense nod.

"Atta girl!" She grins, tapping the tip of my nose playfully with her forefinger. "And don't forget, they can legally order a drink at eighteen here."

The first time I had heard that, I was shocked. Eighteen felt so young, when my whole life growing up in the US, the legal drinking age had always been twenty-one.

Clearly satisfied with my answers, she hands me my new jacket and purse before leaning down to kiss Grumbl's wrinkly brow goodbye.

She locks up the house, links her arm with mine and we head down to the jetty to begin my first real night of work at the pub.

As we walk down the road, Kya turns to me with a serious look on her face.

"Now, do you remember what you do if a woman comes to the bar and asks for Angela?" She dips her chin to my ear, keeping her voice soft to make sure no one overhears us.

When I'd first heard about this, I was amazed to find out what it meant. Had I known about it before now, I can't help but wonder...

Would I have ever been brave enough to ask for Angela?

The stray thought, one that constantly lingers in the dark recesses of my mind—reminding me just how broken I am—sends a ripple of panic through me and I have to draw in a deep breath to steady my nerves before I can answer her.

She patiently watches me and gives my arm a gentle squeeze, reminding me of her solid presence beside me, bringing me back out of my spiraling thoughts.

I blow out my breath and answer her with confidence.

"I stay calm, invite her into the office, and ask if there's someone I can call to come get her. If she says no, then I call for a cab, paid for by the pub, and make sure she's safely inside before sending her home. I let Greg—or Pete, if he's on shift—know, so they can keep an eye on whoever made her feel uncomfortable.

They can ban them if necessary—or, if we feel she or anyone else is in danger, we call the police."

She wraps her arm over my shoulders, pulling me snuggly into her side, resting her cheek on top of my head as we approach the river.

"That's our most important job, Cole," she whispers. "To make sure The Wye Inn is a safe and happy place for everyone."

I wrap my arm around her waist, returning her embrace as we wave to Billy where he waits to ferry us to work.

Chapter 19

Cole

It's Friday night.

Kya had warned me the pub would be busier than what I'd experienced during my week of training, but I have to admit, I wasn't entirely prepared for the crowd of people already lined up, waiting to be served.

The moment we step behind the bar, Kya and I get to work—pouring pints, mixing drinks, and soon I'm right there with her, moving in a practiced rhythm. I have a bit of trouble keeping track of names while Kya greets the regulars, the rapid-fire introductions making my head spin.

"Ah, so you're old Jesse's granddaughter?" A wizened old man greets me through a nearly toothless grin. He removes his flat cap to reveal fine wisps of cottony white hair sparsely covering his balding head. His use of the term *'old'* when describing Jesse makes me raise an eyebrow—*he's got to be about the same age my grandfather would have been before he passed.*

"I'm Tom," he says, extending an arthritic hand across the bar. His fingers linger on mine a moment, his eyes softening, taking on a glassy sheen as he wistfully murmurs, "You have Maggie's look." A soft smile curls the corners of his lips as he holds my hand a moment longer.

Blinking back to the present, he loosens his grip, slipping his fingers from mine.

"Pint of Butty Bach." He says, coughing a couple times, then clearing his throat as he straightens on his barstool.

I smile, already deciding I like Old Tom very much.

"Good to meet you, Tom. I'm Cole. I'll be happy to pour you a pint of Butty, but I'm afraid I'll have to ask for some I.D. first, please. You know... just to be sure," I add, shooting him a little wink as I hold out my hand expectantly waiting for him to produce his identification.

Tom eyes me, his mouth hung slightly ajar, then barks a loud, raspy laugh, fishing his wallet out to show me his I.D.

"You've got a good'un here, Kya Love!" he shouts down the bar.

She peers over her shoulder at him as she pours a cider for one of her customers, grinning and nodding proudly in agreement.

"Only the best for you, Tom!" She sing-songs as she passes the freshly poured drink across the bar and moves on seamlessly to the next customer.

Zavier saunters in about an hour into my shift, his gaze instantly locking onto me. He cuts through the crowd, pushing past the sea of people who have been waiting, making his way over to me.

"How's it going, Cole?" He asks, shouldering in to lean on the bar top in front of where I'm trying to focus on pouring cider for two younger boys—having successfully carded them moments before.

"Fine." I answer him quickly with a tight-lipped smile. I've got a long line of customers who've been waiting for their turn and with so many new faces to learn, it's hard to remember who got here first.

"I'll have a bottle of Newcastle Pale Ale and a double shot of Famous Grouse." He states, already pulling out his wallet, tens and twenties spilling from the side.

"You'll wait your bloody turn, Zavier Johnson!" Kya shouts over her shoulder from her end of the bar without turning. "There are others here who've been waiting longer—and with far more patience than you!"

With her back to him, she misses the way Zavier's eyes darken, the small tick in his jaw, the rhythmic tapping of his fingers against the counter.

But his dark stare and irritated drumming isn't lost on me. All signs that he's losing his patience.

Signs my life has taught me to recognize far too easily.

I can't stand the pressure of him waiting—his typical easy charm stripped away. I glance at the other customers, then quickly uncap his bottle, pour his glass of whiskey and slide them over to him with as big a smile as I can muster, trying to calm him subliminally, just like I've done with *him* for years—trying to quell the fury before the storm erupts.

Relief settles over me when his easy smile returns and he knocks back the whiskey in one swift motion before pushing the empty glass and a twenty-pound note toward me.

"Keep the change." He says with a wink before striding off to a table of familiar faces.

I blow out a breath and return to my customers, trying to ignore the weight of his gaze as it continues to follow me throughout the evening.

Before my shift is even half over, my legs and feet ache, but that ache is accompanied by a new found confidence and a happy sense of accomplishment I didn't even realize I'd been missing.

This persona I've created—extroverted, engaging, laughing along with the customers—feels almost like slipping into a second skin. Feeling bolder now, I emulate Kya's sass more and more, calling out people when they overstep—brazen but good-natured. Each time, more naturally, as I step further into this new, braver version of me.

By his third trip to the bar, Zavier is far less steady, swaying on his feet, his eyes glazed and unfocused.

He slumps onto an empty bar stool and leans on the bar, breathing heavily through his nose.

"N...nother w...whisskyy, Cole..." he slurs, swaying in his seat.

"I think maybe you've had enough, Zavier." I suggest as sweetly as I can, placing a gentle hand on his wrist.

He snatches his hand away, pulling it back hard as he staggers to stand. The familiar movement makes me flinch and I brace myself against the backhand I've come to expect from too many years of experience with intoxicated men.

His eyes blaze, unfocused. "You wann me taa be done?" His slurred words muddle together, almost to the point of becoming incomprehensible. "Okay Cole, I'll be done. But I'll take a kissss fromm uuu innsstead."

Without warning, he leans across the bar, snatching my hand into his, yanking me forward.

I yelp, wincing as my ribs slam hard against the edge of the bar top and he crushes my hand painfully in an iron grip, pinning it beneath his palm.

I freeze.

Unbidden memories rush in, fragmenting the present.

The pub warps at the edges—time slowing, stretching. My heart hammers in my chest as my focus locks on the crushing grip holding me prisoner against the polished mahogany and I feel like I can't take in a full breath.

Everything changes, the world snapping back into motion, when Zavier's grip is wrenched away. I rock back on my heels and stumble back a few steps, holding my hand protectively against my chest.

My senses come back to me in time to see the broad back of a taller, stronger figure moving into Zavier's path.

Brick and Pete close in around Zavier as he staggers backward. They don't touch him, instead they create a solid wall with their bodies between Zavier and the bar as they walk into him—their presence alone enough to force him out the door.

My attention is locked on his retreating form until his loud, blustery voice angrily barks into the night—some complaint about *getting what he paid for.*

"Are you okay?"

The question pulls me back to the present and I look up to see gray eyes locked onto mine.

The Duke... stands in front of me, studying me, a grim look on his face. And he's speaking... directly to me.

I nod mutely, words failing me.

"Are you sure?" he asks again, his eyes dipping to where I'm clutching my hand to my chest.

"Oh." I look down at my hands, quickly dropping them and awkwardly smooth down the front of my apron. "Yes, yes I'm fine. Thank you." I say, though my voice still sounds shaky.

Kya walks in from the back, carrying a case of cider, her eyes wide as she takes in the scene she missed having stepped away to replenish the inventory.

I meet her questioning gaze and give her a nod, reassuring her I'm alright, then straighten my shoulders, willing myself back to the person I was before Zavier ruined the illusion I had built up over the course of the night.

Shaking out of my haze, I turn back to Rogan, forcing myself to meet his eyes again. Plastering on a smile far bigger than I feel, I ask, "So what can I get you, Mr. Cavendish?"

His eyes—grayer than I remember, flecked with lighter lines of silver—hold me for a beat longer before he speaks.

"A Diet Coke. And a pint of Butty for Brick, please, Miss Allbright."

Something inside me flips at the way he says my name. I swallow and give him a single nod, feigning steady confidence, but my legs feel like jelly when I turn to grab a couple glasses and set the soda machine to Diet Coke.

"Ice?"

He nods, long fingers resting lightly on the bar, moving absently—like waves rolling in.

"I'll have a Bacardi and Coke, babe."

The voice is somehow syrupy and sharp at the same time.

I glance over to see a hand tipped in blood red talons, as it wraps possessively around Rogan's bicep, one long nail drifting between the buttons of his shirt.

The woman attached to the hand is stunning—full lips, perfectly arched brows, high platinum blonde ponytail cascading over bare shoulders and a revealing dress, clinging to her very ample curves, matching the same blood red color of her nails.

Rogan's eyes slowly close, a muscle feathering in his jaw. His nostrils flare on a breath then he opens his eyes and nods, "And a Bacardi and Coke for Bethany too, please."

"Double shot. Don't be cheap, baby." *Bethany* giggles, rubbing against him in a way that makes my skin crawl.

I make her drink, then start to pour Brick's ale, when the tap sputters and spits, followed by a hiss of air.

"Dammit!" I curse under my breath.

I glance down to Kya's end of the bar, only to see she's swamped. I quickly scan the room, but Greg is outside, and I don't see Pete anywhere.

"Need a hand?" The deep timbre of his voice pulls my attention back again—calm, steady—cutting through my rising panic.

I blink up at him.

Damn…he's tall.

Disbelieving someone like him would know the first thing about it, I splutter, "Really? *You* know how to change a barrel?"

He smiles, amusement curling the corner of his mouth.

"Sweetheart, when I was at Oxford hosting soirees, at least one of us had to understand the inner workings of a British pub."

Warmth creeps into my cheeks as his words play back in my mind.

The Duke just called me 'Sweetheart'.

Nervously, I tuck a loose strand of hair behind my ear and chance another hopeful glance back toward Kya, who's no less occupied than she'd been a minute ago.

So I force a small smile, swallow down my nerves and dig deep to try and look as calm and composed as possible, before turning back to face him.

"Okay," I shrug, "I guess… if you're sure you don't mind. Please. Follow me, Mr. Cavendish."

Chapter 20

Cole

Bethany pouts as Rogan disentangles himself from her grip.

He hands her the rum and Coke and guides her toward Brick, who holds out an arm toward her, bending at the waist in a chivalrous bow. His effortless charm seems to instantly turn her mood from pissy to pleasant as he leads her to their table.

I lift up the hatch in the bar for Rogan. He rolls up his sleeves as he steps through, and I catch a glimpse of the tattoos I've noticed from a distance each time he's run past the bookshop.

"Thank you." I say quietly as he passes.

His eyes sparkle, a hint of a smile tipping up one side of his mouth as he holds out his hand in mock chivalry, gesturing me forward.

"Lead on, Miss Allbright," he says, voice low and smooth, making my already shaky composure even more unsteady.

"Please," I breathe out. "You can just call me Cole."

"Rogan." he says, lips quirking at the corners as he rests a hand on his chest—clearly calling me out for using his surname a moment ago.

I hesitate at the top of the stairwell, the darkness feeling absolute.

He reaches past me, his broad chest brushing along my shoulder. As he leans over me, I feel the heat of his body against my back as he flips the switch. Tingles rush up my spine at the contact.

Light floods the space, easing a bit of my trepidation and I smile nervously up at him. I'm grateful for the noise of the pub behind us because my heart is slamming so hard against my ribs, I'm all but certain he would be able to hear it if the room were quiet.

Retucking some loose strands of hair behind my ear, I force myself forward, down the narrow steps, scanning the room for the empty barrel, searching for its replacement.

"It's here," he says triumphantly when he immediately locates the spare, lifting it effortlessly over the other barrels in front of it.

"Do you know what to do?"

Greg showed me. *Once.* I swallow.

"Uh... you get a whatchamacallit." I waggle my hand in a turning motion.

That small smile again, threatening to topple me if I'm not careful.

"A wrench," he supplies, with an encouraging dip of his chin.

I nod. "And a hammer."

He hands the tools over to me.

"A *mallet*," he corrects, his amusement evident on his face now, but his eyes never leave mine. There isn't even a hint of condescension in his tone.

With another nod of encouragement, he probes, "Then what?" His deep voice is calm and patient.

"Right. A mallet." I correct myself. "Then, you disconnect the old barrel... and connect the new one..." My voice peters out and heat creeps up my neck as I rack my brain, trying to remember all the steps Greg had shown me the other day.

That can't be all of them. What the hell am I forgetting?

"What about the gas supply?" he says as he reaches over me, his chest only inches from my face. The clean smell of citrus and spice floods my nose, as he flicks a lever with his fingertip.

I swallow again. He chuckles warmly, and I feel the tension inside me begin to ease a bit.

I pull on an oversized pair of thick, leather gloves and take the wrench from him. The gloves are far too large for me and I struggle to grip the tool while attempting to fit it to the coupler on the barrel.

Metal meets metal with a series of rattling clinks.

My hands are shaking. The harder I try to stop them, the worse it gets. I feel my face flame at the loud rattle of the disobedient tool when I can't gain purchase on the coupler.

"Here, let me." he says, gently removing the wrench and gloves from my hands.

I step back and watch him intently, trying to absorb everything he's doing so I can do this myself next time.

The muscles in his corded forearms ripple as he works the wrench. Goosebumps erupt along my arms. I try to convince myself; it's just from the chill of the cellar.

He works with practiced ease—loosening the coupler and lifting the empty barrel with effortless strength.

My mouth goes dry and I swear I've forgotten how to breathe.

"Okay, what do we do next?" he asks, smiling when he catches me staring.

"I, uh..."

Dammit Cole, Get it together and spit it out already!

I clear my throat and try again with as much confidence as I can muster. "Same again, but in reverse?"

He laughs, a genuine rich, warm sound that feels like a warm blanket wrapping around me on a cold day.

"And so the student becomes the master."

I blink dumbly at him for a heartbeat before realizing he's teasing me. Then all at once I feel myself relax and with a soft chuckle, I smile up at him.

For a moment, he just stares at me, a look on his face I can't quite read. I've never had anyone look at me like this before.

It feels... *good*.

With a blink, seeming to come back to himself, he says, "Right then." He moves in, working quickly to secure the new barrel and shifts the coupler.

Pausing, he looks over his shoulder at me.

"Want to do the last bit?"

I smile at him, confidence blooming as I nod and move into place. Taking the tools as he hands them back, his fingers brush mine—sending a jolt of electricity straight up my arms.

I should feel nervous, being alone with him, standing this close to him.

But instead, I feel something else... Not bad. Just unfamiliar.

It's almost like...

As I puzzle through this feeling, I finish hooking up the new barrel. All that's left now is to turn the gas back on, and—VOILA.

Except—

The moment I flip the switch; we're immediately drenched in the finest Wye Valley pale ale.

An involuntary scream escapes my throat as I flail blindly, trying to locate the switch to turn the gas back off while a torrent of ale sprays into my face and soaks my hair.

Rogan leans past me, his chest pressing against my back, managing to get the switch turned off. When the spray finally stops, I wipe my hands down my face and gape disbelievingly down at my clothes. I'm surprised to find I'm nowhere near as wet as I had anticipated.

But when I turn back to face Rogan—he's absolutely drenched.

His normally meticulously styled dark hair is now soaking wet. Droplets shaking loose as he runs a hand through it, his shirt clinging tightly to him, completely sopping wet.

Before I can stop it, laughter bubbles up—bursting into the silence of the basement.

I clap my hands over my mouth.

But when my eyes meet his, he's not angry.

He's laughing too.

And dear God, it's one of the best sounds I've ever heard.

I hand him a bar towel and we let the laughter take over, filling the space until it tapers naturally.

When we finally settle, still grinning, Rogan says, "Shift your arse, Allbright."

Stepping in, he tightens the coupler and carefully restores the gas once more. This time, there's no spray and I blow out an audible sigh of relief.

"I'm so sorry about your hair... and your shirt." I grimace apologetically.

"Nothing to apologize for, Cole." He says, absently reaching out and trailing his finger along my cheek to move the wet hair off my face.

At his touch, it feels like time collapses in on itself and warm tingles travel through my whole body, my breath catching in my throat as I find his eyes in the dim light of the room.

Realizing his mistake, the humor slides from his eyes and he curls his fingers inward, drawing his hand back slowly, his Adam's apple bobbing as he swallows.

For just a moment, he studies me, as if I'm a puzzle he can't quite solve.

The corners of his lips lift into a soft smile and he shifts his focus back to attempting to dry off the front of his shirt with the slightly grubby bar towel.

"But perhaps you'd better leave it for Greg until you get a few more practice runs under your belt, eh," he teases good-naturedly. His face completely transforms into one of the most handsome smiles I've ever seen.

"I think that's probably a good idea." I grin up at him, and silently thank the light in the room for being too dim for him to see how red my face must be right now.

Chapter 21

Cole

I take a few minutes in the ladies' room to dry myself off and try to fix my hair so that I am not a sopping mess for the rest of the night, before meeting Rogan back at the bar to pour a test pint.

I take it slow, ensuring the flow of golden liquid is smooth and steady—only to realize the whole pub is watching, when a roar of applause erupts just as I finish testing the pour. Blushing deep crimson, I tip the tester away, and pour Brick a fresh pint.

I hand Rogan the drinks. "They're on the house."

I can tell he's primed to protest, but, seeing the pleading look on my face, he simply tips his head, gives me one last, lingering look that has heat creeping back up my neck, then turns to carry the drinks to his waiting friends.

A few minutes later, he heads out to the parking lot—only to return a couple minutes later, tugging on a dry T-shirt.

At the briefest flash of extremely well-defined abs, my face flames, surely even redder than when the crowd applauded my successful pour. With a monumental effort, I force myself to focus on my job while fighting back the unbidden smile tugging at the corner of my lips.

As the night slowly winds down, the pub gradually quiets, settling into its final rhythm.

It doesn't escape my notice when Brick steps up to the bar, leaving a tip large enough to cover the drinks I'd given Rogan on the house earlier.

Before I can protest, he grins, raising his fingers to his brow in a friendly salute. "You're doing a grand job, Cole!" he praises before turning and heading back to their table.

Gradually, the bar starts to empty and only a few patrons remain. Brick and Rogan, Bethany draped over him languidly—her shrill laughter grating against the low hum of conversation, makes me shudder.

Among them, a group of rowdy young men linger, their mud-streaked jackets and worn boots marking them as freshly back from a camping trip. I crack my stiff neck, glancing at the clock. Half an hour to closing.

Kya sidles up to me and bumps her hip against mine, her smile playful.

"We can start to put things to bed now. You wanna ring for last orders?" Her eyes flick to the bell hanging on a pillar at the end of the bar.

"Really?" I squeak, grinning widely. I'm not sure why, but somehow it feels like I've won a prize.

She laughs, sauntering away, hips swaying as she wipes down the bar. I pull the short rope, the clang of the bell ringing out across the pub and down to the river.

"Last orders!" Kya calls, her voice carrying easily.

Greg and I chat as we move through the room collecting glasses, then move out to the terrace to tidy up the tables out there.

When we step back in, trays loaded down with drinkware, we notice the trouble brewing at the bar. One of the campers—a young man, barely twenty—has moved behind the counter and is tugging on Kya's arm, trying to coax her out.

She's completely calm, a smile that doesn't quite reach her eyes, locked on her lips as she tells him to let her go.

From the corner of my eye, I see Brick lurch forward, but Rogan grips his arm, holding him back. Brick's jaw ticks, his eyes steely, his whole body coiled with tension.

Why is Rogan stopping him?

I bolt toward the bar, Greg close behind, the heavy-set man panting as he tries to keep up. I reach the bar just in time to see Kya drop her wrist, twisting sharply out of the man's grip. Then, with swift precision, she knees him in the groin.

He doubles over, groaning. It's only then Rogan releases his hold on Brick, who wastes no time getting to her. His long strides eat up the distance between his seat and the bar in seconds. In one fluid motion, he grabs the boy by the collar and hauls him out to the parking lot like he weighs nothing. Greg escorts the rest of the group out, informing them they're not to come back anymore.

"Kya!" I rush to her side, my heart pounding. "Are you okay?"

She wraps her arms around me, rubbing my back as though *I'm* the one who's been assaulted.

"I'm fine, hun." she laughs, her tone light, unfazed.

"Why didn't Rogan let Brick help you sooner?"

She laughs again, holding me close.

"Because he—and Brick—both know I can handle little twerps like that. I've had training, don't ya know?" She pulls back, smiling widely, her confidence unshaken.

"Training?" My brows arch up with curiosity, while I absently twist a bar towel between my hands.

"That's right! Self-defense classes." she says, pushing her shoulders back, a proud smile spreading across her face.

She pauses then, her gaze flicking to Brick and Rogan before returning to me.

"You should come to the next one." she smiles brilliantly at the thought.

"I... I think I might actually like that." I admit.

In fact, that sounds like something I could definitely use in my life.

Finally, the last of the customers filter out.

I lean over the bar, watching as Rogan slips into his sleek, black sports car. My breath catches when his gray eyes find mine across the parking lot, through the open door of the pub. His lips turn up into a small smile, and for a moment, something unspoken passes between us, my chest warming when he lifts his fingers in a little wave.

Brick holds the door for Bethany and waits while she slips into the back. I watch her and feel something unfamiliar claw its way up my chest, that same feeling squeezing at my throat as I try to swallow.

Still, my eyes linger.

Slowly, I exhale, forcing the feeling down, stuffing it into a quiet corner of my mind.

This shouldn't bother me. It shouldn't matter to me who he spends his time with.

Brick pauses before climbing into the car. He turns, gives me a wink, a small salute and beams a radiant smile at Kya, then slides into the passenger seat, saying something that makes Rogan laugh.

But my focus isn't on Brick.

It's on her.

The way she leans into Rogan, her hand resting possessively on his arm. The way she owns her space behind him so easily.

The way he lets her.

I tell myself it doesn't matter.

I tell myself I don't care.

And yet—

There's an unrelenting sharp twist of something inside me.

I glower as I turn away. The sudden loud roar of his engine cuts through the night, startling me, sending a jolt through my already pounding heart.

I stand frozen as the sound of tires crunching over gravel fades into the distance. The thought of her in his bed with him stirs a foreign feeling within me, and my gut twists as I'm hit by a sudden wave of nausea.

I swallow it back, shaking my head in confusion.

Is this jealousy? Why the fuck would I be jealous of her?

The weight of Kya's arm wrapping around my shoulders, snaps me back to the here and now as she pulls me into a side hug, handing me my bag and jacket.

"You did it, Hun! How do you feel after your first shift?"

I scan the empty room, then look up at her as she beams proudly down at me. My chin wobbles as I soak up her warmth and I melt into her embrace. My eyes burn as I tuck into her, wrapping her fully in a hug.

"Thank you," I whisper, against her shoulder, my voice thick as I try to hold back my emotions. "Thank you so much."

She tightens her arms without hesitation and for a few moments, she just holds me, letting the weight of my gratitude settle between us.

"Right then." She says, her own voice tight with emotion, as she gently pulls back and tips my chin up with her fingers.

Her watery gaze finds mine, and when she sees the smile on my tear-streaked face, she doesn't say a word. Instead, she pulls me back into the hug, her arms strong and comforting, rocking me softly.

We stand there, swaying gently, her quiet strength grounding me as the rest of the world fades away.

As I release her, Kya takes my face into her hands and runs her thumbs under my eyes.

"Let's go home," she says with a soft smile.

And for the first time in as long as I can remember, I feel like I can breathe.

Chapter 22

Rogan

As the pub grows smaller in my rearview mirror, my mood sours. Bethany's cloying perfume thickens the air, suffocating in the confines of the car. Her constant touching, her nails scratching, her fingers insistently grasping as she hangs on my arm, make me feel claustrophobic. Her high-pitched laugh and juvenile prattling is grating, relentless, like an insect that refuses to be swatted away. I don't want her near me.

Everything about her feels... wrong.

I need her out of my car. Her hands off me.

She keeps reaching into the front, pawing at me from the backseat and distracting me, pulling my focus. I grit my teeth as I navigate the winding forest roads. My eyes locked on the shadows at the edge of the tree line, watching for deer, boar or any other animals that years of experience driving these roads has taught me could bolt into my path at any moment.

I spare a glance toward Brick. His fingers restlessly drumming on the center console, a clear sign even his seemingly endless patience is being tested by her incessant chatter.

I shift in my seat, leaning my elbow against the door and rub my temple as my head begins to throb.

I find myself praying for a natural break in her seemingly endless narrative, but it never comes. Finally, unable to endure another second, I raise my voice, cutting her off midsentence.

"Where can we drop you, Bethany?" I keep my tone flat, disinterested and firm, brokering no argument.

Her sudden silence is abrupt, her mouth hanging open, the unfinished words still hanging in the air between us. Then, snapping her mouth shut, she slumps back into her seat, folds her arms tightly over her oversized chest and pouts like a spoiled child.

"Monmouth!" She spits, glaring at my reflection in the rearview mirror.

I give her a tight nod, shifting my focus back to the road ahead, the heat of her glare scorching the back of my neck. The ride is blissfully silent—for all of three minutes.

Then she's pushing between the front seats again, her claws wrapping around my bicep. I clench my teeth so hard my jaw pops audibly, drawing Brick's attention back to the interaction.

Bethany, seemingly oblivious to my ire, presses on, her voice a syrupy purr in my ear.

"It's still early, you know? I can hook us up with some of my girlfriends—we could really have some fun."

She flashes a salacious look toward Brick, her smile dripping with innuendo.

"Brick can play with us too, if you want," she adds, her voice husky. "What do you say, babe? I mean, we had lots of fun last time, didn't we?"

She leans in close to my ear. "Wasn't I a good girl last time?" She coos, trailing the tip of her tongue along the shell of my ear before pulling my earlobe between her teeth, biting down lightly.

My knuckles whiten as I grip the steering wheel. Bethany, misreading my actions as excitement, takes it as her cue to step up her game, snaking her tongue up the back of my ear and plunging her hand into the collar of my shirt.

It's all I can do not to slam on the breaks, pull over and toss her out onto the roadside, and be done with her right this second.

Even though everything in me is screaming to do just that, another part of me—the man my mother raised me to be—insists, no woman, no matter how distasteful, deserves to be treated with such disrespect. I had, after all, indulged in her affections just a few nights ago and I was the one who had suggested we invite her to join us tonight.

Brick, reading my body language far better than Bethany, gently takes her wrist, removing her hand from my shirt and guides her back to her seat.

"It's been a long few days," he says, his tone calm but firm. "We've got important business in the morning. I think we're just gonna call it a night, Bethany."

Her brows pinch, her face twisting into an appalled look of horror, as if he'd just slapped her. She slumps back into her seat with a pout, folding her arms tightly across her chest.

The last ten minutes of the drive to Monmouth are blissfully silent, though her glare never stops burning into the back of my skull. When we finally pull up to her place, Brick lifts his seat forward, taking her hand to help her out of the car. The moment she's on her feet, she angrily tugs free of his hold, stomps up her front steps and once inside, turns to glare at us, holding up her middle finger before slamming her door.

As we drive back up the hill, we travel in idyllic silence, both breathing out a sigh at the exact same moment—an unspoken, mutual agreement. Another shared chapter, mercifully closed.

In hindsight, I should never have had Brick call her. I thought what I wanted was someone compliant. Someone willing. Someone I could use to work out my frustrations.

Someone who would let me take what I needed, no questions asked. A distraction. The act, nothing more than a way to clear my head so I could overcome this inexplicable hurdle of Cole Allbright.

My hands tighten once again around the wheel, the leather creaking beneath the strain of my grip. Brick says nothing from the passenger seat. He knows me well enough to recognize when I need advice, and when it's best to just let me sort my thoughts on my own.

Finally, the signs for Verdon-on-Wye appear, and my estate looms on the horizon. My family home. The place where all the Dukes of Wyeholme have lived throughout the centuries. Once, it had been alive, filled with laughter, parties, the voices of children echoing down the halls.

But when my mother died, the life of the Manor seemed to ebb away with her. Now it only serves as a cold reminder of everything I've lost.

Everything I've been forced to give up.

Everything I've been forced to become.

I slow as we near the gatehouse, my eyes instinctively drifting to the path leading to the Allbright's orchard. To the memory of Jesse and Margaret Allbright finding me there, cowering under the old apple tree, bruised, bleeding and broken from my father's latest 'lesson in manhood'.

The same tree where I'd found Cole hiding.

My breath catches.

The memory of her, curled against my chest. Her fingers tangled in the fabric of my shirt. I slow further as I turn onto the drive.

"Drop me here, mate," Brick says, clearing his throat—pulling me back to myself.

The gentle purr of the engine beneath us lulls me slightly as it idles.

"You good?" His brow dips, reading me too well.

When I don't answer right away, he hits me with that damn knowing smile.

"Tell you what—I was gonna catch some replays of the Gloucester-Bath game. You want to join me for a bit?"

He pulls out his keys for the Gatehouse, reaching for the door handle before stepping out.

I see his shift, and I know he won't let this go if I'm brooding too hard so I force a smile.

"Yeah, mate. I'm good. Just gonna call it a night. See if I can finally get some sleep."

One more tight-lipped nod. A clap on the shoulder. A silent promise that he would be there for me, should I need it.

Then he's gone, disappearing through one of the tower doors. I wait until I see the windows light up. Then, finally, I maneuver up the drive, to my cold, empty house.

Verdon Manor has stood for three hundred years, though its foundations—and the small chapel hidden on the grounds—date back to the Normans. There's been a house here since the eleventh century. And always, a Duke.

Split into three parts, it feels empty. Like it's lost its spark.

The farthest wing is mostly sealed off, its rooms stirred to life only on the rare occasions I am expected to host a ball—or when the Monarch and his retinue decide to grace our quiet corner of Great Britain.

The central wing belongs to my staff—maids, a cook, and our old Butler James, who looks about as ancient as the house itself. I will never retire him. The Cavendish family has been his life. If his purpose were lost, so would he be.

Then there's the West Wing. Mine.

My private apartments and the guest rooms reserved for the nights Brick grows tired of his own company in the Gatehouse.

I trudge up the stairs, careful not to disturb the staff, pulling my t-shirt over my head.

As it passes over my hair, the stale scent of Butty Bach hits me full force, right along with the memory of her...

The color of her auburn hair, slightly muted under the dim bulb in the cellar. The way she nervously chewed the corner of her lower lip when remembering what she needed to do. The sound of her laughter that lit up her whole face, and the sparkle of those damn brilliant emerald eyes.

The brush of her fingers as I placed the tools into her tiny hands.

My mind starts to drift as I picture those fingers curled around my length, pumping up and down. Squeezing and turning from base to tip. Running her thumb over my crown...

Suddenly, my gut tightens, an ache building in my balls, the blood rushing to my cock so fast I have to brace myself against the wall on the stairs, breathing out, willing my erection to settle as it presses painfully against the zipper of my jeans.

I gasp, pinching my eyes shut as a torrent of memories of her flash before my eyes.

Green eyes—full lips—the tip of her tongue darting out to lick at the moisture from the spraying barrel—my chest grazing her shoulder as I reach across her.

Feeling the pressure build, I groan as I palm my straining cock, and bolt up the steps two at a time, racing down the corridor to my private rooms. There's no way in hell I'm going to survive this night until I work Cole Allbright out of my system.

I frantically kick off my boots and socks, then strip off my jeans, sighing in relief as I release my aching, throbbing dick from its tight confines. I wrap my hand around it squeezing hard at the base, feeling it pulse against my palm as I stagger toward my ensuite.

I fumble with the faucet, the need to start moving my hand along my shaft consuming me.

Then, I step under the spray, the water still chilled, my impatience pushing me past the point of caring.

Running my head under the slowly warming water, I grab the bottle of shower gel, quickly lathering it into my hair, washing out the smell of the ale, but doing nothing to wash the thought of her from my mind.

The lather slides down my body, gliding down the deep ridges and flat plains of my abs, the combination of the water and soap slickening my body. I tip my head back to rinse the soap from my eyes, then look down at my straining cock.

Breathing hard, I let the memories take hold, my imagination turning it into something so much more.

Bracing one hand on the tiled wall, I slowly slide my other down my stomach. Wrapping it tightly around my shaft, I glide my hand down it once and squeeze the base.

Pinching my eyes shut, my hand becomes hers. Her delicate fingers wrapped firmly around me, working me up and down, lightly twisting, dropping occasionally to gently stroke and squeeze my balls.

My legs begin to shake as my thoughts move to her mouth.

Those soft, full lips, wrapped around my thick crown, her tongue swirling around the top, lapping away the precum, then her cheeks hollowing out, as I slide myself to the back of her throat.

Her stunning half-lidded green eyes looking up at me through lowered lashes. Tears forming as she struggles to take me deeper.

I hear the soft moans she makes, feel the vibration of them as I seat myself into her throat over and over, threading my fingers through her wet auburn hair.

My hand works furiously, stroking, squeezing, twisting, pumping harder, faster and faster, chasing that vision—until I'm roaring as I spill myself down her throat.

My cock strains, then pulses, throbbing hard in my hand as my climax barrels through me, spots of light flaring behind my eyelids as I erupt over the wall of the shower.

As the pulsing slows, I loosen my grip, shaking all over. I open my eyes to see the tiles of my shower splashed with long ropes of cum.

My chest heaving, I take several deep breaths and scowl at the tiles of the shower, as if they've offended me, before I rinse off the mess I've made.

My legs still shaking, I squeeze more of my bergamot scented shower gel into my hand, its fragrance filling the shower as I rub it across my chest and shoulders, down my stomach and back to my cock—causing it to stir yet again as my hands draw near.

I feel powerless as the thoughts of her return, imagining I had taken her in my arms in that cellar. The way her body would soften as she pressed against me. The thought of how she might feel as I slip my fingers beneath her skirt and then as I slowly pump them into her warm, wet cunt. My cock throbs and stiffens again, as I begin to slide my hand up and down my length once again to these new visions.

I imagine her pressing against me, her quiet moans turning into something more primal as I work her. Grinding herself onto my hand, panting, pleading, calling my name as I bring her to climax over and over.

My hand resumes its relentless movement, the friction of the soap and water, playing with my fantasies of how wet she would be as I wrap her legs around me and lower her onto my cock, sliding into her, pressing her down and seating myself deep, pumping, thrusting, rolling my hips up into her wet heat again and again. Then her hand reaching between us, cupping my tightening balls, gently squeezing them until...

Dropping to my knees, my vision blackens around the edges as I erupt again. I come so hard it feels like I've stopped breathing all together. My panting breaths are mixed with soft whimpers as the last of my spend leaves me and washes down the drain.

I'm shaking all over and my ass hits the shower floor. I try to catch my breath while the water spraying down on me begins to cool.

"Jesus Fuck!" I pant, gasping for breath as I run a hand down my face and shake my head.

Who is this fucking woman who has this power over me? When the mere thought of her can consume me like this?

Who are you Cole Allbright and what the fuck have you done to me?

Chapter 23

Cole

"Fuck, Cole. I'm so, so sorry. I don't know what came over me."

Zavier pleads, his face forlorn as he kneels before me on the doorstep of the bookshop.

"I swear, it'll never, ever happen again."

He's holding out a beautiful, but ridiculously oversized bouquet of chrysanthemums, dahlias and roses in an array of fall colors.

"Please get up. This really isn't necessary." My cheeks flame as I glance nervously over my shoulder to see several of the men, who had been working on the bookshop renovations, have all stopped and are now watching to see what's happening in the doorway.

I reluctantly accept the bouquet and tug on his arm to get him to stand back up.

The moment he's up, he sweeps me off my feet. I squeak when he pulls me into a massive bear hug, squeezing me so tightly, I actually hear a few of my vertebrae pop. When he plops me back down, he bends down to plant a big kiss on my cheek.

His teeth sparkle as he flashes me a wide grin, and he hurries out the door, shouting back over his shoulder.

"You're the best, babe. I'm gonna finish up the work in the orchard now. I'll have it all cleaned up for you in no time."

The heavy bundle of flowers hangs loosely at my side and I blink mutely after him, as I'm left standing in the wake of his whirlwind apology.

What in the hell was that?

The next few days pass in a happy, busy blur. My time, filled with painting, decorating, orchestrating handymen—all of us working to breathe life back into the bookshop. Already, I can see the space gradually converting from dim, dusty and dreary to bright, warm and welcoming. Becoming a sanctuary where someone would love to come to escape into a new world, losing themselves between the pages of a good book.

Caring for Hannah and Athena quickly becomes part of my daily rhythm, their quiet presence lending a touch of magic to my days.

The changing colors of the trees in the woods and my orchard are a breathtaking display—reds, ambers, yellows, and golds carpeting the ground in an autumnal mosaic. It reminds me so much of home.

Of before my mother died.

Before my innocence was stolen.

"There's nothing more beautiful than Connecticut in the fall." Her whispered words a sweet echo in my mind as she'd wrapped her arm around my shoulder and hugged me close beneath the Millers' old trees.

Other memories jump to mind... a well-read novel open on her lap, the light scent of her perfume mixed with the sweet smell of the ripe apples in the tree above us—*the haunted look in her tired eyes and the hint of makeup, not quite hiding the yellowing bruises beneath them.*

But here feels like an escape, a new beginning.

In this village, I can hear the nuance of my mother's voice in the people I've met—Kya's broad, vibrant tones, the crisp enunciations of those who frequented the pub. Each one, another tiny thread tying me to this place. Another chord anchoring me whenever the urge to run threatens to rise.

Evenings behind the bar bring unexpected joy. Right from the start, I was welcomed with open arms, very few patrons questioning me as an outsider. Each night, I leave with not only a sense of accomplishment, but with a feeling of genuine belonging, and more like a part of the community.

A warmth spreads through me when I catch the murmurs of hushed conversations like,

"That's Jesse's granddaughter," or

"I can see Maryanne in her—it's like she's come back to us..."

The words float through the room, finding my ears, making me smile to myself.

One evening, as I'm putting some of the freshly washed glasses back on the shelf, the sound of raised voices in the midst of a heated debate and the sound of my name draws my attention. In an effort to listen without seeming obvious, I move closer, busying myself with refilling the garnish trays.

Old Tom, his arm tucked warmly around Kya's elderly neighbor Edna, who's snuggled in closely beside him in her trademark bright, hand-knitted cardigan, speaks up to Miss Braithwaite, whose snide remark has obviously set him off.

Looking satisfied with herself, she sits back as she sips her dry sherry, nose raised in condescension.

I have no idea what she's said that set my nearly toothless knight in shining armor on edge, but suddenly he's standing, leaning into her face, jamming one arthritic finger down repeatedly on the table in front of her.

"That girl has more right to be here than you do woman! Cole's blood is steeped in the St. Briavels Hundred," —*whatever that means*— "and YOU, Edith, are the outsider, since you only moved here from Ledbury!"

Completely aghast, Miss Braithwaite, sits back with her hand to her chest. Fuming, she sets her glass down hard, her eyes seething. Her glare flies to me and then back to Tom as she pins each of us with a tempestuous glare. Gathering her belongings, she harrumphs loudly, then waltzes out of the pub, swinging her oversized rump as she stomps out the door.

As it slams shut behind her, every customer in the place breaks into a loud round of raucous applause, hooting and hollering. Some even stand and direct their applause toward me, where I stand behind the bar, blushing furiously with my eyes wide and mouth gaping, completely dumbfounded by what just happened.

But there's something else too—an untold warmth spreading throughout my chest.

I think Edna is laughing the loudest, cheering for her beau with the enthusiasm of a twenty-year-old cheerleader. Tom mocks a gallant bow to her, before leaning down and resting his lips softly upon hers.

I smile at how sweet it all is. Not only how he defends me in his knightly manner, but how lovingly Edna gazes into his eyes. It's so wonderful he's found someone to spend his time with.

"How far is Ledbury from here?"

I ask Kya as we walk home later that night; Old Tom's quip to Miss Braithwaite about where she's originally from, replaying in my mind.

She tips her head curiously at me. "About fifteen miles away. Why do you ask?"

"So, what did Tom mean when he said, my *blood is steeped in the St. Briavels Hundred*?" I puzzle, trying to make sense of the reasoning behind his argument.

"Ahh, that's right, my butty." She exaggerates her already broad accent, wrapping one long arm around me with a playful grin. "If you were born within the hundred, then you're considered a true Forester."

My brow furrows as I nibble on the skin beside my thumbnail and I wrinkle my nose, a concern still niggling at me.

We continue to walk in silence for a while as I mull that over.

"But I was born in Connecticut." I finally blurt. "Not even in the same country! How does that make me a true Forester?"

"Ah, but see, your mum, your grandparents—they were all born and bred here." Her eyes sparkle as she pulls me closer.

"So that, my friend, is what makes *you* a true Forester."

If I'm being honest with myself, there's another reason I look forward to my shifts at the pub, and it has nothing to do with belonging or needing to feel a sense of accomplishment, but has everything to do with a longing I can't quite understand. A reason that's haunted me since the night Rogan helped me with that damn barrel.

Each night as I lay in bed, I never quite know whether I'll wake up from nightmares of my past or from dreams of him—his presence, his heat, the whisper of his breath against my neck.

While I'm working behind the bar, I catch myself watching the door, listening for the rumble of his engine, hoping it'll be him. Praying he doesn't have another woman hanging off him.

Like clockwork, he strolls through the door, Brick leading the way. So far, my prayers have been answered when Bethany doesn't return with them. Each time she doesn't show, I'm hit with an inexplicable wave of relief.

Regardless of how busy the pub is, he waits for me—even if Kya, Pete, or Greg aren't busy—standing patiently off to the side until the moment I'm free. Before he even has to ask, I pour their drinks while he slips into our unspoken routine, asking how I've been settling in to Verdon-on-Wye, how Greg's been treating me as my new boss and—inevitably—he'll ask how the renovations are going at the bookshop.

I can't shake the feeling, he's asking for reasons other than friendly curiosity. I can't put my finger on it, but every time I mention something going well with the renovations, I catch a glimmer of something like disappointment.

It's fleeting.

There and gone in a blink, but I swear I still catch it.

A reminder that he's likely just keeping an eye on me. Checking in on me, only to find out whether or not I'm failing. The stark truth being, he actually wants me gone, after all.

But then that enigmatic smile returns, curling the edge of his lips and I'm gone—*lost in those damn storm cloud eyes again.*

I live for those moments—when the noises of the pub fade away, for a breath of time when it's just us, causing this strange tingle inside me, like the tiny bubbles rising in his glass, as he lifts his drink to his lips...

Without fail, reality always pushes its way back into focus, ruining the illusion of peace. Another customer will need to be served and he'll step away, a mask of cold indifference slipping into place, hardening the softer features I had seen just a few moments before.

But nothing seems to sour Rogan's mood more than when Zavier shows up and makes his way through the crowd and over to the bar, that glacial stare finding me every time.

From the time he arrives, Rogan goes quiet, his features hardening into a brooding glare that seems perpetually locked on Zavier.

I've asked Kya and a couple other people around the village why those two seem to have such a deep-seated hatred toward one another, but no one seems to know.

The most information I've been able to glean was from Old Tom but all he was able to tell me was that the Johnson's had worked for the Cavendish family for years... right up until shortly after the last Duke, Rogan's father, had passed away.

Old Tom had motioned for me to lean in close, shifting his eyes around the room to see who might be close enough to overhear our conversation, then whispered behind his hand conspiratorially.

"There's been somethin' dark brewin' between those two lads ever since then."

Just one more mystery to figure out in this puzzling little village.

As much as I've been enjoying my shifts working at the pub, between the long evenings on my feet serving customers and the bookshop cleanup and renovations during the day, I have to admit I was more than ready for Wednesday night to roll around—the one night Kya and I have off.

All I've been wanting to do is soak in a hot bath and get lost in the pages of my new book.

This one is about these sisters that get pulled through a portal into a hidden realm where there are hot fae men with wings and magical powers that allow them to control shadows and they can make those shadows do things to the women... *spicy things*. I smirk and feel my cheeks heat just thinking about it.

But when Kya greets me at the door grinning like the Cheshire Cat, it's clear she's got something else in store for our night off.

"Right then, Cole," she declares0 with a clap. I hold the door open for Athena to slink inside beside me and crouch down to ruffle Grumbl's soft head and press a kiss to the wrinkles between his eyes.

"You've got five minutes to get changed—then we're off." She announces, clearly offering no room for argument.

Blinking up at her, I take in the sportswear she's got on—a Lycra top showing off her honey-toned midriff, yoga pants, sneakers and a track jacket slung over her shoulders.

"Off? Off to where?" I ask, trying to figure out what in the world she's got planned for us. With Kya, I've quickly come to learn *literally anything* could be possible.

With a sparkling glint in her eyes, she grins at me, pulling a scrunchie off her wrist and effortlessly twisting her long hair into an impeccable messy bun before propping her hands matter-of-factly on her hips.

"Cole, my sweet! Tonight we're going to self-defense class."

Chapter 24

Cole

Dressed in leggings and a long-sleeve track jacket, I don't feel nearly as stylish as Kya as we step into the dojo—twenty minutes early for the lesson. She moves with easy confidence, while I hesitate for a beat, scanning the space.

The dojo sits toward the center of the village, tucked behind the village hall. Above the entrance, a sign reads:

Iron Oak Gym and Dojo

Specializing in Mixed Martial Arts, Tae Kwon Do, and Jiu-Jitsu

Ladies' Self-Defense Class—Every Wednesday at 7 PM

I take in the room as we enter. The open training area, the equipment lining the walls, the light scent of sweat and aerosols, lingering traces of bodies that have trained here before, mostly hidden by the stronger scent of disinfectant cleaners.

In the distance, I catch the rhythmic thrum of dance music and the low whir of machines as people workout in the gym next door.

Thick blue mats stretch across the floors, their surface worn but sturdy. Wooden racks line the walls, stocked with various types of workout equipment—including, to my surprise, things that look suspiciously like wooden swords. My gaze shifts to a glass-fronted case, where an array of gleaming weapons rests—three-pronged forks, looking like miniature tridents, something resembling a police baton and nun chucks.

To one side, a clearly marked square defines part of the training space, while near the edge of the room stands a sparring dummy—a muscled upper torso and head mounted on a weighted, movable post. From the corner of my eye, I catch Kya's grin as she follows my gaze.

"That's Richard, but we affectionately call him 'Dick,'" she beams. "Dick the Dummy."

Her laughter is bright and mischievous. "That's where we'll get started."

Kya notices my hesitation and gives my shoulder a gentle squeeze of encouragement, pulling my attention back to her. I meet her eyes and give her a timid smile, feeling my throat work as I try to quell my nerves.

I can do this!

Arm in arm, we walk over, depositing our bags and shoes to the side of the sparring ring. She heads to a bin filled with safety equipment and grabs a pair of gloves for each of us.

The gloves are fingerless, padded across the knuckles and the back of the hand. She hands me a pair, and I mimic her movements—slipping them on, fastening the strong Velcro straps snugly around my wrists. She flexes her fingers, adjusting for comfort, and I follow suit, testing the fit.

"Now, you're going to want to get into a defensive stance, like this," Kya says, planting her feet apart—one forward, the other slightly behind and to the side. I do my best to mimic her, nodding for her to continue.

"Then you want to protect your body and face with your hands, like this." She raises one fisted hand in front of her face, the other positioned low near her belly.

I can't help but marvel at how my soft-hearted, gentle friend transforms in an instant. Just by assuming this stance, she exudes a fierce, commanding presence—the warrior version of herself I'd glimpsed in action at the pub.

"Then you give them hell!" she shouts, and suddenly she's in motion. Her fists fly in sharp, rapid strikes, each punch snapping through the air with enough force to make it hiss. She spins, her legs kicking out high and strong, each movement so precise and powerful I'm convinced she could take down even the largest attacker.

I take a couple of steps back, my mouth agape, eyes wide, a huge grin spreading across my face.

When Kya finishes her demonstration, she presses her hands together at her chest in a mock prayer and drops into a deep bow before me. As she straightens, her eyes finding mine and seeing my awestruck expression, we both burst into laughter.

"I don't think I'm quite ready for that yet, but that was badass!" I say as our laughter dissolves into giggles.

Still wiping tears from our eyes, we head back to the dummy. "Let me show you how to hit on 'Dick.'" Kya says with a wink. She strides over to the sparring dummy, dragging it onto the floor and slapping him on the shoulder with a playful, "There you go, Dicky boy!"

Adopting her fighter's stance, she unleashes a flurry of rapid punches, sending *'Dick'* swaying wildly. Then, with a few precise kicks, she sends him tipping back, landing each strike with such precision, skill and power, I can't help but clap when she's done.

Beaming, Kya turns with a brilliant smile and takes a flourishing bow. "Want to take a crack at it?" she asks. Still smiling, I nod eagerly, excitement bubbling up as I step forward.

I position myself in front of the dummy, adjusting my feet the way she had shown me. Raising my fists, I ready myself for my first strike. Trying to emulate Kya's movements, I pull back one gloved fist and swing it into the dummy with all my might.

"OUCH!"

The cry bursts out of me as I clutch my hand, cradling it to my chest.

"Oh, honey! I'm so sorry!" Kya exclaims, rushing to my side.

"I forgot to tell you—it's going to smart a bit until you get used to it."

I flex my fingers a few times, shaking out my hand as I try to muster a reassuring smile. It's watery at best, but I nod anyway. She takes my hand gently, examining my fingers with care.

"You're gonna break your wrist if you lock it up like that when you punch."

The deep voice echoes across the room, sending a jolt through the air, electrifying it. The sudden interruption startles us both—it's as if he's materialized out of nowhere, his presence now so unmistakable, effortlessly filling the space.

Kya lets out a slow, exaggerated sigh, rolling her eyes as she leans toward me conspiratorially.

"Oh goody, it's the Duke," she whispers, catching my eye with a knowing look.

I feel my cheeks heat instantly. *Oh God, he just saw me screw that up so badly. How long had he been watching me?*

"What's he doing here?" I whisper nervously.

"He's one of the instructors, love," Kya shrugs. "It was a 50/50 shot of it being him or Brick."

Dragging my widened eyes from Kya, I turn back to the Duke. He's leaning his shoulder against the doorframe, the last of the evening sunlight streaming in behind him, his features obscured by shadow. As he straightens and steps forward, the light shifts just enough for me to catch the curl of his mouth. Those steel-gray eyes lock onto mine, and I feel Kya's glance flick between us. But I can't seem to look away as he strides toward us, confidence rolling off him like a thick fog.

"You have to let the power come from your body," he says, his voice softer now. He's close enough I have to tip my head back to meet his gaze. The air around me fills with a clean, citrusy, scent—*something familiar... but what?*

Before my brain can supply the answer, he moves to the bin of safety equipment, grabbing a pair of gloves for himself. He fastens them with practiced ease as he strides back to the mat.

My eyes follow his movements, then shift to his clothing. A cotton t-shirt hugs his broad chest, clinging to the deep lines and ridges of his pecks and abs, the sleeves tightly wrapping around his thick biceps. The tattoos I've only glimpsed before are now fully visible, curving and swirling down his arms, stopping just before his wrists. A dress shirt would hide them easily, but here, in the t-shirt, I can see every intricate detail. My gaze drops to his bare feet, then slowly scans upward to his loose-fitting pants, my eyes catching on his—

"Right then!" he barks suddenly.

I jump, my eyes snapping up to his face. His lips are pinched in a tight line, one eyebrow slightly raised.

"I'm sorry," I whisper, feeling like a rabbit caught in a trap.

His brows pinch briefly, his head tilting curiously.

"No need to apologize," he says, his voice gentler now.

I glance over at Kya, who's standing at the edge of the mat. She gives me a wink and a smile before wandering over to our bags to fish out her phone.

"Ready to get started then?" he asks, moving on as if I hadn't just made a complete ass of myself. I nod, forcing a smile and trying desperately to feign a confidence I most certainly don't feel.

Wonderful... this is just the beginning of my embarrassing night.

"Let's see your ready stance," he says, circling behind me and slightly to the side. I glance over my shoulder at him, then position my feet the way Kya had shown me.

"Good. You need to turn your hips a bit, so your body is almost sideways." He reaches down, placing large, warm hands on my hips, gently twisting me into position. My head snaps down to the point of contact, my mouth going dry. The sound of my blood rushing in my ears is so loud, I almost miss his next words.

He leans closer, his voice near my ear like he's sharing a secret, "You'll be a smaller target when you turn like this."

Reaching around me, he takes both my wrists in his hands. "Make a fist," he instructs, the low sound of his deep voice so close I can feel the heat of his breath and it sends a flurry of goose bumps down my legs.

I curl my fingers into fists.

"No, keep your thumb out, so you don't break it when you punch."

His large hand slides up from my wrist to my fingers, gently resetting my fist, the motion causing more goose bumps to travel up my arms beneath my sleeves.

"Good girl," he breathes.

My throat tightens as I try to swallow, my mouth now as dry as the Sahara. But something stirs low in my belly—a warmth, like liquid heat radiating through my core.

He reaches around me, positioning my right hand in front of my face while curling my other fist low, near my belly, his knuckles just grazing the top hem of my leggings. I feel the heat of him behind me, close enough that I swear I can feel his heartbeat.

Or is that mine?

His scent surrounds me, familiar and intoxicating, pulling me into its embrace.

I know that scent, but why?

When I realize he hasn't released my hands yet, I slowly turn to look up at him, only to meet steel-gray eyes already fixed on mine.

My tongue dips out, wetting my lower lip and tug it between my teeth. His gaze tracks the movement, his throat working as a muscle feathers in his jaw.

Kya's phone suddenly trills and the tune *'Don't Worry, Be Happy,'* plays loudly, snapping us out of... whatever that was.

Rogan releases me and quickly steps back and I let out a slow, shaky breath.

"Right," he says, clearing his throat and rubbing the back of his neck. "Let's work on some punches on Dick."

He points awkwardly toward the dummy and heads over to begin.

He watches me as I throw a few punches at Dick's torso. My hits are weak and clearly ineffective. I know I'm being timid—the memory of the pain ratcheting up my arm from my first attempt, still fresh in my mind. That, and his persistent gaze tracking me.

It's... well, it's distracting.

"Where are you aiming, Cole?" he asks after another feeble tap that barely makes Dick wobble, let alone anything that could do any real damage.

I look at him, puzzled, not understanding the question.

He sighs, stepping closer. Behind him, I hear the dojo doors open followed by the happy chatter of more women as they filter in. But the closer he gets, the more their voices fade, like he's the sun, his blinding brilliance obliterating every-thing else around him.

"Watch," he instructs. He doesn't tell me to move, so I stay rooted to the spot, one hand nervously running along the sleeve of my jacket.

"You're aiming here," he says, resting his long index and middle fingers on Dick's sternum. "And that's where all your force is stopping," he lays his palm flat on Dick's chest, "at the surface."

He gestures for me to move aside as he steps back, sizing up his 'opponent' before flicking his gaze at me—a flash of steel-gray eyes—then raises his hands, deliberately throwing a comically weak punch into the dummy.

He looks back at me again, with an eyebrow cocked, "This is how you're punching right now. Do you really think Dick will be hurting after that?" he asks, a playful smirk curling up the corners of his lips.

"No..." I say, a smile prying at the corners of my lips. But the teasing grin that forms on his mouth, the image of his pathetic punch as he emulated my own causes a laugh to bubble up my throat and escapes me before I can stop it.

His eyes widen and his brow crinkles in surprise at my sudden laughter and I clap my hands over my mouth to stifle it, swallowing it back down and rapidly schooling my features and dropping my eyes to the floor in front of me, "I'm sorry..."

"Don't you dare apologize." He cuts in, his gentle, yet stern tone pulling my gaze back up to his. His features turn serious as he scans my face, his jaw tensing briefly as he studies me.

His eyes narrow slightly but then he straightens his shoulders and takes in a breath, seeming to come back to himself, the tension draining from his face. He refocuses his attention on the dummy, resuming the lesson, as if that moment never happened at all.

"If you aim for a point on the other side of him—through him—your punch will naturally hit harder. Remember what I said? The power comes from your body."

I feel myself relax as he smoothly moves us back into the lesson, his gentle training style slipping effortlessly back into place. I nod, my confidence slowly forming when I show him I've remembered what he told me, and he smiles again.

"Good girl." He purrs once more, and my throat tightens all over again.

Then, as quick as a snake, he adopts the stance. His front fist lashes out, as he pivots on his rear foot, his hips swinging forward. Just as quickly, his fist snaps back to guard his face. Dick sways awkwardly from the force of that single punch.

But he's not done. He pivots forward again, his back hand moving almost faster than the first, landing a punishing blow to the dummy's solar plexus.

The group of other women in the class, I realize, have all paused their chatter to watch Rogan as he decimates the poor... er, Dick. And he's not finished yet. As the dummy rocks back, mimicking a counter attack, he grabs the back of its head, pulling it down, while, at the same time, bringing his knee fiercely up to smash into Dick's face.

He releases his hold as the dummy once again leans precariously back. His chest is heaving and there's a slight darkening of the material of his t-shirt where his sweat has soaked through. He looks down, breathing out, running a hand through his hair. My mind whips back to the basement at the pub, the wet strands falling loosely over his forehead.

When his eyes find mine, in the circle of onlookers, he holds my stare for what feels like a small eternity. My heart steps up its rhythm and my grip tightens on my arm. I pull my bottom lip between my teeth. His eyes drop instantly to my mouth, following the movement. The corner of his mouth lifts with a devious smile, causing heat to rush up my neck and blaze into my cheeks, while a tightness forms deep in my lower belly.

Then suddenly he's moving again, spinning around and delivering a powerful flying kick to the side of Dick's head.

This time, the dummy crashes down with a mighty thud.

I flinch—my arms flying up to cover my face as my breath hitches and I slam my eyes shut. The sound—it's exactly the same.

The same as when my mother fell.

When my father's shadow swallowed her unmoving form.

The same as when I hit the wall, my head cracking against the bathroom tiles, the room blurring, my vision blackening around the edges until all I could see was blood—my blood, pooling on the white porcelain beneath me...

Rapturous applause erupts from the women circling around us, sharp and relentless, cutting through the haze, tearing me from the clutches of memory. My eyes snap open and I slowly lower my hands away from my face.

Rogan stands in the center of the ring, his chest heaving, his jaw clenched, fingers curling and uncurling into fists at his sides. His eyes locked on me, blazing with a fierce intensity.

He looks furious.

His brow furrowed, his eyes narrowed as he tilts his head—studying me, like he's piecing something together, or like he's recognizing something familiar.

Heat rushes to my cheeks. I drop my gaze, suddenly fascinated with the Velcro on my sparring glove, blinking against the sharp sting of tears.

Is he angry with me?

Kya sidles up beside me, wrapping an arm around my shoulders, giving me a gentle tug, though her gaze never leaves the Duke.

"Come with me, hun. I think you need a minute," she whispers in my ear. I nod, looking up at her with a glance, grateful she sees so much without truly knowing, as we walk toward our bags at the back of the room.

Kya hands me a water bottle, encouraging me to take a drink. Meeting my eyes, her brow pinched in concern, she asks, "You alright, hun? Do you need to take a break?"

I take a few sips of water, trying to calm my rapidly beating heart as I watch Rogan push the dummy back up, moving it toward the edge of the room. He takes a purposeful swig from his own bottle, his muscles rolling beneath the material of his t-shirt.

You're okay Cole. He's not here. He can't hurt you anymore. Get it together.

I take one last sip and replace the cap, then nod and try to offer her a confident smile.

"I'm good. Just got a little overwhelmed for a minute there."

She holds my gaze for another moment, gauging whether I'm truly alright. Pressing her lips into a thin line, she gives a tight nod, and we head back to the practice ring.

"Find a space," Rogan commands across the room, his back to us, his voice hard.

I stay toward the back, just behind Kya, copying the drills he runs us through. Then he pairs us up, helping us work on our form.

I say us, but for the next hour, it feels as though he's avoiding me. He moves around the room, talking, sometimes even laughing with the other women—even with Kya. And just when I think he's about to give me feedback, he turns away, finding someone else to help.

I try to smile through the training, feeding off the other women's exuberance, but the voice inside my head that's so rarely silent—the voice that torments me, chastising, mocking, belittling—the voice that seeks out the weakest parts of me to needle at—sneers, hissing venom in my ear:

You've done it again, Nicole. You fucked up! You see that? No one wants to be around you. You're worthless. Pathetic.

Why do you even bother? You disgust me. This is why you need me—no one else would ever put up with you and your bullshit. Get the fuck out of my sight! I can't even stand to look at you. You're nothing but a useless, disappointing piece of shit!

The sound of a glove hitting a training pad—*so like the sound of a fist hitting flesh*—shocks me out of my reverie.

At that moment, the sounds, the movement, the smells, the gloves on my hands all feel too tight, too confining. The echo of his voice, always in my head.

It's too much.

Shaking my head furiously, I tear at the Velcro on my gloves, ripping them off and letting them drop to the mat.

I don't bother putting on my shoes. I just grab my bag, *and run.*

I have to get out.

I have to escape.

Not again... Not again... Not again!

I burst through the dojo doors, cross the lawn, and hit the road. Sharp stones and gravel dig into my bare feet, each step slicing, punishing—but I don't stop.

I can't.

I need to go.

I need someplace safe.

I need the warmth of Grumbl pressed against my leg, the quiet reassurance of Athena curling into my lap, her purr steady and dependable.

Someone who won't look at me—or worse... *through me*—like I'm nothing.

So I run home.

Chapter 25

Rogan

After the class ends and the last of the ladies leave, I'm left with a restless energy that won't let me settle.

It builds as I pace, carving a relentless path, back and forth, over and over, like a caged beast. There's a tension inside me, coiling like a viper, poised to strike, but trapped behind an opaque wall, blinded by uncertainty.

It's clear someone has hurt her badly and she's scared.

No, not just scared. She's fucking terrified. And what I saw tonight, only confirmed what I'd suspected that day in the orchard—she's close to breaking.

It damn near killed me, not being able to go after her when she bolted from the dojo, having to stay with the class, in a prison of my own making.

A rumbling breath builds inside me at the thought of someone hurting her, an untold fury boiling inside me as I pace, the sound reverberating through the empty room.

This is my dojo.

My sacred space.

My hallowed ground.

My freedom.

And yet—one look from those emerald eyes, and I want to ruin it all. All of my hard-won discipline and patience, the very foundations of everything I've built, corroding away.

A raging torrent of thoughts and emotions rampage through my mind, caught somewhere between a ferocious need to protect her and an all-consuming need to claim her. To wrap her in my arms, to shield her from whatever—*whomever*—caused her this pain... this terror.

But beneath that desire feels something far more dangerous.

Reminding me of what I once was, what I once had been capable of—and that thought alone is a poison, decimating every ounce of discipline I have left.

Throwing my head back I unleash a roar, the sound ripping from deep in my gut. It echoes off the walls of the empty space, reflecting my own fury back at me. My chest heaves as I draw in ragged breaths and drag my hand down my face.

Dark memories come raging back to me and suddenly, something about the dojo feels off—wrong. The mats beneath my feet feel unstable. The familiar scents, usually comforting, turn sour, sharp—reminding me why I built this space in the first place. What it represents and who it was meant to help. It was created to help take back control. Not for losing it myself.

But seeing her snap, as she curled in on herself, cowering away from the shadow of a demon only she can see—it's unraveling me.

There's a reason she came to this class tonight. Not some vacuous whim like most of the students. Women who show up just to ogle Brick or me. It's not like they're subtle about it and I'd be lying if I said we hadn't taken advantage of their advances in the past—the very recent past.

But not Cole. She came here to learn. To prepare to defend herself against something, *or someone.* I've seen it too many times before to not recognize the signs.

Not only has she been brutalized, but based on how she reacted, I'd have to guess she's been terrorized too. The thought makes my blood boil.

But she doesn't realize how strong she is. Doesn't feel how much power she actually holds. I don't think she sees just how close she is to reclaiming the light and strength that was stolen from her. How she's already becoming who she's always been meant to be. She puts on a good show in the pub, taking on the persona of being light-hearted, happy, bubbly—fully engaged and present.

That is until some fucker like Zavier oversteps and crushes her fragile hold on it, causing her fears to erupt back up to the surface all over again.

I'm hit with flashes of the way she shrinks, folding into herself, as though simply taking up space is a punishable offense.

Apologizing for everything, as though each word out of her mouth needs permission. Hugging her arms around herself, creating a protective barrier between herself and... *and what?*

What the hell was she so afraid of tonight?

Of me?

No.

I shake my head, my fingers gripping my hair at the roots, my jaw clenching so tight it aches.

Not me—*she can't be afraid of me.*

It was in *my* arms where she found comfort when I carried her out of the orchard that day. It was *my* body she burrowed into to hide from the demons that clawed at her mind—*my* shirt her hands gripped when she needed something to hold onto. *My* chest she rested her head against when that feeling of safety finally settled over her.

I was the one she took with her into the dark basement of the pub.

I was the one who stepped in to get Zavier away from her when he wouldn't release her hand.

She *has to* know I would never hurt her—*doesn't she?*

But even as I think it, I know I'm lying to myself.

She knows jack shit about me and she has every right to fear me.

I curse myself for losing my temper the way I had, pouring out the storm I had raging inside me on the dummy. But the way she had looked—her soft features shifting from curiosity to terror in a blink—the feeling that had awoken inside me... I hadn't felt that in a long time.

Shit, if I'm being honest with myself, I'm not sure I've ever felt a rage so all consuming.

"Jesus fuck!" The words tear from my throat, raw and guttural, as I grip the back of my neck and continue pacing. My skin is slick with sweat, my breaths raspy and uneven. I've never had to fight this hard to maintain control. Never had to work like this to control the way I feel around a woman.

My focus whirls to the wall of weapons and I cross the room, hesitating only a moment before choosing.

The tonfas—sturdy and unyielding, like the batons police wield. They're a reminder of the discipline I'm meant to embody.

The nun chucks—Brick's flashy favorite, seem almost mocking in their showmanship.

But my weapon of choice calls to me.

I key in the code on the padlock and yank open the cabinet with enough force to rattle the glass. Reaching in, my hands close around the Sai daggers.

Three sharp spikes, elegant as a trident—a weapon of beauty, but deadly in the right hands. Under the fluorescent lights, they gleam, their center points catching the glow like scattered stars. Reverently, I lift them, spinning them in my grip with practiced movements, reacquainting myself with their weight, their balance—their quiet promise of precision.

The first movements of my kata start slow and deliberate, my body remembering the rhythm, the flow steady and smooth, even as the chaos of my mind rebels. Each step, each strike, is a battle to reclaim the calm I so desperately need.

But she's there.

Green eyes, wide and searching. Auburn hair, soft and wild. The delicate scent of apples and fresh air filling my nose. The feel of her body under my hands as I adjusted her stance, the way her breath hitched when I murmured, "Good girl."

My grip on the daggers tightens, the metal biting into my palms. I pause mid-movement, my chest heaving. The dojo feels stifling, the air thick and oppressive.

I peel off my sweat-soaked shirt, releasing me from the confines of the wet fabric clinging to my skin. I toss it away in hopes the cool air will do something to quell the fire raging inside me.

I close my eyes but my heart races.

Breathe damn it!

In. Out.

In.

Her tongue, darting out to wet her lips...

Out.

Her breath catching in her throat at my touch...

In.

Concentrate, Rogan. Calm your bloody mind.

Her eyes studying me—soft, startled, guarded.

Who the fuck hurt you?!

The unbidden thought crashes over me and I roar—an animalistic sound that feels like it's ripping straight out of my soul, reverberating off the walls of the empty dojo.

My eyes snap open, my body tensed, my breaths sharp and ragged. The frenzy builds to a fever pitch and before I can stop myself, I hurl one of the daggers.

It slices through the air, spinning end over end, gleaming in the stark light before embedding itself deep into Dick's face with a sickening thud.

I drop to my knees, my chest heaving as a trickle of my rage finally seems to ebb away. The silence that follows is deafening.

Until it's broken by the slow, sharp, sound of clapping hands.

My pulse pounds in my ears, hammering like a war drum as I slowly turn my head toward the sound.

Kya.

She's leaning in the doorway, arms crossed and a smirk tugging at the corner of her lips. Her amber eyes shimmer with something unreadable.

Amusement, maybe? Curiosity?

No, there's something sharper beneath.

Judgment?

"Nice aim." She says, her voice steady, deceptively casual. But there's an edge to it, a weight behind it that settles uncomfortably in my chest.

I swallow hard, my throat like sandpaper. The air in the room feels suffocating now. Dick still wobbles from the force of the impact, my damn dagger protruding from his face, mocking me in eerie silence.

Kya steps forward, the sound of her boots against the mats is unnervingly loud, each step seeming deliberate as she slowly approaches.

"Didn't know you were into theatrics." she muses, her smirk deepening, but the sharpness in her tone remains.

I force myself to slow my breathing, to steady the tremor in my hands.

"What are you doing here?"

The words barely make it past my lips, my voice dry, rough.

"I came to offer you some advice, *Your Grace*."

Her use of the honorific drips with sarcasm and sours in my gut and it only gets worse as she continues.

"Cole is vulnerable."

At those words, any of the faux amusement which had initially been there, vanishes from her face. Her usual softness replaced by hard conviction. She keeps her voice steady and calm but her words carry an added edge, as if laying down a steadfast set of rules and brokering no room for argument.

"I don't know what made her run tonight, Rogan—and I can assure you; she is clearly running from something that's got her bloody terrified—but she's finally making a life here. Making friends. Slowly forming some foundations. But in her eyes, they're fragile ones she doesn't feel she deserves."

She takes another step closer, her amber eyes locking onto mine with a barely contained, quiet fury brewing behind them.

"So the last damn thing she needs is someone like you bulldozing through and destroying what she's barely begun to build."

Her eyes drop closed and a tear spills over her lower lashes. She pulls in a long, shuddering breath as she attempts to regain a modicum of the control she normally has before she continues.

"I realize, I haven't known her very long," her voice quieter, but somehow heavier, "but I already love her like a sister, and I am telling you this right now—"

She pauses, turning away slightly to angrily swipe her fingers across her wet cheek.

When she turns back to me, the steel in her has returned as she takes another step closer.

"I know you're after that bookshop and the land Jesse left her. But I can also see the way you've been looking at her—the way you linger around her at the pub."

Her glare burrows into me like a hot drill, searing, relentless.

"I've seen the kind of woman you usually go for, but that's not who she is, Rogan. She's not just some cheap floozy you can hook up with for a few hot, sweaty nights and then throw her away like yesterday's trash."

Her glare is a fiery blaze, cutting into me with a fervency like I've never seen from her before. Her eyes narrow and she takes one last step, closing the remaining distance between us and stabs her finger into my chest like the blade of a knife.

"And so help me, if you hurt her, Rogan, I swear... Nothing... Not you, not Brick, not a pack of goddamn hellhounds, will be able to stop me from making damn sure you suffer for as long as I draw breath!" She hisses, holding my stare.

I don't say a word... *I can't.* Everything she's said about me is true, her words cut to the very heart of me, calling me out for who I am—for who I've become.

She studies me, waiting for me to say... something, anything.

When I still don't speak, she sighs, her shoulders dropping as the ice leaves her eyes and her face softens again.

"Whatever happened to her—she's clearly been through enough. You're going to need to respect that."

My throat tightens and I look away, as the ache in my chest squeezes again.

I hear her blow out a frustrated breath and I can feel her eyes on me.

"Do you hear me, Rogan Cavendish?"

Swallowing past the knot that's formed in my throat, I give her a tight nod.

The weight of her eyes stays on me for a long moment and she sighs again, before turning to head back toward the door, where she stops, resting her hand against it. Her nails drum once, twice—pulling my attention to where she's standing. She looks back over her shoulder, locking her gaze to mine.

Her left brow pops up and she presses her lips into a tight line, the unanswered question still hanging between us, waiting for an impending confirmation.

I nod again, firmer this time.

"Yes, Kya. I hear you. Loud and clear."

"Good." She turns, swinging the door open and waltzing out into the night. It slams shut behind her, the force of it rattling the walls.

Dick wobbles again, the Sai dagger still lodged deep between his eyes—almost like the bastard is mocking me.

Maybe he is.

Chapter 26

Rogan

It comes as no surprise when I get no sleep again, and instead spend the entire night tossing and turning, wrestling with relentless thoughts of Cole while visions of her flash on repeat in my mind.

Kya's promise—correction, her *threat*—is one I have no doubt she'll waste no time following through on, should I go against her.

'Leave Cole alone.'

Sounds simple enough, doesn't it?

The problem is, I need someone to tell my cock to stop constantly hardening at the mere thought of her. The persistent, throbbing ache building, until I'm forced to try to get some semblance of relief—my hand becoming a poor substitute for the warm, wet flesh I crave.

I fuck my hand again and again, imagining it's her hot cunt or mouth, only to repeatedly spill myself onto my shower walls instead.

Shuddering as the last tremors of my orgasm subside, the realization hits—I can't keep doing this. I need to figure out a way to avoid Cole altogether.

I dry off and drop my wet towel to the floor. Without bothering to redress, I collapse onto my mattress and groan. Raking my fingers down my face, I war against the chaos brewing in my mind.

I try to envision how it might unfold. Perhaps, if somehow the expenses were to become too much for her, she might come to see the bookshop as nothing more than a lost cause. A fleeting fantasy built on sentiment rather than solid ground.

I force myself to plot ways to drive up the costs or ways to sabotage her progress. Perhaps I can pull some of the contractors off her job. Offer to pay them more to work on one of my projects instead. Ultimately delaying her to the point that she'll end up missing the six-month deadline Jesse had stipulated in the will. Then she'd be forced to forfeit the property, tuck her tail between her legs and leave.

Then that would be the end of it. Once she's gone from Verdon-on-Wye, everything could get back to normal.

Until then, I'll need to avoid the pub. The pang of disappointment at that thought hits me hard when I think about not going there. Not seeing her smile as she glides along behind the bar, completely oblivious to the brightness and joy she's brought to the space.

The pub has always been a favorite haunt for Brick and I, but her presence there has brought an unexpected warmth and familiarity to the place, that was never there before.

"Fuck." I mutter into my dark room, my chest squeezing at the idea of not going there to see her each night. But I can sense there's an underlying feeling there that I'm not ready to face just yet.

I get up and make my way over to the windows and my eyes instantly go straight to the bookshop, as if there's a magnetic connection to it. The small building is only visible by the moonlight. It reflects off the polished windows that she's been out there cleaning every single day as I run by. That thought makes my heart hammer and I'm hit with the realization that simply avoiding her in the village isn't going to be enough.

If this is going to work, I've got to get the fuck out of here completely.

Maybe I can go to my townhouse in London for a few months. Brick could take over the self-defense classes and handle anything else that might crop up for me here in the village.

If I do that, I could disappear into the quiet spaces between my responsibilities. Get far enough away to be able to drown out the thoughts of her, push her out of my mind and let the city swallow me whole.

But in my heart, I know... I can't do any of it.

How can I possibly stand in her way, do anything that will stop her from succeeding, when the mere thought of her sadness eviscerates me?

I press my forehead against the cool glass, close my eyes and sigh. There's not a chance in hell I can bring myself to do anything that would jeopardize her happiness.

So in the darkness of my lonely room, I give in. I let my thoughts shift back to visions of her smile. Let myself imagine the way her eyes will light up on the day she reopens the bookshop, and how happy she'll be when she succeeds.

That thought changes everything and I'm hit with a torrent of emotions I never knew I could feel. It's that thought that makes me realize...

I *want* her to succeed.

I *want* her to stay.

I. Want. Her.

As I let this new acceptance wash over me, I crawl into bed, settling my head onto the pillow and for the first night in as long as I can remember...

I sleep.

Waking up the next morning, I feel refreshed and ready for the day. I shower, don my running gear, pop in my earbuds and crank the volume up to levels that are bound to eventually deafen me.

But as I lace up my trainers next to the windows, my gaze drifts down to where the autumn sun catches the red and yellow leaves of the orchard, the thatched roof of the cottage and familiar shape of the bookshop, just beyond.

I close my eyes, and I'm hit with a wash of memories and, for a moment, I'm back there again.

In Margaret Allbright's kitchen...

"There you go lad." Mrs. Allbright says softly, plopping a plate in front of me. My mouth waters as I'm instantly hit with the delicious scent of her freshly baked apple pie, still warm from the oven. the reassuring weight of her hand resting softly

on my shoulder. She chucks a finger playfully beneath my chin, as I smile gratefully up at her.

"Made that today, with apples Jesse picked from the orchard just this morning," she says proudly, handing me a fork.

I don't miss how hard she's trying to hide the hint of sadness in her eyes as they flicker over the fresh bruise on my cheek.

I'm glad she can't see the burns from his cigars or lash wounds from his belt on my back...

I shake my head, forcing the memory aside. Turning away from the window, I step out of my room.

Chapter 27

Rogan

The forest is breathtaking at this time of day, especially during the autumn months. With the ferns and other vegetation dying back, the sunlight reaches deeper beneath the trees, revealing glimpses of places usually hidden by shadow. Fallen leaves form a thick carpet across the ground, while the evergreens—conifers, Norway spruces, and mighty redwoods—all stand tall, their green plumage untouched by the season's decay.

A herd of wild boar charge across my path and I have to slow, allowing them to pass. I smile as their loud squeals and grunts carry over the sound of my music, eight or nine piglets bringing up the rear of the group as they hurry by.

The music helps to drown out my thoughts, overriding the chaos of my mind until it's just me, the forest and the rhythmic drumming of my feet on the earth.

As I near the end of my five miles, I realize I've inadvertently taken the path leading to the river—the one that will take me back by way of the bookshop. I check my watch. I could double back, but that will add extra time to my run and then I'll be late for my meeting with Brick.

Or I could risk it. Run past the bookshop, maybe even cut through the orchard and slip back home without incident.

It's still early... *maybe she won't be there yet.*

Decision made—or rather, rationalized—I push forward, breaking free of the trees onto the lane that runs beside the River Wye.

I settle back into my run, losing myself to the music in my ears, breathing slow and steady. I finally feel in control.

Hannah lifts her head as I approach, tail swishing lazily. A pretty tortoiseshell cat perches on her back, leisurely licking its paws, seemingly oblivious to my presence.

I'm almost past the door when the current song playing ends, offering a fleeting moment of silence as it changes to the next track.

Just long enough for me to hear the scream.

I stop so abruptly, my feet slide in the gravel. I kill the music and tug out my earbuds as I scan the area.

Breathing heavily, I listen, turning in place while I try to find the source of the sound.

Maybe I imagined it?

I lift my earbuds back to my ears but I hear it again, louder this time...

It's coming from inside the bookshop.

The cat, startled as I hurry past, leaps gracefully from Hannah's back. The donkey brays, repeatedly lifting her chin in a frantic gesture and flicks her ears toward the door when there's another scream—sharper, more urgent.

Heart hammering, I bolt through the door.

Once I'm inside the bookshop, I hear the sound of rushing water. I squint, trying to adjust my eyes to the dim interior and scan the room to locate where the sound is coming from.

The further I move into the room, the louder it gets. I hear another yelp, coming from the kitchen where there's a puddle of water rapidly spreading out from under the door.

"Shit! Help! Can anybody hear me?! God, please! Someone help me!"

Cole—her voice frantic as she yells, desperate to be heard by anyone as she tries to hold back the rush of water. Her hands are clamped over the tap as water erupts from the pipes, spraying up into her face.

"Cole! I'm here." I shout.

Her head whips toward the sound of my voice, wide eyes locking onto mine filling with a flash of unmistakable relief, briefly overtaking her look of sheer panic.

"The faucet!" she yells over the sound of the water. "It just started spraying and now I can't get it to stop!"

I hurry over to her, the powerful spray drenching me instantly.

"Where are your tools?"

"What?"

"Your tools!"

Her face pales. "Over there," blinking water out of her eyes, she lifts her chin over her shoulder, not daring to let go of the torrent of water spewing from the tap.

Quickly rifling through her sparse tool kit, I come up with a wrench and a screwdriver.

They'll have to do.

I grab them and hurry back to her side. Reaching over her to help her grip the tap, my chest presses against her back. For an instant, I'm all but certain I feel her melt into me, her back fitting against me perfectly. Her wet hair sticks to my chest and an intoxicating scent of apples and patchouli carries on the water rushing over her, flooding all of my senses with her.

I shake off the thought as quickly as it comes and redirect my focus to fitting the wrench around the tap. I give it a twist, but it slips, unleashing an even stronger spray of water. Cole gasps when it hits her square in the face.

I pull her away, moving her off to the side and drop down to the floor, the pool of water spreading rapidly beneath me.

The second I see it; the problem is obvious—corroded pipes and a busted stopcock.

I position the wrench around the rusted nut, trying to turn it.

No good. It won't budge.

Grabbing the screwdriver, I wedge it behind the stopcock, working purely on instinct, and try again.

Muscles straining, I push on the wrench as hard as I can. Finally something gives, the nut turning ever so slightly.

With a guttural exhale, I twist harder and the resistance begins to ease.

"It's... It's working!"

Cole's excited voice is breathless as the water finally slows, until—with one last twist of the tool—it stops completely.

I blow out a long, relieved breath, my hands going slack as I finally let the tension of the moment drain from my body.

I run a hand down my face, wiping away some of the water. When I look up at Cole, I swear her smile could rival the sun.

"You did it!"

She laughs, the combination of the look on her face and that sound sends a rush through me and I'm hit again by that now familiar tightening in my chest. I try to swallow, but my throat is suddenly too dry.

I smile back at her, then start to pull myself up, but she reaches for me, fingers wrapping around mine, steady and sure.

When I feel her tiny hands wrap around mine, I'm hit with a tingling sensation that goes right through my core. With a gentle tug, she helps me out from under the sink. The instant I'm on my feet, her arms are around me, her body buzzing with excitement as she bounces on her toes.

"Thank you! Thank you! Thank you!" She trills. "I don't know what I would have done if you hadn't shown up when you did!"

Her smile is breathtaking, the melodic sound of her laughter making something squeeze in my chest.

I feel my eyes go wide and I blink dumbly down at her, my arms held out awkwardly, not quite sure how to respond to her sudden embrace, her body against mine.

After a few seconds, instinct takes over and I snap out of my stupor, finally wrapping my arms around her, pulling her against me and returning her hug.

The moment she realizes what she's done, I feel her tense against me and I look down in time to catch the subtle shift in her face as her laughter tapers off.

She pulls back slightly, her wide eyes finding mine and her throat works as she swallows nervously.

I'm so close to her now, I can see the different shades of green in those eyes.

I feel my expression soften as I study her features up close. I can't stop myself from sliding the tip of my middle finger along her brow to push aside a tendril of wet hair, tucking it behind her ear.

Her chest presses harder against mine when her breath catches, those mesmerizing eyes, sparkling up at me.

We're both soaking wet and dripping. Our clothes stuck to our bodies, clinging to all of our curves and lines.

Her long-sleeved top, the white fabric now drenched, leaves very little to the imagination. The only thing hiding her soft flesh is the lacy bra she's wearing beneath.

Her breasts are nearly visible, natural perfection, small but firm, her nipples hardened from the cold spray of water. My heart hammers as I think about how well they would fit in my hand, how they might feel as I stroke them with my thumb, or better yet, my tongue.

"Cole, I..."

Kya's warning echoes in my mind, a fragile thread pulling taut.

Don't hurt her.

Her words were a plea, a command, a weight pressing against my chest.

But Cole's hands stay where they are, her fingers resting against the nape of my neck, each point of contact igniting sparks that dance along my skin.

Rising onto her toes, her breath is a warm caress against my cheek, carrying the faintest trace of something sweet.

"Thank you." she whispers as she presses her soft lips tentatively against the corner of my mouth.

I close my eyes and it feels like I can't catch my breath. My fingers dig into her hips.

"Cole," I try again, my voice a rasping breath, low and raw, as my hands tighten around her waist. The fabric of her shirt bunches between my fingers, anchoring me in the moment even as my thoughts spiral.

At the sound of her name on my tongue, she freezes, her lips hesitating a breath's width away. Daring to open my eyes, I find hers searching mine, wide and guarded, an unspoken question swimming in depths of sparkling jade.

Every second staring down at her, I feel my resolve crumbling, but I don't dare move.

I wait.

I won't be the one to take from her. I can't begin to guess what she's been through, but I've seen enough to know it must have been hell.

Her gaze drifts back to my lips.

One heartbeat, one breath… then her lips feather softly over mine—a fleeting, tentative touch that sends a jolt through me, sharp and electric.

The world around us blurs as the air between us charges with something unspoken. My body thrums, every nerve alive, every thought drowning in the simple, undeniable truth of her.

I dip my head toward her, giving her the permission she's silently seeking to take what it is she wants. Lightly, I brush my lips against hers—testing, feeling, breathing in her touch,

Each tentative kiss turns firmer, each brush of our lips pressing harder, growing more insistent. Our hold on one another, gradually tightening until finally, I pull her hips to mine and slide a hand up her back to tangle my fingers into her hair.

Running the tip of my tongue gently along the seam of her lips, an unspoken request, she opens for me. Our tongues slide together, touching, tasting. Hesitant at first, but then, like a dam bursting, the kiss deepens. I pull her body into me, just like I've dreamed of doing all these weeks. Our mouths, claiming one another as she opens for me, her lips molding perfectly against mine as we move together.

The feel of her tongue caressing mine draws a moan from deep within me—a sound I can't suppress, a sound that speaks of my need for her, my desire to hold her, to never stop touching her.

Eventually we break the kiss and her eyes search mine.

Her normally pale face is flushed, her wet hair tousled where my hands have been. She leans back, her fingers trembling as they trace down my abs, over the soaked tank clinging to my skin. Her touch is apprehensive, afraid to leave me, yet afraid to stay.

I can see the war raging within her—her body, her mind, her heart.

"I'm sorr..."

"Don't you dare apologize." I stop her, my voice dropping low.

She blinks up at me as I gently tug her in closer, tenderly cupping the side of her face and tracing the edge of her jaw with my thumb.

"You never have to apologize to me, Cole."

Those beautiful green eyes shimmer in the dim light, her chin trembling slightly, but I feel her body soften as she relaxes into me—the subtle shift as she lets herself surrender.

"Do you have any idea how long I've wanted to kiss you?"

Her eyes widen, lips parting—until she catches that perfect bottom lip, swollen from our kiss, between her teeth. I stroke my thumb over it, watching as her teeth slowly relinquish their grip, her breath slipping out in a quiet exhale. My fingers brush the curve of her cheek, gently stroking her soft skin.

"How long I've wanted to hold you?"

She shakes her head, barely a movement at all and a single tear spills over her lower lashes.

I catch it with my thumb, brushing it away before cradling her head and pressing my lips gently to her forehead.

A soft sob escapes her, fragile and raw, and her shoulders shake. I wrap her in my arms, holding her close, rubbing her back gently, reassuring her of my presents and letting her know I'm right here.

"Shhh... you're alright, Cole. I've got you." I murmur, kissing the top of her head.

I don't know how long we stay like that, her wrapped in my arms, just holding her until she finds herself again. But when I feel her sigh and begin to pull back, I loosen my hold on her just enough to be able to see her face.

"You alright?"

She gives me a watery smile and nods.

"Yes, I'm alright...now."

"Good girl." I say, brushing back a strand of hair from her cheek.

Her breath hitches and her face flushes as her eyes drop back to my mouth, her fingers digging into the fabric of my shirt at those words.

Within a heartbeat, my lips crash onto hers again, a soft lust filled whimper leaving her throat—the sound going straight to my cock.

If the last kiss had turned my world on end, this one set it on fire.

My need for her obliterates my better judgement—Kya's warnings be damned. I need this woman.

I need to feel her against me, beneath me, on top of me.

She meets each of my kisses, taste for taste, stroke for stroke with an intensity that tells me she wants me as badly as I want her.

I pull her to me, holding her so close, but even that doesn't feel close enough. My cock gets painfully hard with my need for her and I can't hold back the groan that escapes me as she presses her body against it.

I grip her thighs and lift her tiny frame effortlessly, wrapping her legs around me and carrying her to the worktop, my feet splashing through the water.

We break the kiss for only a moment, breathing hard as we search each other's eyes. I see something shift in her beautiful, shining emerald stare. She's breathing hard as her hands move down to the hem of my tank, curling her fingers into the wet material, tugging it up. The corner of my mouth tips up and I lift my arms and bend toward her to let her remove it completely.

Her eyes and fingers trace my body and everywhere she touches, my flesh reacts. Her feathering touches travel along the deep grooves of my abs, causing the muscles to contract at the sensation. Her tiny hands tentatively skate across my skin—feeling, exploring, tracing my tattoos.

I can't stop the shiver that rolls through me. Her touch ignites me, stoking me instead of disgusting me, the way the others had.

She grazes along the waistband of my joggers and my heart races, my chest heaving as my breaths come faster. But it's when she begins to dip her fingers beneath the hem that I see them trembling.

When I look back to her eyes, I see the excitement has morphed into something more akin to fear.

She's not ready for this.

Grabbing her hand, I stop her from going any further.

She flinches, eyes shooting up to my face.

"I'm sorry..." she blurts, quickly turning into herself, cheeks turning a bright pink as she tries to tug her hand from my grip.

Keeping hold of her hand, I quickly shake my head and pull her closer, trying desperately not to lose the tenuous hold on the distance we've managed to cross. Sliding my fingers into her hair, I cup her jaw and tilt her face up so she's forced to meet my eyes.

"Shhh... no, Cole. It's alright. I told you, you never need to apologize to me, and I meant that."

She drops her chin, breaking my gaze, "But you don't want me to touch you." It's not a question. "It's okay, I understa..."

Gently tipping her face up to bring her eyes back to me, I interrupt her again.

"No! None of that now." I keep my tone firm.

She needs to believe me.

"This... right here, is the moment I have been dreaming of for weeks on end. I want you to touch me more than I want to breathe right now. I just...," I swallow hard, "I just think we should slow down a bit."

I hold her stare as her eyes dart back and forth between mine, watching as she searches for the lie. When she finds none, her face relaxes a bit, and dropping my gaze, she nods, her voice a bit breathy as a soft smile teases her lips.

"Yeah... you're probably right," she agrees, letting out a long, slow breath.

I lean down and brush a tender kiss to her lips. Her eyes fall closed as I linger there, breathing her in. I stroke my thumb over her cheek, pressing another soft kiss to her forehead. Her eyes follow me as I straighten back to my full height and take her hands to help her off the worktop.

We look around the room at the wet counters and puddles on the floor. Cole, nibbles nervously at her thumbnail and looks a bit lost beside me.

I reclaim my wet tank, giving it a twist to try and wring out some of the water. Pulling the cold fabric back on makes me jump and I gasp loudly when it touches my chest. I look over in time to see Cole's shoulders shaking as she pulls her lips between her teeth, biting down on them to hold back her giggle.

"Enjoying my struggles, eh Allbright?" I grin at her.

"A little," she admits, shrugging playfully and hits me with one of the most stunning smiles I've ever seen.

An untold warmth floods me at the sight and suddenly I'm lost in the wonder of her again.

I clear my throat and straighten my shoulders.

"Right, then." I say.

"Let's get this mess cleaned up, shall we?"

Chapter 28

Cole

After Rogan makes a quick call to Brick to let him know he's going to miss their meeting, we get to work cleaning up the water.

Once we've soaked up as much as possible with towels and some drop cloths the workmen had left behind, we open up all the windows to air out the kitchen, café and bookshop.

"We've cleaned up enough of the water that it should dry well and I don't think you'll have any issues." he says, surveying the room before offering me a reassuring smile.

We bring the wet fabric outside, laying it out flat on the picnic tables and benches to hopefully dry out some before I can have it laundered.

A moment of awkward silence hangs in the air between us when we're done. Then, it only gets worse when we both try to talk at once...

"Can I maybe..."

"Do you maybe want to..."

Our words jumble together and we both stop talking, laughing at the overlapping timing of our questions.

"You go first." I say, still grinning at him, feeling my cheeks heat slightly.

He pauses and clears his throat as he toes the gravel and rubs at the back of his neck.

Is he... nervous?

"I... I was just thinking... it might be nice if we could... I don't know, maybe we could go for a walk sometime? Maybe get to know each other a bit better?" He stammers awkwardly before shyly glancing back over at me.

"A walk?" I ask, feeling my brows lift in surprise, slightly confused by this less than confident, yet incredibly adorable, version of Rogan Cavendish.

"Never mind...," he says, looking off into the trees and shaking his head as if admonishing himself.

"That's silly I suppose..."

Smiling, I step closer, wrapping my fingers around his forearm lightly. "I'd like that."

His head snaps back to me, his hopeful grin widening at my agreement and I feel my own grin widen in response, my face feeling hotter than the sun.

"You would? Okay... okay—great!"

He blows out a loud breath, relief visibly coursing through him, his beaming smile, boyish and triumphant—like a schoolboy who's just won the hand of the prom queen.

"It's a date then! Maybe tomorrow? If the weather's nice." He suggests hopefully. His warmth presses into my palms as his hands close around mine.

"That sounds perfect." I agree, smiling up at him, feeling my nerves alight at the idea of a *date with the Duke*.

His expression sobers and his gray eyes sparkle like liquid metal as he dips down to brush a soft kiss over my lips. When I feel his fingers slide into my hair, his thumb gently stroking the skin of my cheek, my eyes slip shut and I lean into him, my whole body tingling from his touch.

"Tomorrow then." He murmurs against my lips.

I nod.

"Tomorrow."

He lingers, his expression, one of wonder as he studies my face, then tucks a loose strand of hair behind my ear—carefully, reverently.

The backs of his fingers graze my cheek in a fleeting caress, pausing just a moment longer—and then he's gone, jogging down the path, back toward his home.

Chapter 29

Cole

This will be the first time I've ever been on a real date.

Mom had died when I was fourteen and dad... I was eighteen when he died...*was killed.*

Good old Sundance, taking charge of the situation.

I'll never forget what that beautiful creature did for me that day—*after dad had gotten a taste for me.* I was hiding from him in Sundance's stall when he found me. Sundance must have sensed my fear, growing protective of me, he reared up, slamming his front hooves against my father's chest, knocking him back through the stall door.

Whether it was the intense impact, or the shock of it all, we'll never know, but that was the day his heart stopped beating once and for all.

He'd never lay a finger on me again.

After that, I had no one else, so I was on my own for a bit.

But that's when I met him.

When I met *Cain.*

I'd been working more hours on the horse ranch to try to keep up with food and the bills from the house. Dad didn't have much in the way of a life insurance policy. Just enough to cover the cost of his cremation really.

I wasn't making much at the ranch, especially being so young. But I was there every day after school and all day, both days on the weekends. Working as many hours as I could manage, as often as the ranch would allow. But it still wasn't enough. The house still had a mortgage on it and the bills began piling up. It got to the point that I had to choose between keeping the house or being able to feed myself.

Apparently, there was talk about my situation amongst the stable owners. Cain, being one of them, took pity on me, or so I thought.

He started showing up more and more, anywhere I was working. Sometimes he'd even help me with some of my tasks. He would talk to me, complimenting me, always telling me how amazing I was.

He made me feel special, wanted—needed even. Words I had never heard from my own father.

On the afternoon of my nineteenth birthday, he met me at the stables with a cupcake and a candle. He told me to make a wish. I closed my eyes and blew out the flame and when I opened them again, he leaned in and kissed me.

I jolted back from the unexpectedness of it, but he held my wrist, pulling me close again.

He wrapped his hand around the back of my neck and pressed his mouth to mine again. His kiss had been firm, but tender and I was so lonely, and I craved affection. The warm touch of another, soothing my aching soul.

So I kissed him back.

After the kiss, he told me he would take care of me. He was going to fix everything and if I agreed to be his, I wouldn't need to worry about money or a roof over my head anymore. Too stunned to refuse and too desperate for his words to be true, I had agreed.

I had agreed...

And that's when my bad dream turned into my nightmare.

Chapter 30

Cain

"What the fuck am I paying you for?" I scream at the cowering man across the desk from me.

"It's been months! *Months!* And you've got nothing? Nothing at all!" My voice drips with disgust, my dwindling patience with him now all but gone.

"She can't have just vanished! She's around here somewhere and I want her found, goddamn it!" The frames on the walls shake as I slam my fist down on the desk, making the private investigator I hired to find that ungrateful little bitch, jump.

"I've got a few leads I'm working on," the swine of a man snivels, his voice whiny as he grovels for my forgiveness. "But I don't have anything concrete just yet. But I swear, Mr. Brentwood, I should have something for you soon."

Taking in a slow, steady breath through my nose, my hands curl into fists on my desk. Tension rolling over me in waves, I drop my voice to a low, menacing level.

"If you don't find her before this month is out... not only will you be fired... *I. Will. End. You.*"

As I enunciate each of my words, slowly, deliberately, he shrinks back in his chair.

"Yes, sir, Mr. Brentwood sir. I'm on it," he insists.

"Get the fuck out of my sight and don't come back here until you've got something on where she is!" I bark, throwing his worthless folder back at him that he'd brought to try to appease me with his fruitless efforts.

He scrambles to grab its scattered contents and hurries for the door.

He bolts out just as Maria walks past him carrying a tray containing my lunch, my afternoon meeting schedule and my cigars. Her soft brown eyes shift from his departing form to me, but quickly drop down to the tray as she places it on the desk beside me.

Carefully watching the face of my elderly maid as she lays the contents of the tray out in front of me, I narrow my gaze at her. She swallows hard, knowing my eyes are on her, but she never raises hers to meet mine.

"You know where she is, don't you?" I ask, tilting my head as I take her in, my voice low... almost a whisper.

"Know where who is, Mr. Cain?" She answers, her voice shaky. She swallows hard again, her lightly wrinkled cheeks flushing, her weathered eyes never leaving my desk.

"You know exactly... Who. I. Mean." My tone coils tightly, lacing each word with venom, as I slowly rise to tower over the small woman.

"I don't know," she whispers, pressing her hands onto the desk to try to keep them from shaking.

"You do." I growl low in my throat.

"And you're going to tell me."

She's quiet for a long moment, then...

"No."

One word—barely audible. But that's all I needed to hear.

She knows where she is.

"No?" I ask, keeping my voice soft as I walk past her, shutting the office door.

"No." She repeats, her tone firmer now as she finally raises her head to meet my stare.

I move to the windows, methodically closing one blind and then the other. I slowly walk back to the now visibly trembling woman. I stand so close to her, she has to crane her neck to look up at me.

Amazingly, the bold little bitch begins to show a modicum of courage—more than the wretch of a man who was here moments before. Straightening her back and finding her voice she finally speaks.

"You no gonna hurt her again, Mr. Cain. I'm no gonna tell you where she is. I don't care what you do. I don't care what you say. I'm no gonna be quiet and I'm no gonna let you hurt her no more!" She snaps, her accent thick as she takes a small step back, but a fire now blazes in her eyes.

Leaning my face down close to hers, I snap my hand out and firmly grip her shoulder, making her flinch, a small whimper leaving her lips.

"You think you can protect her, huh? Well who's gonna protect you then?" I ask, my lips grazing her ear.

"You know what I can do to you... to your family." I remind her. "You've been with me for a long time, Maria. Haven't you?" I say, not really asking a question.

"I've kept your secret, your family's secret, all this time." I continue, slowly prodding at her conscience.

"If you think you can hide her... if you don't tell me where she is... I'll tell them where *they* can find you... find your family. You don't want that, do you... Maria?" I hiss in her ear, then stand back to my full height to glare down at her.

"No... please Mr. Cain... I can't." She pleads, looking up at me, her brown eyes filled with terror as tears roll down her cheeks.

"You can and you will. Or you... and your family will learn the hard way, that you don't cross Cain Brentwood."

I shove her hard and she stumbles back, falling at my feet.

So fucking weak. I am surrounded by feeble, pathetic fools.

I tug my shirt sleeves out from under my jacket and smooth my hair back against my head.

Perfect. Everything has to be perfect.

I turn away from the quivering woman and move to the door, holding it wide.

"You have one week to decide what it's going to be. Now get the fuck out."

She staggers up, limping slightly as she bolts from the room, her hand held to her mouth.

"Oh and Maria..." I say, my voice halting her escape, "I hear Juan Carlos is doing well in his apprenticeship with the garage. It really would be such a shame if someone were to make a call to immigration and you were sent back. And you know what that would mean, don't you? The Víboras de Sangre will be waiting to welcome you back home with..." a cold laugh rumbles in my throat, "open arms."

She claps a trembling hand over her mouth to stifle a sob, then turns, hurrying down the corridor.

Sitting back down at my desk, I push the plate of food aside and reach for my cigar, snipping off the end with my cutter and lighting it. I draw a long drag of smoke into my lungs as I sit back in my chair.

"I've got you now, Nicole. It's only a matter of when." I say into my empty office.

"You're mine, bitch! I will always find you."

Chapter 31

Rogan

What the fuck is happening to me?

Rogan Cavendish doesn't get shy!

I shake my head, my heart pounding wildly in my chest, as I make my way back to my rooms, my cheeks aching from the grin I can't seem to shake.

I'm so lost in my thoughts of the afternoon; I nearly walk straight into Brick as he strides down the corridor from the suite of rooms he favors when the Gate House begins to feel too isolated.

I school my expression and nod cordially, attempting to sidestep him, but he snags my elbow, pulling me back to face him.

The bastard tries to look stern—but he can't quite hide the flicker of mirth in his eyes as he takes in my current state. Wet clothes, tousled hair and the barely restrained smirk playing at the corners of my lips.

"What in the fuck happened to you?" He laughs as he asks, unable to maintain even a shred of faux indignation.

The words blurt out of me before I can stop them.

"I have a date, mate!"

I swear, I'm bloody beaming.

"A date?" Brick asks incredulously as he releases my elbow, leaning back as if I've physically hit him, his eyebrows damn near reaching his hairline.

"You don't date! At least, not since we were teenagers." He prods, his stunned tone making his voice pitch.

If there wasn't so much truth to his words and I wasn't so high on my current state of bliss, I might be insulted.

When I don't say anything, instead slipping my hands into my pockets and simply standing there with my grin growing ever wider by the second, his curiosity finally bubbles over.

"Who in the hell do you have a date with, mate?"

Giving him a wink, a smile and a small cheeky salute, I step past him without a word, laughing softly to myself.

He calls after me, but I keep my course steady, my sights firmly set on heading straight to my shower. Because there's no denying the effect Cole's kiss had on me.

Her lips, finally on mine, her legs wrapped around my hips. The press of her body as I held her tight against my chest. The look of desire that sparkled in her depthless green eyes.

Nope, I was not going to be hanging around to chat with Brick right now. Not with that memory playing on a persistent loop in my skull.

The second I reach my room, I tear off my wet clothes, kick out of my trainers and head directly into my ensuite—my cock already swollen and heavy, lifting up to meet my navel. I grip the base, giving it a hard squeeze, remembering the sweet taste of her tongue as it danced in tandem with mine.

I wrench on the water and, without wasting a moment, step into the cold spray. Fumbling for the body wash, I manage to snap open the bottle, squirting a large dollop into my palm before stroking my length to the thoughts of her thighs wrapped around my hips, her fingers tracing the muscles of my stomach, teasing the waistband of my shorts.

The vision of her white shirt, wet and clinging to her peaked nipples, taunting me, begging me to pull them into my mouth and suck...

Within seconds I've already worked the gel into a soapy, slick lather, pumping and squeezing my cock furiously, my legs beginning to quake as my balls tighten with my impending release.

With a final memory of her soft moan as she pressed her body against my groin, I spill with a deep, guttural groan. My vision blackens at the edges while my dick pulses. My hand finally slows as I twist lightly and smooth my thumb over the pulsing head, continuing to work out the last of my spend.

Panting, I rest my forehead against the cool tiles of the shower, trying to regain my vision after the hurried session, spots dancing before my eyes.

I shouldn't want this, but everything in me is screaming this is right. It feels like nothing else matters anymore. Like the sun is finally shining for the first time in a world that's been cloaked in shades of black and gray for far too long.

As water drips off the tip of my nose, a huge grin spreads across my face.

I actually have a date with Cole Allbright.

Chapter 32

Cole

As we finish our evening meal, Kya listens wide-eyed, while I recount the afternoon's chaos of the near catastrophe in the bookshop's kitchen and how Rogan had saved me.

I feel my face heat, when I admit I kissed him, having been so grateful for his help. Her expression shifts from one of curious excitement to one of worry, her eyes darkening further when I tell her about his unexpected invitation for me to join him on a walk through the woods tomorrow.

"What is it?" I ask, my fork dropping slowly back toward the plate. I feel something heavy drag through me at the sight of her somber expression. "Is it dangerous? Should I not go?"

For the first time since Rogan asked me, I'm hit with a wave of trepidation about accepting the date.

"No, no. It's fine!" She answers, quickly covering her concern with a hurried smile and reaches out to give my hand a reassuring squeeze.

"I have no doubt you'll be safe with him. Just...," she pauses, as if searching for the right words. Her face is tender, soft concern creasing her worried eyes as she looks into mine. "Just, be careful with your heart, hun."

The weight of her concern for me is palpable in that look, carrying a warmth that could rival the warmest embrace. And I realize it's a feeling I haven't felt since before I lost my mom...

I have to fight against the tears I feel burning behind my eyes.

How on Earth did I get so damn lucky to meet a friend as precious as this woman?

She studies me for a moment. "I know you're not ready to share what's happened to you yet, but you know I'm here for you when you are, right?" Her warm eyes trace my face, her soft tone, gently pleading for me to let her in.

"I know you are." I say, entwining my fingers with hers and offering her a watery smile.

"I'll tell you soon." I promise, dropping my eyes to where my fingers are absently rubbing at my sleeve—the scars I know she's seen, taunting me just beneath the fabric.

A silent tale still waiting to be told.

"There's no rush and I won't ask. But I want you to know, when you're ready to get that weight off your chest, I'll be here to help you lift it."

She smiles warmly, giving my hand another squeeze and dips her chin to meet my eyes again.

There's something in her gaze that tells me, behind her dauntlessness, is a traumatic past. In some interconnected way, her understanding, her patience with me, comes from lived experience.

That at some point, she's been broken too.

But, before I can get my head around this possible revelation, she gives my hand one more squeeze, her face brightening. Within seconds she's up and moving.

"Right then." She sings, scooping up the dinner dishes and carrying them over to the sink, as though the weight of our conversation never turned heavy.

"I've got this tonight, hun. Since you fixed the meal, it seems only fair. You've had a bit of a day anyway. Why don't you go rest for a bit?"

"I think I just might take you up on that." I say, trying to stifle a yawn as I make my way over with the last of the items from the table. I set the dishes beside the sink and wrap my arms around her middle from behind, pressing my cheek against her back, giving her a squeeze.

"Thank you."

I breathe against her shoulder, her familiar scent of patchouli, comforting as it fills my nose. She wraps her hand over the top of my arm, returning my awkward embrace.

"You never have to thank me, hun. That's what friends are for." She gives my hand another quick squeeze and a pat.

"Go on now! You need your beauty sleep for your big date tomorrow, eh?" I can hear the smile in her voice as she effectively shoos me on my way.

"Yes, I suppose I do." I giggle.

Reaching down, I give Grumbl a quick snuggle before snatching my latest spicy book off the counter, and head up to my room.

Boy, these books Kya's got me into really get imaginative with the types of things they have the couples doing together!

I never in my life thought reading something from a book could make me feel something so visceral... *so real*. I never imagined simply reading words in a book could make something deep inside me tighten, to ache for something I've never felt before....

Soaking up the words in yet another spicy chapter in my current read, the hand of the MMC starts to reach between the legs of the FMC. My mind drifts back to the kitchen in the bookshop and the events of the afternoon.

My imagination replaces the man's character in the book with an image of Rogan.

His hands gripping my waist, his fingers curling into my clothing as he pulls me to him. The heat of his tongue, teasing along my lips, gently slipping between them as I open for him. The sounds he made, groaning with need as he pressed into me.

Liquid heat rushes to my core and a dull ache tugs deep inside me.

I've never felt like this before. I've never had this pull, this want for a man to touch me, to kiss me, to hold me close.

A tingling sensation courses through me when I think about the feel of his hands as they gripped my thighs, lifting me to wrap my legs around him as if I weighed nothing at all. My core pulses at the thought of his rigid length as he ground himself against me, his desire evident—I cross my legs, squeezing them together to try to quell the ache building there.

But the more I think about how the afternoon sun had glistened on the tanned skin of his wet abs and how his chest heaved as he hovered over me, I start to squirm.

I need something more.

I don't know what it is exactly, but there's an unfamiliar yearning to be touched. Truthfully, I've never wanted to be touched before, never had any real desire to have any man in that way.

Not since dad found me that day in the orchard.

Cain was so brutal, his touch demanding, cruel—punishing. Only wanting me from behind, his fist gripping my hair, pinning me in place, roughly taking what he wanted. I'll never forget the pain of his belt, whipping me any time I'd lose control and cry out.

Even worse were the times he wanted my mouth.

His fingers viciously digging into my scalp, using my hair to immobilize me and slamming me to my knees. My lips splitting, my throat tearing as he brutally thrust himself into my mouth, over and over again. Seating himself deep in my throat, choking me until my vision darkened as I prayed for him to finish. Or better yet, that I lose consciousness, the momentary disconnect allowing me a brief respite from the pain. I welcomed it, even knowing I would be punished if I did.

The only way I could get through it was to zone out. Go somewhere else in my mind, until it was over—*until the next time.*

But shockingly, it seems Rogan has somehow unearthed something within me, triggering a need for something I never knew I could crave. This heat surging through my center, pulsing at the apex of my thighs, pleading for touch and attention like never before.

His touches gentle, his kisses pleading—never taking.

Each one silently asking for permission, giving me the power over what happens and when. Keeping things on my terms. Never pushing, but instead, letting me decide how far I want this to go.

I close my eyes, remembering the heat of his breath as it coasted across my lips, just shy of pressing onto mine. The slightest tease of his tongue as it grazed the seam of my lips.

I think about the glide of his fingers as they skimmed across my brow and I wonder what it might feel like to have those fingers touching me—*somewhere else*. How it might feel to have the heat of them sliding across my...

Heat floods my core, and I slip my hand between my legs, tentatively running my fingers along my slit, over my cotton panties. Heat seems to spread, and my clit pulses with need. Rubbing harder, I increase the pressure, each stroke of my fingers more insistent, more urgent.

Warmth begins to build, a tingle coursing over the whole of my core. Moving my hips in time with the motion of my hand, I start to chase the ache. My breaths quicken and I start to pant as an overwhelming sensation starts to overtake me.

This feels so good—this building, swelling, throbbing.

It consumes me with an indescribable need to push harder, move faster, chase it higher, until I'm balancing on the precipice of a cliff, willing to dive over the edge, regardless of where it takes me.

I envision the steel gray of Rogan's eyes locked on mine as he presses into me. Feel his lips as they trail down the length of my neck, his tongue tracing lower, circling my breast, the heat of his mouth as he takes the flesh between his lips, gently sucking...

I gasp as the frame of the bed squeaks loudly from my movements, the sudden sound, ripping my attention out of the fantasy.

I jerk my hand out from between my legs, my eyes shooting to the door—hoping, praying Kya's head won't be peeking in to see what the noise was.

Thankfully, it's still closed, my pride unscathed.

Feeling my cheeks flame, I slap both hands over my face and giggle to myself.

Well then... this date should be interesting.

Chapter 33

Rogan

Thankfully, the afternoon offers us perfect weather for the walk I have planned along the wooded trail that skirts the Wye.

I head to the bookshop, taking the shortcut through the orchard, smiling to myself as I peer through the windows of the conservatory into the kitchen beyond.

I hear her before I see her, the gentle cadence of her mellifluous voice carrying around the side of the building. I can't help it. I pause for a moment, and just listen, though I can't quite hear her words.

My cock twitches as I breathe out.

Down, boy, I think to my groin, willing the fire to die down a bit before I turn the corner. Never have I wanted a woman more. Never have I felt content just to listen to her, just to watch her as her expressive face lights up.

Gathering my courage—because, yes, I'm definitely feeling nervous right now—I draw in a steadying breath and step around the corner of the bookshop to pick up Cole for our date.

The late autumn sun catches her just right, bathing her in a glittering wash of gold where she stands with Hannah and Athena.

My breath stills in my chest and I have to take a step back before she notices me, pausing just a moment to take in the sight of her.

She's incredible.

Her touch is impossibly gentle, as the animals lean into her, drawn to her presence. Her lips move, forming quiet words I can't quite make out. But they're listening to her, tilting their heads in silent recognition, absorbing every syllable, like a secret meant only for them.

A smile plays on her lips, as though speaking to her oldest, dearest friends.

That's when I realize I'm smiling too.

Sensing my gaze on her, she looks up, her eyes meeting mine. Her eyes flare wide momentarily, startled for a fraction of a second, then her expression shifts, brightening into a radiant grin as I finally step forward.

"Hello, Little Fawn."

I greet her, as I step closer, stroking a hand down the center of Hannah's face, the donkey nuzzling into my touch.

"Hello."

Cole says, her eyes sparkling and her cheeks turning an adorable shade of pink.

"Are you ready for an adventure?" I ask, cocking up an eyebrow, a smile playing across my lips as I hold my arm out, elbow bent in a silent request for her to take me up on my chivalrous gesture.

"I am!" She says, eagerly swooping her arm into the crook of mine.

"Where are we off to?"

"Let's just see where the afternoon takes us, eh?" I suggest as we begin walking away from the bookshop, and into the shadows of the trees lining the trail.

The afternoon sun is unseasonably warm as we make our way through the trees, dappling the ground with brilliant patches of color against the darker fallen foliage.

As we walk, our feet stir up the dried leaves, dust swirling through the sunlit rays. Cole's eyes widen with joy at the sight.

"Fairy mites!" She squeals happily, her voice taking on an almost childlike sense of glee.

"Fairy what?" My eyes soften as I look down at her, my heart hitching as I take her in and feel her arm tighten around mine as she pulls me forward, her smile lighting up her whole face as she explains.

"Fairy mites!" She repeats excitedly.

"It's what my Mom always called them when I was a little girl."

The excitement slowly ebbs from her voice and her brows pinch as her eyes take on a glassy sheen, filling with a flare of pain. Her throat works as she tries to swallow down the emotion clearly trying to consume her, her gaze dropping to her feet.

I'm hit by a sudden protective instinct, to sooth her, shield her, to take away whatever pain she's feeling in this moment, and to destroy whoever caused her to feel it in the first place.

My mind spirals, winding down an invisible path of retribution to battle against an unseen foe. Tension coils within me as I realize there's nothing I can do to take away this particular pain, when it occurs to me, she's mourning her mother's death.

I'm pulled from my thoughts as her arm loops back through mine and her grip tightens, pulling me closer to rest her head against my bicep, instantly quelling the rage that had boiled up so quickly and anchoring me back in the moment.

For a little while, we walk along arm in arm, a comfortable silence between us before she speaks again.

"So how does one become a Duke, anyway?" She asks, gazing curiously up at me. I turn to face her as a ray of sunlight cuts across the green of her irises, giving them an almost ethereal glow.

Smiling at the question, I nonchalantly shrug a shoulder, running my free hand around my stubbled jaw.

"I guess just outliving my father was the key for me." My non-answer, not offering any further insight on the subject.

After a couple of quiet minutes pass between us, she speaks again.

"Did you and your dad get along?" Her voice is soft, as if she's not sure she should be asking the question.

After taking a deep breath through my nose, I lift my chin, rolling my neck with an audible pop.

"No, we did not get along." I say, matter-of-factly, then pause, looking forward, my eyes hardening slightly at the thought of my father threatening to cast a shadow over our pleasant afternoon.

"To be completely honest, Cole, I can't say as though I'm terribly sorry he's gone, either."

"I know how you feel." Her small voice, almost a whisper, makes me look back down at her as she gazes steadfastly ahead, my eyes widening slightly at her resolute support.

"My dad didn't like me very much either." She pauses, chewing on the tip of her thumb nail. "And I know this probably sounds terrible, but I'm glad he's dead." A touch of venom laces her tone.

We continue forward as another comfortable silence resettles between us. I realize it feels right... peaceful. Just two souls keeping each other company without the need for constant, unnecessary chatter filling the empty air. Her arm through mine, her head resting against me... it just fits. Like pieces of a puzzle slowly, easily, beginning to slide into place, forming a whole.

We make our way closer to the banks of the river. The sound, a soothing compliment to the song of the birds, the rustle of the ferns lining the trail and the crunch of dry leaves beneath our feet.

With an endearing attempt to change the subject, she asks, "So what about your mom? Is she still around?" Her face tilts up and I'm momentarily rendered speechless as my mind goes blank, those damn hypnotic eyes pulling me under, threatening to topple me.

Instinctively, I run my thumb over her fingers, stroking the small hand still resting in the crook of my arm. Reflexively, she lets our fingers lace together and a rush of static flickers through me at her touch.

"I'm afraid that's not a very happy tale either, Little Fawn." I tell her with a sigh. "My mum passed away several years ago—not long after I lost my brother."

My throat tightens at the mention of them.

"I haven't really ever talked to anyone about them besides Brick." Clearing my throat, I continue to stroke my thumb softly over her fingers as we move further down the path. The silence stretches between us, thick with unspoken emotion, until she finally speaks.

"Why do you call me Little Fawn?"

I smile at this, glancing down at her, a chuckle escaping before I can stop it.

"Because from the moment I first saw you, you looked like a terrified baby fawn staring into the eyes of a hungry wolf."

Her brows pinch together, the smile slipping from her lips.

"Oh... I do?" Her voice is nearly a whisper, disappointment coloring her words.

We stop on the path. Gently, I turn her to face me and tip her chin up to meet my gaze.

"That's not a bad thing, Cole. It means you're aware of your surroundings. You're cautious, careful—but still brave enough to try. Finding your legs in a world that feels foreign, standing on your own."

I let my fingers drift to the braid over her shoulder, pressing the soft strands between them.

"And don't forget—the little fawn becomes the mighty doe as she learns and grows. Persevering in spite of her fears, building herself into something stronger, more resilient, and impossibly graceful. Majestic. Stunning. Bold."

I pause, letting my words sink in as my eyes search hers.

"You mystify me, Little Fawn."

Those words hover between us, weightless yet charged, as I tuck a strand of her hair behind her ear, hoping she doesn't hear the tremble in my voice.

She swallows hard, her gaze scanning my face.

"I... I do?"

I nod, dipping down, to brush my lips against hers. They're soft, warm. Her eyes flutter closed and her grip tightens on my hand. When our lips part, she slowly blinks her eyes open, a soft smile brightening her face.

"Okay, I suppose that's not so bad then," she says, a satisfied little smirk playing at the corner of her mouth.

The way her cheeks flush the faintest pink sends warmth through me. I can't help but laugh.

"Not so bad?" I tap the tip of her nose, teasing. "You can live with that then, huh?"

Her grin spreads wide, lighting up her entire face, and my heart tightens at the sight.

I'm mesmerized.

A few too many moments pass as I stare, until I blink, realizing I'm lost in her—*again*. There's a pleasant ache in my cheeks, a quiet reminder of just how long I've been smiling.

"Well then," I say, clearing my throat.

"Shall we?" I offer, gesturing a gallant hand outward, suggesting we continue our hike. Smiling up at me, she nods as we resume our trek.

We walk in companionable silence for a few moments, the sounds of the forest a chorus around us.

Suddenly Cole stops, looking up at me with wide eyes.

"It was you!"

"It was me what?" I ask, confused at her abrupt halt and sudden revelation.

"That day in the orchard... It was you! You were the one who carried me back to Kya's!" She declares excitedly.

"You called me Little Fawn!"

Tipping my head in confusion, "Yes, Cole," I begin. "I found you and got you back to Kya's. I thought you knew it was me."

Shaking her head, her wide fathomless green eyes still looking up at me in wonder, tears rimming her bottom lids.

"It was you...," she whispers, a soft smile lining her lips as her eyes study me, looking at me as if seeing me for the first time.

"Thank you," she says softly, a tear slipping down her cheek as she blinks up at me.

I turn to face her fully, gently cupping the side of her face.

"I'll always find you, Little Fawn. I'll always keep you safe."

The vow had been carved into my soul since the first moment I saw her. My thumb catches the tear sliding down her cheek, an unspoken promise in the touch.

"You never need to thank me for that."

She closes her eyes, tipping her face to press her cheek into my hand. Pulling her into me, I wrap my arms around her and press a kiss to the top of her head, holding her and reveling in the feel of this precious creature in my arms.

Pulling back slightly and tipping her chin up with a finger, I scan her face to make sure she's alright then ask softly, "Shall we continue on our adventure?"

She nods, looping both arms around my elbow and resting her head against my upper arm as we carry on with our hike.

Moving through the forest, I gesture toward the towering, ancient oaks—their gnarled branches stretching wide, resolute. Beech trees, their leaves clinging stubbornly in red and gold, while the fir trees stand tall, holding fast to their needle-like greenery.

I pause before the row of Sweet Chestnuts, my fingers brushing against their ridged bark. Their legend has always fascinated me. It's one of my favorite stories; the kind that's shaped the way I see the world. It's a rare gift to share it with someone who will actually care, not mock me for being a history nerd, like Brick.

"The story goes," I tell her, "these trees took root where Roman soldiers once marched, tossing chestnut seeds into the soft earth as they passed—a quiet, unintended legacy of their conquest."

The pure joy flashing across her face, as if I've just handed her a long-lost secret, sends an untold thrill through me.

Next, I point out the different paths that spread out around us, explaining oftentimes subtle differences between those made by man or by beast.

"So you wouldn't go down a path you suspect was made by a deer or a boar?" She asks, her eyes dance across the landscape, taking everything in with a rare intensity—like she's seeing the world anew.

Instinctively, I pull her closer.

"Oh, I don't know," I chuckle, dropping my voice just a fraction. "Sometimes, the hidden paths lead to the greatest reward."

Pleasure flickers through me as I feel her body respond—though Cole seems oblivious to the signals she's sending. I have to remind myself to go slow, take my time with her. Let her come to me when she's ready—*on her terms.*

But my Little Fawn is brave.

"Now, don't go wandering down those paths alone." I warn.

The thought of her getting lost in this ancient woodland fills me with dread. "A sow with piglets isn't something you want to come face to face with."

"Yes, *My Lord,*" she teases, settling against me.

"It's *Your Grace,*" I correct, arching a brow with mock indignation. Then laughing as I watch her expression shift—uncertainty flickering across her face for a brief moment before an idea sparks.

Spinning out in front of me she drops into a graceful curtsy.

"Pardon me!" She declares with an exaggerated flourish.

"Yes, *Your Grace!*" A wide grin lights up her face when she lifts her head up from her bow, those dazzling green eyes catching mine with a devious glint.

I throw my head back and laugh so loud it echoes through the forest, making her giggle as I pull her back against me.

"Let's go, you little shite." I chuckle as I press a kiss to the top of her head, her snuggling into my side as if she was made to fit perfectly there.

We fall again into an easy rhythm, slipping into comfortable conversation.

She talks about her plans for the bookshop, how she's settling into the village. She picks up leaves and twigs, fidgeting with them as she laughs about evenings at the pub—the antics of regular patrons, the stories they tell.

She tenses when she mentions how Zavier keeps pushing her to quit, urging her to come work on his farm.

Then she chuckles, describing how Old Tom always steps in, defending her honor without hesitation.

It's clear he's one of her favorites at the bar.

She tells me about the types of books she wants to bring into the shop, her cheeks darkening when she admits Kya has influenced some of her choices—especially the spicy books.

I grin at that.

I tell her briefly about my time in the Army with Brick, how becoming Duke was never part of my plan—but after my brother was killed, the duty fell to me. I ramble about the cars I've owned, the future I want to build here now that my title is set. And the longer we walk, the more effortless it all becomes—the conversation flowing, unhurried, shaping its own path.

The forest begins to thin as we approach a clearing. Ahead, a stream trickles into the Wye, the late afternoon sun scattering across the water's surface like shards of diamonds.

"It's beautiful." She breathes, eyes skating over the scene.

A small branch from a fern slips from her fingers, tumbling to the ground. We step closer, but before she can react, her toe catches on a root—unearthed by the recent rains.

With a startled squeal, she nearly topples straight into the icy water. Before she can fall, I sweep my arm around her, turning her into my chest and pull her tightly against me within the same motion.

"Easy there."

My arm presses firm against her back, holding her close. Her fingers curl into my shirt. She swallows hard, breath quickening. I watch the ripple of her throat, my jaw clenching against the instinctual reaction it sends through me. The evening air has started to chill, and with her pressed close, I feel the firm warmth of her body beneath the soft fleece she wears.

"You alright?"

She nods silently; eyes locked onto mine. She's trembling—but whether from nerves or the encroaching cold, I can't tell.

"Are you cold?"

She silently shakes her head. We stay like that, locked in each other's stare. One breath. Then two. Then the tip of her tongue traces her lower lip. My heart pounds, slamming against my ribs.

She's watching me—her gaze dipping down to my lips. My desire takes the lead as I give in to my longing. I lean down and press my mouth to hers. She melts into me, her eyes fluttering shut, a soft moan slipping free as she leans into my body.

Gently, I deepen the kiss, teasing my tongue against her lips. She parts them, meeting my tongue's caress, slow at first—but soon pressing more firmly, branding her touch, her taste into my very soul. A soft whimper escapes her, as I tighten my hold on her. My fingers curl against her, pulling her closer, but somehow she still feels too far away.

I groan as she melds into me and I know, if I don't stop now, I'm not going to be able to. Reluctantly easing back, breathing hard, I close my eyes, resting my forehead against hers—but never loosening my hold on her, keeping her tight against me.

She smirks up at me, her heated eyes, heavy-lidded and sparkling in the last light of the evening sun, her lips swollen from our kiss, her voice husky and soft.

"We should do this again sometime."

A slow grin spreads across my lips.

"Aye, that we should, Little Fawn. That, we most definitely should."

Chapter 34

Cole

I sip my coffee and watch the glimmer of sunshine gradually crest the horizon, the rays casting a hazy glow through the early morning mist across the lawn. A soft smile plays at the corners of my mouth, feeling new and somewhat out of place, as the events of the prior day dance on repeat in my mind.

Remembering the sound of the fallen leaves crunching beneath our steps. The smell of the crisp fresh air, melding flawlessly with the scent of bergamot and spice—the fragrance I've now come to recognize as the intoxicating scent of Rogan—as we walked arm in arm amongst the trees.

The feel of his fingers intertwined with mine and the warmth of his strong arms pulling me against his hard chest, wrapping me into a tight embrace as his lips caressed mine, our tongues tangling as he kissed me beneath the pine covered canopy.

The soothing sound of the stream babbling in the near distance, the last few birds of the day, chirping as they settled in for the evening, serenading us.

It was him, I think, feeling my cheeks tighten into a wide grin as I remember him calling me *'Little Fawn'*

Grumbl yawns loudly at my feet, pulling me out of my reverie.

"Good morning, baby boy." I coo, reaching down to rub the wrinkles by his ears. He groans loudly and pushes his head harder into my hand to deepen the scratch, making me laugh.

"Ready for a walk?" I ask him, slipping off the stool to gather his harness and lead.

He lets out a hefty sigh, as if the effort of going for a walk is a bothersome chore, but begrudgingly gets to his feet and waddles to the door, plopping down to wait patiently for me to fasten his tether and slip on my sneakers and jacket.

As I'm about to reach for the door, I hear the sound of Kya's footsteps. She skips down the stairs while effortlessly tying her hair up into a perfect messy bun on top of her head.

"Where are you off to, hun?" She asks, making her way over to us to slip into her own shoes.

"I was just going to take our little buddy here, out for a wee." I tell her, smiling down at Grumbl as he struggles to bring a short back leg up to scratch behind an ear, grunting and groaning at the challenge, making both of us laugh at his rather futile efforts.

"Alright if I come with ya?" Kya asks, reaching for her jacket in the same breath, clearly planning on joining regardless. "Looks like we're going to have another lovely day. Doubt we'll have too many of those left before winter takes hold." She says, looking out the window as she shrugs on her coat.

Having spent enough time with her now to know full well she's more interested in finding out the details of my date with Rogan, than the nature of the weather, I give her an impish grin.

"I wouldn't dream of excluding you from our wee-date."

She jovially bumps her shoulder into mine, giving me a sly wink, making us both giggle again, as we head out the door, Grumbl leading the way, and Athena slinking out the door with a soft chortle to indicate she'll be attending our walk too, just before Kya closes the door behind us.

With our arms looped at the elbow, Kya and I walk down the street toward the village as I recount the events of my date with Rogan. Kya listens intently, nodding and encouraging in all the right places.

When I tell her about Rogan saving me from going for an impromptu swim in the stream that led to that heart stopping kiss, I look up at her to see her beaming at me like a loon.

"What?"

My cheeks flame but I meet her grin with my own.

"It's going well then?" She asks, a hopeful sparkle in her eyes, radiating more warmth and love than any words ever could.

"You know, I really think it is." I smile back at her.

"Oh honey, I'm just so damn happy for you!" She beams, pulling me into a huge hug, almost making me see stars from how tightly she's gripping me.

She pulls back from the hug, still holding my shoulders as she studies my face.

"I truly am hun. I just want you to be happy. But please, please just take it slow." she implores.

"I know you've been through some shit, and I couldn't bear it if you got hurt again on my watch."

There's no question she means it, the passion in her words blazing like the summer sun.

"About that..." I say, trailing off.

Her expression shifts, her playful smile dropping away, she dips her chin once, giving me an encouraging nod.

"I think I'm finally ready to talk about it."

My throat gets tight, but there's a lightness that follows too. It's time to let her all the way in.

"Alright," she says, "If you're sure, then I'm here to listen, hun."

She loops her arm back through mine and scans our surroundings, her eyes catching on a stile nestled within the hedgerows. Beyond it, a field stretches toward the horizon, belonging to one of the farming families that border the village.

A weathered sign, marked with the familiar arrow of the 'Wye Valley Walking Trail', tilts at an angle, pointing the way. Without hesitating, her hand closes around mine and she leads us down the path, away from the village and away from the ears of nosy villagers that might listen in.

After we scale the stile, Grumbl squeezing beneath it, I clear my throat.

"I know you've seen the scars on my arms, that you've seen most of them on my body."

I pause for a beat, taking in another slow breath to steady myself. "And you know I'm running from something."

My eyes drop to the ground while I prepare myself for my next words, for my truth. Kya grips my hand, lacing our fingers together and gives it a reassuring squeeze.

"Yeah, I have, hun. And I've gathered there's something that's got you scared shitless. Bad relationship?" She offers, her brows pinch together at her question, her chin dipping to meet my eyes again.

"You could definitely say that." I nod, taking a deep breath before continuing.

"Bad husband." I admit, wincing at the taste of copper when a bit of the skin tears where I'm biting alongside my thumbnail.

"Did ya..." she pauses one beat...two. "Did ya try to..." She trails off again. Her eyes flick briefly to my wrists before she turns her head, swallowing hard, unable to finish her question.

Realizing what she's asking... the conclusion she's likely to have come to based on purely circumstantial evidence, I hurry to answer her.

"Oh, no Kya, no!" I turn and grip both of her hands in mine, turning to face her fully.

"I didn't try to kill myself."

"No?" Her watery gaze scanning my face in search of a lie. When she sees the truth in my eyes, she pulls me into a tight hug.

"Oh thank God!" There's an audible flood of relief in her voice.

After a long hug, she blows out a breath before releasing me. Then we continue walking.

"So if you didn't try to...," she clears her throat before she's able to get the words out, "kill yourself, what the hell did happen to you?" Confusion and horror lace her tone.

I try to find the right words, where to begin, what to say. After a long bit of silence, the grass of the field blowing in the breeze around us, I finally build up the courage to continue.

"He didn't like the soup..." I whisper.

"What?" Kya asks, clearly not understanding. "He didn't like the soup?" She repeats my words, as if there's no way she heard me correctly.

I nod, tears now flowing freely down my cheeks. I'm glad Kya had the foresight to take us somewhere quieter, more private.

"He... he didn't like the soup. He said if I couldn't even make a decent dinner, then I wasn't worth keeping around anymore." I tell her, my voice shaking.

As we come up to a bench opposite a cropped part of the hedgerow, overlooking a breathtaking view of the village and the shimmering waters of the Wye, Kya leads us over to sit down. I can just make out the thatched roof of Haven and the tiles of the bookshop in the near distance.

She turns me to face her, taking both my hands into hers.

"Alright hun, go on then. What happened after he said that?" She asks, encouraging me to continue unloading my truth on her, her thumbs brushing soft strokes over my knuckles, reminding me she's here—comforting me, holding me, her grip steady and waiting, ready to catch me should I fall.

"He... he threw his bowl against the wall...," I start to tell her, feeling my eyes haze as I fall back into the memory of that night.

"This soup is fucking disgusting!" He snarls.

I lift a shaky spoonful to my lips, the weight of his glare boring into me from across the table. Keeping my eyes down, I try to make myself as small as possible... try to go unnoticed, but I know full well, if he's got his sights set on me, there'll be no hiding from him... no escaping the beating that's coming.

The crash of porcelain shattering against the wall makes me jump and I curl tightly into myself.

"Did you fucking hear me? You answer me when I'm talking to you!! What the fuck did I tell you Nicole!?" He screams, throwing his napkin down on the table. Terror floods my veins when he stands, his chair scraping loudly across the floor.

I jump again as the back of the chair hits the floor behind him with a loud bang and I drop my hands into my lap.

"I'm sorry." I whisper, keeping my head down, my eyes pinned to my hands in my lap.

My fear ratchets up at the sound of his boots stomping across the floor as he rounds the table. Then my head is wrenched back, his fist gripping my hair, forcing me to look up at him.

"Stop your fucking sniveling you pathetic little bitch!" He grits out through clenched teeth and gives me a rough shake. I wince in pain as some of the strands of my hair rip away from my scalp.

"I'm sorry." I say again, trying to keep my tears from falling, knowing they'll only make him more mad.

"I'm so fucking sick of this shit! Why the fuck can't you do anything right?" he seethes. "It's fucking soup, Nicole! How fucking hard is that?"

There's no right answer here. This is a trick question.

If I answer him, I'll get a beating.

If I don't... I'll get the same.

Pain bursts through my eye socket as his fist collides with the side of my face. Then I'm vaguely aware of the sound of my soup bowl smashing on the floor beside me as he slams my head down on the table.

"I'm sorry!" I scream, "I'm so sorry, Cain. Please stop. I'll do better." I beg, blinking the blood out of my eye that's now weeping from the large gash on my forehead.

"I'll do better. Please stop. I'm so sorry, Cain." He mocks in a feminine voice.

"I've heard it a thousand times, Nicole. You're such a worthless piece of shit! Now clean up this fucking mess!" He bellows, throwing me onto the floor, my hands and knees sliding across the broken pieces of china.

"Yes sir." I whisper, scrambling to sweep the shattered pieces of bowl and the puddle of soup into a pile in front of me with my hands.

Blinding pain rips through my side as his boot connects with my ribs, his kick sending me sprawling face first into the puddle of soup and broken glass, the air leaving my lungs in a rush.

"What the fuck is that going to do, you stupid fucking bitch?" He snarls, reaching down to fist another handful of my hair, lifting me to my feet and slamming his fist into my stomach, making me instantly vomit.

With disgust radiating off of him, he growls, dragging me to the bathroom down the hall, my feet barely touching the floor the whole way. Weakly, I try to cling to his arm to lessen the pull of my weight on the hair still gripped in his fist.

"Clean yourself up!" He roars, throwing me full force into the tub, my head cracking painfully against the tiles.

I can't stop the tears anymore, even though I know how much they anger him. There's just too much pain... too little hope. I just can't do this anymore.

"Please... stop..." I beg weakly. "I just want it to stop." My last words are said more to myself than to him, as my head spins, my vision growing hazy.

He grabs me by the throat, squeezing hard as he pulls me right up to his face. The acrid smell of the whiskey on his breath burns my nose and makes my stomach churn. My head pounds and I can't take in any air with how hard he's gripping my throat.

Then a fresh flood of terror rushes through me when his next words drip with a false sweetness, his tone taking on an eerie calm.

"You want it to stop, Nicole? I can make it stop. All you have to do is tell me that's what you want."

Fear and despair pour off me in waves, my consciousness growing dimmer by the second as my head swims.

"Please...," is the only thing I can manage, the word nothing more than a weak whimper.

He throws me back into the tub, so hard my teeth jam together, biting my tongue, the familiar taste of hot copper filling my mouth.

He turns to the sink to rummage through the drawers. When he turns back to me, I see the glint of metal in his hand.

"No...." I whisper, too weak to do more than slightly shake my head and squirm as my consciousness threatens to leave me.

"I'm done, Nicole. You want it to stop. I'll stop it for you." He says, roughly pulling my arm up by the wrist.

"You've got your wish you useless fucking bitch. Just make sure you die knowing you did this to yourself!"

Then the sharp bite of metal cuts into me as he slices the blade of the straight razor down my wrist, ripping a scream from my throat.

Weakly, I try to pull away, futilely trying to fight against him when he grabs my other hand and repeats the slice down my other wrist. Whaling in pain, true fear floods my senses as my tenuous grip on my life ebbs down the drain.

"No... no, Cain, please..." I beg, my fingers fumbling weakly as I try to grip at his sleeves, my vision fading.

He tosses the bloody blade down next to my hand.

"Don't say I never gave you anything. I gave you exactly what you asked for."

The last thing I see are his eyes—cold, soulless, careless, unforgiving, remorseless. And then he was gone...

Chapter 35

Cole

There's a long silence between us as I finish telling Kya my truth. Blinking back from the haze of the memory, I angrily wipe the tears from my eyes and scan the horizon as I let out a long, slow breath.

When my eyes come back into focus and land on her, I see her cheeks are glistening, huge tears brimming and falling from her horror filled eyes in quick succession. Her hands holding mine so tightly her knuckles have turned white.

"Oh, Cole..." She whispers, her voice cracking— a sob catching in her throat as she tries to speak. She clears it and tries again.

"I... I don't even know what to say." She croaks, blinking rapidly as more tears spill down her cheeks.

"How did you ever survive?" She asks, her voice raspy as she tries to speak through her tears.

"Maria." I state bluntly, wiping my cheek on my shoulder as I realize my face is once again soaked with tears too.

"Maria?" Kya repeats, "Bless her... the angel!" Letting out a short sob, and with a shake of her head she asks, "Who's Maria?"

"Cain's maid. She had already left for the day, but thankfully had forgotten her bag. She must have just missed him on her way back to get it. She saw the mess in the dining room and followed the trail of blood to the bathroom where she found me just in time.

"She wrapped my arms tightly in towels and called for help. She saved my life."

My love and appreciation for Maria fills my chest, my voice cracking with the weight of everything she's done for me.

"She's been helping me try to get away from him for years. But she's undocumented and he always told her he'd have her deported if she didn't keep her mouth shut. So she's been secretly helping me.

"She set up a bank account and helped set aside money so, when the time was right, I could get away from him... for good this time."

"This time?" Kya asks, her tone laced with concern. "He's done this before?"

"It's never been this bad before. There were plenty of times I thought for sure he was going to kill me, but it was nothing compared to that night. It was just the beatings and the burns."

"Just?" She asks incredulously.

"My God Cole! I'm so sorry!" She sobs, pulling me into her tightly, her whole body shaking as she weeps onto my shoulder.

When she releases me I continue.

"I've tried to get away from him before, but he always finds me." My voice is a whisper, as if he'll somehow hear me if I say it too loud. I'm not quite able to bring my eyes up to meet hers.

"But I was extra careful this time. No digital footprint. No paper trail. Nothing pointing to where I might have gone. Nothing in my name. Honestly, my grandparents leaving me the bookshop really couldn't have come at a better time." I admit, running my sleeves under my eyes. "I'm just sorry I never got to meet them."

"Me too." Kya says, with a small smile. "Because they would have absolutely adored you, Cole." She blinks, a couple more tears trailing down her cheeks.

"So your name... is it Baker?" It's not quite a question. More of an offering. A guess wrapped in quiet understanding.

I shake my head. "No, it's not. It never has been. My mom never married my dad, so I've always been an Allbright." I exhale, the truth sitting heavy in my chest.

"But my married name is Nicole Brentwood."

With a sniff, Kya grips my hands again.

"Well your secret's safe with me... *Cole Allbright*." She confirms, assuring me by using my 'new' name.

"Can I ask you something else?"

"Hmm?" I answer her absently, with a small nod.

"Where is he now?" She asks, her voice quiet, as if she doesn't really even want to ask the question.

"I assume he's probably looking for me." I tell her, a shudder slipping down my spine as I involuntarily glance around me, the habit of keeping an eye out so deeply ingrained.

"The last location he had on me was a hospital in London. I left without the doctors or nurses knowing I was gone. Maria snuck me my travel bag and the money I had saved and I just got on a bus to come here. All I had was Grandpa Jesse's letters and my hopes to go on." I shiver as the memories trail a line of unbidden fear down my spine.

"Well you're here now, and you've got me!" She declares, wrapping me up in a tight hug. "And I'll never let anything happen to ya!" she says into my hair.

Holding her tightly, comforted by the loving embrace of this amazing woman, I whisper into her shoulder, "I love you Kya."

"I love you right back, hun!" She pulls back, her smile watery.

"And, if I'm hearing you correctly," sniffing as she straightens her shoulders, plastering a huge smile on her face, as if physically brushing off the heaviness of the prior conversation, "it sounds like you've got a strapping new man in your life that will certainly kick the shit out of anybody who's stupid enough to threaten ya from here on out!" She states with a wink.

Blushing furiously, I can't help but return her smile as thoughts of Rogan flood my memory.

Sniffling and beaming all at once, I say, "You know, Kya... I really think you might be right about that!"

Chapter 36

Rogan

Working my way through some equipment orders, needing to get these damn things squared away before our New York partners take off for the Thanksgiving holiday, I sit in the office at the dojo, cursing Brick for leaving this task for me. He knows how much I hate bloody paperwork.

I glance at my watch when I hear the sound of the door to the training area opening and slamming shut. We don't have any classes today. There shouldn't be anyone here.

I flip the monitor over to the CCTV screen, only to see Cole, looking aggravated as she scans the semi darkened room.

Seemingly coming to a decision, she storms over toward Dick, kicking off her trainers then tossing them and her bag off to the side. She shakes out her hands as she settles into a defensive ready stance, setting herself up perfectly for sparring.

She's come such a long way since her first day here. The day she ran from the dojo—ran from me and my overzealous punches and kicks as I showed off, trying to impress her, only to have it send her spiraling into some horrific memory from her past.

Since then, she's been steadily improving. Her movements growing in strength and confidence every week. Within just the first few lessons, I watched her really start to step into this stronger version of herself as she mastered each maneuver with surprising speed, some unspoken determination seeming to spur her on toward her goals. I have to admit, it's been one of the most astonishing transformations I've ever seen, the fight in her, unwavering.

Her slight frame has turned from thin, almost gaunt; to lean and trim, her limbs now lined with toned muscles. Her time spent in the sun as she's worked in the garden of the bookshop and Haven, has turned her once ghostly pale skin to a lovely light honeyed tan. Her tiny freckles, all now a bit more prominent.

Smiling at my student with a teacher's pride, I watch as she begins going through her katas, preparing for whatever battle she's planning on waging against Dick today. Her motions, smooth and flowing, begin to pick up speed, her chest starting to heave.

Then she turns to the dummy and unleashes her fury—punching, kicking, twirling around to slam solid roundhouse kicks into it—Dick swaying violently with each assault, Cole meeting each of his returning sways with even more ire.

Finally, with a yell that echoes through the empty building, she turns and lands a powerful spinning back kick into the dummy, sending it toppling backwards onto the mat, dropping down to her knees at the same time.

I bolt up in my chair the moment her knees hit the mat, leaning in close to the computer, then enlarging the video screen. Cole is on her hands and knees, her body shaking violently. There's no sound on the CCTV, but it looks like she's crying.

I stand up so quickly, my chair rolls across the room and slams against the opposite wall of the office. My heart hammers in my chest, the need to get to her—to find out who hurt her, drowning out any sense of reason. I storm out of the office and race toward the training area.

"Cole?"

I say her name softly, approaching slowly, like one might approach an injured animal, trying not to spook her.

Who the fuck hurt my Little Fawn?

I'm close enough to hear her sobs now, the sound of each shuddering breath shredding pieces out of my heart. But she doesn't acknowledge me, she mustn't have heard me. Crouching beside her, I reach a tentative hand out and gently brush my fingers against her shoulder.

"Cole..." I say again, but this time, she jumps. Her whole body pulls away.

"NO!" she yells, scrambling backward across the mat. I quickly pull my hand back.

Everything in me is screaming to pull her into me, to help her, calm her. A fiery rage builds in me, writhing beneath my skin, demanding I seek out and destroy whoever could have made her this upset.

Her eyes are frantic, unfocused and she's shaking her head, curling in on herself. I try again softly, "Cole, it's just me, darling. What is it? What happened to you Little Fawn? Did someone hurt you?"

At the sound of my voice, my name for her, her head snaps up, her glassy gaze finally shifting and focusing on mine. The tension visibly drains from her body, her face crumpling as she slumps and lets the tears fall.

Hit by a wave of relief, confident I can now approach her, touch her without causing her to spiral further, I drop to my knees beside her. I wrap my arm around her shoulders and take her hand in mine. I gently pull her to me and feel her body soften.

She turns into me as I hold her against me. Sobs wrack her body and she trembles all over, her hands twisting into the fabric of my t-shirt. I stroke her hair softly, soothing her as I rock her gently.

"Shhh. You're alright, Little Fawn. You're alright. I've got you. I'm not going to let anyone hurt you. You're safe now." I reassure her, keeping my voice low.

Her sobs eventually turn into soft sniffles and her body begins to soften, slowly relaxing away from my tight hold. I lean back slightly, not wanting to let her go, but sense she's ready for some space. Her eyes are red, swollen and puffy from crying, bright pink blotches cover her neck and cheeks, but she seems clearer now, calm. Her face is as lovely as ever, regardless of the tears staining her cheeks.

"Can you tell me what that was all about, Cole?" I dare to ask, still keeping my voice as calm as I can, even though everything in me is raging over what could have possibly happened to her.

She's quiet for too long, the minutes of silence stretching on for what feels like an excruciating eternity and the wait to find out what's happened to her is driving me fucking mad.

She pulls in a sharp breath and sniffs again, her eyes glued to her hands in her lap, never meeting mine. She opens her mouth to speak, closes it again, then shakes her head and shrugs.

"It's nothing. I'm okay. I'm sorry…"

Her eyes flash up to mine the moment those last two words leave her lips, a tiny knowing cringe before I can admonish her for the apology she knows I'm going to tell her is unnecessary.

My jaw clenches, but I'm not angry with her. I hate the fear I see in her eyes, hate that she feels like she has to hide whatever it is that's happened from me.

"Alright." I say, a look of quiet understanding sliding across my face, as I trace a thumb under her eye, wiping a tear off her cheek. "Let's try that again," my tone is gentle but firm, "but the truth this time, right?"

She studies me, her eyes flitting back and forth between mine, worry etched across her pretty face—a decision being made. At last she breaks my stare, looking down and nodding, seeming to accept me as a safe space to let go of her truths.

"It's really nothing," she starts, but meeting my eyes again, she quickly continues, sensing I'm not going to accept that as an answer again, "It's just that I went out with Zavier…"

Chapter 37

Rogan

At the sound of Zavier's name, I see red—fury blazing through my veins like a volcanic inferno. My teeth clench so hard, I'm almost certain I'll crack a tooth and my breath rumbles low in the depths of my chest.

Hear her out Rogan, you fucking arse. She just needs you to listen right now.

Working hard to keep the evidence of my internal turmoil from my face, I nod, encouraging her to continue.

"He insisted I owed him a date after he'd helped me clean up the trees in the orchard. I didn't really want to go, but it seemed harmless enough and I figured if all he wanted was to go to dinner with me, that didn't seem so bad, right?"

I stay silent, her question clearly rhetorical, and nod, silently encouraging her to keep going with her story.

"So, we went to the Chippy and had dinner and everything was fine. We were just hanging out like usual. Our conversation seemed normal enough, but he kept badgering me about quitting my job at the pub so I could go work for him on his farm instead. He says it's so he can 'Keep an eye on me'." She rolls her eyes, making air quotes with her fingers, obvious aggravation lacing her words.

"But then when we got ready to leave, he insisted we needed to stop at the pub for a drink too. I just figured; I probably owed him that much. The orchard really was a mess, after all. So I agreed."

She sniffs, pausing her tale, seemingly lost in thought. Settling back a bit in my arms, she absently fiddles with the tab of her zipper at the base of her track jacket.

"What happened at the pub, Cole." I ask, gently urging her to continue, desperately needing to know just what the fuck Zavier did to her.

"He had *a lot* to drink. He just kept ordering glass after glass of whiskey." Her lip curls as if the word tastes sour on her tongue.

"I tried to tell him he'd had enough, that I wanted to leave, but he just got angry. Pete finally stepped in and cut him off. I thought that would be the end of it, that I could finally be done with this damn date, but Pete getting involved only seemed to make him more mad."

Her eyes turn distant as she continues, telling the tale as if from an old memory, disconnecting from the here and now, her eyes unfocused.

"He was quiet, sulking on the boat the whole ride back as we crossed the Wye. But when he was walking me back to Kya's, just as we got to the alley right before 'Lover's Lane', he grabbed my arm and pulled me into the dark."

Tears well in her eyes, and I feel her body start to tremble.

My arm stays firmly around her back, holding her steady as my fingers stroke a soft, soothing rhythm up and down her arm, a silent offer of comfort and support.

But inside me, there's a torrent of rage boiling as my thoughts drift to the memory of finding Zavier with Tessa, our maid—the image of him holding her by the throat, pressing her against the wall as he groped her, tugging at her skirt. The anger in me turns to molten lava and it's taking everything in me to keep my hands from shaking.

The hitch in her voice as she fights to continue speaking past a broken sob, pulls me back from my raging thoughts.

"He pushed me up against the building, and pressed himself against me, pinning me against the wall. He said I still owed him more for his services and that he'd take my mouth as payment. That he wouldn't consider my debt paid in full if I didn't give him what he wanted.

"But I told him, no. That we're only friends and I don't feel that way about him... but he said it didn't matter... he would *make* us more than friends. His eyes were so cold, vacant—like he wasn't even there."

A tear tracks down her cheek and her throat works as she tries to get the next part out.

"He was so close, literally no space between us, no room to turn away. The next thing I knew, his lips were on mine and he was pushing his tongue into my mouth. I tried to scream, to push him away, to use the lessons you've taught me here..." her eyes turn to me pleading, begging for something.

"But he was digging his fingers into me so hard, had me pinned so tightly to the wall—and he's just so goddamn big!"

She's shouting now, frantic panic strangling her words.

"I tried, Rogan, I swear I did, but he's just too strong," she says, sounding defeated.

"Then he started grabbing at me, pawing at my clothes,..."

Her face morphs to a look of disgust and she cringes, shrinking down into herself.

My tension turns damn near volatile, and I honestly have no idea how I'm managing to hold it together—but for her sake, I will. I bite back my fury and let her finish telling her story.

"The whole time, I just kept thinking... *This can't be real. This can't be happening. Zavier wouldn't do this.* But, when he grabbed my throat... that's when I really panicked.

So, the next time he put his tongue into my mouth, I bit down until I tasted blood. He pulled back just enough for me to twist out of his grip and that gave me enough room to bring my knee up into his balls, HARD!"

A look of blazing satisfaction flares in her eyes.

"When he let go of me to grab himself, I was finally able to push past him. Then I ran home as fast as I could and locked the door behind me the second I got into the house. But I'm so mad, Rogan! So fucking pissed off! I'm just so tired of... of..." she begins to sob, losing her words as her face crumples again.

I pull her against me and wrap her in my arms.

"It's okay Little Fawn, it's over now." I soothe.

"He's not ever going to fucking touch you again." I promise.

"I won't ever let anyone hurt you again."

She goes still, then slowly sits back again, her wet eyes scanning my face.

"*You* won't?" The echo of my words rings back to me.

I did say that, didn't I?

I sigh and slide my thumb along her dampened cheek and nod.

"Yes, Cole. *I* won't let anyone or anything hurt you again... because I've got you."

The silence sits heavy in the air between us as the weight of what I just said sinks in for one breath, then another...

Then, as if whatever's been holding her back releases its grip, she leans in, her eyes dropping to my mouth, and then her lips brush against mine.

Gently, I press into the kiss and a soft moan slips from her throat. Blood rushes straight to my cock at the sound. I pull her tighter against me, and slide my hand into her hair, tilting her head to deepen the kiss. Her tongue teases the seam of my lips, testing, asking, and I open, granting her unspoken request. Our tongues tangle in a slow dance, tasting each other, moving together in a sensual swirl, losing ourselves to the essence of the kiss.

Cradling her head, I lower her to the mat, hovering my body over hers, keeping my weight off her as I follow her down. Her hands trail up the muscled plains of my chest and move across my shoulders, then loop around the back of my neck as she weaves her fingers into my hair.

She moves into me, rolling her hips against my groin as she presses her tiny frame up at the same time tugging me down, needing to be closer, so I settle a bit more of my weight on top of her.

Small, needy gasps and whimpers escape her between kisses and I groan, pressing my aching bulge against her, chasing the delicious friction I've been fantasizing about for months now, desperate for her touch.

Her hands rove, exploring my body. Curiosity mixes with a frantic need, building until she's tugging at the hem of my shirt. Breaking our kiss, I reach over the back of my head and grab my collar, pulling it off in one swift movement. Her eyes heat as they trail down my chest, my muscles tight as I hold the bulk of my weight off of her.

She's breathing heavily and the brilliant green of her eyes is nearly eclipsed by her dilated pupils. They sparkle in the dim light of the barely lit dojo as they move across my body. Her chest rises and falls, the swell of her perfect breasts pressing against the top edge of her sports bra, the tender skin begging to be licked, sucked, caressed.

For just a moment, I stop to take her in where she lies beneath me, letting me touch her, kiss her, hold her—and I realize—she's perfect. I stare at her in wonder, completely awestruck by her sheer, natural beauty.

I'm suddenly overwhelmed by her.

I lean in and press another soft kiss to her lips, then run the tip of my finger over her brow, along her jaw and skim it down her neck, settling my hand over her heart.

"You're stunning, Cole. Absolutely... fucking... stunning."

I say, breathless, completely dumbstruck by her.

She swallows hard, her head shaking in silent disbelief. A single tear rolls down the side of her face; her eyes locked on mine.

Wiping it away with the pad of my thumb I nod, trying to make her see the conviction of my words through my stare. Make her believe the truth of what I see when I look at her. Try to let her see her beauty through the mirror of my eyes.

Her chin wobbles, but she smiles softly, a tenuous glimmer of acceptance.

I press my lips to her forehead, then her temple, next her cheek. Then I kiss the corner of her mouth, my lips a feather-light whisper as I move to graze the line of her jaw and she shivers beneath me.

Trailing the tip of my tongue down the side of her neck, I alternate between tasting her and peppering light kisses along the column of her throat. When I run my tongue along her collar bone, she gasps, her fingers digging into my shoulders. I can't stop the roll of my hips as she lifts up to wrap her legs around my waist. The groan that escapes me is near feral when I feel the heat between her legs as she lifts her hips, matching my movement.

I move lower, down across her chest, grazing my teeth lightly along her creamy skin and smile at the goosebumps rising in the wake of my touch. Her breaths are quick and uneven, her body writhing beneath me. I trace the small swell of her breast that's pressed up slightly above the top of her sports bra, the tip of my tongue barely touching her skin.

I'm practically salivating at the taste of her.

I want more. I *need* more.

Her body feels like heaven as I slide my hand down her side. My thumb skates along the underside of her breast as I wrap my fingers around her hip and she lets out a needy whimper at the sensation.

The sounds she's making are driving me mad. I want to devour her. Lose myself in her. Plunge my cock into that sweet oblivion between her thighs and rut into her like an animal until we're both falling into that sweet abyss with feral need.

But no. As fucking divine as that sounds, I need to hold back. I won't take from her and I refuse to be someone else she needs to fear. I can't chance breaking this fragile trust that's slowly growing between us.

This isn't just another one-night stand.

No.

Cole is special.

My eyes move back up her body to find her watching me, her eyes heavy lidded, pupils blown with desire. Smirking, I take the zipper at the top of her sports bra into my mouth and hold it loosely between my teeth, with my heated stare locked on hers, silently asking permission. Her chest rises and falls on a heavy breath and I see her throat move as she swallows back the last of her trepidation—then she gives me the barest of nods.

Permission granted, I hold her gaze as I slowly slide the zipper down with my teeth, the Lycra popping open when I reach the bottom of the clasp. The sight of her perfect pale breasts spilling out elicits a growl that vibrates from somewhere deep in my throat. My cock throbs painfully, the material of my pants feeling too tight, too restrictive and I grind my hips down again.

Her dusky pink nipples are hard, tight and perfect. My mouth waters as wild need begs me to devour her. I cup my hand around her breast, then run my thumb gently over her nipple, lightly kneading the soft swell of flesh. She watches as I lower my mouth down, gasping as I swirl my tongue over one of the hardened peaks.

"So sweet…"

My words are a breathy groan, before I drop my mouth over her breast, taking it in fully, sucking, licking and lightly grazing my teeth over her soft flesh, only to move over and repeat my ministrations on her other breast.

Cole's breaths are nothing more than quick gasps as she pants. She threads her fingers into my hair, holding my mouth against her as she writhes beneath my touch.

"Rogan." She says my name like a prayer on a breathless whimper and my dick grows impossibly harder at the sound. Her finger nails dig into my scalp, driving me insane with need.

I move my mouth and tongue down, down, down. My movements getting more desperate, more frantic with need. I drag my nose along the waist band of her leggings, then grip the fabric between my teeth, tugging it down, just barely an inch, releasing it again to lick along the newly exposed skin of her stomach, looking up to see those stunning green eyes, half-lidded as she watches me.

"I want to taste you, Cole." I breathe, lightly raking my teeth over her bare skin again.

Her eyes widen and she lifts up onto her elbows.

"Wh…what?" She asks, apprehension lacing her tone. "What do you mean, you want to *taste me*?"

My voice is husky when I answer her, desire coursing through my veins, my attention fully focused on her body.

"I want to pleasure you Cole… with my hands," a kiss to her sternum, "my mouth…," a swirl of my tongue beneath her navel, "my tongue."

I rake my teeth over the thin fabric standing between me and the sweet heat between her legs and she draws in a sharp breath.

"I want to *taste* you, Little Fawn."

She goes completely silent, the only sound in the room, our ragged breaths. At her stillness and the weight of her stare bearing down on me, I finally look up.

Her brows are pinched with confusion, worry... *fear?*

I tilt my head, only now considering her question.

And then I get it.

"Cole... has anyone ever pleasured you with their tongue before?"

Her face flames a deep shade of crimson.

"No." Her voice is barely a whisper, but her heated eyes find mine again.

At her admission, I feel a swell of primal possessiveness and a low, hungry growl rumbles deep in my chest with savage need.

"Then I beg of you," I say, curling my fingers into the hem of her leggings, "may I have the esteemed honor of being the first, and hopefully only man to learn your taste?"

Her whole body trembles, her chest rising and falling with quick breaths as she considers my request.

I don't move, holding her stare, waiting for her to decide, my heart beating wildly in my chest.

Then, even though her eyes look unsure, she dips her chin in a single, tight nod.

"Good girl." I purr, dropping my mouth back down to run my tongue along her hip bone as I slowly peel her leggings down to expose the delicate white lace panties beneath. Once I've pulled her leggings completely off, I begin to make my way back up her body.

I lick, kiss and nip up the curve of her calf. Sucking, nibbling and teasing, raking my teeth gently along her tender skin. The evidence of the effect I'm having on her is obvious as I reach the apex of her thighs, the fabric of her panties darkened by her arousal.

"You're soaked for me, Cole." I groan, as I drag the tip of my nose up her center, my touch making her jump. I breathe her in and the scent of her sweet honey makes my cock throb.

I run my tongue over the wet fabric, and she whimpers. Sliding my hands under her ass, I slip my fingers into the waistband of her panties, slowly sliding them down over her hips. Her body goes rigid as I shift to the side to remove them, and I pause immediately.

"You alright, Cole?"

But she's not watching me anymore. Instead, she's dropped her head back, her eyes locked on the ceiling and her breaths are coming in short, uneven gasps, sounding less like pleasure and more like fear.

"Hey now. It's alright, Cole. We don't have to do this. We can stop anytime you want, love. There's no pressure here." I tell her softly as I settle her panties gently back against her hips. She lifts her head, watching me with wide eyes as I rise up to kneel between her legs.

I run my thumb in soft, soothing circles on her leg, waiting for her breathing to slow, for her to decide if she wants to stop, or if she wants more.

Her eyes shimmer as she opens her mouth to speak, "I... I think..." she stammers nervously as she tries to find words.

"Shhh, it's alright, Little Fawn, just breathe." I interrupt as I lower myself down to lay beside her, curling my hand around her fingers and folding her hand into mine.

"Can I ask you something, Cole?"

I pull her into my side and tuck her hair back behind her ear and she nods.

"Do you know what a safe word is?"

I feel her body start to relax into me as she answers.

"A safe word? No." She shakes her head as she stares curiously up at me, her breathing slowing as her fear slips away.

"It's a word you say if you ever feel like you're uncomfortable, or if anything feels like it's too much for you and you want to stop. And no matter what's happening, no matter what we're doing, if you say that one word, we stop. No questions, no consequences, nothing bad will happen. Because it's the word you use to feel safe." I explain.

"Something like 'pineapple', for example."

Her nose crinkles and I laugh. Her lips turn up at the corners at my laughter and I'm hit with a flood of warmth just from the way she's looking at me.

"Okay, *not* pineapple then. So, you'll want to think of something that makes you feel safe. Something you can easily remember, but try to make sure it's not something you would normally say during sex." I laugh again, making her grin.

She pulls her bottom lip in between her teeth and lifts her eyes in thought. After a couple seconds, she says, "Sundance. That was the name of my favorite horse when I was a little girl." She explains.

"Alright then, Sundance can be your safe word. You say that anytime anything ever makes you feel uncomfortable and you want it to stop. Good?"

She smiles gratefully and nods. She cups my face, trailing her fingers through my beard, her green eyes sparkling as she looks at me.

"Thank you for helping me feel safe, Rogan." She says softly.

"You're welcome, Cole." I lean down and kiss her gently on the lips. She slides her fingers behind my head, pulling me into the kiss, opening for me, her tongue slipping between my lips. She pulls me into her and I move back over her.

Before I know it, my hands are roaming back down her body, caressing her breasts, my cock swelling, throbbing against my zipper.

She melts into the kiss, meeting me hungrily with each press of our lips, her hands roving curiously across my skin as much as mine are on hers. Moving my lips back down her body, I start working my way back toward her sex, making sure to glance up to check on her between kisses the lower I go.

I glide my hands along her hips, stroking my thumbs across the soft flesh of her lower belly and tease my fingers beneath the waistband of her panties.

When she meets my eyes this time, there's no fear in her stare, just a heated hunger as she nods, giving me the permission I need to keep going.

I slip the fabric off of her legs and settle between them. Gently, I lift one leg, and kiss along her inner thigh. She gasps again, but relaxes into my touch. I lower down and place her leg over my shoulder.

"Beautiful." I breathe as I run the tip of my nose over her glistening seam. She takes in a quick gasp of air and flinches, but doesn't speak, so I flick the tip of my tongue lightly against her clit, making her squeak and buck her hips.

"Shhh... you're alright, Little Fawn." I soothe, but I don't know if it's her I'm trying to calm or myself, as the taste of her bursts across my tongue, driving me half mad with desire.

I gently, but firmly press my palm onto her lower stomach to steady her, then flatten my tongue, licking her from the base of her pussy all the way to her clit.

Cole's low moan echoes in the room and my dick swells at the sound. I have to grind myself down into the mat to keep from erupting in my pants.

I start to work her then, sucking, licking, delving my tongue deeper into her hot, wet center—then dragging my tongue back up to flick at her clit.

"Rogan."

She pants, her breaths short and fast, as she threads her fingers into my hair, pulling my face harder against her weeping pussy.

I groan at the sound of my name on her lips and the taste of her on my tongue as she writhes beneath me, the combination making me light headed—I swear every ounce of blood in my body has rushed to my dick at this point.

I continue to lick and suck on her clit as I bring one hand up to my mouth, rolling my tongue around one thick finger before slowly slipping it inside her.

I ease it in, working it deeper as I devour her, sucking her clit harder with each thrust of my hand.

Cole's legs start to shake and she begins to shudder beneath me as the inner walls of her pussy quiver and grip tighter around my finger. I pull my hand away and bury my face between her thighs, plunging my tongue deep inside her.

"Mmmm... God, Rogan! I... I... It's... I need..."

She stammers, whimpering and squirming, until she's rolling her hips, taking her own pleasure from me. Her nails bite into my scalp as she tries to pull me closer, needing something more to send her soaring over that precipice.

She's so close, right there...

I move my hand back, this time adding a second finger and slide into her, curling them upward with each pulse of my hand, alternating between flicking my tongue and sucking hard on her clit.

"Oh my God, Rogan!!" She screams, her body convulsing, her pussy throbbing. Her thighs grip the sides of my head as she pushes her pulsing cunt up against my mouth, her inner walls rippling and squeezing as she comes undone.

I press my fingers deep, rolling them against her inner walls and lap gently against her swollen clit, slowly easing my ministrations as her tremors start to subside to avoid making her overly sensitive.

Once I'm sure she's come down from her orgasm, I place a kiss to her inner thigh, before moving back up her body. She's panting, breathing as if she's just run a race. Her cheeks are rosy and a lovely pink flush colors her neck and chest. I grab my t-shirt to lay it over her body as I lean down to kiss her gently.

"What the hell did you just do to me?" She asks breathlessly, as I settle back over her. Her eyes half lidded, a drunken smile on her lips.

"I've never felt *anything* like that before."

I blink down at her, my brows pulled together. "Has no one ever given you an orgasm before?" I ask, incredulous.

"Apparently not," she giggles, "because that was the most amazing thing I've ever felt in my life!"

Nothing can stop the boastful grin that spreads across my face at her admission, and she laughs, swatting me on the shoulder, which only makes me laugh harder. When our laughter turns to contented smiles, I lean down and place a tender kiss on her lips.

"Well then. I'll be sure to make you feel like that again as many times as you like."

I settle down next to her, holding her close, relishing the feel of her in my arms as she snuggles against my side.

It feels like bliss as we lay there in comfortable silence, but my cock is still rock hard and pinned tightly against my zipper, so I reach between us to adjust myself. I feel her body start to stiffen and she shifts away from me.

Curious, I look down at her to see the smile has faded from her lips and her face has fallen. Her expression shifting, turning distant, her eyes clouding. When I look into her eyes it's like she's looking right through me.

Her hand moves to her neck, her fingers absently stroking along the column of her throat. Swallowing hard, she moves to sit up.

Confused by this abrupt change in her, I push up on my arm and lean back, giving her space to move past me.

She turns to face me but her eyes are unseeing. She rises to her knees, her movements almost robotic.

I'm hit with a sudden surge of concern. Something is wrong. It's like she's not there.

"Cole, what are you doing?" I ask, sitting up beside her.

Not meeting my eyes, she just stares at the floor, unblinking.

"I'm ready, Sir." Her voice sounds hollow, empty. None of the sweet, happy Cole I've come to know.

"Ready for what, Cole?" I ask, confused. She's really starting to scare me now. She still won't meet my eyes.

"Little Fawn, what the hell is going on?"

A slow blink is my only response, her eyes still unfocused as she kneels.

"Cole?" I ask again. But it's as if she's not there. Almost like she's sleepwalking.

Then it hits me. She just called me *'Sir'*.

I look at her again... the way she's sitting.

Kneeling, eyes down, her hands resting palms up on her thighs...

The picture of the perfect sub.

But I'd have to guess, she was never a willing one.

My stomach churns when I realize—when I start to envision what's been done to her.

Fuck! She thinks I'm going to take what I want from her now. That I'm expecting some form of compensation. Someone has made her feel like she's had to perform, to gratify them sexually for any pleasure she's been allowed to receive.

I reach up and cup her cheek. As my fingers touch her skin, she flinches ever so slightly, as if she's fighting against the movement.

Because flinching will earn her punishment, I realize.

I keep my touch gentle but firm and turn her to face me.

"Little Fawn, look at me, my darling. You're safe word... you remember what it is?"

She blinks once, twice... and finally, there's a subtle shift as her eyes refocus fractionally.

I try again, "Tell me your safe word, Little Fawn."

"Sundance." She remembers... the word a broken whisper as her lip trembles and a tear slips from her eye.

"See, nothing is going to happen now. Everything stops, right?" I promise, gently brushing the tear from her cheek.

She blinks again, her eyes finally lifting to mine, her vision slowly clearing. Her eyes flutter, as if waking from a dream and her throat works like she can't quite catch her breath. She tries to smile, but it's weak, broken—her face crumpling when she sees the worry in my eyes.

"I'm so sorry..." she starts.

"Ah-ah, no," I whisper, not letting her finish her apology.

"We never, and I mean NEVER do anything you're not comfortable with. Is that clear, Little Fawn?"

"But... I...you..." gasping between her words, her voice broken as more tears spill over her lashes.

"Fuck, come here." I say, pulling her into me and cradling her head against my chest. Kissing the top of her head, I vow to her,

"Never again, Little Fawn. No one will EVER fucking hurt you again."

It's then, I make a silent promise to myself...

I'm going to fucking destroy Zavier for doing this to her, and I swear I'm going to kill whoever this mother fucker is that hurt her.

Chapter 38

Cole

Glowing beams of sunshine slowly stretch across the floorboards of my room while I lay in bed the next morning. A persistent smile tugs at the corners of my lips as memories of the way he touched me flash through my mind.

The heat of his bare chest pressing against me as he slid down my body. His tongue as it trailed across my skin... the extraordinary sensation as he slipped it into my aching center. My thighs squeeze together at the thought of his breath against my most sensitive area, my hips shifting at the sudden tug of need deep inside me.

You'd think I'd be dwelling on the horrific way my so-called *'date'* with Zavier had ended, but instead I woke up feeling euphoric, alive... *reborn*.

Like my very being had been awakened for the first time. A reincarnation of my former self, finally made whole by the presence of this one incredible man. I never knew a man's touch could be so gentle, so caring... *so decadent*.

I close my eyes and let the memory of his touch erase all the dark sins of the night. Let the thought of his fingers on my skin tear away every page laced with evil from my story, rewriting each one with his own gentle words, telling a new tale all our own.

Lingering under the warm spray of water in the shower, my fingers feel different now when I trail them down my body. Each touch a new sensation as I prepare to explore the hidden places his clever mouth introduced me to—his wicked tongue, and his expert fingers having woken up a part of me I hadn't even known existed.

My whole body tingles, my fingers tracing along the same lines of my body he had kissed and licked. An ache tugs low in my belly at the thought of his hands as they caressed my body, his touches gentle and reverent, like I was something precious. Like I was something worthy of being adored and worshipped.

My fingers dip between my thighs, tentative and light. But the moment my fingertips graze over my clit—already swollen and sensitive from thoughts of him—suddenly, I crave more.

Adding more pressure, I slide them deeper between my folds, dipping my finger into my center. It's slick, warm and I gasp, my hips tilting on their own, chasing this new desire.

I press my thumb against my clit and push my finger deeper, imagining his warm breath ghosting against my skin. His voice, a vibrating tenor, low and insistent as he spoke in hushed tones against my neck.

I want more.

I whimper; my head dropping back against the cool tiles of the shower wall and lift my leg giving myself more access to press in even deeper.

But it's still not enough...

More. I need more.

Trying to emulate what he'd done, I imagine my touch as his and dip a second finger inside me. Instantly, I feel a heavy need tug at my center and I begin to work them in and out, grinding the knuckle of my thumb harder against my clit. My hips move of their own accord in time with my hand, each curl of my fingers driving the tingle in my spine closer to that euphoric edge he sent me off of last night.

I envision the heated look in his eyes. Hear his husky whisper, growling, *'Good Girl'.* Feel the heat of his breath as he dipped down between my legs, his tongue teasing my clit as he nipped and sucked places no one had ever tasted on me before. A sudden rush of heat pulses inside me and my legs begin to shake.

Yes, that's it. That's the feeling he introduced me to. The one I've only been craving more of ever since.

I chase the feeling until the sounds of the rushing water around me go distant and my insides tighten, a swelling need growing, surging, pulling me toward the edge until finally... *I'm falling.*

Waves of pleasure crash over me and I drive my hand harder into my pussy, holding it there while the tightness squeezes in time with my racing heartbeat and pleasure courses through me from my very core.

Spots dance before my eyes as the pulses slowly start to ebb and the waves grow further apart until eventually, they fade completely. I slump against the shower wall, breathing hard, my shaking legs all but giving out beneath me. Reluctantly, I slip my fingers out from between my thighs and instantly feel a needy emptiness.

I blow out a slow breath and laugh disbelievingly.

What the hell has this man done to me?

Once I've finished showering, I dry off, dress and head downstairs. I take out the french press and set the kettle on to boil, then pop a few slices of bread into the toaster.

I scoop up Athena to give her a cuddle. She instantly starts purring like crazy and making biscuits on my chest while snuggling her head up under my chin, returning my love tenfold. Planting a couple kisses on top of her head, I set her back down and fix her a dish of tuna before pulling the now steaming kettle off the stove to pour over the coffee in the press—the toast popping up to be buttered just as I finish my pour.

I absently nibble at my toast while I let my mind wander back to memories of Rogan, giving them free reign to run through my mind on a steady loop. Letting myself fall into them deeply, I'm suddenly there again, in the dojo, Rogan above me...

His eyes sparkling like molten silver, his chest rising and falling heavily, like he can't catch his breath, his muscles rippling and flexing while he braces his weight above me.

The heat of his body as he settles between my thighs and the feel of his lips as he traces them along my skin, learning each curve of my body. The heat of his mouth as it closes around each of my breasts, the slick feel of his tongue as it trails down my belly until finally dipping between my...

"You look well."

Kya's cheerful voice jolts me out of my vision and I nearly drop my toast.

I have to blink a few times and give myself a quick shake when I realize I've been standing at the counter, waiting for the coffee in the french press to steep for far longer than necessary. Kya laughs at my dazed expression, her eyes twinkling with a knowing mischief, concealing her smirk poorly behind the rim of her mug as she takes a sip of her steaming tea.

When the hell did she even make that?

I push the plunger down and finish making my coffee—the dark liquid in the press having steeped far longer than necessary while I was daydreaming—all the while, fighting the giddy smile threatening to take over my face.

The thought of confessing the delightfully devious things that happened to me last night with her, sends a sudden thrill through me. I've never had someone in my life I've wanted to share anything like this with before—never had anything like this I'd ever wanted to share.

Heat rockets to my cheeks, turning them a shade that could rival the ripest of apples and my jaw aches from attempting to hold back my smile.

Fuck it.

I blow out a deep sigh, releasing my last bit of hesitation. I don't want to keep this a secret anymore. When I meet her eyes I let my smile run free and let her see the pure, undeniable joy plastered all over my face.

"Blimey! You must've had a *really* good evening!" Her eyes widen as she grins wickedly at me.

"I really did." I reply, still grinning like the Cheshire Cat.

I shift my attention to the cabinets to pull out a mug for my coffee, taking my time to pour it while leaving her palpable curiosity hanging in the air between us.

I can feel her stare as she watches me, waiting for me to elaborate on the events of my *'date'* with Zavier.

When I hear her huff and set her mug down with a little more force than necessary, I know I've just about met her threshold for patience, her curiosity nearly at its peak.

"Cole!" She says, her voice raised in mock indignation.

"Anddddd...?"

Unable to stop myself from teasing her just a little longer, I cross the room slowly, bringing my mug and the french press over to the table. I'm not sure her eyes can go any wider and her impatience is nearly a living thing hanging in the weight of her stare. But I drag it out just a tiny bit more with a coy smirk playing on my lips as I purposefully take my time to stir a spoonful of sugar into my mug, then straighten my cup and brush a few imaginary crumbs off the table. A wicked smile plays on my tightly sealed lips.

"Damnit, Cole! Spill it already!" She nearly shouts, eyes wild with frantic excitement and her mouth held in a gaping smile, knowing full well I'm egging her on and loving every minute of it.

"Okay, okay!" I giggle, finally relenting. "It's quite a story, and you'll be glad you're sitting down for this one."

I take a sip from my mug, wincing at the bitter brew and pull the sugar bowl closer, spooning another scoop into my cup.

"I'll start by saying, Zavier is a fucking asshole!"

Immediately, Kya's brows meet and her eyes darken, the smile falling completely from her face, her eyes narrowing with murderous intent. Her mouth drops, gaping further the longer I speak, as I recount the start of my evening with Zavier. She moves her mug away to lean in, settling her chin on top of her fingers, her eyes never leaving mine, as though she's afraid she might miss something if she even so much as blinks.

The change in her was obvious, her mood morphing into a protective rage, when I tell her how he had dragged me into the alley. I go quiet while I prepare to tell the story again.

"What did he do, Cole?" She shifts in her seat, her voice low, but I can hear the storm brewing in her tone. Her nails tap impatiently on the table, once... twice...

I exhale, long and slow, willing the anger I feel from the memory to settle, "He wanted more than I was prepared to give." I finally tell her, unable to force myself to relive the whole thing all over again so soon.

Her eyes flame and she inhales sharply, her fingers curling into claws and I hear her nails scrape on the wood of the table.

"So..." I pause, deliberately relaxing back as I raise my coffee to my lips, cocking a satisfied smile with an arch of my brow,

"I bit his tongue and kneed him right in the balls."

"Atta girl!" She shouts triumphantly, slapping her hand down hard on the table making the spoon rattle against the sugar bowl, her eyes alight with pride.

I nod with a smile filled with unconcealed pride of my own, meeting her eyes with steady resilience. Her reaction was exactly the assurance I needed and I feel even more justified in my actions.

My brow furrows as I take another sip of coffee and continue, "I was so fucking angry, you know? With him, yes... but more with myself. For letting myself get into yet another vulnerable position... *again*. When the fuck am I going to learn to recognize these warning signs for what they are?"

Dropping my chin, I tap my fingers absently on my coffee mug and sit in my anger for a minute, ruminating on my stupidity. Furious with my ignorance and my goddamn trusting nature. My insistent naivete in believing his intentions had been good, when all the warning signs were right there all along, practically screaming at me to pay attention.

But then I feel the tension in me ebb, when I think about what I chose to do to let go of some of that fury and at that, my wicked smile returns.

"I was so pissed, I just needed to hit something, so I went to the dojo to... I don't know...," I shrug absently, "just work out some of my anger—except, well... I ended up kind of having a private lesson... with Rogan..." I let my words trail off.

When I lift my eyes and I'm met with Kya's gaping stare my grin widens at her awestruck expression—sitting back in her chair, eyebrows raised and hands planted out wide on the table.

She whistles, long and low.

"Wow... A private lesson, huh? With the Duke?" Her eyes brighten, her smile returning to her face.

"And did he? Help you... work out some of your anger?" She asks teasingly, her tone dripping with innuendo, little knowing how right she actually is.

Rolling my lips between my teeth to try to hold back my giggle, she throws back her head and laughs, leaning forward to grab the french press.

"Right then." She declares, refilling my coffee mug and pushing the sugar bowl over beside it. "I think you need to get to telling me everything about last night, hun. And don't skip any of the good bits!"

Sitting back into her chair, she wraps her fingers around her mug and settles in while I prepare to tell her all the details of my night with the Duke.

Stirring a spoonful of sugar into my almost overflowing mug of very strong coffee, I take a deep breath, preparing to confide in my dearest friend about things I never dreamed could happen to me.

Chapter 39

Cole

I arrive at the bookshop to see Hannah nuzzling into the palm of a tall, familiar figure.

Rogan.

The smile that paints itself across my face is starting to feel like a welcome friend as I stop and just watch them for a moment—the way the watery winter sunlight seems drawn to him and the natural warmth he radiates as he runs his hand down Hannah's neck. Athena weaves her lanky body between his legs and he stoops down to smooth along her flank. She lets out a little chirp when she spots me standing off to the side.

Following her curious gaze, Rogan lifts his head. The moment our eyes meet, there's a shift in him, his body visibly tensing and relaxing at the same time. But it's when he smiles, I feel that same shift in me. The strangest combination of a thrill of excitement mixed with a soothing calm. I have to look away, suddenly needing to catch my breath.

Get a grip, Cole.

I swallow down my nerves and force myself to lift my gaze back up to him, only to find he hasn't looked away.

Embarrassment coloring my cheeks, I lift my hand in a timid wave.

If possible, his smile beams even brighter and he waves back, standing back up to his full height. Giving the donkey's neck one more gentle pat, he makes his way over to me.

He's not dressed in his usual attire. No crisp dress shirt and perfectly pressed slacks. No running gear, showing off all his finely toned muscles. Instead, he's wearing a beat-up pair of running shoes, a sweatshirt with a frayed hole near the neckline and paint splashes decorating the sleeves. But it's the worn gray sweatpants that make my mouth go dry as he steps closer, each purposeful stride drawing my attention to the outline of his...

"Hello, Little Fawn."

"Hi," I croak, my voice catching in my throat as if I haven't spoken in days. I swallow my nerves and try again.

"Hi." I utter softly, the word now clear, but fading to a whisper as his hand gently cups my face, his thumb stroking tenderly across my cheek.

I automatically lean into his touch, the bright scent of bergamot and spice, an instant comfort.

His gaze softens as he looks down at me. He wraps his hand around my waist, pulling me in close enough to feel the rise and fall of his chest, the warmth of his body radiating right through his clothes.

My legs go weak and I sink into him, losing myself in his smokey steel gaze. I have no idea how much time passes as we stand there in each other's arms.

Finally, remembering why I've come to the bookshop in the first place today, I blink out of my lust-fueled fog and ease out of his hold. He releases me without question, his fingers lightly trailing along my body with quiet reluctance as I step away.

I clear my throat and try to keep my voice calm and light as I move past him toward the door of the shop.

"So, what brings you here today?" I ask, pulling the keys from my pocket and slipping them into the lock.

"Brick told me you had some tradies coming today."

"Tradies?" I ask, arching a curious brow as I turn to look over my shoulder at him. I twist the key and push the door open.

He smiles sweetly, a spark of realization in his eyes at his choice of words.

"Tradies, you know... tradespeople. Plumbers, electricians..." He explains, chuckling softly.

"Ohhh!" I laugh, slapping my palm lightly against my forehead. "Tradies! Got it!" I roll my eyes and grin back at him as I step into the foyer, logging yet another

British idiom into my mental notes. I have to admit, it's probably been one of the most interesting things, learning all these little tidbits about this wonderful world I now call home.

"Well, thank you for the language lesson," I tease, "but that still doesn't explain why you're here." I say, grateful the dim interior hides my face—so he can't see just how completely beside myself I am at his unexpected visit. Honestly, I think he could tell me he was here just to be a nuisance, and I'd still be overjoyed to be with him right now.

"Thought I'd come by to see if I could give you a hand."

He lifts a tool bag from beside the door, giving it a shake, the tools clanking together lightly, then follows me inside.

He closes the distance between us as the door snicks shut behind him. Lowering his tools down to the floor, he brings his arm around my waist, pulling me against him, pressing his body against mine as he slowly rises. The heat of his whispered breath sends chills across my skin as he brushes his lips against my ear.

I can hear the smile in his voice as he whispers, "You've seen how handy I can be with your plumbing."

I suck in a breath, his double meaning all too clear and my heart starts to gallop in my chest as the heat of his body sears my back.

Thank God for the darkened room. I know my face has got to be a bright shade of scarlet, but I settle back against him, eternally grateful for his strong grip around my waist, since I have to squeeze my thighs together so tightly, I can barely stand.

His hands move over my body, the tips of his fingers grazing the bare skin beneath my shirt, and I melt into him.

"What time are they due to arrive?" He purrs into my ear, his breath hot against my skin as he trails his lips along my neck, his hands moving smoothly across my body.

"Nine..." I breathe, leaning back into him, my eyes fluttering closed. I slip my fingers around his neck, threading them into his hair, pulling him closer with each tease of his lips across my skin. There's nothing I want more in this moment, than to savor this feeling, wishing we could stay like this forever.

"Mmmm...Good." He growls, spinning me in his arms. He tilts my chin up, bringing my eyes to his, and I swear I feel the intensity of his gaze in my soul.

His lips brush against mine, so soft, so tender—pulling an aching sound from deep within me. He presses his growing desire against my belly as his tongue gently traces my lips, parting them to tangle with mine. Teasing at first, then more urgently as he deepens the kiss. His hands stroke along my body, softly, reverently—gentle yet urgent touches, showing me just how desperately he craves me. Making me realize just how desperately I crave him in return.

He leans into the kiss, slowly walking me backward, further into the bookshop.

"I've missed you." He whispers against my mouth, breaking the kiss only to move his lips down my neck. His hands curl into my jacket, absently tugging at the fabric. Finding the bare skin beneath my shirt, his fingers flex, dimpling my flesh.

"Rogan, I...," I breathe, my thoughts a jumble while I desperately fist my fingers into his shirt, gasping and pulling him closer as his tongue trails along my collar bone, "but..." I suck in a sharp breath as he nips lightly at the skin of my neck, "the workers... will be here... any minute."

"I don't care." He pants, his kisses turning frantic. "I need you, Cole. I'll never get enough of your lips," a heated kiss, "your body," he grips my ass firmly, kneading it gently, "your taste..." his head dips, his tongue trailing along my neck, his teeth lightly grazing my skin.

He lifts me, wrapping my legs around his waist.

"Rogan!" I squeak and giggle as he hurries us into one of the alcoves between the bookshelves and settles me down onto his lap, trapping his hard length tightly between us.

His arms wrap around me, holding me to him, as his talented mouth and tongue dance along the column of my throat, briefly finding my lips again only to work his way back down to my chest, seconds later.

I push out of my jacket and let it drop to the floor. He pauses just long enough to grab the back of his collar, tugging his shirt off over his head, then tosses it down beside my jacket.

I lean back to admire the freshly revealed, solid wall of muscles that had been hidden beneath his ratty old sweatshirt—the whorls of his tattoos rising and falling rapidly with each breath. I trace along the lines of one of them, my touch barely grazing his skin.

Goosebumps rise in the wake of my touch and I feel his eyes on me. Realizing I've lost myself in the sheer beauty of his form, I smile at him to find him watching me with ravenous hunger. The gray of his eyes has all but disappeared, swallowed up by his pupils, his desire consuming them.

The look of want in his eyes sends a thrill through me, empowering me with a sudden surge of bravery. I slide my fingers along one of the designs that wraps over his shoulder and down across the muscled wall of his chest, then lower my head to trail the tip of my tongue lightly along the thick line of ink.

He breathes in sharply, his eyes falling closed. His fingers dig into my hips as he pulls my center down against his hard length. The pressure does untold things to me when he hits just the right spot, a rush of wetness soaks my panties and I can't hold back the moan.

"Cole..." His voice is a pained whisper, an urgent plea.

The way he comes undone beneath my touch only emboldens me to keep going.

"Hmm?" I hum against his skin and continue to run my tongue along his chest and neck, alternating between kissing and licking his heated flesh, savoring the taste of him on my tongue.

"Cole...fuck, Cole..." my name becomes a reverent chant as he drags my center against himself again and again, harder each time.

His obvious need fuels me and, growing bolder still, I grip his shoulders and slowly start to rock my hips against him, testing the feeling.

It's divine. I do it again... and again, until I'm moving faster, chasing that delicious friction only he has ever made me feel. I want more of it.

I want more of him.

Locking my eyes with his, I lean in, kissing him again, then begin to rock myself against him more urgently.

"That's it, Cole." He watches the point where our bodies meet, his hands locked on my hips, gripping me and holding me close, pulling and pushing in time with each roll of my hips. "That's it. Ride me. Take what you need from me, Cole. I'm yours."

He lifts his hips, meeting me roll for roll, thrust for thrust, dragging his rock-hard cock against my throbbing center. I feel all of his rigid length, the thin layers of fabric, all that separates us. He wraps his arm around my waist, pulling me in close, lifting and pushing, thrusting and grinding in perfect time with me.

"Oh Jesus, Cole... fuck yes. You feel so fucking incredible and I'm not even inside you yet." He groans, burying his face into my neck as he grinds himself against my center. I feel that now familiar tingle starting to build, heat pulsing in my core. His words pushing me ever closer with each panted breath, each maddening grind of his cock against my aching center.

"Don't stop." I whisper, panting against his skin. "Please, Rogan... don't ever stop."

Our movements grow frantic, building, climbing to that enticing precipice, somehow so much higher than the one I'd reached on my own.

"Oh God, Rogan, I... I'm... ahhh!" I throw back my head and scream as my body crests the peak, diving off head first as my core pulses, pleasure coursing through me like fireworks exploding in the night sky.

"Oh, Jesus fuck! Cole!" He whimpers, crying out as his hips stutter beneath me. He presses himself up hard against me and groans into my neck as his cock pulses and throbs between us.

Locked in each other's arms and breathing hard, we slowly settle back to Earth. I snuggle my head against his neck, lightly stroking my fingers against the skin of his chest, his hold on me never loosening.

I feel him swallow hard, his chest still heaving. His eyes are locked between us as he stares at the darkening fabric of his gray sweatpants, his cheeks a bright pink.

Sensing my eyes on him, he lifts his dazed stare and smiles sheepishly.

"Well then…" he chuckles softly, "that's something that hasn't happened to me since I was a lad." He runs a shaky hand through his hair, giving it a disheveled look that still somehow looks absolutely perfect and blows out a long breath.

"Looks like I'll be needing a fresh pair of sweats before those tradies get here, huh?" His smile is sweet and boyish and all at once a deep wave of affection washes over me for this man.

Grinning widely, I giggle and snuggle back into him, his large arms pulling me tightly against his chest in a warm embrace.

"Thank you for *coming* today." I snicker playfully into his neck, my tone dripping with innuendo.

"You cheeky little shite!" he says grinning widely.

He tickles my sides until we end up tumbling onto the floor, both of us laughing hard. He peppers my entire face with kisses, until inevitably they turn heated once more. We kiss until there's a knock at the door as the first of the tradies arrives for the day.

Chapter 40

Cole

After pecking one more, tiny kiss to the tip of my nose, Rogan strides confidently past the tradie standing in the doorway. The man's eyes widen at the darkened material by his groin. Rogan smirks and gives him a cocky salute then, without saying a word, takes off along the trail to jog back to the Manor to grab a fresh pair of sweats.

The man's wide eyes shift from Rogan's retreating form, back to me, a questioning expression on his face. My cheeks flame, but I offer him nothing in the way of an explanation. Instead, I bite back my grin and usher him toward the kitchen where the actual plumbing awaits maintenance.

The rest of the tradies arrive, setting to work immediately. When Rogan returns he finds me sorting through a stack of paint chips, comparing the colors as I hold them up to the sunlight. He steps up close behind me, the warmth of his body grazing my back and I immediately close my eyes and lean back against him.

"So, what's next?" he asks, resting his big hands on my shoulders, his thumbs stroking gentle circles along the back of my neck as he glances around the room. His hands feel divine on my skin.

Will I ever get enough of this man's hands on my body?

Dropping my head back, I tip my chin up to look at him. His gray eyes sparkle as he meets my gaze and I lose myself for a moment.

My eyes track over him, admiring his features—his strong jaw, the dark lines of his perfectly kept beard, the arch of his brow, the sharp angles of his cheekbones, the warm pools of liquid mercury staring back at me—I practically feel weightless, like I'm floating within them.

I suck my bottom lip between my teeth and his eyes drop to my mouth, following the movement. His pupils blow wide and his grip on my shoulders tightens. He breathes in deeply and licks his lips.

I blink, straightening quickly as I realize how lost we've gotten in each other again. Stepping out of his hold, I move over to the supplies. I try to clear my head by clearing my throat and stoop down to grab a broad brush.

"Eh-hm... Umm... painting. We... we umm, we need to paint." I stammer, finally coming back to my senses... somewhat.

"Painting?" He takes the brush, lifting an eyebrow, a sly smirk still playing at the corner of his lips. "And what, pray tell... will we be painting, Little Fawn?"

I tip my head toward the back of the bookshop, where the dimmest corners lurk beneath a solitary hanging bulb. Glancing in the direction I've indicated then back to me, he twirls the paintbrush between his long fingers as a slow, devious smile spreads across his face.

"And... will you be joining me?" He asks, taking measured steps, closing the distance between us. His voice is low and smooth, but there's an awareness in his posture—his eyes flicking occasionally to where the men are working, noting just how much we're not alone. His words are restrained, but I know exactly what he wants to say.

What I want him to say.

He wraps his arm around my waist, pulling me against him, and feathers the edge of the bristles lightly along my cheek, trailing the brush slowly down my neck, his eyes heating as they follow its descent.

My core pulses at the ravenous look in his eyes and I tilt my head, giving him better access to my neck.

"Mmm hmm," I nod, glancing between him and the workmen in the next room. "Give me five minutes to sort out the *tradies.*"—his smile sparkles at my use of his slang term— "and I'll be right with you."

I lift up onto my toes and brush a quick kiss to his lips, his mouth chasing mine as I lower back down. I grin up at him with a devious smile of my own, then turn out of his arms to head toward the kitchen.

"The paint's already down there." I call back over my shoulder.

My grin widens when I see the hunger in his stare, his eyes planted firmly on my ass as he watches me walk away.

"Cole, darling...," he calls after me, his eyes tracking my movements.

"Don't be too long."

A tingle of giddiness snakes up my spine and I give him a quick nod and hurry off to go talk with the workmen.

The rest of the day passes in a whirlwind of activity. The workmen move through their tasks while Rogan and I take to the walls, painting the bookshop a soft, minty green—cool, calming, a space where hopefully, readers can come to enjoy themselves, relax and just be.

As we work, we talk, the conversation flowing with a natural ease, as if we've known each other for years instead of just a few short months. He asks about my plans for the bookshop, about what changes I'm thinking about making. Then he tells me what he'd have done with it if Grandpa Jesse had agreed to sell it to him.

"Outdoor activity center?" I pause mid-stroke, looking down at him from my perch atop the ladder as he skillfully paints around the light switch.

Looking up from his work, he nods, "Yeah, it just makes good business sense with the Wye right here." He says, gesturing in the direction of the river just beyond the garden in front of the bookshop.

"Really? So what activities would you run?" I ask, my curiosity tugging at me.

"Canoeing, mostly," he replies, turning back to refocus on his task. "Rock climbing, kayaking, cycling. You know..." he says, shrugging one large shoulder as he looks back up to me, his gray eyes finding mine, that easy smile playing at the corners of his mouth, "the usual sort of thing."

Stepping down the ladder to refill my paint cup, my foot slips off the third rung from the top. My arms start to pinwheel, but there's no stopping my fall. Fully expecting to go crashing to the floor, all I can do is brace for impact, but before I hit, Rogan is there, one big hand gripping my thigh, the other on my waist.

Realizing too late I've been saved from falling, instinct overrides logic and I grab for something—anything to stop my fall. I grip onto his shoulders, but failing to release the paint brush I'd been wielding, I end up streaking a long mint green stripe down the side of Rogan's face.

It's at that moment, my heart stalls.

I've marked him. Painted him. Made a mess—*on his face*. Heart hammering, I quickly pull away from him, the paint brush slipping from my fingers and clattering to the floor. I clamp my hands over my mouth, my eyes going wide with terror as I see the evidence of my crime taunting me across his skin.

I'll be punished. No, no, no, no, no! Fuck! I'm fucking dead!

What the fuck is wrong with you, Nicole? Look at what you've done! This is a two-thousand-dollar suit and you've fucking ruined it, you clumsy bitch! How are you going to pay for this, you worthless cunt? On. Your. Knees...

"Oh my God, Rogan I'm so sorr..."

My words fall away entirely as he streaks a cold, wet line of paint up the side of my face. Shock freezes me in place and my eyes flare wide with surprise, my mouth gaping open like a fish out of water.

He steps forward, wrapping an arm around my waist to pull me into him, until there's barely a hair's breadth between us. His fingers tuck under my chin, tilting my face up, his touch light but commanding and my mouth snaps shut.

"Now, what did I say about apologizing, Little Fawn?" His voice playful, though he deepens his tone.

"N-not to." I stutter.

"Mmm hmmm." He purrs, pulling me tighter against him. I feel my nerves ease and my body relaxes into him.

He's not Cain.

His mouth lowers toward mine, and now my heart is racing for an entirely different reason. Anticipating the kiss, I smile softly up at him and close my eyes, but instead of his lips, I feel a cold, wet blob of paint streak right down the center of my nose.

Shocked, my eyes fly wide open.

"Oh my God! Rogan!" I squeal, giggling as I push out of his arms, wiping at my face with my sleeve. He's laughing so hard, he has tears in his eyes as he backs away, his whole body shaking as he tries to catch his breath.

"You started it!" He gasps between fits of laughter.

I turn my back to him, unable to stop the grin from taking over my whole face.

I work to school my expression, stooping down to pick up my paint brush and try to make my voice sound serious and calm.

"You're right, I suppose I did..." I shrug, nonchalantly and walk over and dip my brush into the bucket of paint, then move back toward the wall I'd been painting.

"And I'm also going to finish it." I spin... swiping fresh paint across his shirt, an arc of mint green splattering across his tattered sweatshirt.

Then... It's war.

Brushes, hands, streaks of color, giggling laughter and squeals of joy—sounds I didn't even realize I remembered how to make. They peel from me in waves as we playfully tussle between the shelves. Until finally, he catches me, pulling me into a tight embrace. We're both breathing hard, but his grin is brilliant, lighting up his whole face, an adorable dimple pulling into his cheek.

His eyes track over my face, tracing my smile. Our eyes meet and when I see the heat burning in his stare as he looks down at me, I have to lean into him harder, my legs going weak at the instant wave of desire, threatening to consume me.

Our chests rise and fall together, panting as the laughter fades, slowly shifting to something more. Swallowing hard, he leans down, lowering his mouth to mine and brushes a soft kiss against my lips.

He lowers us down onto the drop cloth in the darkest part of the bookshop, his kiss turning deeper, more urgent... like he hasn't kissed me in a hundred years.

His hands trace my body, slipping beneath my sweater. My fingers dig into his shoulders, then slide to his neck, threading through his hair, mindless of the sticky paint that's tangling into the strands.

"Safe word...," he murmurs against my lips, his beautiful face streaked with color, his eyes intense—heavy lidded with desire as the weight of his body settles between my legs.

"Mmmm... huh?" I mutter incoherently, lost to the feel of his lips and tongue on my skin.

"Your safe word, Cole. You remember it?" He repeats, his words coming fast as he drags his teeth lightly across my jaw, then moves his lips and tongue down my throat.

"S-Sundance," I stutter back, barely able to catch my breath, my hands gripping his neck.

"Good girl," that devilish smile playing on his lips as he moves further down my body, pushing my sweater up so his tongue can trail down the dip in my belly, before moving lower.

His hands stroke over me—my hips, my thighs. Kneading, feeling, smoothing up and down my heated flesh. My core pulses, that knowing ache building as his mouth continues to kiss and suck at the skin on my stomach, his tongue gliding across my hip to my belly, grazing the hem of my leggings.

His fingers curl into the waistband and he lifts his eyes to mine, never stopping the movements of his magical tongue and lips.

"Tell me Cole... tell me you want me to taste you." His voice is a rough plea, needing permission, refusing to go any further without my approval.

Flicking a quick glance to the entrance of the bookshop, confirming we're still alone back here, I give him a shallow nod, lifting my ass a bit so he can easily slip my leggings off of me.

Permission granted he wastes no time stripping them from my body, and then I'm gasping while that clever mouth of his sends me back to that place where I no longer know whether up is down, left is right or what my friggin' name is.

But I don't need to know my name when his name is the only one I want to know. When it's his name on my lips as his tongue delves deep into my core, feasting on me like a starved man. And it's his name I groan as he brings me to the height of pleasure again and again, in between the bookshelves of my shop.

"Rogan..."

Chapter 41

Cole

Going to work in the bookshop starts to take on a new shape after that and I find myself giddily anticipating going there each day. Rogan's guise of *'helping'* with the DIY projects is fooling absolutely no one, but I'm certainly not about to complain when each project inevitably leads to more indecent activities in the darkened back corners between the shelves.

His hands and mouth seek out my skin and before long each task gets forgotten, turning instead into a heavy petting session where I completely lose myself in his touch—the shadowed alcove quickly becoming one of my favorite places in the whole shop.

Zavier hasn't shown his face since the night of our *'date'*, thank God! I guess he at least has enough sense to keep his distance from the bookshop and the pub after what he pulled. I really don't know how I'm going to handle seeing him again.

In a village this size though, I'm sure it's only a matter of time before I'm going to have to face him. But that's a worry for another day, I suppose.

Even though I've been expecting him, I still struggle to hide my disappointment when I open the door the next morning to find Brick instead of Rogan on the other side. He greets me with his usual wide, easy-going grin as he massages his fingers into the fur of the snuggly little tortoise shell purring wildly in his arms.

While Rogan had told me he was going to have to go to London for a couple days on business, there's no denying the pang of longing that twists in my chest at his absence today. I'd be lying if I said I wasn't quickly becoming addicted to our daily rendezvous between the bookshelves, his gentle, intoxicating touch—my drug of choice.

Brick, ever observant, notes the slight falter in my smile when I open the door, but instead of taking offense, he effortlessly switches on his debonair charm.

Doffing an imaginary cap, he sweeps into a low, exaggerated bow, releasing Athena as he nears the ground with a gentle flourish.

"Ahh, fair maiden! Fear not! Though Sir Rogan, your knight in shining armor, has had to travel far to tend to wars untold across the lands, I am here in his stead to be at your beck and call, m'lady!"

I burst out laughing at his over the top mockingly chivalrous antics. Adopting a similar persona, I step back from the doorway, theatrically gesturing him into the bookshop with an exaggerated twirl of my wrist. Straightening back to his full height, he glides past me, his grin broad and sparkling as he smoothly shifts back to his true self.

"Hey, Red!" He says with a wink. "Ready to get started?"

Before long, I can clearly see just how adept Brick is at DIY and why Rogan didn't hesitate to send him in his place. He scales ladders with ease, secures heavy bookshelves to the walls as if they weigh practically nothing, and seems to know how to do just about every single thing that needs doing without requiring anyone's assistance.

I watch him as he balances on a ladder, installing the new lighting at the back of the shop. My cheeks warm when it occurs to me he's brightening up the little hideaway where The Duke and I tend to spend the majority of our time when we're not working to improve the bookshop.

He glances down from his perch atop the ladder to find me watching him.

"Would you mind handing me a Philips screwdriver from my bag there, Red?"

My cheeks flame, even though there's no way he could possibly know where my thoughts had just been. I smile awkwardly, then dip down to dig through his bag to locate the tool.

"You're pretty handy."

"Well, thank you for noticing." He beams proudly down at me as he skillfully twirls the wire cutters in his hand like a miniature baton.

"These are the kinds of things Ro and I worked on together back in the Army. He's a whiz at plumbing and carpentry—I always had more of a knack for the electrical side: wiring, motors, that sort of thing." He pauses, a shadow gliding across his usually jovial face.

"Came in handy more times than I can count..." The light in his brown eyes dims as his gaze grows distant—his thoughts slipping sideways—down some darker path.

My curiosity piques at his mention of their time together in the Army. Rogan hasn't told me more than a few bits and pieces, and whenever he gets to the darker parts of his tales, his eyes take on the same look as Brick's have now... going distant as he grows quiet.

I study him as he fiddles absentmindedly with the tool in his hand, seeming a bit lost in his thoughts and can't help but wonder exactly what he and Rogan have been through together that would cause the same distant look to creep in for both of them.

I open my mouth to ask more, but snap it shut again when his eyes lift back to me, deciding it's probably none of my business.

"Seems like you're a good team." I say instead, smiling at him warmly. He smiles back, his usual playful glint returning as if it never left and he gives the wire cutters in his hand another twirl. But I swear I see a soft look of appreciation when his eyes lift to mine this time. A silent thank you for not pushing too hard.

"Yeah," his voice is stronger, more boastful... more... *'Brick'*. His pride in what he and Rogan have accomplished together, then and even now, written clearly across his face.

"The best there is!" He agrees, giving me a wink. "Now hand me that screwdriver, would ya? I think we're nearly done here!"

"Yes, Sir!" I tap the tool lightly to my forehead in a mock salute before passing it up to him, earning me one of his hearty laughs I've come to look forward to whenever he's around.

I place the tool in his outstretched hand, his focus shifting back to the wiring harness he'd been securing and I pull out a stack of carpet samples to review.

"Hey, are you getting hungry?" I ask offhandedly holding a swatch up to the sunlight streaming in through the window, "Because, Kya said she'd be stopping over with some lunch later today and...,"

A metallic clatter cuts through the air and I nearly jump out of my skin—the carpet sample I'd been holding flipping right out of my hand.

I glance over in time to see Brick scrambling after the screwdriver as it tumbles out of his grip, hitting every single rung of the ladder on its way down, making the metal steps clang loudly with every bounce. It clatters to the floor and he hurries down the ladder after it, muttering something under his breath and running a hand through his hair, stooping to reclaim the fallen tool with a little too much force.

I bite back my smile and quickly bend down to pick up the carpet sample to hide the fact I've noticed his sudden lack of coordination at the mere mention of Kya's name. It's endearing, watching his reaction whenever she's nearby.

He clears his throat in an attempt to regain his composure. "Eh... uh... okay, cool... yeah, I could eat." He stammers, then makes his way back up the ladder and gets right back to his work, like nothing happened.

As promised, Kya arrives with lunch a little while later, Grumbl trundling along at her side and we huddle together under a blanket at one of the picnic tables in front of the bookshop.

We chat with each other, enjoying the meal she's brought, her wicker basket practically overflowing with delicious foods—sausage rolls, drumsticks, salad, and cheese sandwiches. When she flourishes a bottle of sparkling fruit juice, we laugh together, drinking it like it's the finest champagne, watching Hannah methodically crop the low grass nearby.

Once we've finished eating, we pack up the remains of the picnic and prepare to head back inside, the air getting too cold to remain sitting outside as the late Autumn sun begins to dip behind the trees.

Brick carries the basket into the bookshop for us and Kya and I stand, working together to fold the large blanket.

Our backs are to the road when we hear the sound of gravel crunching beneath boots. Turning toward the sound, every muscle in my body freezes as Zavier strolls up to the fence. He slows, narrowing his frigid stare right on me.

Without hesitating, Kya moves to my side, wrapping one arm protectively around me, tucking me behind her, just as Brick steps back out of the bookshop–bristling as he takes in the scene before him. In a flash, he moves, putting himself in front of both of us—his body effectively blocking us from Zavier's view.

Brick flares out his shoulders, setting his feet wide, his hulking stature massive in comparison to the man standing in the road. He somehow looks taller and broader than I've ever seen him before.

"Zavier…," his tone is measured—calmer than his body language would imply, yet laced with warning. "I think you best be on your way now."

His words sound like a suggestion, but the way he's looking at Zavier, clearly doesn't offer even the slightest bit of room for discussion, his hard stare locked on Zavier's icy one.

Silence hangs in the air like a weighted cloud as Zavier considers his next move. His jaw ticks, his eyes like glacial shards of ice as he looks past Brick to me and Kya, then back to Brick again. His hands loosely fisted at his sides, he flexes his fingers a few times before taking a careful step to the side, setting his sights squarely back on me.

"Cole… I wanted to…" he starts, taking a single step forward, his words trailing off as Brick visibly tenses, giving him a warning tilt of his head, the movement a silent threat, *'don't you dare come another step closer'.*

Zavier takes a cautious step back, snapping his mouth shut, his eyes narrowing at Brick as he swallows down his rage. He flicks one last penetrating glare past Kya, his searing gaze, slicing into me like a blade.

"I'll be seeing you, Cole." He says cooly, his tone laced with venom, holding my stare for one more solid beat. Then, spinning on his heel, he finally leaves, heading back in the direction of his farm.

I lean into Kya and blow out a long, shuttering breath. Both Kya and Brick visibly relax, then Kya spins to look at me and gently grips my shoulders.

"You alright, hun?" She asks, her mother-hen protectiveness in full effect.

With my attention still locked on the road, even though Zavier has long since disappeared from view, I give her a shallow nod.

Brick makes his way over to the picnic table and picks up the crumpled blanket from the ground where we'd dropped it.

"Oh, by the way, Cole...," his voice, calm and conversational, as if none of that just happened, "Rogan's back later tonight, and he asked me to invite you to the dojo..." he refolds the blanket with ease with just a few practiced flips of the fabric, "said something about... private lessons?"

Kya's eyes go comically wide, her face shifting from concern to a playful, knowing smirk and just like that, the intense fear I'd just felt melts away, instantly replaced by excitement for Rogan's return. I never would have thought it could be so simple, but with her and Brick stepping up, literally putting themselves between me and danger, I feel like I can breathe now.

She grabs my hands and giggles, tugging me with her into the bookshop.

"Wait, what did I miss?" Brick asks, arching a puzzled brow as he follows in behind us.

"Nothing Brick..." Kya and I sing-song in unison, laughing even harder at his confusion.

Kya stays and helps around the bookshop the rest of the afternoon with Brick going out of his way to help her with her tasks, even when she clearly has them under control. And for whatever reason she lets him, her smile bright as they banter playfully while they work.

Grumbl goes scuttling by with the corner of a drop cloth held between his teeth, while Brick clambers awkwardly behind trying to catch him, throwing both Kya and I into fits of laughter.

Kya steps in to help as Grumbl easily evades Brick's pursuit, yapping happily from beneath a table, just out of Brick's reach.

I feel a comfortable warmth settle over me as I watch them laugh with one another and I realize the smile on my lips is starting to feel familiar, comfortable. I take a moment to let myself just be here, taking in the ease of this new life as the rest of the day unfolds around me, settling deep in my bones as I wonder again—how this all happened.

How I finally ended up lucky enough to have friends like this.

Chapter 42

Cole

Rogan's invitation to the dojo was indeed for private lessons, but not the kind I was expecting. He guided me through maneuver after maneuver, teaching me how to break out of different holds. Pinning me down in lots of different ways to show me how to disengage from each and every one, regardless of the size of my opponent.

We practiced for hours until I'd mastered each one, both of us drenched in sweat and panting from our exertion, but with my confidence soaring by the end of the night.

"Whoa..." I pant, wiping sweat from my brow.

"That was intense!"

"You know you'd cool down faster if you take your track jacket off." He suggests, fiddling with my zipper as he moves in close, his voice taking on a suggestive tone, the look in his eyes turning heated.

I feel my smile drop and swallow hard. I take a small step back and tug at my sleeves, pulling them down a little further on my wrists. My spine goes rigid at the thought of him seeing my scars and my heart hammers hard in my chest.

—broken china, soup splattered across the floor, sour whiskey on his breath...—

Somehow, I've managed to keep them covered up until now, our intimate times together never getting to the point of either of us being fully undressed.

At my unexpected retreat, a frown pinches between his brows, a concerned look immediately replacing the heat which had been there only seconds ago.

"What is it, Cole? You don't have to hide anything from me. You know that, right?" Worry coats his words, but his eyes are warm, coaxing.

—his fist, unrelenting, his boot slamming into my ribs, his vicious grip tearing my hair…—

"I…eh um… It's…" I blow out a frustrated breath, as I stammer, trying to make the words come out. There's a part of me that wants to tell him the truth of what lies beneath the fabric of my sleeves, but panic seizes in my chest and the words just won't come.

—the taste of copper, the room spinning, a flash of metal, searing pain, blood, blood, blood… so much fucking blood…—

I grip my hair, pinching my eyes shut. I grit my teeth and shake my head, trying to make the visions stop.

"No…," The word is a whisper if I even utter it aloud at all, lost in the horror of my memories. My whole body is shaking as hot tears wet my cheeks.

Rogan's warmth surrounds me as he steps in close, wrapping his arms around me, pulling me gently against him. I instinctively melt into his body, instantly comforted by his unwavering strength. His soothing touch, driving the visions away, almost as if they never existed at all.

"Shhh… it's alright, Little Fawn. You don't have to tell me anything you're not ready for."

He kisses the top of my head, the heat of his hand stroking soothingly up and down my back.

"Some other time then."

Nodding against his chest, I wrap my arms around him, sinking deeper into his embrace, reveling in the feel of his strength and warmth as he holds me in the safety of his arms.

"Thank you, Rogan. I will tell you… soon." I promise, even though I'm really not sure it's the truth. If I'm being honest with myself, I don't know if I'll ever be willing to let another man fully into my world.

Chapter 43

Cole

The scent of old ale and yesterday's gossip hangs in the air as I enter the quiet bar room the next afternoon. Every time I prepare for a new shift, I'm hit with a wave of eager anticipation for all the different people who will pass through the main doors or wander up from the ferry below.

I set about my opening routines; checking the restrooms are fully stocked, lighting the kindling in the large fireplace and checking we have enough wood to keep the fire burning well into the evening.

Then I restock the fridges with bottles of fruity ciders, wines and soft drinks and ensure we have enough chips—no wait, *crisps*, I remind myself with a smile—and nuts on display, as well as double checking the supplies in the box under the bar so we can quickly replenish the products on show as they begin to dwindle.

Greg lugs up a large case of prosecco from the basement and sets it down on the bar top with a grunt. I give the room a final once over, mentally checking off each item needing to be done. Once satisfied, I give Pete a nod and he unlocks the front and back doors.

I'm hit with a small frisson of excitement every time I hear those locks click open, eagerly anticipating another afternoon of chats with Old Tom, of meeting visiting families on the terrace, of slipping effortlessly into a smooth rhythm of filling drink orders while enjoying the company of new friends.

Of Rogan... the weight of his tender gaze following me as I work, his watchful presence, warm and comforting. The thought of his heated stare sends a tug low in my belly and I suck in a deep breath at the welcome pull.

Trying halfheartedly not to let my mind wander to the hidden corners of the pub, imagining he might coax me into one, his fingers and tongue doing wonderful things—the mere thought makes my pussy clench and my toes curl...

"Ow bist, my butty?" Old Tom's cheerful greeting shakes me from my reverie. "I think that old glass is clean enough, love, don't you?"

He chuckles, his gap-toothed grin breaking across his withered face, his clouded blue eyes scrunching merrily at the corners.

I shoot him a quick smile and hastily tip the pint glass I'd been polishing within an inch of its life, under the Butty Bach tap.

"Usual?" I ask, shooting him a wide grin while pulling down the tap. He nods, his eyes twinkling as he removes his flat cap, cottony wisps of gray hair sticking up in every direction. He leans against the bar, steadying himself as he settles gingerly onto the barstool. I finish pulling the pint and carefully hand it over the bar to him.

"Now that..." he takes the glass from me gratefully and holds it up to the light reverently, "is a perfect pour, my dear!" His eyes linger admiringly on the rich amber liquid for another moment before bringing the glass to his puckered lips.

He takes a long sip, closing his eyes, then lets out a long, satisfied sigh as he lowers the glass down to the bar, a bit of foam lining his upper lip. He reaches for the bowl of nuts and I note an obvious tremor in his hand. I watch as he cracks open a few peanut shells, his gnarled fingers quaking as he struggles to liberate the nuts from their casings. He smiles warmly at me when he catches me watching him, then chuckles.

"You remember that first pint you pulled, Cole?" He asks, his tone teasing, a playful smirk on his lips.

"Ughh... don't remind me!" I groan theatrically, pretending to hide my feigned shame behind my bar towel. "The pint that almost never was!"

I roll my eyes comically, both of us falling into good-natured laughter at the memory of my chaotic first day behind the bar.

He gives me a kind hearted wink, still chuckling and I grin back at him, moving down the bar to serve the next customer.

The first few hours of my shift pass in a blur. As autumn gradually fades, winter nipping at its heels, the darkness of the early evenings brings people to the pub sooner than usual and the room fills up quickly. Though many still linger on the terrace, still a welcoming space, with the artificial warmth from the propane heat lamps, allowing them to enjoy a mercifully dry evening.

One such group includes four or five young men from the village, their happy voices and loud laughter drifting through the doorway, adding to the cheery air that seems to fill this space so completely.

I am happily engrossed with serving my customers while listening to bits of conversations, checking in on Old Tom, and making a mental note to clear table four. I'm pleasantly distracted, until the sound of a loud, deep voice carries over the din, shattering my sense of calm and making the hairs on the back of my neck rise up as an icy chill trickles down my spine.

Zavier.

Daring to look up, I'm instantly met with the arctic blue of his eyes as they lock directly onto mine, burning into me.

I swallow.

All the easy happiness and the sense of safety and comfort I was feeling just moments ago, dissipates as quickly as frost brought near a flame.

In a few long strides he crosses the room, strolling straight over to me, his grin wide—cocksure and bold.

"Hiya, Cole..." The sound of his voice slithers down my spine like the cold underbelly of a snake—dark, foreboding.

"Zavier," I reply, my tone cold and clipped.

His smile falters ever so slightly, but then returns, his eyes piercing into me like frozen daggers. The way they rake over my body makes my skin crawl. I can't stop myself from retreating a single step as he approaches. I suck in a breath and clear my throat as he leans against the bar.

"Eh em... What can I get you?" I ask, trying to keep my tone as professional and clinical as possible, while making a show of wiping down the already clean bar.

His lips curl into a knowing sneer, his eyes never leaving my face, his cold smile never reaching his eyes. There's a long pause before he answers, then finally he says, "Give me a whiskey and a pint of Stella."

His order is deliberately rude and it grinds at my temper.

I'm so done putting up with men treating me like shit. Even though I want to smack that smug smile off his face, I give him a stiff nod and get to work pulling his lager and his shot of whiskey.

"Double," he instructs sharply as I press the glass under the optical. I close my eyes and blow out a slow breath, trying to hold on to the small remaining scraps of my patience.

Greg's watchful eye doesn't miss the interaction as he looks on from his end of the bar. His eyes flicker between me and Zavier, immediately reading the situation, his years as a pub owner giving him a keen sense of when something's amiss. He waves a finger between himself and me—an offer to take over serving Zavier.

I shake my head and try to give him a reassuring smile.

No, I can do this. I refuse to let him bully me.

I turn back to face Zavier and force a saccharine smile on my face, pushing the drinks over the polished dark wood surface toward where he's tapping a credit card on the bar. I pull out the card reader, happy to almost be done with him.

"So..." he begins as I type in his bill. "How've you been?"

I will not be bullied; I repeat to myself. *He's just gotta pay, and then he'll go away and I can breathe again...*

I look up, leaning my legs against the bar so he can't see them shaking.

"Fine." I keep my tone clipped and lace my response with as much frost as I can manage. I proffer the machine and wait as he taps his card against it.

But it beeps, an error code flashing on the screen.

The corner of his lips curl higher, his smug smirk deepening, knowing full well I'm stuck here with him for as long as it takes to complete this transaction. Moving slower than necessary, he inserts his card, typing in his code at a snail's pace.

It beeps again. Wrong PIN number.

"Oops," he says, sounding theatrically unapologetic, as a vicious grin slides across his face and lifts his shoulders in a mock shrug.

I grit my teeth and glare at him, losing my grip on my frustration with his antics, my anger starting to get the better of me. I repeat the process a third time, entering his bill again, then reoffer the machine and wait as he makes his third attempt to pay.

Time seems to stretch, the icy cold I was feeling before, has now turned to sweat. I can feel it track down my back as it rolls to the band of my skirt. I quickly wipe away the fine beads of moisture I feel forming on my upper lip, entirely aware he's still watching me.

The machine beeps with another error message.

"Damn, I'm just being so clumsy tonight, Cole." He drolls, removing his card again and handing the card reader back toward my outstretched hand.

Just as my fingers curl around the machine, his hand closes over mine, pinning it between the machine and his iron grip, holding me prisoner.

"See what you do to me?" He leans in, tugging me forward until I'm practically laying across the bar and forcing me onto the tips of my toes—his voice a low growl so no one else can hear his words as I try... and fail, to tug free from his grasp.

My heart hammers in my chest and it feels like the room contracts around me—my breath caged in what feels like a perpetual exhale, the sound of the crowd in the room muting, as his hand traps me in place.

"Let. Her. Go... NOW!"

With a whir, the room resets. Air rushes into my lungs, sharp and sudden, as a stronger, steadier hand, closes around Zavier's arm.

Familiar tips of dark ink just barely hidden beneath the sleeve of his shirt. Hands whose gentle touch have sent me reeling, spiraling into such bright, aching bliss I could almost believe heaven may be real after all. Fingers whose tender touch wiped away my tears and held me until I felt safe again.

Now they grip with intent.

I swear, I can almost hear Zavier's bones creak, as Rogan's grip cinches down, targeting those very same pressure points he showed me last night in the dojo.

The second Zavier's grip loosens on my hand, I rip it away, the machine clattering loudly to the bar top. I rub my hand across my apron as if trying to wipe off his touch.

Rogan's menacing glare is locked on Zavier, but when he speaks, it's to me, his voice hard but controlled.

"How much does he owe you, Cole?"

I glance between the two men, Rogan's unflinching hard stare and Zavier's seething glower. I grab the machine and glance down at the total—I have to work hard to keep my voice from shaking when I answer.

"£12.50"

"You have cash?" Rogan asks him quietly. Zavier seems to consider this for a moment, his bravado now somewhat diminished, his hand still crushed tightly in Rogan's unrelenting grip.

Finally, he nods, and awkwardly pulls out some notes one handedly from his wallet.

"Let's make it an even twenty shall we? Tip the lady, Zavier."

Zavier winces, snarling as Rogan's knuckles whiten, his grip tightening even more, his tone leaving no room for discussion.

Shooting me a scathing glare, Zavier tosses two ten-pound notes in my direction.

It's only then Rogan releases his wrist, giving him a hard shove.

Zavier stumbles, his arms pinwheeling before regaining his balance. Rogan plants himself in front of me, right where Zavier had been standing, then sliding his drinks down the bar with the side of his hand, effectively dismisses the seething man.

Zavier snatches the drinks and retreats toward a table near the door—only to spot Brick sprawled nearby, one arm draped lazily across the back of Kya's chair. His legs spread wide, clearly taking up more space than necessary, his posture loose, effortless—but his gaze is cold, pinned on Zavier with quiet precision.

With the slightest flick of his fingers, like he's shooing away a fly, Brick makes it clear... Zavier won't be sitting inside the pub tonight.

Zavier swallows, glancing between me and Rogan one more time, then back to Brick and Kya, before making a show of deciding perhaps the terrace is a better place to sit on this unexpectedly clement evening.

As soon as he disappears from view, Rogan turns his full attention to me. He studies me, my eyes locked on the door to the terrace and wringing the life out of the bar towel I've got twisted between my fists. He watches me, his fingers tapping out a slow, steady rhythm on the bar, as if weighing something unspoken.

"Be right back," he mutters, knocking his knuckles lightly on the bar top, then moves down the bar toward Greg.

I glance around the room and notice Pete isn't by the front door anymore. He's drifted over to the terrace instead. Even Old Tom has turned on his barstool, his watery eyes trained on the door Zavier exited through, his bushy eyebrows pulled together in a tight scowl.

Tears sting my eyes when I look around at all these people—people who didn't even know me a few short months ago, who are now here... *for me*. People who are looking out for me without any agenda other than they like, care for and maybe even... *love* me. The realization hits me like a truck and my eyes burn, unsure what to do with this new feeling of being secure, cared for... *protected*.

I drop my head into my hands and lean against the bar while I try to make sense of this, until I feel a warm hand smooth down my back.

I look up at him as the weight of his arm circles my waist and sink against his side, letting him guide me out from behind the bar. He leads me toward the front door, away from the terrace and the noise of the pub.

"Rogan, I can't go... I'm working," I begin, glancing back toward the busy bar area. But he keeps walking, hugging me closer to his side. His fingers brush under my chin coaxing my attention to him as we walk. He leans down and kisses me so tenderly, it makes everything else feel inconsequential, a wave of comfort settling over me like a warm blanket.

"Shhh, Little Fawn," he whispers against my lips. "That's what I was discussing with Greg. You're just having your half hour break a bit early tonight."

"Oh, okay." I sniff, smiling against his lips. His thumb glides softly across the line of my jaw, his eyes warm as he smiles down at me.

"And what did you have in mind for this half hour?" I ask, settling back against his side as we step into the parking lot. There's no denying there's a part of me needing him to touch me the way he has so many times now... but truthfully, my insides are so churned up—first with fear, then with the unfamiliar feeling of being safe and loved by other people and now whatever this feeling of elation is every time this man is near me. I honestly don't think I can handle anything more at the moment.

"We can do whatever you want, my...." He pauses, his breath catching in his throat.

My eyes search his, holding my breath as I let myself imagine how he might finish his thought, my heart clenching in my chest.

His smile softens and he clears his throat, his brows pinching ever so slightly, "my darling," he finishes, pecking a quick kiss to the tip of my nose.

I wrap my arms around his waist, then lean my head against his chest as we walk toward his car.

"Rogan," I whisper.

"Yes, Little Fawn?" The deep bass of his voice rumbles beneath my ear and I hold him tighter, pressing myself further into the warmth of his body.

"Would it be okay if we just... sit?"

He pulls back slightly, looking down at me, his face unreadable under the stars as they peer out from behind the clouds.

"Sit?" He repeats, a small smile playing at his lips.

My throat feels tight as I nod and I tuck myself back against his side, bracing myself for the inevitable anger I'm expecting, having rejected any potential intimacy. But finding my voice, I continue.

"Yeah, just sit. And..." I swallow hard, trying to hold onto my courage, "m-maybe... I don't know... do you think maybe you could just... hold me?"

He stops walking and slips his finger beneath my chin again, gently tilting my face until my eyes meet his.

"Little Fawn..." his gray eyes twinkle as bright as the stars as they meet mine, the moonlight reflecting off his dark hair. My breath catches at the sheer beauty of him, and I lose myself in his stare for a moment.

"There's literally nothing in this world I wouldn't do for you." He wraps his arms around me, holding me tight against his chest. I hear the gentle thrum of his heart through his jacket and nestle against him, releasing the long, slow breath I'd been holding onto for far longer than I'd realized.

We make our way over to one of the benches beneath the trees.

"Stay here. I'll be right back."

He jogs over to his car, returning a few moments later with a blanket he'd pulled from the trunk. He settles down next to me on the bench, wrapping it around us both.

There in the silence, our backs to the pub, his warm arm wrapped snuggly around my shoulders and my head tucked against his chest—he holds me.

Chapter 44

Rogan

After a long, slow kiss which leaves me aching, an unfamiliar yet welcome sense of hunger settles into me with a feeling I can't quite put into words.

She moves back behind the bar, lifting her fingers in a quick wave to me as she seamlessly slips back into her role of bartender, picking up on a conversation with Old Tom, laughing easily as Greg makes some sort of joke.

I can't help but watch her, losing count of how many times her eyes seek me out, of the way she transforms into something breathtaking, her beautiful face lighting up with a radiant smile every time she finds me in the crowd. Each time our eyes meet, a strange tightness pulls in my chest, the air in my lungs feeling insufficient. The only time I feel like I can breathe fully is when she's close to me. Only then do I feel... *whole.*

"You okay there, pal?" Brick teases me. Kya smirks beside him as she sips her drink—her little dog snoring happily across their feet.

"Fuck off," I volley back, smiling as I take a sip of my Diet Coke.

The three of us—well, four with the pup—sit chatting about everything and nothing. I rarely take my eyes off the mesmerizing barmaid who undoubtedly has me under her spell. But when I notice Brick stiffen, his back straightening, I snap my attention to where his gaze is locked on the terrace door, as Zavier walks back in.

"Next rounds on me." He declares, rising from his seat to stride purposefully toward the bar. He blatantly muscles in front of Zavier to start up a conversation with Cole, deliberately angling his broad body between them to block her from his view.

Zavier pins the back of Brick's head with a sullen glare, finally throwing his arms up in disgust and redirects his focus toward Greg to place his next order.

It doesn't escape my notice his orders have solely turned to glasses of whiskey, the lager now long forgotten–his inebriation now more obvious as he staggers back out to the terrace with his full glass in hand.

Glaring as I watch this fucking pig of a man stumble back out through the doorway, my molars grind together, my thoughts turning murderous as I envision getting my hands on him and...

"Ro..." Kya's gentle but firm voice breaks me out of the internal war I'd been waging with Zavier, her hand closing over the top of mine where I've got a napkin fisted so tightly, my knuckles have turned white.

"He's not worth it." She gives my hand a gentle squeeze, keeping her tone calm and reassuring.

She's right. Zavier Johnson is a fucking bottom feeder. He's not worth my time. But I swear to everything that's holy, if he ever goes near Cole again I'll...

"Rogan!" She barks, snapping me out of it again. She gives my hand another squeeze, encouraging me to release my fist.

She watches me carefully; her eyes locked on mine until I finally meet her stare. "Okay?"

I let out a long, slow breath down my nose, closing my eyes and forcing myself to calm, only opening them again once my self-control has returned.

I nod once. "Okay."

"She's fine, Ro," Brick states quietly as he sets our fresh round of drinks down on the table. "She's confident, happy and just about ready to wrap up her shift for the night."

He smiles over at me as he settles back into his seat next to Kya, draping his arm over the back of her seat. Grumbl well... grumbles, as Brick gently nudges the toe of his boot back under the pup's jowls.

I shoot a quick glance at the large clock behind the bar. In about twenty minutes, the last orders bell will be rung and I've already decided I'll be waiting for Cole to take her home when she's finished.

The bar has already started to empty. Old Tom left about an hour ago, after taking Cole's hand in his to place a kiss on her knuckles and tipping his cap toward her before disappearing out into the night. Her smiling gaze watched him depart and I shook my head, chuffing a laugh.

Don't tell me I have to compete with Old Tom Vaughn for Cole's affections? I muse humorously to myself.

The only people left are Kya, Brick and myself, as well as a rather large group of lads wandering in from the terrace, noisily shouting over one another about the score of some Rugby match as they make their way back toward the bar for a final round of shots.

I haven't seen Zavier for nearly an hour. Hopefully, the slimy prick has fucked off back to whatever hole he crawled out of.

Glancing once more at the clock, I stand. "I'm just off to the loo," I tell Brick. "I won't be long." I glance toward Cole and back to him, meeting his eyes. He nods, understanding.

Keep an eye on her.

When I return, I instinctively scan the room, seeking her out, but find she's nowhere in sight.

"Where is she?" I thunder at Brick, my heart rate ratcheting up as a sudden pang of panic surges through my veins.

"Ro..." Brick raises his hands as he lifts out of his seat. "I'm sure she's fine, mate! She just went out to the terrace to collect some glasses and..."

A scream carries over the loud voices of the men arguing at the bar followed by the sound of breaking glasses hitting the concrete floor of the terrace.

My blood turns to ice.

Without hesitation Brick and I move, leaving overturned chairs and tables in our wake. We rush past Pete, who's struggling to get through the crowd of men from the bar, now clamoring in the doorway of the terrace to see what's going on out there.

I slam my body toward the front of the crowd, frantically scanning the terrace. I look left, right, then back again, but I don't see her.

I rake my hand through my hair, my eyes wild with a combination of fear and rage, my chest heaving in quick, painful gasps.

"There!" Brick finally shouts, pointing into a dark corner where a tall figure looms, the moonlight reflecting off his blonde hair, a small form struggling against his hold. Loose strands of her auburn hair sticking to the Artex on the wall, her shirt torn, hanging in tatters, his thigh thrust between hers, pinning her to the wall as his meaty hand gropes her...

Time slows to a crawl.

Struggling to push my way past the crowd, I see it all. The way he leans into her face, his hand tightly gripping her throat, squeezing her, forcing her to look up at him... I see the tears shining on her cheeks, the terror in her eyes, but there's something more there... *fury.*

Before I can make my way there, her hand snakes around his thumb and...

With a sharp yank—her own hand positioned perfectly at a pressure point I'd shown her only the night before—she twists his hand away, forcing his arm into an awkward angle, a surprised yelp tearing from his throat.

That's my girl, the more lucid side of my brain praises her. But the protective beast in me, the one currently ruling my decisions, imagines wrenching this fucker's arm clean off at the shoulder and ramming it straight up his ass...

Unrelenting, Cole slams her free hand down onto Zavier's elbow, forcing him away, driving him to his knees.

I push my way past the crowd, but it feels like I am moving through fog, through mud. Time somehow moves too slowly and too quickly all at once. I'm vaguely aware of Brick on my left, readying himself to step in if needed.

Just as I make my way there, she brings her knee up and lands it solidly under Zavier's chin. His head rocks back, straight into my waiting hand.

I grab a fistful of his hair and force him to his feet. With a quick glance behind him, I note Kya's made her way over to Cole and has her arm wrapped protectively around her, quickly leading her away.

Good.

Time settles back into its normal speed and then I move.

I hit him with a swift strike straight to his throat, slamming the ridge of my hand against his Adam's apple, hard enough to incapacitate him, but not take him out of commission. I want this piece of shit to hear my words.

I release my grip on his hair and give him a hard shove. He staggers back, his body slamming against the wall. Choking and spluttering, he grips his throat, wheezing as he tries to draw in a breath.

I step into him, grabbing a fistful of his shirt, pressing his back against the wall. I move in so close; he's forced to look up at me.

Nose to nose, I speak—my voice a low, menacing growl.

I enunciate each and every word. Every syllable said with slow, deliberate precision. There will be no confusion, no debate. This rotten fuck will get this through his thick skull if I have to drive it in there with my fist.

"If you ever even *think* about going near her again..."

I let the words hang in the air between us.

"I... will fucking... *gut you!*"

Zavier's throat works... his glare dropping from mine, fury blazing in his glassy eyes.

I feel Brick's hand settle on my shoulder, pulling me away.

Zavier grunts as I give him one last hard shove into the wall and turn to walk away.

"Hey Rogan," Zavier's venomous tone stops me in my tracks.

"Fuck you!"

I turn back to face him just as his fist slams into my cheek, rocking my head to the side.

I work my jaw from side to side and run my tongue along my bottom teeth, tasting copper. I spit the blood to the terrace floor, a slow smile gliding across my face and a low heat igniting in my gut. He's just thrown a flaming match into petrol.

"You know what, mate," Brick says, stepping back with his hands raised. "Go for it. Teach this stupid mother fucker a lesson."

Zavier laughs, his attention now on Brick.

"A lesson? In what? How to get into Cole Allbright's pants? How to make her moan against a wall? How to..." His words cut off when my fist slams into him with a brutal punch to his solar plexus.

He doubles over gripping his gut, gasping out a loud groan. He drops to his knees, blood and spittle spewing from his mouth.

I'm vaguely aware of the onlooking crowd, the lights from their camera phones flashing in my periphery. But I tune them out. Nothing else matters at this moment.

He touched what's mine.

Hurt what's mine.

A wave of visions hit me all at once—Cole's terror filled eyes, his hand on her throat, the tears on her cheeks...

Fury consumes me and *I see red*.

I grab a fistful of his hair and thrust his face down to meet my knee, turning him just enough to avoid breaking his nose. As much as I'd love to feel his bones crush, I'm not quite ready for him to pass out...

Not yet.

I step back, linking my hands behind my back and forcing my shoulders down, giving him a moment to regain his equilibrium, letting him believe I'm finished with him.

Brick likes to refer to this as the 'vipers trap'. The moment when the snake goes deadly still, its body appearing relaxed—calm. Luring its prey into a false sense of safety when, in fact, it's waiting for the perfect opening to deal its final strike.

Zavier, clearly ignorant to the trap I've laid before him, staggers back to his feet and spits a glob of bloody saliva onto the floor. He wipes the back of his hand across his mouth, then charges at me with a roar.

I pivot smoothly to the side, sidestepping his attack and watching as he crashes into a table—glasses smashing and the dregs of alcohol spilling everywhere.

He pushes himself back up, growling as he charges again.

Once more, I step to the side, but this time, it isn't a wooden table breaking his fall, but the immovable wall that is Thaddeus Brickton the Third.

Brick laughs, squeezing Zavier's face in his giant hand, lifting him effortlessly, forcing him onto the tips of his toes. He holds him there briefly before sending him back toward me with a hard shove.

Zavier's met with my fist slamming straight into his temple.

He staggers, dazed, but the blighter still won't give up.

As he readies to charge at me again, I bounce on my toes, lining up the timing perfectly to land a solid roundhouse kick to his head.

This time, he goes down—*hard*.

He groans against the concrete, coughing up blood and bile. The acrid stench of piss burns my nose and my lip curls in disgust at the wet pool spreading beneath him, darkening the patio floor.

I've been training for most of my life. I know how to kill a man with one strike to his throat. I know where to punch a man so he pisses blood for the rest of his life.

But I also know how to simply incapacitate someone. This bloody wanker will not only live, he won't even need medical care. After a few days with an ice pack, he'll be up and operating normally again. Well, semi-normally after he's had the shit kicked out of him anyway.

What he will need to do however, is get the fuck out of my sight... *immediately*. If this dumb piece of shit keeps coming at me, then I'll be more than happy to dole out a harsher punishment than a mere ass kicking.

I draw in a long, slow breath, flexing my jaw again to make sure the fucker hadn't done any lasting damage, and force myself to calm down.

Turning back toward the tavern door, I hunt for Cole in the crowd, but I'm met with a rowdy onslaught of all the remaining patrons, a loud round of cheering and clapping echoing into the chill night air, several of the men coming over to clap me on the shoulders, congratulating me for a fight well fought.

I finally spot her over by the wall, her head buried against Kya's shoulder as she consoles her. Kya's somber eyes meet mine and she gives me a subtle shake of her head.

Her message is clear—Don't come over here.

Fuck.

My heart sinks, a hollowness settling in my chest.

Of course I shouldn't go over there.

After seeing me beat the shit out of Zavier—seeing the violence I'm capable of... *seeing the monster inside me.* It's the side of me I'd hoped she'd never have to see. A part of me I thought I'd buried a long time ago. But as much as I hate that part of me, as much as I want to forget that part of my life...

I can't deny the pleasure I'd gotten each time I landed a hit. Or the surge of satisfaction I'd felt as he'd crumpled to the floor at my feet. The rush of adrenaline at the sight of his blood...

Bile burns the back of my throat, sickened by what I've become.

Pete and Greg push their way past, grabbing Zavier and pulling him roughly to his feet. Greg grips him hard by the back of his neck and barks in his ear.

"Let's go you bloody wanker. That's the last time you'll ever show your fucking face in my pub!"

The thought of Cole never having to serve that smarmy fucker ever again eases something in my chest. Greg continues shouting at him as they march him down to the boat—going on to say, if he ever comes in the place again, the police will be called and he'd better not even so much as hear a whisper of any police visiting the Manor, because everyone tonight saw what he did to Cole and he was the fucker who threw the first punch.

Pete gets on the boat with Billy, manhandling Zavier into one of the seats, holding him by his collar as they make the crossing.

Greg trudges wearily back up, rubbing his hands together to warm them against the cold of the night and stops next to me.

"How long?" I ask, my eyes watching the men on the boat, my arms crossed over my chest.

"How long for what, Your Grace?" Greg asks, confusion coloring his tone as he stands watching the boat depart beside me.

"How long will I be banned... for fighting in the pub?" I ask, knowing I've left a wake of destruction in my path.

He turns toward me; one bushy eyebrow arched in puzzlement.

"Don't be daft, son! I'm not barring you from the pub. In fact," he grins widely at me and claps his large hand on my shoulder, "You'll be getting free drinks for a week!"

He pulls me in a little closer, the smile dropping from his lips, his jaw tightening as he glances behind us and lowers his voice.

"You did what you had to do."

I offer him a tight-lipped smile and dip my chin in a shallow nod of thanks, then return my attention back toward the river.

"And Cole?" I watch Zavier's dark form as the boat approaches the far shore, flashing red and blue lights approaching in the distance.

Greg turns to look back toward the pub and scratches his jaw, considering the question.

"I think she's earned a week off, don't you?"

Relief floods my veins as the boat bumps against the opposite bank of the river and I turn to glance in the direction of Greg's stare.

Silhouetted in the soft glow of the Christmas tree the Wye Inn displays on the terrace every year, I see Kya as she cradles Cole in a protective hug. My Little Fawn's head tucked under her chin as she gently strokes her loose auburn hair away from her tear-streaked face.

Behind them, Brick stands tall—his full height a wall of silent warning—arms folded tight across his chest, the muscles in his jaw rigid. His unblinking gaze, locked on Zavier as he's escorted off the boat and met by the police awaiting his arrival.

Swallowing hard, I turn back to the large man beside me.

"That she does." I agree with another firm nod. "You're a good man, Greg." Taking his hand in mine, I give it a tight squeeze. "And don't worry, I'll take care of the damages to the bar."

"Your Grace," his grip on my hand tightens, "you just look after our girl, won't you?" His eyes flick back toward Cole, a clear fondness softening the corners.

"She's a great kid. There's really something special about her."

Again, my attention pulls back toward the terrace, finding her instinctively, the magnetic pull she has over me drawing me in—like honing in on my true North.

"That she is, Greg." I say, softly. "I will."

Walking back up toward the pub, the crowd of spectators waits, ready to pat me on the back and congratulate me for a fight well fought, but all I see is Cole.

As I make my way to her, I can see the tears staining her cheeks, her hair in disarray, but as I get closer, the lights on the terrace illuminate the darker patches starting to form across her throat–the clear shape of a hand pressed into her skin and I grit my teeth.

Tracking my gaze, she raises her fingers to her delicate neck, the torn sleeve of her shirt falling away from her arm and hanging loose at her side.

For the first time, I see the bare skin of her forearm, revealing what she's been hiding under the long sleeves of her shirts and track jackets all this time—what she wasn't ready to share with me yet.

My chest squeezes, a fissure splitting my heart in two at the sight.

Gregg heads back to close up the pub while Brick, Kya, Cole and Grumbl make their way over to join me. Without hesitation, Cole immediately steps into me and curls into my chest.

Relief floods me as I wrap my arms around her, hugging her tightly and rocking her gently, my lips pressed to the top of her head.

"Rogan, would you and Brick mind walking us home?" Kya asks. "I think Cole has had more than enough excitement for one night."

She shivers and Brick drapes an arm around her shoulders pulling her into his side—her head falling to his shoulder. I nod mutely, kissing the top of Cole's head, as I begin to understand a glimmer of her trauma.

I note the clouds overhead have darkened and the air begins to smell of a brewing storm.

Without another thought, I scoop Cole up into my arms, wrapping her into my chest. Her body relaxes against me, her head resting perfectly under my chin and I kiss her hair as we head down to the boat. Her fingers absently play with the zipper on my jacket, so much like they had with the buttons of my shirt the day I found her in the orchard all those weeks ago.

Once on the boat I settle her onto my lap, unwilling to let her go until we're back at Kya's house.

I literally have to force myself to set her feet down on the doorstep. Releasing her, but not wanting to let her go.

As the door closes behind her, the first heavy drops of rain begin to fall.

Chapter 45

Rogan

My hair and clothes, still dripping wet, soak the carpet as I pace.

What do I do? What do I do?

I tug at the roots of my hair frantically trekking back and forth across my room. It felt so wrong to leave her there, even though I know she's safe with Kya.

"Go to her."

His calm voice makes me jump and I turn to see Brick leaning casually against the door frame.

How fucking long has he been standing there anyway?

"I mean, I worry about the state of your carpet if you keep pacing like that, mate."

Dropping my hands to my sides, I stop pacing but my chest rises and falls as if I've just been running.

"Seriously, Rogan. For fuck's sake, just go to her. Stay there with her, or bring her back here. But you know you're not going to rest and you're going to drive yourself mad unless you have that woman safe in your arms tonight."

He steps into the room to stand beside me, then points back toward the door, giving my shoulder a gentle nudge.

"So fucking go."

With a nod, I turn to move toward the door.

"Go and get the woman you love before I drag you there myself."

I stumble to a stop, gripping the doorframe to keep from toppling over. I slowly turn back to face him, my mouth hanging open as his words sink in.

"Love?" I rasp.

"Yeah, you bloody fool. Fucking love." He laughs, walking over to grip me by the shoulders and gives me a hardy shake.

"Go, you fucking idiot! Go get your girl."

I stare at him wide eyed for what feels like an eternity letting the truth of what he's said register, until I feel the smile tugging up the corners of my lips, the reality of his statement hitting me like a freight train.

Well, fuck... he's right!

This foreign feeling I've been struggling with all this time... the one I've been unable to name up until right now... *is fucking love!*

I'm in love with Cole Allbright!

Without another word, I spin, sprinting down the corridor with Brick's laugh echoing off the walls behind me.

I take the stairs two and three at a time, skidding at the bottom, my hand on the newel post the only thing keeping me upright as I propel myself through the front door and down the driveway.

The storm is raging now, thunder and lightning flashing across the pitch-black sky.

I'm nearly to the Gatehouse when a bright bolt flashes, illuminating the dark path, lighting up the small figure running up the drive toward me.

The moment we see each other, we stop.

Then, as the thunder rolls, rain pouring down all around us, we cover the remaining space between us, our steps quickening the closer we get to one another.

The moment I reach her, I pull her tightly to me, our bodies meeting in a clash of arms, mouths and tongues.

She presses against me, as I pull her up into my arms. Her hands thread through my wet hair, her mouth seizing my lips as if they were her last breath of air.

I pull back just to look at her. She's here... my Little Fawn, safe in my arms—and she's come to me on her own, clearly needing me as much as I'm needing her.

She wraps her arms around my head, the fabric of her torn sleeve exposing her bare arm to me. I turn my face against her skin and gently brush my lips against the thick white scars lining her skin. She sobs, tucking her face against me and I feel the warmth of her tears mingle with the cold rain.

I lift her higher to kiss the side of her face, murmuring against her temple, "I've got you, Cole. I've got you."

She clings to me, her fingers sliding through my hair, tenderly stroking down my neck and back up again.

I turn, carrying her back to my home, my heart thundering so loudly I'm all but certain she can hear it over the storm.

If Brick is right—if this *is* love—then I have to go slowly, gently. I have to prove to her she's safe with me. She saw a side of me tonight I had never wanted her to see. I need to show her the creature she saw, the one more beast than man, the one who made Zavier pay for what he'd done to her, isn't who I am. I need to prove that part of me would never, *ever* come near her.

And if this is love, she needs to choose it for herself, in her own time. She needs to feel in control—even as I teach her how to surrender to it. How to fight back.

If this is love, then I'm already lost to it—*to her*.

I'd give my life—my everything—to make sure this woman never feels pain or fear again.

If anything in this world tries to get in the way, I'll burn the fucker down for her.

Chapter 46

Rogan

Cole curls into me, her arms wrapped tightly around my neck, her head tucked snuggly under my chin. Both of us are drenched, soaked through by the deluge of rain from the storm and she shivers against me.

As I cross the threshold, her head lifts, slowly scanning the grand hall while I carry her toward the staircase. Her eyes dance across the trove of statues, vases and framed paintings. I smile, watching her take it all in, realizing this is the first time she's seeing the inside of my home.

She finally turns back to me, her eyes wide, her mouth slightly ajar—a look of wonder and awe.

It occurs to me it's likely the same look I have on my face whenever I watch her, taking her in, discovering the beauty and wonder that is Cole Allbright.

Brilliant green eyes lock on mine and my throat tightens. Cole is here... in my home... in my arms. My heart squeezes as the magnitude of what I'm feeling begins to seat itself into my reality.

Love...

So this is what it feels like to love someone.

I'm lost to her. She has me so completely, so wholly, it feels like I'm drowning and if I can't touch her, hold her, feel her against me... *be* with her... then I might as well let myself go under, because I simply can't breathe without her.

She is my air.

My life.

My everything.

I don't know when it happened. From the moment I glimpsed her from my window that first day she was in town, my world just hasn't been the same. And now that I have her... I can't imagine my existence without her anymore.

She shudders in my arms, snapping me out of my stupor.

I curse, inwardly chastising myself.

Rogan, you bloody, fucking idiot!

Here I stand, gawking at her like a fool. Completely awestruck by her, while her poor body is racked with cold—no coat, her blouse torn and soaked through from the rain.

I pull her tighter against me, willing my own body heat into her—my efforts futile, being just as sodden as she is—and head toward the staircase.

She shivers violently, her teeth chattering loudly as she smiles up at me.

I rush down the hall, shouldering open the door to my room and stride straight for my ensuite.

"First thing we need to do is get you into a hot shower. Warm you up." She nods against my lips as I whisper into her hair, and burrows herself deeper against my chest.

I gently lower her down, keeping a steadying hand on her waist before moving toward the shower.

Once I've got the water warming, I turn back to face her, her eyes are glued to me. Her arms are wrapped tightly around her waist as she tries to quell the shivering, her teeth chattering loudly. But there's something different in her eyes. A fire I hadn't seen before.

Returning to her, I move the wet hair away from her neck, gently running my thumb along her bruising skin. A muscle feathers in my jaw as my teeth grind.

Her gaze follows me as I tilt her chin to get a better look at the damage. My heart clenches as I watch the delicate muscles of her neck contract as she swallows.

"You did so well tonight, Little Fawn." My voice is hoarse, nearly a whisper—my eyes burning with visions of the night playing on repeat in my mind.

Cole pinned against the wall.

Zavier's hand around her throat.

Her torn sleeve exposing her scars...

Those fucking scars...

Jesus.

The room begins to steam, the humidity of the hot shower filling the air with a warm, dense vapor laced with the scent of bergamot.

"I should let you shower." I say, moving to step toward the door, but her fingers curl around my wrists, keeping me there.

"Stay."

Her soft voice is barely a whisper, that one word clenching something inside my chest.

For a moment, all I can do is stare, studying all her features as if only now, truly seeing them for the first time.

The smattering of tiny freckles dusted across her nose and cheeks; the brilliant shine of her emerald eyes, sparkling like rare gemstones, dancing between mine before dropping to my mouth, then back again.

Her tongue dips out, wetting her plush lower lip, instantly ensnaring me with the movement. My cock swells and my heart feels like it's about to beat straight out of my chest.

Unable to hold back a moment longer, I lean down and lightly press my lips to hers.

She moves into me, deepening the kiss, her body settling against me. The moment our tongues meet, a soft moan escapes her throat. I hug her, pulling her tighter against my chest, wanting to hold her close, but with everything in me screaming to be gentle, to take care of her.

Reluctantly, I break the kiss, both of us breathing heavily as I rest my forehead to hers, our lips but a breath's width apart.

"We need to get you out of these wet clothes." I whisper against her mouth.

She nods. She locks her eyes on mine as she steps back, kicking out of her shoes. Her fingers hook into the waist of her skirt. With a little shimmy that dries my mouth and makes my cock twitch, she pushes it down over her hips, letting it drop to the floor.

Taking her time, she slowly unfastens the buttons on her blouse. My eyes trail her fingers as her shirt falls open, exposing more and more of her pale flesh with each button undone.

The lace of her bra clings to her milky breasts, her dusky nipples pebbled into hard, tight peaks showing through the chilled, wet lace.

Sliding my fingers across her collar bones, I push the fabric down her arms, lightly grazing her skin with the tips of my fingers as the shirt slides away from her, the wet material falling to the floor.

Gently turning her hand, her breath stills as I slowly bring her wrist to my lips.

My eyes on hers, I barely—just barely—brush a tender kiss to the risen white flesh. The darker line of red at its center tells of its depth, its savagery.

"Does it still hurt?"

She shakes her head, as a large tear spills over her lower lashes and tracks down her cheek.

"Not anymore," she whispers.

I nod, my eyes falling closed as I will my heart to stop aching for her.

Moving my lips up her arm, up the length of her scar, I start to notice the other marks on her arms. More marks I've not seen before. More marks I didn't know she'd been hiding.

Round, puckered scars–some big, some small and all looking like they're in different stages of healing. Some are older, I realize, while others are more recent, still with a redness to their centers as opposed to the stark white of the older ones.

I look back to meet emerald eyes. Her watery gaze locked on me, watching me take in her scars one by one.

"Who did this to you, my Little Fawn." My voice, a broken whisper.

Her chin only trembles, more tears slipping down her cheeks.

Tugging her into me, I bring my mouth to hers, wrapping her tightly into my body. She buries her fingers in my hair, pulling me closer to deepen the kiss.

Then her hands are sliding down my chest, down my abs until she's pulling at my shirt, untucking it and lifting it up.

She struggles to get it over my shoulders, letting out an adorably frustrated little growl.

Laughing, I break the kiss just long enough to help her get my shirt the rest of the way off, before moving back in to reclaim her lips.

Her hands trace along the muscles of my shoulders, sliding down the ridges of my biceps and back up again. Then her hands are on my chest, her fingers running down the deep ridges of my abs, slipping lower until they reach the button on my jeans. My muscles clench as they graze the dark trail of hair leading into my waist band.

"Cole," I pant against her lips as our tongues dip in and out, tangling with one another. My hand gripping her waist, my fingers curling into the thin fabric of her lace panties, while the other cradles her jaw, my fingers threaded into her hair, tilting her head to angle deeper into the kiss.

Hot vapors from the steaming shower swirl around us, our chill from the rain long forgotten, our bodies now coated with a light sheen of sweat.

"I want this, Rogan," she breathes, pressing her body into me. "I want *you*."

She finally manages to get the button of my jeans open, then lowers my zipper. When her hand wraps around my cock, I swear time stands still.

With a jolt, I groan into her mouth... every bit of air leaving my lungs in a rush. It takes everything in me not to dig my fingers into her soft flesh.

"Jesus, Cole..." I moan, unable to stop my hips from bucking forward into her touch.

"We shouldn't... You've been through hell tonight." I wrap my hand around her wrist, dropping my head to her shoulder.

"I don't care, Rogan. I don't fucking care!" She yells, releasing my cock and pushing my chest back to look up at my face, but she doesn't pull out of my arms.

Her eyes lock onto mine, a fury burning in them that could scorch the world... but it's her next words that rock me to my core.

"My *whole life* has been fucking hell!

"For as long as I can remember, I've lived in fear. Feeling hated, unwanted... used and useless—all at once. I've been shamed, beaten, burned, raped, cut and nearly fucking murdered, by the men who were *supposed* to protect me!

"But, I survived, goddamn it!

"*I! Fucking! Survived!*"

Tears spill over her lower lashes as she takes in a long, shaky breath.

Nodding, I smooth my thumbs through the wet tracks on her cheeks, swallowing hard, as she surrenders her truth.

"So I'm done being scared, Rogan.

I'm so... fucking... done... being a victim. And I refuse to wait one more goddamn minute to finally *live.*"

Her lip quivers as she pulls in a long, shuddering breath.

"I've found a life here in Verdon. A life I never, ever dreamed I could have—never even imagined could exist."

Unblinking, those beautiful eyes shimmer up at me.

"But the most incredible thing I've found here... *is you.*"

For a long moment, the running water from the shower is the only sound in the room. Steam swirls around us in thick, damp clouds—the drumming of my heart nearly deafening in my ears.

Cole's eyes shine with angry, unshed tears as she waits for my reaction to the deluge of nightmares she's just divulged.

My eyes burn and I feel the wet heat of a tear as it tracks down my cheek. Her eyes follow its path, her chin trembling. The lump in my throat threatens to suffocate me when her tiny fingers reach up to swipe it away and I turn my face into her palm.

Her hand wraps around the back of my neck to pull me down to her. I follow her willingly, pressing my lips to hers, my eyes squeezing shut as more tears track down my face, the reality of her abuse gutting me. I curl her into me, holding her in a tight embrace, my face buried into her neck.

How could someone hurt this magnificent creature?

My Little Fawn...

My Cole...

"Shhh, I'm alright now." She soothes as her hands stroke my neck. "You saved me."

Pulling back to look at her, I shake my head.

"No, Little Fawn. I didn't...

"*You* saved you."

Her breath hitches, but she raises her chin, her lips pulled tight with a look of... pride in her eyes.

That's it, my Little Fawn. You are so fucking incredible.

Be proud.

I smile at her, my brows pulling together in awe over this phenomenal woman standing before me.

"Yeah, I guess I kind of did, didn't I?" She says as she smiles back up at me, roughly batting away the tears from her cheeks.

"You sure as hell did, Little Fawn." I smile proudly at her, leaning down to run my nose against the tip of hers.

Her teeth sink into her bottom lip as a devilish glint sparkles in her eyes. With a giggle, she grabs both my hands and pulls me to her, backing us both straight into the shower.

Chapter 47

Rogan

Cole laughs as the warm water pours over both of us, soaking my jeans even more thoroughly than they'd been from the rain. She looks down and gapes, clapping both hands over her mouth, her eyes sparkling with mirth, when she sees I'm still wearing my boots.

I smirk down at her, reaching up and twisting the shower head to spray directly on her, making her squeal.

Pushing the hair out of her eyes, she gathers a mouthful of water, spraying it at me like a fountain. Laughing, I wipe one hand down my face and wrap my arm around her waist, pulling her into me.

Grinning down at her, her beautiful smile beams up at me and once again, I'm pulled into her. I lean down, pressing my lips to hers. She opens immediately, sweeping her tongue against mine, her hands wrapped tightly around my neck, pulling me deeper into the kiss.

Without parting our lips, I kick out of my boots, knocking them outside the shower as I slide my hands down Cole's back, finding the clasp on her bra to unfasten it. I peel the wet lace off her body and drop it to the shower floor, then pull her into me. The feeling of her soft breasts pressing against my chest has my cock hardening instantly at the sensation.

She pushes at the top of my jeans, struggling to move them down my hips—the thick, wet material stubbornly resisting the descent. Grinning against her lips, I help her push them down the rest of the way, the head of my hard cock peeking up past the waist band of my briefs, the fabric no longer able to contain it.

She runs the pad of her thumb over the tip and I pull in a hissing breath through my teeth. Her eyes jump to mine.

Confidence growing, she does it again and I close my eyes, humming low in my throat and press my hips into her hand when she does it a third time.

I grab her waist and pull her into me, swallowing her mouth in a frantic kiss, needing to taste her more than I need to breathe right now.

She gasps, the fervent kiss taking her by surprise, but returns it just as frantically, our mouths tangling in a fury of lips, tongues and teeth. Gentle nips woven with smooth strokes. Cupping the back of her head, I delve my tongue deep into her mouth, the way I've delved it into her pussy—the way I want to delve my aching cock into her.

Her wet body slides against mine in a delicious friction, the bare skin of her stomach sliding against the exposed head of my cock, driving me nearly insane with need.

Breaking away from the kiss, I slip my fingers into the string of her panties, sliding them down her thighs. As they lower down her legs, I follow them down the length of her body, trailing my tongue down her neck and across her chest, pausing to suck one peaked nipple into my mouth. She moans when I pinch it lightly between my teeth. I move down to her stomach, grazing my teeth across the soft flesh below her navel, moving lower still, sliding the tip of my nose along the skin over her hip bone before bending to slip her panties completely off.

I feel her eyes tracking me as I make my way back up her leg, peppering her with soft kisses as I slowly make my assent, only pausing once I reach the apex of her thighs. Dropping to my knees before her, I grip her hips, plunging my tongue into her bare center like a man starved, then gently tease her clit with the tip of my tongue before driving it back inside her again. She gasps, rocking back on her heels, both hands gripping the back of my head and pulls me further into her.

I eagerly sink my tongue deeper, lifting her leg to rest on my shoulder, giving me better access to her sweet, pink pussy. I wrap my arm around her thigh, gripping a handful of her ass, tugging her dripping cunt harder against my mouth, stiffening my tongue to drive it deep into her core.

"Rogan...," Cole moans, looking down at me with a heavy-lidded, lust filled gaze and rocking her hips in time with the motions of my mouth. I meet her eyes and run my tongue back over her clit, taking it between my lips and sucking hard. Her head drops back against the shower wall on a long, low moan. I groan against her sex, her sounds of pleasure spurring me on, my hunger for her only ratcheting up higher with each stroke of my tongue.

My eyes track up her body while I continue to lave at her, mesmerized by the rivulets of water cascading across the delicate swells of her breasts only to join with the beads rolling down her stomach. The erotic combination of her taste on my tongue as I stare up at the body of this goddess while I worship on my knees for her, has my cock pulsing with painful need.

She's a vision of pure ecstasy, and she's really here. The number of times I've come to the image of her in this very shower and now, with her pussy on my mouth, my tongue deep inside her, it's so much better than any imagined version of her I could have ever dreamed. Yet I still want more.

I want all of her.

Lifting a hand, I glide a finger into her soaking center, curling it against the spot I know will drive her closer to the edge. Her legs start to quake, panting out my name in a whispered chant, again and again as her inner walls begin to quiver and pulse.

She's so close.

Adding a second finger, I roll my tongue rhythmically against her clit alternating between licking, nipping and sucking at the swollen bundle of nerves.

"Oh God, Rogan... I'm... I'm going to..." her back arches and her hips jolt forward. She throws back her head, letting out a low, guttural groan, her thighs shake violently as she grips them tightly around my head, her fingernails digging into my scalp, as her inner walls seize, clamping down hard on my fingers, a surge of wet heat soaking my hand.

"That's it! That's my good girl. Give me everything you've got, Little Fawn." I praise, continuing to move my fingers gently inside her until the last tremors of her orgasm slowly subside.

I slip my fingers out of her and grip her hips to steady her, just as she slumps against the wall of the shower, her legs shaking, her chest rapidly rising and falling as she tries to catch her breath.

I carefully lower her leg back to the shower floor and rise to standing, bracing a hand on her hip, until I'm sure she's steady on her feet. Reaching past her, I grab my body wash, squeezing some into my hand, then smooth it over her body, working the soap into a thick lather.

"What about you?" She asks, her eyes following me while I begin to wash every inch of her. Without a word, I smile, leaning down to press a soft kiss against her lips.

She watches me as I move my hands methodically over her body, rolling my thumbs into her tight muscles before rinsing away the suds.

I wash her hair last, massaging her scalp. Her eyes fall closed and she lets out a soft sigh.

Once I'm satisfied, I've thoroughly cleaned every inch of her, I drop my briefs down my thighs so I can wash myself. Having just effectively stroked my hands and fingers over every part of this stunning creature before me, my still very hard cock slaps back against the wet skin of my stomach when I pull off the soggy fabric. I glance over to see Cole staring wide-eyed at my erection, standing at full mast, well past my navel.

I bite back a grin when her cheeks pinken. Hurrying to wash myself, I rinse off quickly and then reach past her to turn off the shower. Stepping out, I fasten a towel around my waist and grab another to wrap around Cole, meticulously drying her, pausing occasionally to drop a soft kiss to her skin.

She silently watches me, her eyes never leaving me, tracking my every movement.

Once we're both fully dried, I lead her into my room. She slowly looks around, taking in the space, her gaze finally landing on the large bed at the center.

"Are you tired?" I ask, walking across the room to pour her a glass of water. Wrapped in nothing but a towel, she shakes her head, stepping over to the wall of windows overlooking the dark village below.

I move in behind her, wrapping one hand around her hip, pulling her against me and circle my arm in front of her, handing her the glass.

She settles against me, her head resting against my chest as she tips back the glass, taking several long swallows, quickly finishing the cool liquid.

"Thank you." She says, turning in my arms to face me, the empty glass in hand, her lips still glistening with moisture. My mouth waters as her tongue tips out to run over them, my chest rising as I inhale a deep breath, my cock firming once again beneath my own towel between us.

Taking the glass from her, I set it on the table beside us and turn back to see her heated eyes locked on my towel, the fabric beginning to tent as my dick thickens, hardening more and more as my eyes trail over her barely clad body in the dim light of the room.

She stretches up on her toes, wrapping her arms around my neck, pulling me down to her lips. I greedily oblige, my hands moving to grip her hips as I bend to meet her—our mouths opening, our tongues tangling in a slow, sensuous dance. The kiss heats, turning more fervent and our bodies begin to move together, instinctively knowing exactly how to move and where to touch.

She reaches between us, unfastening the twist of her towel, letting it drop to the floor. The only thing standing between us now is my own towel wrapped loosely at my hips.

Letting her take the lead, she slowly backs us toward the bed, pulling me with her, her mouth never leaving mine. I feel her hand move to my waist, her fingers teasing the fabric—a silent question in her eyes as she watches my face at her touch.

Giving her a small nod, I feel her smile against my lips as she curls her fingers into my towel, tugging it open. My cock, hard and heavy, rises between us as my towel hits the floor.

The light graze of her fingers is tentative as she glides them up the underside of my shaft, trailing along the thick vein and I pull in a hissing breath.

"Fuuuckkk..." I groan against her mouth, my hips involuntarily driving forward into her touch.

She wraps her small hand around my cock, gripping me gently, moving up and down in a hesitant stroke. I'm almost embarrassed by the pained whimper I hear come from my throat, but the sound seems to encourage her. When her grip tightens and her strokes become more deliberate—more confident, I break from the kiss, my eyes falling to where her hand grips me. I can't help but watch as she works me, just like I'd envisioned so many times in my fantasies.

Feeling her eyes on me, I slide my fingers into her hair, pulling her face to mine, driving my tongue into her mouth again in another desperate kiss. My legs start to shake as my hips roll in time with her movements, thrusting up and pressing into each stroke of her hand, trapping my cock between her body and mine, needing more, to be closer to her—needing to be inside her.

My balls start to tighten, a heated tingle teasing my spine, I gasp, breaking the kiss and grip her hand, pausing her strokes. "Wait…" I pant, swallowing hard, my heart racing in my chest. "Not yet… I just… not yet."

She pulls her bottom lip between her teeth, her grin turning wicked. She tugs my mouth back to hers, and lightly runs the tip of her tongue along the seam of my lips and gives my cock another squeeze, sending a bolt of desire searing through me. I growl, claiming her mouth and bend to sweep my arm beneath her legs, lifting her up to place her gently on the bed, following her down and settling my weight between her thighs.

"Mmmm…Rogan." She purrs, threading her fingers through my hair. She hums softly as I trail my lips along her jaw and down her neck, lightly grazing my teeth along her collar bone. The sound makes my dick grow impossibly harder, my hips roll into the mattress, chasing the friction I so desperately crave.

I slide my hand down her body, until my fingers reach the hot, wet apex of her thighs. I press two fingers into her, and she groans. I curl them up and circle softly, sliding them out only to push them back in again and repeat the motion.

"Rogan… I… Oh God, Rogan I need…" She breathes, struggling to find her words while her hips buck up into my hand.

"Tell me, Little Fawn. Tell me what you need…what you want. Say the words and you'll have it. Anything you want… ask it of me and it's yours."

She writhes beneath me, her fingers digging into my shoulders as I work mine in and out of her pussy. Her eyes heated, her breath coming in heavy gasps.

"You." She pants, finally finding her words. "I want... ahh..." She groans, arching her back, her head falling against the pillow when I hit a spot deep within her.

"You... I need you... *inside me.*"

My nostrils flare, my hand stilling between us.

"Are you sure, Little Fawn? We don't have to if you're not ready."

"God, Rogan... yes!" She rolls her eyes, dropping her head back in frustration.

"I promise, I'm not going to break! I want this! I want *you.* I don't think I've ever wanted anything more in my life." She pleads, her hips grinding up into my hand, my fingers buried deep inside her.

I press a long, languid kiss to her lips, pulling back to look into her eyes.

"It would be my greatest honor, Little Fawn."

I stretch across her and pull open the drawer of my nightstand, pulling out a condom. Then, tearing open the foil packet with my teeth, I reach between us to roll it on.

My chest tightens, my heart hammering violently as I brace myself above her, lining up the head of my cock with her glistening entrance, her legs wrapped tightly around my hips, the tips of her nails lightly grazing my skin as she grips my arms.

"Tell me your safe word, Cole." My eyes lock on wide emerald ones staring back at me, my cock throbbing in my hand, begging to thrust into her.

"Sundance." She whispers. Her body relaxing ever so slightly beneath me, her eyes softening at my gentle reminder—she's in control.

I nod, locking my eyes on hers, then begin to push into her with a slow, steady thrust. Her mouth falls open on a breathless gasp, the air stilling between us as I sink into her, inch by glorious inch.

Her eyes go wide—nails digging into the skin of my shoulders as I push into her perfect, tight cunt until, finally seating myself fully to the hilt.

Her eyes roll back, then shutter closed as she lets out a long, slow breath.

My body trembles as I hold myself there, not moving... giving her time to adjust to my size, sweat beading along my brow as I struggle not to thrust again.

She finally takes in a new breath of air, when a single tear slips from her eye.

My heart cinches in my chest as I watch it disappear into her hair.

"Little Fawn..." I ask, dread creeping up my throat as I gently cup her face, sweeping away the trail of moisture in the tear's wake.

"What is it? Are you alright? Do you want to stop?"

Was it too soon? Did I go too hard... too fast?

Her eyes flutter open, sparkling as they find mine, a soft, adoring smile taking over her lips and she shakes her head, leaning her cheek into my touch. Her voice... barely a whisper, laced with wonder and awe as another tear slides into her hair.

"It doesn't hurt..."

Chapter 48

Cole

It doesn't hurt.

Rogan's cock throbs deep inside me as he holds perfectly still, gauging me, reading me, needing to know I'm alright before he moves again.

His body shakes as sweat gathers on his brow, his chest rising and falling heavily between us.

Tentatively, I shift my hips, testing, feeling...

But no... it really doesn't hurt.

Instead it feels...

Incredible.

Smiling up at him, I give him a small nod, and shift my hips again, letting him know I'm okay. He breathes out a tortured moan, relief washing over his face as he lowers his mouth to mine.

"I'll never hurt you, Little Fawn..." he whispers, before gently parting my lips with his tongue as he slowly begins to move his hips. He slides his thick cock nearly all the way out, before slowly pushing back in again and I moan against his mouth when he seats himself deep within me. He stills once again with his cock buried in me to the hilt—a low groan vibrating in his throat.

"Fuuucckkk..." he purrs as he drops his face into the crook of my neck, his breath fanning across my collar bone as he pants. I hear him swallow, his breaths heavy as he works to hold himself back. His cock seated inside me, unmoving aside from a slow steady, torturous pulse within me, making me ache with need. The lack of movement drives me wild beneath him. Everything in my body needing him to thrust again—a desire I've never felt before, making me squirm.

"You feel even more incredible than I ever could have imagined."

His breath is hot against my ear before his teeth lightly drag over the lobe, sucking it into his mouth, sending chills cascading down my neck.

Slowly, he begins to roll his hips, the thick shaft of his cock stroking along the walls of my pussy in a slow, measured caress.

Gentle at first, his pace gradually increasing—uncontrollable sounds of pleasure escape me as I wrap my hands around his lats, gripping the large muscles of his back—needing something... anything to hold onto as I let myself go, losing myself to the bliss of this moment—of this man.

My body craves him... needs more of him, closer, faster, deeper.

More...

More...

More...

The unbidden chant repeats in my mind as I begin to roll my own hips in time with his, the cadence of our thrusts in perfect time with one another as I curve my body up to meet his, my pussy gliding along his thick shaft, a primal need taking over my body as he continues to sink into me over and over.

Soft groans and needy whimpers escape his throat, as he gives in to his own desire, thrusting his hardness in and out of me. His panting breaths hot against my skin as he alternates between kissing, licking and nipping my neck, lips and breasts.

My pussy clenches around him as we continue to move together. Raising himself up on one arm, he reaches under me and grabs my ass, lifting me up into each driving arch of his hips, thrusting himself deeper, as he angles into me. The decadent drag of his hard cock sends unimaginable pleasure coursing through me, the smooth head rhythmically stroking a place deep inside me, my toes curling with each teasing caress.

That now familiar heat builds, throbbing in my core as tingles begin to radiate down my spine—my inner walls beginning to quiver. I arch my back, as I feel pleasure start to coil deep in my core, a crescendo of ecstasy growing closer and closer with each and every delicious thrust of his hips.

I lift my head to watch his thick cock, slick with my arousal, as it drives into me again and again. The sight, so licentious, it drives me even closer to the brink of euphoria.

As my orgasm begins to crest, I throw my head back, unable to control my body as the waves begin to overtake me.

"Rogan... Oh God, yes, yes... Oh, Ro... I'm going... I'm going to..."

He reaches between us, rolling his thumb over my clit in firm, tight circles, applying just the right amount of pressure, as he continues driving into me.

"That's it, Little Fawn...Let go. Give it to me... I need to feel you come around my cock. Come for me, Cole."

I break... his words sending me over the edge and I scream as pleasure erupts through my body, my pussy tightly clamping down on his hard shaft, pulsing hard as my release barrels through me. My legs clamp around his hips, my heels locking around the backs of his thighs, pulling him into me as my fingers dig into his skin.

"That's it..." he grunts, "good girl..." he praises breathlessly, continuing to drive into me as I writhe beneath him—his hips picking up speed, thrusting harder, impossibly deeper, as he chases his own release. The rapid drag of his cock along the inner walls of my pussy prolongs my orgasm, making me cry out as another wave of pleasure crashes over me.

"That's it... give me one more. Squeeze my cock with that perfect pussy, Cole. Fuck, but you were made for me."

Rising to his knees, he grips my hips, thrusting himself deeply inside me again and again. Snapping his hips faster, harder—his thrusts beginning to falter, his cock swelling, somehow becoming even more rigid inside me, sending me over the edge yet again, bringing me to climax once more.

"God yes!" He growls, "That's it, Cole. Fucking hell, but you're perfect."

He pulls my hips hard, his cock seating firmly inside me with a final hard thrust, his hips still as he roars his release... his cock pulsing, the thick muscle rippling in deep waves, throbbing within me.

For a few moments, his heaving form towers above me in the shadowed room, our chests rising and falling rapidly as we work to catch our breath—our souls once again settling back to earth.

With his cock still inside me, slowly softening, he lowers himself down to press a tender kiss to my lips. He drags the tip of his nose along mine, his big hand cupping my face while his thumb gently strokes my cheek.

His eyes sparkle with wonder as he silently gazes down at me, then he finally utters one word.

"Magnificent."

My eyes sting and blur at the unfamiliar sense of adoration I hear in his voice. I blink rapidly, trying to clear my vision, not wanting to ruin this moment with more unnecessary tears.

He kisses me again, "You took me so well, Little Fawn. I honestly don't know how I'll ever get enough of you."

He presses his lips to mine as he gently slides out of me, then rises from the bed, heading to his ensuite. He returns a few moments later with a warm, wet cloth, laying down beside me, kissing me deeply while he meticulously moves the cloth over me, reverently cleaning me with soft, tender strokes.

Discarding the cloth in the hamper, he returns to the bed, laying down beside me only to pull me into him, wrapping his large arm around me, tightly cocooning me into his body.

Pressing a soft kiss to my temple, and tucking my head into the crook of his neck, he whispers against my ear, "Rest now, Little Fawn. I've got you."

And for the first time in my life, I feel safe as I fall asleep in a man's arms.

Chapter 49

Cole

I wake to the feeling of Rogan's lips as he kisses down the side of my neck, his arm wrapped tightly around me as he gently pulls my back tightly to his chest—his hard cock nestled into the crease of my ass.

As I stir, he begins to move, pressing his hips forward and grinding his hardness against me, his hand slowly working its way down my stomach, reaching my already soaking pussy and lightly grazing his fingers in between my folds, gently circling that sensitive bundle of nerves.

The heat of his breath fans across my neck, sending goosebumps down my arms and legs and I press myself into him as a quiet moan escapes my throat.

"I need you, Little Fawn." He whispers into my ear before pulling the lobe into his mouth, gently dragging the skin between his teeth.

I reach my arm around his neck, running my fingers up through the short hair at his nape and turn my face to his, pulling his mouth to mine.

He groans into my mouth, thrusting his hips forward again, dragging his straining cock upward against the seam of my ass.

"Are you sore?" He asks, his movements becoming more urgent.

I nod, and grin against his lips. "Yes," I giggle, "but only in the most delicious way." I tell him before thrusting my tongue between his lips. He groans again, his mouth capturing mine as he pushes two fingers into me, pulling my backside against his rigid cock.

He works his fingers in and out in time with the thrusts of his tongue, our kisses turning frantic. Then his fingers slip out of me and he moves his hips back, only to slide his hard cock between my thighs, gliding it along the seam of my pussy, coating his shaft in my arousal. Moving his fingers back to my clit, he thrusts himself along my wet core, the feel of his hot skin as it drives along my aching center, teasing but never entering me—a delicious yet maddening friction—causes an aching throb to pulse, tugging at my core.

I reach between us to feel the smooth head of his cock as it pushes forward, past my thighs. I cup my hand around him, allowing him to fuck into my hand at the same time as he slides himself along my wet center.

"Jesus, Cole... mmmhh..." He pants into my ear. "You're... fuuuck... you're so goddamn incredible. Need... mmmhh... need to... be inside you..."

Suddenly, he stops... pulling his cock and his hand from between my thighs—his abrupt absence making me whimper at the sudden loss of contact. I turn to face him, only to see him fumbling with the drawer to his nightstand, his hand hurriedly rummaging through its contents, emerging triumphantly with a condom.

He tears the foil with his teeth, quickly sheaths himself and tugs me back to him. Trailing urgent kisses along my neck and shoulder, he slides his leg between mine. Raising his knee, he opens me to him, his hand reaching between us as he lines himself up with my center before pressing his full length into me in one, smooth thrust. His movement is slow but firm and steady as he buries himself inside me—my head falling back onto the pillow as he fills me. My lips part as I gasp at the sudden fullness, but it quickly turns to a moan of pleasure as he rolls his hips, seating himself fully.

"Fuuuucckk..." he growls as he begins to thrust, pumping his hips, driving his huge cock in and out of me at a fevered pace.

"I'll never get enough of you, Little Fawn. Even when I'm inside you, I want more... *need* more!

It will never be enough. Never... mmhhhh...enough."

"Yes, Rogan... mmm...more..." I plead, pushing my hips back in time with his thrusts. "I need you, Rogan. Please, I need... ohhhh...God yes!"

He rolls us forward, his body on top of mine, before rocking back on his knees, lifting me with him, pressing my back to his chest—his strong arm splayed across my front, holding me to him, his big hand gripping my shoulder. I straddle his lap as he drives up into me, kissing, licking and nipping along my neck.

I turn my head, working to capture his mouth. His dick hitting me even deeper at this angle than I ever could have dreamed possible. Heat starts to bloom inside me, a wave of ecstasy settling into my core as we move together.

He brings his fingers to my clit, massaging in a firm, tight circle. For every thrust of his hips, he counters with a rolling gyration that works his cock inside me in a way that triggers all new sensations, causing me to cry out as a new surge of liquid heat floods my already soaking center.

I can feel my insides start to quiver and tighten, heat blooming as my climax begins to crest.

"That's it, Little Fawn. Come for me. Choke my cock with that beautiful pussy." He growls in my ear, his movements never ceasing as I feel his dick grow harder inside me.

He slides his finger into me between his cock and my clit, keeping the heel of his hand in a steady pressure on that tight bundle of nerves. With the combination of his hand pressing against my clit, his finger inside me and each rolling surge of his cock driving into me... I explode—screaming in ecstasy as my orgasm overtakes me—my pussy squeezing his cock hard as he thrusts up into me once...twice... a third time...

He plunges himself into me fully, stilling his hips as his own release barrels through him.

"FUUUUCK!!" He roars as he spills himself, his cock rippling in hard, rapid pulses inside me.

He grinds himself into me, swirling and grinding his hips, prolonging the sensation, my inner walls pulsing in time with him as another flurry of pleasure ripples through me.

As we come down from our orgasms breathing heavily, I lay my head back on his shoulder.

Rogan's big arms hold me to him in a warm embrace as he kisses along my neck, nuzzling his nose into my hair, then whispers into my ear.

"An eternity inside you wouldn't be enough." His heated breath sends elated chills down my body.

I lift off him to turn in his arms, straddling his lap again and wrap my arms around his shoulders, burying my face into his neck—his arms enveloping me into a tight hug, holding me against him.

"Thank you."

"What are you thanking me for, Little Fawn?" He asks, arching a confused brow and smiling as he studies my face.

"I never knew it could be like this. I've never felt anything like this before." I tell him, his gorgeous, gray eyes looking intensely back into mine. He leans down and presses a tender kiss to my lips.

"The truth of the matter, Little Fawn is... I've never felt anything like this before either. Never did I ever imagine having someone in my bed, where I longed to wake up with them in my arms. With you, I not only want to be inside you... I want to be *beside* you... be with you in every way. I truly can't seem to get enough of you, Cole."

We lose ourselves in a long, languid kiss as he slowly lowers us back down to the bed. We stay like that, kissing until our lips are tingling and swollen.

Eventually, Rogan leads me to the ensuite where he walks me into the shower and cleans us both from head to toe.

Once we're dried off, we return to the bed, lightly dozing in each other's arms as the morning sun slowly brightens the room.

Chapter 50

Rogan

Cole and I lay in bed, watching the sun crest the horizon, her head nestled against my chest while her fingers absently trace over the ink of one of my tattoos as I hold her tucked in close to my side. Before long, I hear her breathing slow, her fingers stilling against my arm and realize she's dozed off again.

Once I know she's fallen deeply asleep, I carefully slide out from beneath her, slip on a pair of gray sweatpants and head to my mother's wing of the castle. This section of the Manor has remained practically untouched, aside from the light cleaning the maids do to keep the dust from accumulating. Mother was about the same size as Cole. I gather some of her clothing so she'll have something to wear, instead of having to put on the torn, wet clothing from the night before.

When I get back to my room, Cole's awake. She's standing in front of the windows looking down at the town below. Wrapped in a bed sheet, her hair tousled from sleep and well... our other activities—and damn it if she isn't just a fucking vision—the mere sight of her making something in my chest pinch.

Not wanting to startle her, I softly clear my throat. Her lips turn up in a brilliant smile when her eyes meet mine and fuck... that twinge in my chest pinches again.

Meeting her smile with my own, I cross the room to her, bending to kiss her and offer her the clothes I brought.

"What's this?" She asks, looking at the clothes in my hands with a raised brow.

"As much as I'd love to keep you naked in my bed all day, my sweet Little Fawn," I pull her into me, "I fear if I don't let you recover, you'll begin to chafe!" I say playfully, bending to kiss her on the tip of her nose.

She laughs, wrapping her arms around me and snuggles into my chest.

"Thank you." She says, but then pulls back.

"Wait… but… whose clothes are these?" She pauses, her brow pinched, a look of apprehension on her face.

I smile down at her, realizing she's probably worried they belonged to some other woman. I pull her back into me, stroking my hand down her back.

"They were my mother's, my darling."

She relaxes against me, snuggling into me again.

"Oh… okay then. Thank you, Rogan." She huffs a laugh, her lips so close to my skin I feel them brush across the muscles of my chest.

My groin starts to pulse again, blood heading back toward my cock—ever the vigilant soldier—clearly believing his services will be required again. Clearing my throat, I give her a quick kiss on the top of her head before stepping back slightly, knowing full well if I hold her much longer, there will be no leaving this bedroom any time soon and the poor girl is probably starving.

As if my thought alone evoked it, Cole's stomach growls loudly and her cheeks immediately turn a deep shade of pink.

"You must be starved after all that… *exercise* last night." I give her a cheeky grin and wink, waggling my eyebrows suggestively at her. If possible, her cheeks pinken even further, but she giggles and nods.

"I actually am very hungry."

"Splendid! I'll get us some breakfast and then we can do whatever you want today. Sound good?" I ask, briskly walking across the room to pick up my phone to call down to the kitchens.

"Mmm hmm." Cole replies absently, picking up the clothing and admiring it before starting to dress while I order the food.

We decide, since Greg gave her the whole week off, we'd start with a tour of the Manor and then just let the days take us wherever they may from there.

James brings us our meal and we eat in my room at the very same table where I sat with Brick the day I learned about Cole Allbright.

Watching her sink her teeth into the ripe flesh of a strawberry, before lifting her coffee cup to her lips, I can't even believe this is the same woman I'd wanted gone, not so long ago. This same woman I now can't even stand to be away from for more than a few minutes at a time without feeling something inside me go wild with need.

She's consumed me in a way I never believed was possible... in a way I don't even think she realizes.

I find myself just watching her, mesmerized by her every movement. The way her jaw moves as she chews, the way her throat works as she swallows, her tongue as she licks the small drop of berry juice from her lips...

She's intoxicating and I'm beyond drunk on every part of her. Enraptured by her very being. This foreign feeling in my chest overtaking my entire life.

Brick had said...*love*. And goddamnit, but I think the bastard might be right.

Walking through the halls of the Manor, I'm reminded of our first date as we walked through the woods. Cole's arm linked through mine, her head resting against my bicep as we walked and talked about everything and nothing.

We stop occasionally so I can explain the tales behind different portraits or statues she finds intriguing and I point out different architectural details I feel will spark her interest. She seems fascinated by every single detail, seemingly never growing bored of my ramblings, always having dozens of follow up questions to the items I tell her about. She also seems to sense when certain pieces are of greater importance or value to me, because I feel her lean into me, asking more in-depth questions when we stop and talk about them.

When we get to the main hall, we stop at a family portrait, framed in silver, sitting atop the large fireplace. This one is of me, my parents and my brother—right before he left for the military.

I feel Cole's eyes on me as we stand there looking up at the picture, her grip tight on my arm. She watches me intently, waiting patiently for me to tell her about the portrait. We stand in silence for a while, until I feel her give my arm a light squeeze. I clear my throat and stroke my thumb across her knuckles before finally dragging my gaze off the photo to smile down at her.

"Are you okay?" Her sweet eyes study my face with genuine concern.

I give her a tight-lipped smile and nod.

"Yes, I'm alright."

I let out a long breath, preparing for the story behind the image that both haunts me and brings me peace.

"This is my family. My mother, father, brother and, of course... there's me." Clearing my throat again, I struggle to swallow past the lump in my throat, blinking as my eyes burn.

Cole nods, her eyes tracing the faces of each person in the picture before looking back to me, patiently waiting for me to go on.

When I don't say more, aware the silence is growing heavy between us, she shifts on her feet, never letting go of my arm.

Tentatively, she whispers, "What was his name?"

"Devon...," I smile down at her. "His name was Devon."

"Devon," she repeats thoughtfully, the corners of her mouth turning up as her eyes go back to the image of him on the mantlepiece. Stepping up to the portrait, she traces her fingers reverently along the outline of Devon's face. Feeling the absence of her touch, I find myself awkwardly unsure of what to do with my hands, so I push them into my pockets and rock back on my heels as I watch her studying his image—an unfamiliar tug tightening in my chest.

"You look like him."

Peering back at me over her shoulder, her voice is soft, wistful. Her wide green eyes, glassy as they trace over my own features. Somehow understanding the pain I feel without knowing the whole story—the ache in my chest tightening even further, threatening to cut off my air.

I nod, my throat tight and my eyes stinging as I fight the tears wanting to form there, the ever-present phantom ache, nagging at the corners of my mind.

"Your mom was a beautiful lady."

Her focus returns to the portrait again, her finger skimming the diminutive form holding onto Devon's arm.

"You have her eyes."

"She was...," my voice cracks as a hot tear tracks down my face.

I offer my hand as she steps back to me and she threads her fingers through mine. The moment they're joined, I feel grounded again—whole. The connection inexplicably allows me to breathe again.

She reaches up to brush away the tear I hadn't even realized had escaped my eye, brushing the pad of her thumb across my cheek, then wraps her arms around me, pulling me into her, burying her face against my chest.

"I'm so sorry, Rogan. I know how you feel. I miss my mom too..."

I fold my arms around her and I pull her tightly into me, and for the first time I can remember, truly let myself feel the loss of my mother and brother in the presence of another.

Chapter 51

Cole

I blink my eyes open as the first glimmers of soft winter sun peak through the wide windows. The fire burned down to embers, the cool air of the room caresses my body, lightly stroking the places newly awoken by his touch. I can feel the heat of his body as he lies beside me, his usually rugged features softened by sleep, making him look younger—a tiny glimpse of the boy he once was.

His normally meticulously styled hair, falls haphazardly across his brow. A smile teases the corners of my lips as I reach over to gently brush it back, but the dark locks disobey me, immediately falling back down across his forehead.

Pushing up on one elbow, my eyes trail leisurely down his body as I take the opportunity to appreciate his stunning form. The sleek muscles of his back slope downward before curving back up to his perfect, tight, bare ass. His long legs, lean and strong, are sculpted from years of running, honed to perfection. Those same legs on which he knelt before me, gazing up at me with a look of reverence before dipping his mouth between my thighs.

The muscles in his leg, slightly bent between us, flex and shift—as though, even in sleep, the need to move continues to drive him.

As my gaze trails back up his body, I bite back a wicked grin when I see the tiny pink marks I've left on his skin. Slightly raised crescents from where my nails dug into his flesh when I desperately needed to hold onto something as he drove his steely length into me again and again. Showing me with each thrust of his hips, each word of praise whispered into my ear, that sex could be so much more than pain and punishment—taking me to heights of pleasure I never even knew existed, over and over and over again. The sensations, so new, so incredible as he brought me to the brink of heaven, then ushered me back down to Earth on a cloud of gentle, blissful ecstasy.

His broad shoulders slowly rise and fall with each relaxed breath. One large arm framing his head, the other curled into a loose fist, just below his chin. His fingers twitch slightly against the onyx silk sheets.

My attention moves to the ink decorating his back. Not wanting to wake him, I carefully lean in, looking more closely at the extensive and highly detailed tattoos mapping his body. Dark Celtic symbols and thick lines of tribal art scroll across his shoulders, then branch across to run down the deep ridges of his thickly muscled arms. Another one sits proudly on his bicep and looks to be an Army insignia of some sort—a sword framed by wings, flared wide on either side of the blade.

I lightly trace the thick lines of one of his many tribal designs, marveling at the artwork, but as I continue to move my fingers along the ink, I feel the ridges of what I hadn't seen before.

The unmistakable rise of a thick scar.

I flinch, pulling my hand away and sit up straighter. My eyes flick to his face, where he still sleeps peacefully. Desperately hoping not to wake him, I carefully lean in to try to get a closer look.

Having discovered this one, the rest all seem so obvious now. Each one hidden under the dark designs etched into his skin.

Reading his body like a book I've read a thousand times, I understand all too well what caused the marks I now see.

Round burns, roughly the size of a quarter...

I lightly smooth my finger over one on his back, then trace along a similar one on my own arm—*cigar burns.*

Now in tune to what was previously hidden from view, I locate the longer, deeper scars, marring his back with crisscrossed hatch marks. My throat tightens and my eyes burn knowing they're likely the result of being struck with a belt buckle, whipped at him with enough force, to not only break the skin, but so much, it left a long, deep gash in the wake of each and every brutal lashing.

I cover my mouth, trying to stifle a sob as my eyes spill over, unable to hold back the massive wave of grief and anger that barrels into me. The sudden realization that this strong, seemingly unflappable man, actually has a far deeper understanding of what it means to be abused. So much more than just the compassionate sympathy I'd assumed it to be, as he listened to my own tale.

I press my fist hard against my lips, my eyes squeezing shut as my heart breaks for him and the secrets, he's felt the need to keep locked inside. I know the feeling all too well and just how crippling and exhausting it is to carry the weight of it all alone.

He shifts beside me. My eyes fly open and dart to his face. I freeze, praying I haven't woken him. He doesn't need to see me crying yet again. Especially over something he's apparently gone to great lengths to disguise and keep hidden from the world.

He mutters something in his sleep, his eyes flitting back and forth beneath his eyelids as his fingers clench, tightly gripping the sheet in his fist. I hold my breath, but he stills again, sleep pulling him deeper into its embrace.

I let out a slow, shaky breath and quickly swipe the tears off my face. I lean in and brush a soft kiss over one of his hidden scars, then slip from the bed and pad into the bathroom.

In the mirror, I study my pale face, my eyes red and puffy from the tears I've been trying desperately not to shed.

"Get a God damn grip, Cole! Enough with the fucking tears already!" I chastise myself, swiping angrily at my wet cheeks. I blow out a harsh breath and wrench the tap harder than necessary to splash some cool water on my face.

"It's none of your damn business and it's not your place to pry. He'll tell you when—," I shake my head, "*if* he's ever ready."

I pat my face dry with a towel and sigh, bracing my hands on the countertop, frowning down into the sink.

"NO!"

Rogan's loud shout from the bedroom jolts me from my thoughts and I jump back from the sink, clapping my hand over my mouth to stifle a yelp of my own.

"STOP!"

He barks again. I slowly move to the bathroom door, tentatively pressing my ear to the wood. Eyes wide, I listen, trying to figure out who he's shouting at.

Has someone broken in?

Is he fighting them off?

"THE GIRL! BRICK! THE GIRL!"

The girl?

What girl?

Does he mean me?

My mind scrambles to think of what could be happening, immediately assuming the worst.

Dear God! Has Cain *found me?*

My heart thunders in my chest as silence descends on the room beyond the bathroom door again—so deep I can practically feel it seep into my bones. Pressing my ear harder against the door, straining to listen, I hold my breath, waiting for any more sounds.

It's silent for such a long time, my curiosity finally gets the best of me and I reach for the door handle. As I start to turn it, Rogan's voice breaks through the silence again and I pull my hand back, listening again.

His voice is quieter now—meeker... and he's... pleading.

"Papa... please...

I'm sorry, no please, Papa...

I'm sorry...

I'm sorry... Papa, please stop..."

Cold realization hits me when the truth of what I'm hearing dawns on me...

He's having a nightmare. His unconscious mind has him trapped in a hellish loop of memories past.

Knowing all too well the torment and horror those types of dreams can evoke, I throw the door open and run to the bed. He's rolled over on his side, his knees pinned up to his chest, his arms raised, shielding his face, attempting to protect himself from the blows his past memories are forcing him to relive, believing they're about to be doled out, yet again.

Doing the only thing I can think of, I climb onto the bed and kneel at his side, gripping his wrists to try to pry them away from his face in an effort to wake him from his nightmare.

He flails beneath me, his body coated in sweat. It takes all my strength to keep hold of him as he swings his arms wildly. His wrist connects with my cheek bone and pain flares through the side of my face, but I grip his wrists harder, forcing them down as I work to straddle his writhing form—pinning him between my legs, laying my body across his and encircling him in a tight hug.

"Rogan! Rogan, wake up!" I call loudly to him, his skin hot against my cheek. Using all my strength, I strain to hold on to him as he bucks beneath me.

"Rogan—it's okay! I'm here! Rogan! Wake up!"

His movements are so visceral, so violent, his cries so heartbreakingly cutting. My chest aches for him as he struggles to outrun the ghost of a threat from his past, still haunting his present.

His unseeing eyes are wide open, but he's not conscious, his tortured mind locked in the throes of his nightmare. I continue to hold him, calling to him, trying to pry him free from the jaws of his invisible attacker.

"Rogan, baby, it's me. It's Cole... I'm right here! Please wake up! You're alright, it's not real! Come on out of it baby, please just wake up!"

I can barely keep hold of him, my hands slipping on his sweat slickened wrists, so I wrap my arms around his chest, burying my face against his neck, holding onto him with every ounce of strength I have as he writhes beneath me, fighting against my grip—all the while telling him it's okay. Trying desperately to reassure him he's not alone, I'm here and none of this is real.

Gradually, his thrashing movements begin to calm, his breathing starts to even out and his heart beat eventually slows—though I can still feel its heavy thrum as it pounds hard against the ear I have pressed against his chest.

Holding him tight, unwilling to let him go, I refuse to let him suffer through this alone. As his consciousness slowly returns, his fingers skate lightly up my spine, threading into my hair. I lift my face to his, his gray eyes finding my green—deep fathomless windows peering between two shattered souls.

"Cole?"

He studies me, looking a little lost. His voice rasps, rough from screaming. I slide up his body, bringing my face to his. Tracing his damp brow, I brush the hair off his forehead, then stroke my fingers down the side of his face, lightly raking my nails along his stubbled jaw.

"I'm here, Rogan."

He cups my face, softly running this thumb along my reddened cheekbone and his brows pinch, his lips pulling into a tight line as his jaw clenches.

"I hurt you."

My heart squeezes... his first concern, for me instead of dwelling on the trauma he's just relived.

"No." I hurriedly shake my head and quickly press my lips to his just as a tear slides down my cheek.

He pulls his head back into the pillow, trying to study my face. His knowing eyes scan me, seeing everything, while his thumb gently strokes along my cheekbone. I offer him a small smile while I try to convey everything I want to say with that one look.

Everything is okay.

I'm here... with you.

You're not alone.

We *are not alone... anymore.*

"Fuck! Cole, I'm so goddamn sorry." He whispers through clenched teeth, pulling me to him and tenderly kissing my forehead.

Releasing a bit of tension, I let a small laugh break free.

"Hey, what is it you always say to me? *'Don't you dare apologize, Little Fawn'*" I parrot in a terrible mock British accent.

"You told me that word is banned, remember?"

A small smile lifts the corner of his mouth while his fingers lightly feather across my cheek. His body trembles slightly beneath me, his eyes tracing over my face as if he's seeing it for the first time.

I lean into him, our mouths meeting softly, then I snuggle into him as his arms wrap around me, holding me close and our hearts beat against each other—a sense of peace, belonging and trust, descending upon us with their combined rhythm.

Chapter 52

"We were on patrol, on our last tour..." I tell her as we sit in bed together, our backs resting against the headboard, the covers pulled over us, a mug of coffee in her hand, a tea in mine. She's pressed against me, my arm wrapped around her shoulders, my fingers feathering lightly up and down her ribs. Those attentive green eyes watch me while I tell my story.

I take a sip from my mug, then rest my head back, feeling my eyes get hazy, staring off into the distance while my fingers continue to dance across her skin, anchoring me in some small way to the present, while I relive one of my worst nightmares.

"Brick and I were formidable. Even in a group of hard-asses, we were known to be the hardest. If there was a mission deemed impossible, we were the ones they sent in. Either to run it or execute it, but more often than not, we were doing both."

I pause, taking another sip from my mug and relishing the feel of her warmth against my side, her fingers absently trailing through the hairs on my chest.

"Brick's skill at disarming any bomb could effectively knock the power out of any enemy insurgent's base in mere minutes. He was always two steps ahead of everyone else, tackling problems with his signature, easy calm."

I feel her smile against my chest. My skin pebbles as her breath skates over me and I pull her deeper into my side.

"That bloody eidetic memory of his meant he only had to look at a route or a plan once, and he'd have the damn thing memorized. He knew all the ways in and out of a compound, secret rooms, hot spots, even the areas where civilians were most likely to be.

"My forté was for fixing problems. Manipulating weak spots and figuring out how we would be able to get done what everyone else had deemed impossible. That and not really giving a shite about what we had to do or how we did it." My unsaid words hang heavy in the air between us. I put my mug down on the side table and take a long, slow breath before continuing.

"In the SAS, we say, *'Who dares, wins.'* And that was the motto we lived by. And we always won... Always..." my nostrils flare and my insides tense, "that is until our last mission."

Cole's wide eyes meet mine. She sits up a little straighter, turning to deposit her mug on her own side table before tucking her body in close to my side. She wraps her arms around me and gives me a reassuring nod as she looks up at me, patiently waiting for me to tell her something I've never shared with another soul outside of the Army.

"We'd scouted that compound for days..."

Our source had assured us, the family with children would be leaving soon, so we focused on readying ourselves for the next phase of the operation. It's hell hiding in this damn souk, the time dragging on for what feels like an eternity. By the fifth day, the men are getting restless, sand sticking to our sweat soaked skin while we watch, essentially waiting in our own version of purgatory for our chance to make our move.

The tension is palpable. The men wound tight and ready to pounce when the night finally came that the family left. So it doesn't take us long before we've executed our plan, rolling truckloads full of armed men into the compound.

The plan is simple... get in, capture the leader, destroy the weapons and bring back any intelligentsia we can find.

We've all got our roles. Me as lead in command, Brick my second. Then there's Rabbit, a sniper with an impressive list of kill shots.

Patch, our medic and his dog Roxy—the best damn sniffer dog in the Army. And the kid... Joey. A cocky little fucker who just passed into the ranks of the SAS, this being his first live mission. Damn kid is so pumped up; I wouldn't be surprised if he jizzed in his pants. Ready to go, cock sure and full of hell, sights locked on earning his first stripes.

It should be easy... just a quick mission. We all know our objectives forward and back.

Rabbit, true to his name, moves quickly, taking out the guards in the towers and at the gates, while I deal with the ones at ground level, the blade of my knife taking care of things quickly and quietly.

Patch and Roxy are on my six, Roxy working that extraordinary nose of hers as we come up to the main gate. I motion for them to stand back while I place a small device against the lock and detonate it, allowing us entry.

Brick is making his way around to the other side of the compound to do his thing, Joey at his side. There's a flash from Rabbit's light—our code indicating it's safe to proceed. Inside the compound we can see the trucks, loaded with covered crates filled with rifles, rocket launchers and bomb making materials. Roxy goes crazy with all the scents she's trained to find assailing her.

But I can't shake the feeling there's something off. Something's not right. It's eerily quiet... and there isn't a single person here.

Not one.

*Everything about this feels...*wrong.

Brick and Joey head toward the center of the compound having reconned the rooms and come up empty. There should have been more resistance... more hostiles. More than just the men outside, guarding the site.

This is too easy...

I shake off the feeling and decide to radio it in, to bring in the reinforcements to move the contraband out. But just as I reach for my radio, all hell breaks loose.

There wasn't a single plan showing that hidden cellar—not one.

Multiple trap doors hidden... right there in plain sight.

We didn't stand a chance as they burst through, guns blazing. Roxy is the first to be hit. The sound of her whimpering cries as Patch pulls her behind a crate will haunt me for the rest of my life.

Brick's pinned down behind a large stack of crates, forcing Joey's head down as he quickly assesses the situation, looking for the best path for us to get the fuck out of here. We share an unspoken message when our eyes meet across the short distance that now seems insurmountable.

Brick and I have always had our own way of communicating without words. One we'd adopted as kids at school and then, summers at the Manor on the days I was avoiding my father.

Silently we form a plan. A distraction so we can get to the truck and get the fuck out.

"We were nearly there Cole," I barely recognize my own voice, my words a raspy whisper in the dim room. I look down to see I have both her hands gripped in mine, my knuckles white as she listens, looking up at me with wide, horror-filled eyes.

Loosening my grip on her hands, I kiss her forehead, brushing her hair behind her ear, then pull her against my side again. The warmth of her body, a soothing balm, easing the pain before I slip back into the memory.

Rabbit's providing cover for us, while Patch loads Roxy's bleeding body onto the bed of a truck. I take out everyone that gets in my path as I make my way to the cab of the truck. I wrench open the driver's door and scramble in, ready to get us the hell out of here. But Brick and Joey are still pinned down, unable to move.

I turn the key and the engine grinds, turning over again and again, but it won't catch. I pump the gas a couple times and try again, my eyes locked on where Brick is now struggling with a flailing Joey. I can't hear what's being said, but they're arguing. Brick is shaking his head, grabbing at Joey as he pulls away. Suddenly, Joey turns on Brick, punching him in the jaw. Brick's head rocks back, dazed by the unexpected blow.

I don't know what the hell's gotten into him, but once Joey's broken free of Brick's grip, he stands, just out of his reach, unloading his gun everywhere. He's not aiming... just... pulling the fucking trigger and screaming at the top of his lungs like a mad man.

Brick is still shouting at him, trying to pull him back down, but the bloodlust has Joey in a stronghold now. He fires until his gun is empty, continuing to pull the trigger even after all the bullets have been spent. Then he's leaping over the wall, straight toward a crate of rifles...

That was his fatal mistake...

I watch it all play out as if in slow motion. Behind Joey, an insurgent rears up, his machete raised. He swings it down in a brutal arc, bringing it down right toward Joey's neck...

Brick's bullet hits the bastard with the machete right between the eyes, but not before his blade cleaves Joey's head from his body.

Bile lurches up my throat and I retch out the window of the truck. I'm breathing hard, trying to get my head around what the fuck just happened. I don't know how long I sit there, like a dazed fucking asshole, the world around me feeling like it's moving too fast and too slow all at the same time, before I hear Brick screaming my name—reminding me some of us are still alive. Living souls that I need to get the fuck out of here.

That snaps me out of it and I jump back out of the cab, pulling out my gun to provide cover fire while Brick throws Joey's body up over his shoulder. He bolts toward the truck, stooping to grab Joey's head as he runs. He tucks it under his arm, holding it close to his body like a goddamn rugby ball and my stomach lurches again at the sight.

There's a spray of blood from his shoulder and he stumbles forward, as a bullet slams into him, but the big bastard barely misses a step as he continues to barrel toward the truck.

After tossing Joey's remains onto the bed next to Roxy and Patch, he climbs up himself—hands coated in Joey's blood. I jump back into the driver's seat, and gun the engine. This time it roars to life, but before we can move, a bullet tears into the side of Patch's neck, hitting his jugular.

He's dead in seconds.

Brick pounds his fist on the cab of the truck, screaming for me to go. I stomp the pedal to the floor and drive, ploughing right over insurgents without a second thought. I don't stop until we crest the hill, when we're back at the rendezvous point, meeting back up with Rabbit.

We've lost three good soldiers.

Good men...

Friends.

Every one of us is caked in blood and sand.

Bloodied, broken...

Defeated.

Rabbit had seen it all and already radioed for an emergency evac, the transport already on their way.

That's when I see her.

The girl.

She can't be more than twelve or thirteen years old. Tears tracking through the dust on her face as she walks steadily toward us. I step out of the truck and slowly start to approach her. My first thought is she's somehow been entangled in the mess below and needs our help.

She looks so... young...

So innocent...

I can't seem to catch my breath as tears streak down my face. Holding a fist over my mouth, I pinch my eyes shut—chest shaking as the pain of reliving this memory out loud washes over me.

Blowing out a shuddering breath I wipe roughly at my eyes and push forward, to get through to the end of my story.

"Rabbit was closest to her when she detonated the bomb she had strapped to her body. The blast blew me back and knocked me clean out. I didn't know anything more until I woke up in the sick bay, concussed, confused and so fucking pissed off, raving like a fucking lunatic.

"Four soldiers lost. Four fucking *friends* lying dead in the sand."

My shoulders shake as I try to draw in a ragged breath.

"I was so frantic, Brick was the only one who could hold me down. The only one who even stood a chance of getting through to me."

My words fall away and I let the silence hang in the air for a couple minutes, just breathing through it. Cole waits patiently beside me until I find my words again.

"It was just three days later; we received our new orders. I was told my father had died, that I was now the Duke of Wyeholme and my stint in the Army was officially over. Brick decided to leave the Army with me."

Her hand slides across my body, curling into me, hugging me close. A silent reassurance, quietly letting me know she's still here.

"Going home presented its own set of problems." I continue, my fingers finding her skin again, feathering lightly up and down her side.

"My relationship with my father was... *strained*. My mother had died several years before and his beloved first born had died in service not long before mum. To this day, I think my father died from shame because his spare had survived what his heir had not."

I sniff, swallowing back the lump in my throat as my anger for my father moves to the forefront of my emotions.

"Devon was a good few years older than me. When he left to join the army, and without my mum to protect me, my father took out his frustrations on me."

Cole moves to sit up, gently resting her hand on my shoulder, motioning for me to lean forward. Her fingers lightly trace the scars hidden beneath the tattoos covering them.

Her voice is soft, almost clinical as I feel her touch lightly slide over one of the dark circles in a Celtic tattoo on my shoulder blade. "He burned you... with cigars," she continues, tracing her fingers along a particularly wide welt, "and whipped you with a belt, right?"

I feel my skin pebble beneath her touch, and even though I instinctively want to pull away, I don't.

Instead, I nod, confirming what she's already figured out.

"It was worse when he was in the whiskey," I huff a cynical laugh, "which was most of the damn time."

I shift back and slide my hand softly down her bare arm, bringing it to my lips to press a tender kiss to one of the circular burn marks there before running my thumb over it gently.

"I wish I could wipe these away for you," I hear my voice break and another tear escapes over my lower lashes. "I wish I could have protected you from the fuckers who hurt you."

"I wish I could have done the same for you." She whispers back, her hand coming up to cup my cheek, catching the tear with her thumb and wiping it away as her emerald eyes lift to mine.

"I haven't slept properly in years," I confess, "and definitely not with anyone else in my bed. It's one of the reasons why Brick stays close. So, he can talk me down before the dreams drive me mad."

I swipe a hand across my eyes again, staring defeatedly at the glistening tears I've been holding back for so goddamn long.

"I owe that big bastard my life." I sniff, chuffing a laugh.

She slides down in the bed and motions for me to lie with her. I follow her down to the mattress, settling my head over her heart. Her arms come around me and pull me in tight against her.

I wrap my arm around her waist and melt into her. I can't hold back the shudder that rolls through me as she runs her fingers through my hair.

"Shhh... It's over now. And we can keep each other safe from now on. Sleep now, Rogan. I've got your six."

Her arms tighten around me and I breathe out a heavy sigh.

"Thank you, Cole." I say before finally letting my body relax completely against her. Her fingers continue to stroke through my hair and she starts to hum softly. Something about the tune is familiar and I realize it's a song my mother used to sing to me when I was a little boy. One more tear slips from my eye.

Soon my breathing deepens, my heart rate settling. Slowing until I gradually drift into a deep, dreamless sleep—as the sun continues to rise, bathing the room in the soft, golden glow of dawn.

Chapter 53

Rogan

When we return to the Manor after our afternoon at the bookshop, Cole takes me by the hands, pulling me with her as she backs into the bedroom.

"I want to try to do something for you."

I laugh happily, curiously watching her eyes sparkle as I follow her in.

"You don't need to do anything for me, Little Fawn, but if it's something you want, then anything your heart desires is yours." I say, watching her with a besotted smile on my lips, as she tugs me closer toward the bed.

She stops, sitting down on the edge, moving me to stand in front of her. She licks her lips, bringing the side of her finger to her mouth, nibbling nervously at the cuticle—a pensive look settling into her eyes.

I gently remove it from between her teeth and smooth my thumb over the reddened edge of skin, then bring her hand to my lips, pressing a light kiss to her knuckles.

Studying her anxious expression, I'm compelled to ask, "What's going on, Little Fawn?"

"I..." her voice cracks and she takes a deep breath before trying again. "I want to...," she pauses, licking her lips, "taste you," she whispers, her voice barely audible.

I lower down to my knees in front of her and tuck a thick lock of her auburn hair behind her ear before cupping her cheek and bringing my mouth to hers, kissing her deeply.

"You know you don't have to do that, Cole."

She nods against my hand, her wide emerald eyes flitting back and forth between mine.

"I know I don't have to but..." she licks her lips again, "it's something I really want to do for you, Rogan."

My heart squeezes in my chest. Far be it from me to deny this woman anything she wants, but to hear her say she wants to *taste me...*

Fucking hell!

The thought of her lips wrapped around me sends a surge of heat sprinting to my balls, blood rushing straight to my cock and my pants tighten uncomfortably at my groin from the rapid swell.

I dip my chin and study her eyes, making sure she's not pushing herself past a point she's not yet ready for.

"You're sure?"

She meets my stare—determination blazing in her eyes and nods.

"Yes, I'm very sure." She says, her face shifting with serious conviction as she confidently stands up, pulling her shirt off over her head. My eyes drop to her breasts, my mouth watering at the sight of her pale flesh, her nipples hardened into peaks, visible through the thin lace of her bra.

I groan, my mouth dropping immediately onto the swell of her perfect tits, pulling her into me as I suck the soft flesh into my mouth, soaking the fabric.

Her arms wrap around my head arching into me and holding me against her as I suck and nip at her breasts. I unclasp her bra and pull it down her arms, returning my mouth to her bare breast, gently raking my teeth over her nipple and swirling my tongue before sucking it back into my mouth. She moans, her hips pushing forward involuntarily.

I curl my fingers into her leggings and panties, taking them both down her legs at the same time, quickly removing them from her body.

I press her back down on the bed, toss her legs over my shoulders and plunge my tongue into her hot, wet center, consuming her like I've only known famine—my hunger for her, insatiable. Drinking from her as if parched—my thirst for her, unquenchable.

She writhes beneath me, her fingers digging into my hair, pulling me tightly to her as I lick into her perfect cunt, driving my tongue deeper, groaning as I lose myself in her taste.

I slide two fingers into her, curling them upward as I thrust in and out of her, my tongue dancing over her clit.

I look up to see her watching me devour her, her eyes molten pools of jade. With a twist of my fingers and rapid flick of my tongue, her head drops back on a gasp, "Rogan, oh my God, Rogan!"

She starts to tense, her hips rocking frantically in time with each thrust of my hand.

"That's it, come for me, Little Fawn." I demand, then drop my mouth over her clit and suck. With a cry, she explodes—her pussy clamping down hard on my hand, pulsing and squeezing as a rush of wet heat coats my fingers. I plunge my tongue back into her center, sucking and licking at her, drinking down every drop of her pleasure, until she slowly comes down, her orgasm gradually ebbing to gentle tremors.

Her chest heaves as she tries to catch her breath and loops her hand behind by head to pull herself up. The green of her irises is nearly swallowed by her pupils and she leans in, taking my mouth and plunging her tongue between my lips.

She pulls me to my feet and dips her fingers into my waistband, making quick work of the button and zipper, freeing my aching cock. I grunt as it slaps against my abs. She grips it firmly, stroking her hand up and down, pumping it with hard, confident strokes.

She slides down to the floor, resting on her knees and leans in, tentatively licking the shining pearl of precum from my tip, her eyes jumping up to mine as I hiss at the contact.

She runs her tongue over her bottom lip and I cup her jaw, staring at her adoringly. She closes her eyes, smiling as she lightly tugs her lip between her teeth and hums low in her throat, leaning into my touch.

"Fucking perfect." I purr, running my thumb along her jaw.

Opening her eyes, they hungrily trace up the muscles of my stomach, eventually landing on mine again, the emerald shining like gemstones beneath her long lashes. My cock twitches in her hand in anticipation when one side of her mouth curls into a soft, knowing smile.

I return her smile, my chest rising and falling more rapidly as my breathing starts to quicken.

"Take your time. Your bare skin against me is more than enough."

I instinctively slide my hand to the nape of her neck, threading my fingers into her hair, cradling her head in my hand. Applying no pressure, just holding her reverently—stroking my thumb gently beneath her ear.

My cock twitches again and her lips part. Flattening her tongue, she presses it solidly to the base of my crown, applying the perfect amount of pressure before swirling it around, gently squeezing her hand on my shaft.

My hips buck forward slightly and I bite my lip, drawing in a quick breath, my nostrils flaring as I use all of my strength to resist pushing my cock further between her plump lips.

Emboldened by my reactions, she licks the tip again and I groan, my eyes falling closed. Gaining confidence, she widens her mouth, gradually stretching her lips over the head as she slowly takes my crown into her mouth.

"Good girl…" I growl, my voice more breath than sound.

I pant, straining against my desire to thrust further into her perfect mouth. The corded muscles in my neck tense as I swallow down my need.

Again, I feel her widen her mouth a bit further as she slowly starts to take in more of my length. The hot, wet slide of her tongue along the underside of my shaft makes my balls tighten—my grip on her neck tensing slightly as my fingers begin to curl into her hair.

Her eyes find me again, and the lust I see in her gaze combined with the feel of her lips wrapped around my cock—her cautious descent, a slow, sweet torture like nothing I've ever felt before, already has need barreling through me and my spine tingling.

"Yes, that's it, love. Mmmmm... You're doing so well, Cole." I meet her gaze, my voice gravely when I speak.

Breathlessly I ask her, "Do you think you can take just a bit more?"

The corners of her lips curl up just enough that I catch her smile, her eyes sparkling devilishly as she hums her agreement around my cock. She bobs her head up and down in a shallow nod—the movement and vibrations have my hips bucking again. I grit my teeth and have to clench my muscles to stop myself from driving forward.

Widening her jaw, she pushes her mouth down my shaft, sliding it rapidly all the way to the back. She gags and pulls her mouth off of me quickly, her eyes watering.

"I'm sorry..." She starts to say as she gasps for breath.

"Ah, ahh. What did we say about apologies, Little Fawn?" I gently admonish her, smiling as I shake my head. I stroke my thumb beneath her eye to wipe away the moisture.

"Everything's alright. Do you want to stop?"

She shakes her head, "No... no, I can do this. I *want* to do this."

"Alright, then... only when you're ready." I tell her, my fingers threading back into her hair as she moves forward again.

After taking a few slow breaths, she leans in, her lips stretching over my cock again, slower this time. She gradually takes in more of my length, beginning to bob her head, gliding her mouth up and down my aching cock, stroking her hand in time with the movement, seating me deeper and deeper each time she lowers her mouth.

My hips begin to move in time with each bob of her head. "That's it, Cole... that's it, love." I grunt, gently thrusting my cock between her lips. I bite down on my bottom lip to hold back from fucking into her mouth as hard as I'd like.

I look down at her, watching each time my dick disappears further between her beautiful lips. The sight of her on her knees before me, my hard cock slick with her saliva, her swollen lips wrapped around my shaft, my fingers threaded through her soft, auburn locks. The vision ratchets up my desire tenfold, making my balls ache with an urgent need to come.

Suddenly, she pulls her mouth off of my cock, panting as she looks up at me, her hand still sliding rhythmically up and down my shaft.

"Tell me how..." She pleads, then glides her tongue along the full length of my cock, wrapping her lips around the crown and sucking it back into her mouth before releasing it again.

"I want to know how to take you deeper."

"Cole... I... you don't have to..." I tell her shaking my head, my hips moving of their own accord in time to meet each stroke of her hand, my grip now tight in her hair.

"Please Rogan, tell me... show me. I want to... no, I *need* to do this."

I drag my thumb across her lower lip, slowly pulling it down exposing her bottom teeth. Her tongue darts out to lick at my thumb before wrapping her lips around it, her cheeks hollowing as she hungrily sucks it into her mouth, her eyes never leaving mine—my knees damn near buckle at the sight.

"Alright! Jesus fucking hell, alright." A pained groan escapes my throat.

She releases my thumb with a pop, licking her lips as she grins up at me. I swallow hard, returning her grin.

"Have mercy, Little Fawn. You're going to be the fucking death of me." I chuckle.

Sliding my hand down her neck, I place that same thumb at the center of her throat and stroke gently.

"When you take me in, relax your throat and breathe through your nose. If you need to stop, just tap my thigh and we'll stop immediately, alright?"

She nods, her lust filled eyes moving off mine and dropping back to my cock. I feel her swallow against my hand before she opens her mouth wide, slowly stretching her lips over the head of my cock and sliding it all the way to the back of her mouth. I feel her tense up as my crown hits the back of her throat and she fights the urge to gag, but pulls back just a bit and takes another deep breath, then slides her lips up and down my shaft a few more times—each time taking a bit more of my length further into her mouth.

I feel her jaw flex, her mouth widening further as she opens her throat to stretch around the head of my cock as it slowly begins to seat deeper with each bob of her head.

I groan as the tightness of her throat squeezes me, feeling the movement of my cock in her throat with the hand I still have wrapped around her neck, as I slowly pump in and out of her mouth.

"Jesus fuck, Cole... yes!" I grit out through clenched teeth. "That's it... That's my good girl." I growl, losing myself as my legs begin to shake. Sliding my other hand into her hair, I start to pull her head forward, moving her mouth in time with each pump of my hips, my balls tightening as heat blooms up my spine. She relaxes her head and neck, letting me take over as my cock seats in her throat again and again, tears spilling down her cheeks as her eyes sparkle adoringly up at me.

"Little Fawn... mmmhh, I'm so fucking close." I breathe, as the movements of my hips begin to falter.

I start to pull away knowing I'm about to come, but she grips my hips, her fingers digging into the muscles of my ass, effectively pulling my cock even deeper into her throat. I look down to see her wet eyes blazing up at me with determination.

Her nails dig into my skin and I feel her throat work as she swallows down on my cock. My eyes roll back in my head and my legs shake at the tight squeeze.

"Fuck, Cole... you're gonna make me co..." but before the words are out of my mouth, my climax barrels through me.

"Fuuuuuckk!!"

I roar, my cock pulsing hard as I spill myself down her throat. Her eyes go wide, but she continues sucking me, gripping my hips tightly, her throat squeezing down on my cock again and again as she works to swallow every drop.

Once the most powerful pulses of my orgasm subside, she slides her mouth off of me, and licks her lips. Panting hard she wipes the back of her hand across her mouth. Her eyes are watery, but she's beaming up at me with a huge smile on her face.

It's the sight of her like this that takes the last of the strength from my legs and I drop to my knees before her, my limbs feeling like my bones are made of jelly. I grip both sides of her face and capture her mouth with mine, tasting the salt of my release on her lips.

Breaking the kiss, I press my forehead to hers, panting hard as I try to slow my racing heart, the combination of what she's just done and everything she's overcome to be who she is today, completely taking my breath away.

"You are the most extraordinary creature that's ever existed, Little Fawn."

I draw in a shuddering breath and take her face into my hands, swiping the tears off her cheeks. My eyes trace over every lovely feature, etching her into my memory, never wanting to forget this moment.

"You mystify me with everything you are..."

As I lose myself in the pools of her eyes, I know with everything I am and everything I will ever be, my next words will be the most important words I ever speak.

"I am so... in love with you, Cole."

Her eyes turn glassy as they flit back and forth between mine.

Her chin quivers as her lips lift into a soft smile, her hand reaching up to cup my face.

"I'm in love with you too, Rogan." She whispers as one tear spills over her lower lashes.

"So, so much."

I feel my brows pinch, my eyes dropping closed, my forehead falling gently against hers as I let out a long, slow breath. The relief at her words washes over me in a crashing wave. The tightness in my chest releases, replaced by a euphoric warmth that spreads all the way through me.

I capture her mouth with mine and we kiss, long and slow, the world around us be damned. I cocoon her in my arms, losing myself in her touch.

Her warm, naked body writhing beneath me.

Her soft skin, an intoxicating caress against mine.

Before long, I'm hard again, pressing up between her perfect thighs until I'm buried inside her, making desperate love to her right there on the floor beside the bed.

Chapter 54

Cole

My week off is nearly over, but what a week it's been. Blissfully shut away in our own perfect, little bubble, blocking out the rest of the world for as long as humanly possible. Happily ignoring the weight of responsibility, if only for a short time.

It's been absolute heaven. A full week loaded with seemingly unending pleasure as we've gotten to know one another, spending our time exploring the Manor, the grounds—and each other's bodies.

Any worries about recrimination after the events at the pub slowly slip away, Zavier now nothing more than a passing thought—a black stain in our memories.

We're pleasantly surprised by an unplanned visit from Kya and Brick.

"Just stopping by to make sure you two are still alive and breathing." Brick jokes, laughing loudly as he claps Rogan heartily on the back.

Kya sweeps me into a brutal hug, practically squeezing the air clean out of my lungs, beaming widely at me when she finally releases me.

Her ever-watchful eyes scan me from head to toe. Apparently satisfied I'm still in one piece, she giggles, her eyes taking on a devilish glint when she grabs me by the hands and pulls me into the next room, wanting all the juicy details of what the Duke and I have been up to for the past few days.

Once she's satisfied with the scandalous tidbits I'm willing to divulge, we move on to more mundane topics. Even though Rogan had promised he would see to their needs, Kya assures me I have nothing to worry about since she and Brick have been taking great care of Hannah and Athena for me in my absence.

Brick has taken upon himself—*I later found out Rogan had put him up to the task*—to keep a firm hand on the tiller, overseeing the workmen for me at the bookshop, making sure they stay on task, keeping them on a rigid schedule.

I have to admit, it feels like a huge weight has been lifted from me, and it goes a long way toward assuaging any lingering feelings of guilt I've been having at abandoning my pets and my responsibilities while I bask in the wonder of this new found version of my life, and of this man who's consuming not only my every waking thought, but in ways I never even thought were possible.

And who, *apparently*... feels the same way about me.

As we rejoin the men in the foyer, I move into Rogan's side. He smiles warmly at me and wraps his arm around me, pulling me into him as I snuggle against his chest. Kya catches my attention and gives me a knowing wink, her smile sparkling, sensing our unspoken wish to be alone.

She pokes Brick in the ribs with her elbow and lifts her chin toward the door, indicating it's time for them to take their leave of us. He hands her Grumbl's leash, but as she searches for the pup to get him tethered and ready to leave, he's nowhere to be found.

Rogan, Kya and I start to look around, but Brick lets out one quick, sharp whistle. In immediate response to the sound, the chubby puppy comes barreling out of the coat closet, proudly carrying one of Rogan's expensive looking leather shoes in his wet mouth.

"Grumbl!" Kya scolds, both she and I stooping to greet the little thief. I hold his shoulders while Kya wrestles the obviously destroyed shoe out from between his teeth. We look at each other wide-eyed, cringing and wrinkling our noses at the long line of slobber that pools out of the shoe.

Looking a bit sheepish, I hand the wet shoe back to Rogan, who looks at the pup with one brow lifted in a stern expression.

Grumbl doesn't miss a beat, sticking his little round rump up into the air and gives him a gruff bark before bouncing happily around his feet, completely unaffected by Rogan's look of condemnation.

I see the lines of Rogan's mouth tighten as he fights back the smile, but when Grumbl bounces a bit too high and flops clumsily onto his back, struggling to roll back onto his feet, he can't contain any semblance of sternness a second longer. He bursts out laughing, bending down to rub Grumbl's fat belly and then helps roll him back onto his feet, ruffling the wrinkles on the little dog's head once he's upright again.

Grumbl greedily leans into his touch, groaning loudly with pleasure as Rogan digs his fingers in to deepen the scratch.

"No wonder we haven't heard a peep from you this week," Kya leans into me conspiratorially. "If he can make Grumbl groan like that from just a scratch on the head, I can only imagine what those fingers can do when he—"

"Kya!" I whisper-shout. My cheeks flame and my eyes flare wide as I clap my hand over her mouth. She squeals, muffled laughter bubbling out around my fingers.

I shoot a quick glance over at Rogan, whose attention is seemingly fixed on Grumbl, but I see a deep dimple in his cheek where he's obviously trying to hold back a grin.

Brick, somehow missing the whole exchange, stands in the doorway, Kya's coat in hand looking confused.

Kya smiles and rolls her eyes when she sees his dumbfounded expression.

"Never mind, Brick. Just grown-up talk. You wouldn't understand." She grins up at him and pats him on the cheek, her fingers lingering there for a few seconds longer than necessary. The moment his eyes lock with hers, his expression shifts. Something in his eyes softening, like chocolate melting over the rim of a fountain. She gives him a wink, then turns to slip her arms into the sleeves of her jacket as he holds it out for her, his question about the previous interaction long forgotten.

She tugs me into another tight hug, clips Grumbl's leash to his harness, then quickly ushers Brick and the pup out the door. We watch our friends, closer to us now than family, as they walk down the long drive. Brick gallantly holds Grumbl's lead, while *accidentally* bumping his broad shoulder into Kya. Her happy laugh echoes back to us as Rogan's arms settle around my waist. He tucks his head into my neck and lets out a long, slow breath.

I shiver, relishing the sensation of the goosebumps rising along my arms and skirting down my legs, as he places soft kisses along my neck.

"He doesn't have a clue, does he?" I ask quietly, my hands lightly resting over his, his thumbs skirting the underside of my breasts.

"About Kya?"

His breath is warm on my skin as the tip of his tongue lightly glides along my neck, his hand moving up higher to cup my breast, gently massaging the tender flesh.

"Mmmm..." I hum in agreement, leaning back against him, my eyes dropping closed.

"Not one bloody clue," the warmth of his laugh sends a rush of heat to my core, my knees going weak as his grip tightens on me. I loop my hand around his neck, pulling his lips more firmly into my skin. He lightly grazes his teeth along my flesh and I can't hold back the moan that escapes my throat.

"Has he ever made an attempt to— mmmm...," I breathe, pausing to rock my hips back into his hardening length as he presses it against my backside, while trying to find the word I'm after.

"... tried to *woo* her?"

I feel his lips shift into a grin, his breath coasting across my skin, huffing out a small laugh.

"Woo?" He asks teasingly.

I turn to look back up at him, cocking up an indignant brow, gently elbowing him in the ribs.

"Yes, Rogan... *'woo!'*" I repeat with mock exasperation, but I can't hold back the grin when I'm met with his devilish smile, his eyes sparkling down at me with playful mirth.

His expression turns wicked, his attention shifting to my mouth, "Mmmm... kinda like this?"

The next thing I know, he's swinging me up into his arms, I squeal, but his mouth finds mine a split second later, swallowing the sound.

"I thought they'd never bloody leave!" his breath and teeth against my lips, our tongues tangled in a heated kiss as I thread my fingers into his hair and melt into him.

Kicking the door shut behind us, he carries me up the stairs.

Chapter 55

Cole

The night had been splendid. Rogan worshipping my body, delivering me to new realms of ecstasy—each time somehow greater than the last—followed by a restful, dreamless sleep.

Waking up naked in his arms, completely wrapped around his body, feels like nothing short of heaven, until...

Bang, bang, bang!

Rogan stirs beneath me, grumbling under his breath, but only tugs me closer, burrowing his face deeper into my neck.

Bang, bang, bang!

"Bloody hell..." He blows out a frustrated sigh. He buries his nose into my hair, breathing in deeply, then kisses my neck, before gently untangling our limbs and slipping off the bed.

He pulls the covers up to my chin and tucks them around me, leaning in to kiss my forehead, his knuckle trailing lightly along the line of my jaw, lingering a moment longer.

"Keep it warm for me, Little Fawn."

His sweet smile melts something in me and I return it with one of my own. I tug my arm free from the cocoon of blankets he's got me tucked into and reach up to stroke his face, brushing his sleep tousled hair away from his eyes. He turns into my palm, placing a lingering kiss against my wrist.

Bang, bang, bang!

His face shifts from soft adoration to anger at the persistent knock.

"Grraahhh! I'll be right there, God damn it!" He growls, whirling around and stomping toward the door. He stops to swipe a discarded towel from the floor, roughly wrapping it around his waist before gripping the handle and wrenching the door open with so much force, I'm almost worried he'll yank it right off its hinges.

I can't see who's at the door, but as Rogan waits for them to finish speaking I can tell by the set of his shoulders, he's not happy with whatever they're saying.

He glances over his shoulder at me, his expression grim, then turns back to whomever is on the other side of the door.

"They can wait. If they wanted an audience with us they should have scheduled a fucking appointment. Tell them we'll be down in a bit. Get them some tea and have them wait in my office."

After the door shuts, he pauses, his hands bracketing the door frame.

With a sudden rush, he spins, snatching his gray sweatpants from the back of the chair, hurriedly pulling them on, the towel dropping to a pile in the middle of the floor. I sit bolt upright, the covers clutched to my chest, my eyes following him as he moves determinedly around the room.

He grabs his phone off the table, yanking it free from the charger, before frantically running his fingers over the screen—the light from the display reflecting in his serious, gray eyes. His fingers still when he finds whatever he'd been searching for.

"Shit," he mutters under his breath.

When his eyes meet mine, I know our happy, carefree bubble has officially just popped.

"What is it, Rogan?" My body begins to tremble, sensing the tension rolling off him—an ingrained fight or flight reaction from years of leaning into those self-preservation instincts.

He walks over to me, sitting down on the side of the bed, taking my hands into his.

"That was James. The police are here."

"Police?" Shaking my head, I begin to pull away. The urge to run, seeping into my bones.

"No... no, no, no, no, no...," I vaguely realize I'm whispering the words as my thoughts begin to spiral and fear floods my veins.

He's found me again.

He's sent them to collect me.

He's coming for me.

It's over... It's over... It's all over!

He'll make me pay for what I've done.

He almost killed me last time and now...

Jesus, now I've actually fucking cheated on him!

Oh dear God—he's going to come for Rogan...

Tears sting my eyes as any hope of keeping hold of my new found happiness washes away. I try to pull my hands away from him, but he holds firm, gently tugging me closer, his hand cupping my cheek, pulling my focus to his face. He tips my chin up, meeting my eyes, pulling my attention out of the maelstrom of my spiraling terrors.

"Shhh... hey... hey now, Little Fawn. It's alright. Everything is all going to be alright." He soothes, his voice is strong and firm as he strokes his warm hand across my cheek, gently keeping a tight grip on my hands as he tries to soothe my frantic nerves.

He locks his eyes with mine. "I'm not sure what's got you so nervous, but you have nothing to worry about. I promise."

I close my eyes, trying to focus on his touch, on his words. I want to believe him... want to dig my heels in and stay, but if there's any chance he's found me... *if he's found a way to figure out where I am...*

"What do they want?" I whisper.

"They just want to talk to us about what happened the other night at the pub. It looks like a couple of lads filmed the fight."

He rolls his eyes and smiles, clearly trying to put my mind at ease. "They posted it all over social media and it's apparently gone bloody viral."

My eyes widen, the tremors racking my body instantly becoming more violent as his words sink in. He reaches behind him and picks up his phone off the bed, holding it out toward me. He presses play and a video comes to life on the screen.

I take the phone with shaky hands and watch as the scene plays out, transporting me right back to that night. My skin crawls at the memory of Zavier's hands on me, his relentless grip, pinning me against the wall. His fingers squeezing my throat as he tore at my clothes, groping and pawing at me. The sour stench of whiskey and beer on his breath, burning my nose, while he spat his vitriol into my face.

But a deep, fierce feeling of pride bubbles up in me as I remember how it had felt to bring that bastard to his fucking knees. The euphoric feeling of breaking his hold on my throat—*my* hand doling out the punishments for once, as I wrenched his fingers away, breaking his grip, crippling him with nothing more than a clever twist of my wrist, with the self-defense techniques I'd learned in the dojo.

But as the video plays, it only shows Rogan, his hands gripped behind his back and shoulders squared as he easily side steps Zavier's charging attacks—two... no, make that three times. Each time Zavier barrels past him, making a complete ass of himself as he crashes through tables, chairs and at one point, slamming solidly into Brick.

Rogan finally delivers a solid roundhouse kick to his head, the fight ending with Zavier crumpling limply onto the floor, groaning and pissing himself all at the same time.

The video gets shaky as the men hoot and cheer, spinning the camera back toward themselves, the scene changing to close ups of their faces as they excitedly holler and drunkenly try to emulate some of Rogan's moves, high fiving one another as though they've just won a game.

I relax a bit and sigh, feeling some of the tension drain from my muscles, until it gets to the last few seconds of the video—

There in the background...

Kya stands off to the side of the terrace. Her attention isn't on the fight scene or the men filming the video. She's entirely focused on the person beside her, her arm wrapped around their shoulders...

My red hair stands out like a fucking beacon. My tear-streaked face, on full display—crystal clear as the camera captures the last few moments of the video. There I stand, plain as day for anyone who has access to fucking social media, to not only be able to see who I am—but *where*.

My eyes flick to the tag in the caption below the video as it comes to an end, the image stilling on my face.

Location: The Wye Inn & Pub - Verdon on Wye

And it's gone fucking... *viral*.

I feel my blood run cold, a bone deep fear washing over me, driving out all reasonable thought, all rational judgment. I drop his phone and push out of his arms, scrambling off the bed.

My head spins as a jumble of thoughts attack me from all sides. All the measures I'd taken to stay hidden. Keeping away from social media, to stay out of sight—all destroyed with one, stupid fucking video.

Every fear I'd harbored in the back of my mind, rushing to the forefront at once, each one pushing and shoving their way toward fruition.

"No, no, no, no, no..." I mutter over and over and over, as I flit from place to place, frantically tugging on my clothes.

I'm vaguely aware of Rogan calling my name, but his voice is distant, clouded, like he's speaking through cotton.

Panic sinks into my bones as I spiral. My blood rushes in my ears, everything in me screaming to run.

He's going to come.

He's going to find me.

I have to get out of here... have to get away... have to run.

I can't let him find me.

He'll kill me... He'll kill HIM!

I have to go, have to leave, have to run!

I pull on my shoes and make for the door, only to meet Rogan's immovable presence. He grips me gently, but firmly by the shoulders.

"Let me go." I beg him, my voice a broken cry as I struggle out of his hold. He releases me, but stands his ground, blocking my escape.

"Please, Rogan... please. You have to let me go!" I meet his eyes, frantically pleading for him to understand—to let me by.

I can't let Cain get to him. I just can't...

Worry lines his face as he looks into my eyes and he shakes his head in confusion. I try to move past him, but he shifts into my path again, holding his palms up, keeping me there.

"Stop! Please, Cole. Jesus, just stop and fucking talk to me!" He nearly shouts.

He softens his voice, a silent apology in his eyes, when I flinch back from him.

"Please... just tell me what the fuck is going on? I'm not going to let *anyone* hurt you, Little Fawn."

He moves in closer, cautiously resettling his hands on my shoulders, his thumbs stroking soft circles along my skin as he studies my face, his eyes pleading for answers.

"You don't know him, Rogan...," I cry, gripping his wrists.

The urge to lean into him pulls at the corners of my mind and all I want to do is bury myself against his chest, but if I stay, he's in danger.

I can't. I just fucking can't.

"You don't understand! He'll *destroy* anyone who stands in his way. Please, just let me go...," my voice breaks.

"Who, Cole? Who are you so fucking worried about? Please, just let me in." He pleads.

"I'll keep you safe. You're safe with me, I promise you."

"I don't fucking care about me, Rogan! Don't you get it?" My teeth clench as I beg him to understand.

"I can't let him hurt *you*!" I scream, slamming my fists against his chest.

His hands close over my fists, holding them in place as he tries desperately to make sense of my fury.

"Who, Cole? Who are you so bloody afraid of?"

"My husband...," I say weakly, my strength slowly waning, my chin dropping as the shame of my admission washes over me.

"I couldn't live with myself if something happened to you because of me, Rogan. Please... *please!* You have to let me go."

His mouth snaps shut, his eyes softening with pained understanding as he turns my hands, exposing the scars along my wrists. He gently glides his thumbs along them.

"He did this to you."

I can hear the ache in his voice and I watch as his haunted eyes follow the trail of his thumbs up my arms.

"Your fucking husband?"

I nod.

"So, wait a minute... you want to leave... to protect *me?*"

"I don't want to leave but, I'm not going to give him a fucking reason to hurt you! If he finds me with you, there's nothing he won't do to get me back. He'll use you to punish me. He'll hurt *you* just to make me pay for leaving him."

I draw in a shuddering breath.

"It's the only way."

Defeat coats my words as I slip my hands from his. I let my arms fall to my sides, my eyes dropping to the floor as the last shreds of my fantasy dissolve into more bitter tears.

Strong arms surround me in a tight embrace, blanketing me in a solid wall of security and strength. He holds me to his chest, his hand stroking softly down my back, his other cradling my head, rocking me in his arms and whispering assurances into my hair.

I succumb to his hold, melting against him as my own strength drains away. I sob against his chest allowing myself a few more moments of his warmth to comfort me.

"You don't need to be afraid anymore, Little Fawn. If he thinks for one second I'll let him anywhere near you ever again, he's sorely mistaken. I can protect you, Cole. I can protect *us*."

He pulls back to look at me.

"Please... just stay."

My eyes rocket back and forth between his. Everything in me wanting... no *needing* to believe what he's saying could be true.

I don't want to give up this new life. I don't want to give up this wonderful man. But, fuck! The thought of Cain... *hurting Rogan.*

I'd rather let Cain have his way with me, destroy me, *kill me...* than to be the reason anything bad happens to Rogan.

My chin quivers as my mind slams me with image after image of the horrid things Cain could do to Rogan and a fresh wave of anguish washes over me, a new flood of tears rushing down my cheeks.

My legs finally give out, the last dregs of my strength giving way as I collapse against him. The grave I had thought I'd buried my greatest fears and my worst nightmares in, not deep enough—as their imminent resurrection threatens to bring them back to life. The weight, more than I can bear.

He grips me tight and tugs me into his chest, settling us both down onto the carpet by the door.

I'm not sure how long we stay like that, just holding each other. Rogan rocks me softly, whispering the sweetest words against my skin. A sense of calm finally settles over me as I let a small piece of me believe his promises of safety, desperate for them to be true, but knowing... I really have no choice here.

Sensing my calm, Rogan shifts back, wiping away my tears.

"So you'll stay?" He asks, his eyes hopeful as he studies my face.

I nod, offering him a thin smile, but I know it doesn't quite reach my eyes. He presses his lips to my forehead, holding me a moment longer.

Bang, bang, bang!

The loud knock from the door behind us makes us both jump and his arms tighten around me, a deep scowl marring his brow.

"I'll be down in a bloody minute!" He barks angrily, his jaw tight.

He lets out a frustrated sigh, his eyes searching mine again.

"I need to go see what the police want, love." he says reluctantly.

I nod again and try to make my smile more convincing, praying my guise of peace holds. Praying that Rogan, usually seeing everything, doesn't read the thoughts running through my mind.

"Go splash some cool water on your face and take some deep breaths. Let yourself calm down a bit and I'll speak to the police first to get an idea of what's going on. Then, when you feel like you can—come down and join us."

He helps me to my feet, kissing the top of my head as we stand.

"It's going to be alright, Little Fawn. I promise." He insists, leaning down to press a soft kiss to my lips.

"I love you." He whispers against my lips, his hands cupping my face and I can't stop the single tear from spilling over my lashes.

Then, he grabs a shirt off the chair and turns to head out of the bedroom door, slipping the shirt over his head as he heads down the stairs to meet with the officers.

Alone in the massive bedroom, I blow out a shaky breath, my eyes slowly trailing over every feature, locking every detail in my memory. Making sure I have just one thing Cain can never take from me.

I make my way to the bathroom, glaring at the bloodshot eyes staring back at me in the mirror. I grip the counter so hard my knuckles turn white. Fury floods my veins at knowing Cain can still affect me like this—that he still has this much power over me.

Angry tears spill down my cheeks when I think about leaving the one place I've ever had that I could call my own. My new friends, the village I now love so much... *my home.* Leaving behind the best things, the best people I've ever had in my life, once again, losing *everything...* because of him.

It dawns on me that I'll have to go back to Kya's and get my things. My gut clenches, my blood turning to ice at the thought.

What if Cain finds out about Kya and Brick? What if he finds out about the animals? Dear God, the things he could do to them just to hurt me...

I spin, dropping to my knees in front of the toilet, throwing back the lid just in time to empty the contents of my stomach into the bowl.

I spit, wiping the back of my hand across my mouth and rest my head against the cool porcelain and my heart screams as I make my decision.

I *won't* let him hurt them.

I'll leave Verdon so the people I love—

So the man I love—

Will be safe from him.

Chapter 56

Cain

With a fistful of her hair, I snap my hips hard, driving myself deeper into her throat. I look down at the once perfectly curled hair and pristinely made-up face of my current secretary—the whore I'm currently face fucking—her tears streaking muddy tracks of mascara down her face, her cheeks stained an angry shade of red.

Her eyes are wide, her nostrils flaring as drool spills down her chin, choking and gagging as she struggles to breathe around my cock.

The sight of her torment only spurs me on as I force the head of my cock past the back of her throat. She bucks, panicking at the lack of air, shoving against my thighs as she tries to pull back, but I hold her tight, pushing her down harder and twist a fistful of her hair until I feel some tear away at the roots.

Heat tingles up my spine, my cock swelling. I speed up my thrusts and grit my teeth, grabbing her head with both my hands to hold her face down fully on my cock.

I roar my release, my climax erupting deep in her throat. Her eyes flutter as she loses consciousness. Her body slumps against me and she goes limp. I grab her neck, squeezing to feel my cock pulsing in her swollen throat.

My eyes roll back and I picture the face of the treacherous bitch whose throat I'd rather be ruining right now.

The blonde hair in my fist turns auburn, the vacant, watery blue eyes turn green and it's Nicole's face I'm fucking. It's Nicole's tears turning her mascara to blackened tracks down her face. The bright red lipstick I made her wear, smudged from her lips, meeting the purpling bruise welting on her cheek—the beating she'd earned for thinking she could refuse me my rights as her husband.

As my orgasm wanes, I shove the whore off my cock—her limp body slumping to the floor at my feet, her drool and my cum running out the side of her mouth.

I curse my bitch wife and that backstabbing wretch of an old maid who helped her escape, even though the fucking wetback bitch knows the threat I made on her family is real. The truth of that threat, happening even now.

The Cartel are on the move, and they'll be ready to do whatever I say, when I decide exactly what I want done with that old bitch and her mongrel family.

My mind shifts back to Nicole again, remembering the way she always submitted to me. I could do anything to that sweet body, that innocent looking face, that fucking tight cunt—how she would roll over and just take it. The memory of what it felt like to come inside her as I slammed my cock into her, my belt tight around her pale throat like the reins of the horses she loved so goddamn much when I first claimed her as my property.

My cock thickens at the thought of fucking her again. I sigh, collapsing back into my desk chair. I stroke my length, still wet from this whore's mouth.

She groans as she regains consciousness and groggily pushes herself up onto her knees. Dazed, she spits, her hand shaking as she swipes the back of it across her swollen lips. It comes away bloody from where they'd split open while I fucked her face.

I snatch a fistful of her hair, dragging her up to her knees. She yelps as my fingers dig into her wet, blotchy face, dimpling her cheeks, pursing her lips. She whimpers as the split there widens and a mixture of drool, cum and blood dribbles down her chin.

Her nails bite into my skin as she grips my wrist. She struggles to speak, but it's nothing more than a pathetic whimper.

I pull her face closer to mine. She struggles to twist out of my hold, but my grip on her jaw is unrelenting, keeping her right where I want her.

"What did you say, Little Whore?"

"P-please..." she croaks, begging me through her ruined lips.

"Begging for more... already?" I sneer, knowing full well her plea is for mercy. *She'll find none here.*

She tries to shake her head, her eyes falling closed as fresh tears roll down her cheeks.

I yank her hard, pressing my nose against her cheek. I drag it along her cheekbone, my lips brushing the shell of her ear as I speak, my words a vicious whisper.

"You thought it would be fun to fuck the boss, huh? You thought you'd win me over? Raise yourself up through the company ranks?"

I don't expect a response.

I'm not really asking.

I rise to stand, dragging her with me. She scrambles, trying to get her feet beneath her, her eyes flaring wide. She shakes her head violently in my grip, clawing at my hand as she struggles to break free from my hold.

"Feel *important* yet, Little Whore?" I growl—my words, pure acid as I snarl through my teeth.

I spin her around, forcing her face down on my desk, tightly squeezing the back of her neck. She cries out as I crush her cheek against the unforgiving oak.

Fuck, how I love it when they squeal.

With every scream, every cry, the sounds a symphony—a delightful chorus of pleas, begging for me to ruin them.

'Take me! Fuck me! Make me scream!'

My cock turns to granite as she squirms against my grip, desperate for a mercy she'll never get.

I kick her legs apart, flipping her skirt up onto her back, then tear her panties off—the thin lace breaking away easily. I crack my palm across her ass with a punishing blow. She jolts and squawks, her pale skin instantly welting, flaring a bright red.

I scan my desk, my eyes landing on the sleek, black stapler. I grab it, turning it backward and shove it roughly into her cunt. She screams as I ram it deeper into her, dragging it all the way out only to slam it back in again. My cock aches at the sound of her cries.

She bucks under my hand, so I press down harder, pinning her to the desk by her neck. After tormenting her with a few more hard thrusts of the stapler, I rip it out of her cunt, toss it back on the desk in front of her face and move between her legs. I line the head of my cock up with her pussy and slam inside her.

She mewls, spluttering incoherently as I take my pleasure from her—her pleas falling on deaf ears, as I continue to fuck her.

I drive into her harder, faster until I feel my balls start to tighten as my release begins to crest. All the while imagining Nicole's tight cunt gripping my dick, ready to take everything I have to give her.

A loud knock on my office door rips me from my vision.

"Arrrhhhhhh, FUUUCCKKKK!!" I roar, and give the whore's throat one more tight squeeze before roughly pulling my cock out of her and cramming myself back into my pants.

I drag her up to standing again and throw my handkerchief at her.

"Clean yourself up and get the fuck out. You're fired."

Sobbing, she hurriedly pulls down her skirt and picks up her stiletto heels, shakily wiping at her face with the cloth.

She lets out a pitiful yelp and flinches when I grab her upper arm, leaning in close to snarl into her ear.

"And don't get any ideas about reporting any of this..." I growl, keeping my voice low.

"You know what I can do to you if you do."

I give her a hard shove and she stumbles away, scrambling out the door.

I pick up a cigar, snipping off the end. I run it under my nose, breathing in the sweet smell of the tobacco and lower into my chair.

Straightening my tie, I watch disinterestedly as she pushes past the PI.

"Well?"

The asshole is still hanging in the door, mouth agape, watching the whore as she runs sobbing down the hall.

"What the fuck do you want?"

The man swallows, his eyes fixed on her as she leaves, testing my patience.

"Is... is she okay?" He stammers, hooking his thumb over his shoulder in her direction, finally stepping into my office.

"Door."

"What?"

"Close. The fucking. Door."

I'm surrounded by fucking imbeciles!

He swings the door shut and scuffles toward me, his hands wringing together.

I pay him little attention as I meticulously reorganize my desk.

"Sit."

"Huh?"

"SIT!"

"Oh... oh yeah, sure, sure." He hurriedly drops into the chair, still fidgeting with his hands. His eyes nervously watch as I methodically straighten each item on my desk.

"Speak."

Jesus Christ, I feel like I'm talking to a fucking dog!

"Oh... yeah...uhhh, well there's been a, well a... development." He rambles, stuttering over his words.

"A positive one I hope." I pick up the stapler, streaked with a mixture of blood and her wetness. My lip curls as I toss it into the trash can—the loud metallic clang makes him jump in his seat.

"A social media post has gone viral of some, uhhh, royal guy. A Duke, I think. Yeah, he's got connections to the Royal Family or something. The video showed him getting into a fight with a guy in a pub in a little village in a..." he fumbles with his phone, tapping on the screen a few times to bring up a social media app, "in Gloucestershire."

My molars grind as the fucking idiot scrolls through different pages on his phone and I swear if he doesn't get to the goddamn point soon, I'm going to put a bullet in his fucking skull!

Narrowing my eyes, I hiss at him, "And why the *fuck* would I give two shits about some Duke having a fight at some no name pub in the middle of fucking nowhere?"

He leans over the desk holding out his phone. He sets it down and gives it a shove, sliding it across the expanse of my desk—a video playing on the screen.

I watch indifferently, seeing nothing more than a group of inebriated assholes leering and cheering about some over-dressed neanderthal, kicking down a big, drunken fool.

My anger starts to boil over at the stupidity of this fucking piece of shit. This worthless fucker who I've paid good money to. Not for him to show me some loser in a bar fight, but to *find my fucking wife*!

I'm near the breaking point, ready to end this fucker's existence, until the video comes to an end.

The image stills, the scene stopping, focused at the back of the patio, just beyond the faces of the men filming the footage—

There, in the background, two women stand side by side. A taller, dark-haired girl with her arm wrapped protectively around a small framed woman...

A woman with blazing, auburn hair.

The screen on the phone scrolls to a new video, automatically starting to play.

I jolt forward, grabbing the phone from the desk.

"Wait! Go back! Go to the end! Make it larger!" I command, anxiously thrusting the phone back toward him.

He takes it from me, his hands shaking as he moves his fingers across the screen until the video lands back on the previous one. He slides the progress bar until it reaches the end, hitting pause, then snaps a quick screenshot. He opens the saved image and slides two fingers outward on the screen, blowing up the image of the redhead's face...

Nicole's. Fucking. Face.

"It's her..." I growl beneath my breath.

"What village is this?"

"Verdon-on-Wye, Sir."

"When was this taken?"

"Three days ago."

"So, there's a good chance she's still there…" I say absently, my fingers raking across my jaw while I stare at my traitorous wife.

She's crying and her shirt is torn. Looks like our *Duke* was playing the hero.

My mind works as I plot out exactly how I want to approach this bitch. She can't know I've found her.

"Send me that screenshot. Then, I want you to go to Verdon-on-Wye. Take photos. Confirm it's her. Then, I want you to find out more about this *Duke*," I spit out his title, "and the name of the man he was fighting. Report back to me in three days. Understood?"

He nods, pulling his phone back, his fingers rapidly tapping the screen, sending me the image. My phone pings a moment later with a text notification.

"Three days." I reiterate. "Now get the fuck out."

He rapidly nods his agreement and hurriedly pulls himself out of the chair, then rushes out the door.

Once it closes behind him, I press the intercom.

"Gloria?"

"Yes, sir?"

"Get paperwork together to terminate the new secretary. Her contract isn't working out. Find me someone…" I lick my lips, "more flexible."

There's a long pause before she replies.

"Yes, sir."

I'll be celebrating tonight.

Nicole is nearly back on her leash.

Back where she fucking belongs.

A wicked smile slides across my face at the thought of getting my hands back on her. Of fucking her until she can't stand, then beating her until she can't breathe.

I rock back in my chair, lighting my cigar and taking a long drag. The ember at its tip glows a bright cherry red.

I admire it, blowing out a thick plume of smoke, anticipating the smell of her burning flesh as I press it into her skin.

Chapter 57

Rogan

As I make my way down the stairs and enter the foyer, an older woman with a severe expression and even more severe bun in her dark hair, stands from her chair, her steps determined as she approaches me, hand outstretched.

"Your Grace," she begins. Her voice, nasally and gruff. Her intelligent eyes not missing anything as she takes me in, while glancing past me up the empty stairwell.

"My name is Detective Inspector Petra Olubanjo."

I give her a tight nod and take her hand. She gives it one hard, no-nonsense shake, her grip firm, then releases me just as quickly. She steps to the side, ushering forward the younger man beside her.

"This is Detective Constable Wayne Kerr."

I cock an eyebrow high and smirk, glancing disbelievingly between the two officers, sure I've misheard her as he steps forward, reaching his hand out to take mine.

"You're joking." I ask, fighting the smile as I take his hand.

He chuckles good-naturedly as he gives my hand a surprisingly firm shake.

"I know, I know… Trust me, I've heard all the razzin' over my name no less than a thousand times before." His smile is warm, his eyes gleaming with the kind of eager confidence that only exists in the young and unbroken.

"American?" I ask, picking up on his accent, a hint of southern drawl curling around his words, though it's somewhat muddled with a hint of someone who's lived in the North West of England.

"Yup. I'm originally from the states. Born and raised in Georgia." He beams proudly.

"My family moved here when I was a teen. Imagine going through the last couple years of school in England with a name like *Wayne Kerr.*" He clenches his teeth and pulls his head back, tucking his chin in a mock grimace, though the smile never leaves his eyes.

I find myself liking the young man immediately.

"And then, of course, the police academy here was brutal! Caught my fair share of jibbin' there as well. Just call me Kerr, it's far less embarrassing."

He flashes me a grin full of brilliantly white, perfectly straight teeth, a dimple sinking deeply into his right cheek.

He leans in, bumping his elbow against my arm and hitting me with a conspiratorial wink. "I can't complain too much though. The name is certainly a conversation starter and the ladies seem to love the accent."

I smile back at him easily and nod my agreement. His candor and good nature, instantly putting me at ease and taking the edge off the nature of their visit.

Olubanjo clears her throat with obvious impatience.

My smile drops as I shift my attention back over to her, meeting her stern expression.

"Can I ask what this is about?"

Seemingly satisfied she's regained control of the conversation; she quickly rifles through her handbag and pulls out a small notebook.

"Is there somewhere we could sit and talk, Your Grace?" She asks, eyes flitting expectantly around the cavernous space.

I look to James and he tilts his head, almost imperceptibly toward my father's study, ready and waiting for us to take our meeting.

Like I've said... the perfect butler.

"This way." I walk past them, leading the way through one of the tall doors.

We pass through the library, morning sunlight streaming through the tall windows. It was my mother's favorite place in the whole Manor. Her books line the shelves as if waiting for her return, quietly hoping she'll come back and reclaim them any day now.

We move on through the long dining room, to the far end of the Manor. The door here is a heavy, dark oak.

How I hated being summoned to this room.

It emanates a false sense of masculine strength. The kind meant to belittle, to unnerve, to denigrate. But considering the obvious waves of accusation rolling off Detective Olubanjo, it feels like the perfect place to meet with these officers.

The room is large. A massive mahogany desk, passed down from duke to duke, sits opposite the door so my father could see exactly who was coming and going.

A smaller room sits off to the side, dark and foreboding, furnished in faux comfort—where he would entertain some of his *special* guests.

An unbidden memory flashes in my mind; of the one time I'd dared to peek in as a child.

A naked woman strapped to the bed, her legs stretched wide, each tethered to a separate bedpost. My father pacing beside her, stroking his erect cock. And he was whipping her...

Over and over, he struck her, the sound of the riding crop swishing through the air, only to crack loudly as it connected with her bare flesh. With each strike, she'd cry out, bucking her hips and struggling against her restraints. The look of dark satisfaction in my father's eyes would blaze at the sounds, his hand moving faster as he stroked himself. Then there were other women, lounging around the space in various degrees of undress, moaning and touching each other.

I was too young to understand everything I was seeing, but even then, the scene had made me feel sick, as something inside me screamed it was all so very wrong. Especially, knowing my mother was laying battered and bruised in her room while he entertained his *guests*.

Devon's hand had gently squeezed my shoulder, turning me away from the debaucherous scene. His finger was over his lips shushing me as he scooped me up into his arms and silently carried me away from the sight that would later haunt me for years to come.

"Want some ice cream, Little Man?" He'd smiled at me, hitching me up high on his hip.

Even at fourteen, he'd felt like a giant to me. He was lean and tall; his young body already lined with tight muscles from several years of playing rugby. I was convinced he was the strongest person in the world.

My hero.

I don't remember the ice cream. But I do remember his laugh as he told silly jokes to try to distract me from the truth of our family unraveling around us.

It was the first room I gutted after my father's death. Now it's used for storing away the things I can't seem to bring myself to get rid of, but can't bear to look at any longer.

My father's study? That's a different story. Some part of me needs this reminder of his cruelty, so I never forget what he put me through—so I never make his same mistakes.

A board room table lies across the other half of the room, where James has already set up five chairs, a cafetiere of coffee gently brewing on a silver tray along with a carafe of milk and cubes of Demerara sugar. He'd even placed some shortbread rounds on a plate, though I doubt any of us will be eating those.

Kerr quashes that prediction when he reaches across the table and quickly snatches two of them off the tray. Olubanjo rolls her eyes, but the young man seems unbothered by her frustrations. I can't help but wonder just how good he actually is at his job.

James moves to pour our coffees.

Kerr's eyes dart toward the other empty chairs positioned around the table.

At his notice, I speak up. "I hope you don't mind; I've asked for some legal representation to join us this morning." I take my seat and lean back, the chair creaking slightly beneath me. I keep my smile kind, but watch them closely to gauge their reaction to my unexpected guest's announcement.

I'll be in charge of this meeting, whether they realize it or not.

Olubanjo straightens in her chair, pulling on the seam of her cardigan. She clearly hadn't anticipated this, no doubt assuming she'd be leading the charge.

"Your Grace, there's really no need for all that. This is an informal meeting just to get some more information on the incidents that happened the other night at The Wye Inn. You're welcome to have an attorney present of course. That is you're right... but it's entirely unnecessary at this point in time."

"As you said, it's my right. It's also my home and you've come here without an appointment. So you'll forgive me if I don't entirely trust your motives, detective." I give her an unapologetic shrug as my smile drops away, replaced instead with a look of irritation.

"To be honest, it feels a bit like you were hoping to ambush me. Perhaps hoping to catch me unaware?" I suggest, arching a brow in silent accusation.

"Of course not, Your Grace. We were just hoping to..."

As if on cue, the door swings open admitting my *'legal representative'*.

Brick heads straight over to the detectives, his long legs eating up the space between the door and the table quickly, his massive hand outstretched. They shuffle to their feet and he shakes their hands in turn, introducing himself with a quick squeeze of each, then settles himself into the chair across from them, hitting them with one of his brilliant, disarming smiles.

His hair is a mess, his rugby shirt ruffled and untucked—I'd clearly woken him up with my call to get him over here in a hurry.

But Brick doesn't give a fuck if he's in a suit or a disheveled rugby kit. And he also doesn't give a fuck what anyone thinks about it either. He knows he's good, and sometimes, mollifying people with his appearance before he strikes, is the best way to land the hardest blow. I have to hide my smile behind my fingers as I settle back into my chair and watch him work his magic.

"So...," he smiles, all white teeth and sparkling eyes.

"What's all this about then?"

The detectives settle back into their seats, and Olubanjo fumbles through the pages of her notebook. Kerr takes a bite of his biscuit, while his wide eyes observe the mountain of a man sitting opposite him, a few stray crumbs tumbling down the front of his shirt unnoticed.

"Your Grace," she begins, her cheeks slightly pink as she forces herself to look away from Brick's brilliant grin and back to me.

I flick up my hand to stop her.

"I hate that title." I state dismissively.

"Please, call me Mr. Cavendish."

She snaps her mouth shut, looking affronted at my abrupt interruption—the fact that she's on my turf suddenly sinking in. Her original bravado and confidence she'd come into my home with, slowly slipping away.

Her eyes shift between Brick and me, her jaw flexing. Conceding, she finally nods before starting again.

"Mr. Cavendish." She corrects, looking more than a little annoyed. "We're part of the serious crimes division, including cyber and hate crimes. A social media post has been brought to our attention." She checks her notes, "It was made last Saturday night, and has raised a lot of questions for my team. Are you aware of this post?"

I shrug, feigning indifference. Brick flicks his eyes to mine. He's seen it as well.

"Well, Your Gra..., *Mr. Cavendish*," she corrects herself when my eyes flash to hers, "it shows a man, and excuse my language, getting the shit kicked out of him..." her dark eyes meet mine, "by you, sir."

I hold her stare with a blank expression.

Kerr leans forward, brushing the crumbs from his jacket and tie, then fishes a notebook out of his shirt pocket.

"We understand the man who you fought is one," he makes a show of checking his notepad, "Zavier Johnson." He looks back up, and suddenly I realize why Olubanjo brought him. It's clear in his eyes, he may be a puppy, but he's a rottweiler if ever there was one.

"We will, of course, be going to speak to him as well as Greg Turley at the Wye Inn after we've finished here. But we thought, considering your, er, *standing* in the community and your connections to..." he swirls his hand and lets his words trail off.

To the Royal Family. Distant cousins but still connected.

"We wanted to hear your side of the events first."

He leans back; a smug smile spreads across his face now that he's said his piece. Now that he thinks he's gotten one over the hoity toity *'Royal'* upper class.

My eye catches Brick's. I incline my head a fraction, giving him permission for him to continue the conversation on my behalf.

"I've seen the footage," he begins, folding his arms in front of himself on the table as he leans forward. The picture of easy grace and charm. "I would say it's grainy, dark even? Hard to tell who's doing what." He lifts his shoulders in a dismissive shrug, his eyebrows furrow as if he doesn't see the problem.

Olubanjo digs in her bag and pulls out her iPad, opening the social media app. It's quite clearly me on the screen, although it is dark, and the videographer is jostling so much, presumably in drunken excitement, that Brick's argument could potentially hold up in court.

"As you can see here," she pauses the video at the moment before I land my strike, my face illuminated by the fairy lights strewn around the terrace. "There are moments of clarity where the assailant and victim are clearly visible."

"Victim?" Brick's voice, incredulous, interrupts her. "And who, pray tell, is the victim?" The shift in his tone is subtle, nearly imperceptible, but I see it for what it is—he's setting up for his own deadly, acerbic strike.

"Zavier Johnson, clearly." Kerr quips pointing at the stilled image on Olubanjo's iPad, his expression, cocky—thinking he's matching Brick's demeanor.

"Zavier Johnson is no victim." Brick scoffs, his voice low, menacing as he sits back in his chair, his demeanor shifting from smooth charm to courtroom serious.

"Any counter measures His Grace, The Duke of Wyeholme," I bite back my smile as he stresses my full title, "enacted, were made in defense of the real victim. Any moron on any jury will see that. And be grateful men like him still exist to defend others from, and excuse *my* language detective," his eyes lock on Olubanjo as he throws her own words back at her, "*cunts* like Zavier bloody Johnson."

"Okay, okay...," Olubanjo holds up her palms toward Brick, flinching slightly at his choice of words.

"So then who, Mr. Brickton, are you saying is the real victim here?"

"I am." Cole's quiet voice answers from the doorway.

Chapter 58

Rogan

Cole stands in the opening of the doorway, her eyes wide as she scans the faces sitting around the table. Her tension visibly lessons the moment they lock onto mine. I smile warmly at her and motion her into the room, standing to walk over to her side.

Stepping behind her, I rest my hands on her shoulders, reminding her I'm here and that she's not facing this alone.

"Detectives. This is my partner, Cole Allbright." She curls her hands over mine, her fingers softly gripping me. She presses back a fraction, fitting herself against me as my hands flex across her shoulders, my thumbs stroking the nape of her neck.

Moving beside her, I take her hand in mine and guide her over to the table. I can feel her shaking, a persistent tremor that remains no matter how much reassurance I try to push into my touch. No matter how much I silently will her to believe I'm not going anywhere and that I will destroy anyone who dares to threaten her.

After a brief introduction, I pull out the chair next to mine and gesture for Cole to sit. Once she's seated, I settle in beside her, reclaiming her hand and giving it another reassuring squeeze.

They ask her a few questions about what instigated the events of the evening.

Her voice is shaky and timid at first, but as she recants the chain of events that led up to this point, I see a fierceness start to build in her. A determination to not let this hold her down any longer.

She tells them everything, from how she had originally met Zavier to him pinning her against the wall in the alley. My insides roil as I fight through my anger. Hearing it again only makes me wish I had done more damage to the fucker that night on the terrace.

She goes on, explaining how the night of the fight had begun, detailing him assaulting her earlier in the evening with the card reader, then the gruesome details of what he had done to her outside.

I'd be lying if I said I wasn't raging inside, hearing her explain, step-by-bloody-step what that piece of shit had done.

The memory of his hands on her as she'd fought against his hold. The feeling of utter terror I had when I'd been unable to break past the crowd to get to her.

The officers take thorough notes, a deep furrow forming in Olubanjo's brow, her eyes darkening, as Cole reveals each part of how Zavier's been tormenting her for the past several weeks.

But as she explains how she brought Zavier to his knees, Olubanjo's eyes spark, a hint of admiration crossing her features. She doesn't speak it aloud, but a proud smile tugs at the corner of her mouth and she nods, scribbling Cole's statement into her notepad.

Once Cole's told the whole story, the detectives sit back and exchange a resigned look.

Olubanjo, her expression much softer now, addresses her directly.

"Ms. Allbright, considering these events and what Mr. Johnson has put you through, I would highly recommend you file for a temporary restraining order. Furthermore, I would suggest filing assault charges against him."

Cole looks to me, a worried expression marring her brow. I give her a reassuring nod, encouraging her to make her choice.

She straightens her shoulders, rolling them back as she exhales a long, slow breath and shakes her head.

"I just want him to leave me alone."

She takes in another deep breath, closing her eyes as she blows it back out, trying to calm her nerves. Resigned to her decision, I watch as she draws on the reserves of strength she keeps hidden from the rest of the world, her shaking hand lifting toward her lips...

"Can you please just file the restraining order for me?" She says, biting at the skin along her cuticles. I gently take her hand away from her mouth and smooth my thumb over the tattered skin, soothing the angry edge of her nail.

Kerr hits her with that brilliant white smile and gives her a nod, silently reassuring her as he adds her request to his notes.

"Of course, Ms. Allbright. We'll get that order filed immediately for you and if he tries to contact you again, you give us a call and we'll take care of it, alright?"

They rise from their chairs, tucking away their note pads as they head toward the large oak study doors.

James stands beside the doorway, still as a statue, back straight, nose slightly upturned, one arm tucked behind his back while the other holds their two coats. Putting on the perfect show.

Standing with them, I watch Kerr as he slips on his coat. His eyes wide and jaw slack, he takes a moment to gaze around the ostentatious room. He blows out a quiet whistle and Olubanjo jabs him in the ribs with her elbow, shooting him a disgusted glare before they both step out the door.

I must admit, the space does look like the epitome of opulence—the sort of place that visitors would pay lots of money to traipse around gawking at the finery, trying to get a glimpse of how the other half lives.

Personally, I've always hated it. Hated the show, the pomp, the fucking arrogance of it all.

My private suite of rooms, the corridor they're on and the one where Brick stays when he's not in the Gatehouse, are more modern, more me.

Yes, I know what it means to be born into wealth and privilege, of never having to worry about the next paycheck or feeding the mouths of those you're responsible for. But all of it came with a price.

It cost me my mother, my brother, and then, with the death of my father, it cost me my dreams. My freedom.

But Cole has stirred something in me. Rekindling some of those discarded dreams I thought I'd lost when I had to become The Duke. She's making me believe I can be that *and* the man I had once dreamed of becoming.

This woman has never seen me as anything other than who I truly am—who I *want* to be.

She sees *me*.

Sees past the title, past the money.

Past the pompous, arrogant and foreboding Duke of Wyeholme.

She only sees me—Rogan, the man.

To her, it wouldn't matter if I was poor, if I had nothing. I swear to God, I think she would be happy if we lived in a tent in the bloody orchard.

As my mind drifts to thoughts of the orchard, my hand tightens on hers, remembering finding her curled beneath the tree that day—trembling, frightened. I tug her gently into my side, wrapping an arm around her as I recall the moment I felt her sink into my chest, settling there, finding a sense of comfort, of safety, of home... *in me*.

Without hesitation, Cole curls into me again, softly sighing as she tucks herself against my side, wrapping her arms around my waist. I can feel the tension in her body lesson the more she settles into me.

A deep ache tightens in my chest at the feel of her held protectively against my side. I know now, I would do anything for this woman. Anything to make her feel safe. To take away her pain, her fears and to ensure she feels nothing but utter happiness and peace for the rest of her life.

Chapter 59

Rogan

We watch the detectives climb back into their black sedan.

"That was very brave, Cole." Brick says as he stands beside us.

Cole's teeth click together as she nips off a tiny piece of skin from her cuticle and glances toward him. She gives him a tight smile, but goes back to chewing her finger, her attention shifting back to the car as it pulls down the drive. It's clear she's still not alright with all of this.

When Olubanjo had asked if there were any other witnesses, other than the three of us who could back up her story, we put together a list of names of everyone who'd been at the pub that night, who'd seen the events play out.

"He has a history of this kind of behavior..." I had told the detectives, finally deciding it was time for the truth behind the reason why I had to fire Zavier all those years ago, to come out.

I hated admitting I had known what he had already proven capable of. Cole's eyes felt heavy on the side of my face as I told the detectives of what I'd caught him doing to our maid, Tessa.

It makes me sick to think I could have prevented all of this if only I had reported him back then. The guilt of it eats at me like a festering rot. There's no denying I'd questioned myself for years about not doing more at the time. His attacks on Cole, only further proving I should have.

But at the time, I'd believed I was doing what was right for Tessa, for her life. She had pleaded with me not to say anything, not to report it to the police. Zavier's threats had clearly gotten to her. She was terrified of what he might do in retaliation should she turn him in.

Young, naive and having just stepped into my role as the Duke, I was out of my depth. I hadn't considered he would ever try something like this with anyone else, let alone the person I loved.

It's certainly a mistake I won't be making again.

Brick steps forward, his gaze locking onto a tall, slender shape moving up the drive. Her long, colorful skirt billowing out around her legs, a roly-poly pup, trundling along beside her. A tiny, lithe shadow darts in and out of the bushes lining the drive alongside her.

She moves aside, letting the police car drive past.

Brick jogs out the door, hurrying to meet her, taking the basket from Kya's arm and carrying it for her as they approach Cole and me.

"Thought you might want some girl time, Hun." She smiles brightly at Cole, pulling her into a hug, "After living with all this testosterone for nearly a week."

Cole melts into her friend and laughs, squeezing Kya tightly before bending down to scoop Athena up in her arms. She hugs the little tortoiseshell cat close to her chest and buries her nose into her soft fur.

She looks up at me, lifting her face to mine, smiling sweetly. I can't resist leaning in to steal a kiss from her lips.

"We won't be far." Kya boldly states, linking her arm through Cole's and pulling her away.

"Give you two some time to sort out this mess, and me some time with my bestie after you pretty much kidnapped her." She laughs playfully, looking back over her shoulder at me with mock exasperation.

She snatches the basket back from Brick then leads Cole down to the lawn in front of the Manor.

"James, please see that the ladies have some warm blankets for their picnic. Perhaps bring them something hot to drink to help keep some of the chill out of their bones."

I can already think of a few ways to warm Cole up later on...

"Of course, sir." James replies, turning to head further into the house to gather the requested items.

I harrumph slightly as Brick slaps my shoulder, forcing me to spin away from watching the women as Grumbl yaps happily, rolling onto his back so Cole can scratch his belly.

"Come on then. We have a lot to do. Starting with an invitation to attend a meeting at Abelridge Group in London tomorrow. The CEO is very keen to meet you."

"Tell him I can't make it!" I bark angrily, my thoughts solely on Cole.

"Can't do that, mate, sadly." Brick runs a hand around his chin.

"They're the ones funding that deal of ours, with our company in Dublin. They're threatening to pull out if they don't meet with you soon."

He shoots me an imploring look then rolls his eyes.

"They said something about wanting to ensure our values match theirs because they've seen the bloody pub video." Clearly irritated with their reasoning for the meeting.

"They just want to make sure you're not some mad, dangerous fucker." Brick grins devilishly.

"I mean... you are, so you'll have to really act the part..."

His smile fades when his attempt at humor misses its mark and I growl low in my throat.

"Calm down, mate. You'll be there and back in a day, I promise. Back to fuckin' your girl in no time."

I grab his arm and he flinches back.

"Whoa, whoa! Easy Ro! I was just bustin' your arse..." He grins playfully at me, until he meets my eyes, his grin quickly shifting to concern.

"I need you to promise me something." My tone is dark, serious.

"While I'm gone, you do not let Cole out of your sight, you understand?"

He looks at me, scanning my face.

"She's had a shock today, and she may seem good right now, but you didn't see her earlier. She lost her shit, mate." I stare into his eyes, driving my message home.

"I'm worried she's been shaken enough; she might run. She said something about wanting to keep me safe."

He cocks a brow, "Keep *you* safe? What the fuck from?"

"She's sure her husband is going to find out where she's been all this time from that bloody video and she's worried he'll come after me if I get in his way. I'm worried about her, Brick." My hand clenches and his arm contracts under my grip.

"She needs to know that nothing and no one will hurt her here. I..." I swallow, hard—my gaze dropping to his chest, my voice breaking.

"I can't fucking lose her. Not now that I've found her."

Without a word, he nods, understanding how badly I need his help right now.

I loosen my grip on his arm, but give it one more squeeze, gentler this time—showing him my silent gratitude.

"Jesus... her husband, eh? Shit. Alright then. Let's sort out all this fuckery then, shall we?" He replies, his tone reassuring. Once again, without question, without ceremony—he's got my six and I can't thank the universe enough for bringing him into my world.

We head back up to my office to begin making phone calls, to make sure everyone's story from the pub matches up.

Not for my sake. I couldn't care less.

It's all for her.

For my Little Fawn.

Chapter 60

Cain

The pictures strewn across my desk only fuel my rage.

Nicole. *Smiling.*

Nicole. *Laughing.*

It makes me feel sick to see her looking *so... fucking... happy.*

The expensive dresses I'd paid for—Gone.

The high-end shoes that made her legs and ass look incredible—Gone.

The makeup that turned her face into my own private fuck toy—Gone.

She's mine.

I own this body.

I own this mouth.

I own *her.*

The years of work I'd put into her, creating her, molding her into exactly what I wanted. Turning her into my perfect little submissive plaything—all replaced by shapeless hoodies, jeans and sneakers.

Bile climbs my throat as I try to swallow back my disgust, my fury becoming uncontrollable, unrelenting.

I will have her again.

I flip through the pile to find the photos of him.

The Duke.

Close-up shots of him standing naked behind her, brazenly moving his hand over her body as they stand at his window, her body clad in nothing but a towel—*Mine.*

His hands on *my* property.

His mouth and tongue tasting the flesh I've bought. I've paid for—*Mine.*

His hands stroking down her torso as she turns her face to him, putting his mouth on hers—*Mine.*

She's a whore. My wife is a fucking *whore—MINE!*

Maria had walked in when the PI had first given me the manilla folder filled with the images he'd taken.

All my rage exploded at her the moment he left the room. Every ounce of it focused on the woman who'd helped make this all possible.

The site of her broken and beaten, sniveling on the floor, quelled something within me. But it didn't stop me from landing one last kick in her ribs before telling her to clean up the fucking mess she'd made, her vomit tinged with blood puddled on the carpet beneath her.

She didn't show this morning—*sniveling little bitch.*

Another maid had served me my breakfast instead. No doubt Maria is still off licking her wounds.

Well, I laugh to myself, *if she doesn't report for work tonight, her family is fucking finished.*

My intercom buzzes.

"What?" I snap. My patience frayed.

"The Duke of Wyeholme is here, Sir."

I crack my knuckles before gathering the images toward me, tucking them back inside their folder and shoving them into my desk drawer. I press the button on the intercom.

"Send him in."

I run my hands over my hair and fix a smile onto my face.

This bastard isn't going to have the first clue what's coming for him.

I stride to the doors and throw them both open wide.

"Your Grace!" I beam at the tall man on the other side, dressed in an impeccable gray suit. His hair carefully slicked back, perfectly groomed dark stubble lining his jaw. He studies me, an air of privilege rolling off him like smoke as his eyes track over me.

I swallow down the instinct to get my gun out of my desk drawer. I would give anything to see the back of his goddamn skull painting the wall behind him.

But not yet.

Leaning into him, I extend a hand.

"Cain, Your Grace," I say, careful not to use my surname in case he makes the connection between me and the fucking whore.

"So glad you could come on down." I over exaggerate my American accent, adding extra drawl where there normally isn't any.

The bastard merely grunts as he takes my hand, his steely gray eyes narrowing.

His grip is firm. I make sure I match it and wait for him to release our hands first. It's my game he's playing now. My world he's in and I'll be sure he knows his place.

I step aside, ushering him through the doors of my office and step past him into the outer office. "Bring in some coffee would you, Sweetheart?" I smile at Gloria. Her brows arch in confusion at the term of endearment. I've never called her sweetheart.

"Y-yes, Sir." She replies, pushing up from her desk.

"Oh, and Darlin'," my faux southern drawl leaks a bit thicker than before. "Be a dear and ring Maria. Check if she's okay to work later? The poor love took a terrible spill yesterday."

She nods, eyes still wide, catching the smirk on my face, before placing the handset to her ear and hurrying to press one of the speed dial buttons.

The Duke has made his way across the room and is standing at the windows, looking out over Canary Wharf, glass giants reflecting the sun as they stand over the river far below. People moving like ants buzzing around, doing whatever it is poor people do.

"Quite a view, huh?" I move to stand beside him, clapping him on the shoulder, surprised to feel the solid bulk of his muscles hidden beneath his finely tailored suit.

He turns his head, eyes dropping to where my hand rests on his shoulder, then over to my face. I give him one more solid clap on the back, and give his shoulder a hard squeeze, before moving toward my desk. His eyes flare, but he says nothing.

"Nothing but the best here at Abelridge, am I right?"

"Unusual name." His voice is deep, cultured, but his tone is aloof as he turns his attention away from the window and over to me.

"Hmm, yes I suppose so. My father named it for his brother, Abel. Poor fella. He ended up having a bad run of things there for a bit. Quite unfortunate." I hum, hanging my head a bit, working to look the part.

"I see he didn't steer far when naming you."

"Ha!" I fake laugh. "You know your bible stories! I confess, being Cain in a company named for Abel is ironic."

His lips quirk up quickly, but the smile doesn't linger, then checks his watch. He clearly wants to be here even less than I want him here. But I need to know who he is, what makes him tick. What his weaknesses are.

"Well, my father was nothing if not ironic." I motion toward the sitting area. "Please, come, sit. Let's talk."

He follows me to the armchairs surrounding a low coffee table. Effortlessly chic, screaming of wealth.

Gloria brings in a tray with two black coffees and a small pitcher of milk.

I gesture for Gloria to pour. "Milk?" I ask him.

"No, thank you." He holds up a hand covering the cup, but addresses his reply to Gloria, giving her the first genuine smile I've seen from him. The bitch smiles back at him sweetly.

My teeth grind as I fight back a retort.

Sensing my irritation with her, she turns her attention to me, dropping her eyes to the floor.

"Sir, Maria isn't answering her phone."

My fingers flex, and I catch the Duke's eyes landing on my bruised knuckles.

"Boxing injury." I tell him quickly, running my thumb across my knuckles and chuckling. His overly observant gaze is unsettling as it flicks from my hand up to my face, the muscle flexing at his jaw.

"Afraid I don't know my own strength when it comes to a punching bag."

Gloria shifts uncomfortably on her feet.

His eyes narrow as he studies me, shooting a quick glance toward her, then back to me. He leans back in his chair, legs spread wide. He rests his fingers along his lower lip, tapping them lightly as he watches me.

"That'll be all, Gloria." I say, dismissing her from the room, effectively removing her telling fidgeting from his unbearably observant eyes.

"Oh, and please keep trying Maria." I say, laying the concern in my tone on extra thick.

"I'm terribly worried about her."

She gives me a quick nod, keeping her eyes on the floor then finally hurries out of the room. As the door clicks shut behind her, I lean back, mirroring his pose.

"Why am I here?" His voice is low, rumbling across the space between us, his tone impatient.

"I'm sure you've seen the video making its rounds on social media at the moment?" He doesn't move, doesn't blink, but his eyes narrow slightly.

"Like I said, Your Grace. We're a family business. We're built on strong Christian values of respect, of love. To have one of our partners acting so... so... brazenly, to be frank, has made a few of our board members a little uneasy."

He remains immovable, his gaze unblinking, so I decide to push harder, digging into something I think will salt the wound and get under his skin.

"Did your eight years as a Major in the SAS not teach you respect? Humility? How to contain your violent instincts?" I admonish. The only sign I've hit a nerve is the subtle flex of his jaw and the slightest twitch of his eyes.

I lean forward, invading his space. "The fact is, Your Grace, if you want Abelridge Group to continue funding your little project in Dubai..." I let my voice drop, taking on a threatening tonality.

"Dublin." His eyes narrow.

"Ah yes. My mistake. In *Dublin*. If you want our funding for your project in *Dublin*, then I need to be able to tell the members of the board, Cavendish Holdings is in stable hands. That their CEO won't be bringing their company—and by association, *my* company—into disrepute."

"And?" He asks, his tone dripping with annoyance.

My blood boils. This man seems to be unflappable. He has the gall to be annoyed? *With me*? The fucking balls on this mother fucker!

I'm renowned for ferreting out an adversary's weaknesses, but this cunt is like fucking granite.

"We need assurances, *Your Grace*." I nearly spit his title, my façade beginning to drop as my patience wanes. I can feel my rage bubbling, and soon I won't be able to stop myself from shooting this bastard dead.

"Assurances that nothing like this will happen again."

A humorless smile spreads across his face.

"I can assure you, *Cain,* your company will not be brought into any form of disrepute by Cavendish Holdings." He states, with no ceremony he stands, pushing his massive frame up and out of the chair—for a moment towering over me.

"You can expect a call from my legal advisor, Thaddeus Brickton."

He reaches out a hand in my direction, signifying our meeting is over.

How has this worthless Army grunt dressed up in aristocracy managed to get the upper hand?

I stand quickly, not allowing him to stand over me a moment longer and take his hand in mine. I squeeze harder than I should, pulling him closer.

"I look forward to it." I flash my perfect white teeth, my grip tightening even further, but then I feel his returning squeeze, feel the cartilage in my hand grind, the pressure deadening my hand and I'm forced to tug out of his grip. I stick my hand into my pocket and flex my fingers to try to regain the feeling.

For a moment, he holds my stare, two predators eyeing each other up.

"I'll show myself out."

Turning on his heel, he strides out the door and then he's gone.

As the door clicks shut. I upend the coffee table, then toss the chairs, screaming as I turn my fury to the furniture. Coffee cups smash loudly to the floor, the coffee staining my cashmere rug.

Rushing over to my intercom, my hair in disarray, my body shaking from pent up aggression, I slam my finger down on the button to page Gloria.

"Get me the number for Zavier Johnson! NOW!" I pant, dragging in deep, ragged breaths. My cock throbs with the need to fuck someone, watching as I choke the life out of her eyes.

"And a whore. Get me a goddamn whore!"

I move behind my desk, sinking into my chair and wrenching open the drawer. I pull out the pictures and my 9MM. My hands shaking with rage, I pull back the slide. A thrill runs through me as the gleam of the shining metal casing on the hollow point slides into place, loading the chamber. All that's left is to pull the trigger and I can put a bullet into his fucking skull.

Dropping the gun down onto my desk, my lip curls, a smile slithering across my lips.

The fucking Duke's dead...
He just doesn't know it yet.

Chapter 61

Rogan

As soon as the door closes behind me, I pull the folded image out of my inner pocket.

It's a photo of Cole, sitting with Kya, wrapped in blankets on the front lawn, the Manor behind them. She looks beautiful.

But there's no question, this was taken only yesterday.

While Cain spoke to his secretary, I'd noticed it sticking out from under his desk blotter, the image of her unmistakable. I'd snatched it up immediately, tucking it away inside my jacket before he came back into the room.

The picture proves the threat on Cole's life is real, not imagined. She's right to be terrified. Her husband is having her watched and it's only a matter of time before he makes his move to try and get her back.

The only thing I can't figure out is how the owner of Abelridge Holdings is involved and why he's got a photograph of her.

There's no question he'd invited me here today to get me away from her and to check me out, clearly sizing me up. Likely trying to get a read on me and figure out just how much of a threat I'm going to be.

I swallow down the sheer fury I have to go back into that pompous pricks office and show him exactly what Army justice looks like.

I turn to Gloria. She looks at me nervously, her eyes wide as they meet mine.

I turn it over in my mind, trying to make sense of it all. I'm struck with a sudden, sickening thought.

"What's your boss's name?" The color drains from her face at the seemingly benign question.

The sound of furniture smashing followed by a loud roar of outrage rumbles from behind Cain's office door, both of us turning toward the direction of the sounds.

I turn back to Gloria, her face ashen. She's visibly trembling.

"His name, Gloria!" I snap at her, no longer asking.

The time for a gentle approach, now long over as my need to get back to Cole rapidly intensifies, the pieces starting to fall into place.

Her eyes flick indecisively between his office door and me. She takes a deep breath before answering, a look of resolve crossing her face.

"Cain... Brentwood, sir."

My blood goes cold.

Brentwood.

Cole's married name.

I just had a face to face with her fucking husband.

The very same son of a bitch who gave her those fucking scars.

Rage scours my veins, everything in me screams to go back through that door and gut the bastard that hurt my Little Fawn.

I fight through my fury, trying to get my head around what his plans could possibly be. What the hell game is he playing at by getting me here today? Was this just a distraction? Has he got someone going after Cole right now?

"This Maria..." My mind works quickly to make the connections, "She's his maid, correct?"

Gloria nods, her eyes flitting between me and the sound of her boss losing his shit in the next room.

"Give me her address and her phone number. Then get the hell out of here, alright? You're worth more than working for a piece of shit like him!"

She nods again as fat tears spill over her lashes and roll down her cheeks. She turns back to her desk, pulling up a screen on her computer. After hitting a few keys, she jots down the information on a notepad, then tears it off and hands it over to me.

"If you need help, call this number." I say, pulling a card from my pocket and handing it to her. She takes it, hands shaking violently. "Ask for Brick. He'll help you, alright?"

She nods again, jumping as a shrill buzzing comes from the phone next to her. I lock eyes with her.

"Answer it, but don't let him know I'm still here."

She nods quickly, wiping at her cheeks and tries to compose herself, then presses the button to respond.

"Yes, sir?"

"Get me the number for Zavier Johnson! NOW!"

He's breathing heavily and there's a pause.

"And a whore. Get me a goddamn whore!"

"Yes, sir." Gloria answers, doing an impressive job of keeping her voice from shaking.

Releasing the intercom button, she turns her attention back to me.

"What should I do?" She asks, her voice soft, broken.

"Give him the number, but don't call for an escort. No woman is safe around that man today."

She does as I ask, sending Zavier's information to Cain on her computer, then grabs her coat and bag. I usher her out of the building, get her a cab and pay enough for the driver to take her anywhere she wants to go. Out of London, if necessary.

My gut roils as I pull out my phone. Missed calls. Lots of fucking missed calls.

Shit!

I hit Brick's name.

"What's happened?"

I don't waste time with any preamble. Brick wouldn't call me unless something urgent had happened.

"It's Cole. She's gone."

Ice pours down my spine.

"I was with her all day, Ro. I just went to take a piss and when I came back she was fucking gone. I tried to catch her but by the time I'd found her, she'd gotten on a bus. I wasn't able to stop her. I've been trying to find out what bus it was, but I haven't had any luck yet. Fuck, Ro! I'm so sorry. But she's gone."

Fuck!

I could tell she wasn't alright when I'd left her. The look in her eyes spoke volumes. Cole is a determined woman. If she wants to run, it would only take seconds for her to get past Brick if he was distracted. Hell, she's been trying to escape her nightmare husband for years. The girl knows how to slip away unnoticed if she needs to.

I glance down at the address Gloria gave me.

Maybe there's one person who will know where Cole might go.

Chapter 62

Cole

I spend the morning in Rogan's rooms, the carpet flattened where I've paced repeatedly while watching the viral video over and over again on my phone. Letting it play on a constant loop; the entire scene is burned into my mind. Regardless of how many times I watch it, or how much I wish for it, the final scene of me and Kya standing at the back of the patio, fairy lights illuminating my face, never changes.

Heart pounding and hands shaking, I hit replay, pausing when my face comes into focus yet again. Silent rage bubbles up in my chest, tears stinging my eyes, knowing... *knowing* Cain's going to find me, and this fucking video will be exactly how he does it.

Hot tears spill over my lower lashes and drip onto the screen of my phone, blurring the image.

Why can't I just be free of him?

Why won't this nightmare ever fucking end?

My gut churns, fury boiling my blood. He's going to ruin this new life I've created, destroy what I've built and take it all away. Whether he finds me or not, my bliss is over. I can't take the chance of him finding *them*...

My friends.

My family.

My love...

I have to leave.

My chest aches, the weight of my decision heavy as I resign myself to this feeling, knowing soon, this empty ache will be my constant companion.

Is this what true heartbreak feels like?

But I remind myself, I'm doing this to save him. To save all of them.

They'll understand... won't they?

My anger finally boils over and I hurl my phone across the room, the screen cracking as it smashes against the stone hearth of the fireplace, a sob ripping from my throat.

Dropping to my knees, I let myself sit in the pain for a while, until it feels like I just can't cry another tear—raw determination taking over in place of my pain and grief.

Sniffing and swiping angrily at my wet cheeks, I head into the ensuite and wash my face, holding a cold cloth to my eyes to try to get the puffiness to subside. I apply a bit of concealer and use some eye drops to disguise my red, blotchy features.

If living with Cain has taught me anything, it's how to hide the truth on my skin.

Giving myself a final once over in the mirror, I straighten my back, snatch my phone off the floor—shocked to find it still working even with the large crack in the screen—and head for the door. I'll need to figure out how to get past Brick if I'm going to be able to leave before Rogan returns.

When I come down the stairs, Brick is sitting at the kitchen island, watching a rugby game on his phone. I clear my throat and his head snaps up.

"Hey Red! How's it going?"

His voice is jovial, but there's an intensity behind his gaze, always seeing way more than he's letting on.

"Umm...," his gentle tone throws me off. A moment of hesitation, of regret, bubbles to the surface and I almost give in to the overwhelming desire to stay. It's taking everything in me to go through with this and it feels so wrong to lie. To deceive these people who have never been anything but kind and accepting of me.

He'll only hurt them if I stay. I remind myself.

I swallow hard, digging deep to find my resolve again.

"Do you, umm... do you think we could head over to Kya's for the day, instead of staying here in the Manor? It just feels a little odd being here without Rogan and I think I could use a little girl time anyway." I smile at him, trying to not only make him believe me, but to keep convincing myself this is the right thing to do.

His warm smile damn near breaks me as he immediately stands and pockets his phone.

"Of course we can, Red. Grab your coat and we'll head over right now."

As soon as we arrive, Kya sweeps me into a tight bear hug, the warm scent of patchouli instantly giving me a sense of home. I sink into her hug, dreading the fact that this may very well be the last time I get to feel it.

We settle around the table, a card game between us, Kya and Brick seemingly oblivious to their own flirting. My eyes sting as I let their light hearted banter burn into my memory.

Grumbl and Athena race around the room, Grumbl ambling along clumsily, while Athena banks off the furniture around him with graceful ease.

I excuse myself to use the bathroom and quickly detour into my room, retrieving the bag I've kept packed for this exact situation. A change of clothes, my passport, and cash. Enough to get me out of the country—to get me far away from Verdon. Somewhere I could maybe learn to live without them... *without him.*

I think I've always known in my heart this was only temporary.

While Kya and Brick are distracted dealing out another hand of cards, I drop the bag quietly by the door, tucking it behind one of Kya's oversized plants, then rejoin them at the table.

Before long, Kya has to head off to work. She gives me another tight hug, promising we'll share some fish and chips and a bottle of wine when she gets back later tonight.

Then it's just me, Brick, Grumbl and Athena.

We continue playing cards and chatting. Brick is so easy to talk to, so skilled at making any situation feel warm and comfortable.

My heart squeezes when the moment I've been waiting for finally happens, when he excuses himself to use the bathroom.

Now is my chance.

As he rounds the corner, I move toward the door, quietly retrieving my bag and jacket and slipping them on. I listen carefully to the sound of his footsteps growing distant as he reaches the top of the stairs. The moment the bathroom door clicks shut—I open the cottage door and run.

Yes, *run*.

As fast as my legs can take me, my heart racing, my breath coming out in short, quick pants, all but certain my sweet beast of a friend is going to find me missing and come after me before I can escape.

I sprint up Lover's Lane, hitting the village high street. I cast my eyes up and down the road, sure I'll hear Brick's feet pounding after me at any moment, but when I look back, I'm still alone.

In the distance I hear the hiss of air breaks.

The bus to Gloucester. *Perfect timing.*

I bolt toward the bus stop, meeting up with it just as the doors start to close. Squeezing through the narrow opening, I leap up the steps, throw some money at the driver and quickly take my seat.

As the bus starts to pull away from the curb, I see him. Racing toward it, picking up speed. It doesn't take but a few seconds before he's at my window, keeping pace with the bus, his face bobbing beside me.

"Cole!"

His shout is muffled through the glass of the window.

"Cole! Stop! You don't have to do this!"

My brows pinch as hot tears pour from my eyes, my face crumpling with the sheer agony of my heart breaking. I lay my palm on the glass and try to let him see the apology in my eyes. His slap on the window as the bus finally gains more speed than he can keep up with, reverberates through me. I face forward, clutching my bag to my chest and let myself completely break down into sobs.

"Are you alright, dear?" I jump, turning to look into the cloudy eyes of an elderly woman sitting across from me.

"Bad break up, eh?"

I wipe at my wet cheeks, my forced smile not fooling anyone as I nod, more tears spilling down my face.

"Ah Love, we've all been there. You're doing the right thing getting away like this. Life's too short to stay when you know in your heart it's time to leave."

My chin quivers and I look back out the window, Brick's handprint glaring back at me on the glass.

I play the old woman's words over and over in my mind. As the Forest of Dean speeds past, I watch as it gradually changes from dense woodland to the wide-open fields of the valley of the Severn.

God, I hope so.

Chapter 63

Cole

It takes nearly two hours to reach the Gloucester bus depot.

After cleaning myself up again in the ladies' bathroom, I head back out. I scan the area and see the train station just across the road.

I pull out my phone, carefully sliding my finger across the shattered screen, to bring up the transit app and choose a destination.

Edinburgh, Scotland.

That should be far enough. I'll have to make a change over in London—the thought of going back there makes a chill run down my spine. But London is a big city and Cain won't know to look for me there yet.

From there, I'll head north, find somewhere to stay, to lay low, to plan, before I fly... somewhere even farther away from here. The more distance I can put between myself and Verdon, the safer they'll be from him.

I still have a few hours to wait before my train arrives, so I buy a coffee, a magazine, and try to distract myself in the small station cafe. Anything to try to stop my thoughts from racing, my memories from surfacing, my unrelenting nerves to get the better of me.

As I wait, nursing my paper cup of rapidly cooling, bitter liquid that barely passes as coffee, I flip aimlessly through my magazine with unseeing eyes. An unbidden memory of Rogan floods my mind, making my confidence waiver, fresh tears stinging the backs of my eyes.

My chin drops, my eyes closing as I think of how his arms felt as they held me. How his fingers, feather light, tenderly grazed my skin with such care as he brushed a lock of hair from my face. The way he felt inside me, moving with me, bringing to light pleasures I never knew existed.

The way he held me while I slept, chasing away the nightmares with his presence alone. His words of love and assurance driving out the darkness I've carried with me since I was a child.

Moisture leaks from my eyes as I realize how much he's needed me too. He's been sleeping so deeply lately. Blissful, dreamless sleep, because when I'm with him, his nightmares stop too.

"God damn you, Cain." I curse under my breath through my teeth, my decision to leave feeling more and more wrong the longer I sit with it.

Damn you for ruining everything... again.

My eyes snap open when I hear the legs of the chair across from me scrape across the floor. I keep my head down and pull the hood of my jacket further over my face, curling in on myself, trying to make myself look smaller.

A large form settles into the chair and I feel their eyes on me, my pulse ratcheting up. As casually as I can, I gather up my belongings, rise from my chair and slip my bag over my shoulder, moving to walk away. I make it just a few steps when...

"Stop."

I gasp, a sob escaping me before my hand can clasp over my mouth. Crushing my eyes shut, I shake my head. I can't move, my legs frozen to the spot where I stand.

I can't turn around. I can't look. He can't be here. No one knows where I would go. I didn't even really know.

"Look at me."

I shake my head again. This can't be happening. I almost made it. I was almost gone.

I feel the heat of him as he steps up behind me, close but not touching. A beat of silence hangs in the air as he waits for me to comply, my heart hammering in my chest.

"Look at me, Little Fawn." His tone is soft, pleading, but with an air of command.

Fresh tears pour down my cheeks at his nickname for me and I can't stand it a second longer.

A loud sob rips from my throat, as I spin and barrel into his arms, my bag dropping to the floor at my feet. He crushes me to his chest, his big hand curling over the back of my head. The crisp smell of bergamot and spice fills my nose as I breathe him in deeply—instantly soothing me, calming my frayed nerves.

My fingers tangle into the fabric of his jacket, holding onto him like he's the only thing keeping me afloat in this sea of despair I've been so lost in. Every reason I had for leaving, now seems so small, so insignificant.

Rogan.

He's here. I have no idea how he found me, but right now I really don't care. Having his arms around me validates every doubt I had for leaving.

I feel completely boneless in his tight grip, his strength, the only thing keeping me from collapsing to my knees.

My rock.

My everything.

"Where are you going, Little Fawn?" He murmurs into my hair, his voice cracking slightly as his strong arms squeeze me a little tighter.

There are so many things I want to say. So many worries I've been ruminating on that I'm so terrified will come to fruition if I don't leave now.

I want to tell him I love him so much, that it hurts to be apart from him. Tell him everything.

But the only words I can manage are, "I'm sorry."

He doesn't reprimand me for the apology like usual—just presses soft kisses to the top of my head. I can feel his body trembling too.

"Come home, Cole. Please. We're going to get through this together, Little Fawn. You don't have to do this alone."

He pulls back slightly, his finger tipping my chin up.

"I know you're worried about me, but you don't have to be. I've got you."

Staring into his steely gray eyes, I realize, I can't fight it anymore. I don't even want to. I'm tired of running, of being afraid, and I really don't want to do this alone. I don't want to give up this life; give up everything I've worked so hard to build—give up Rogan.

I nod and I feel him breathe out, his breath shaking with relief, then leans in, pressing his lips to mine.

"Let's go home." He murmurs, resting his forehead against mine, his eyes close as the tension slowly ebbs from his body.

He bends down to grab my bag, and tugs me into his side—his strong arm holding me close. Wrapping my arms around his waist, I lean in to his side as we head toward the exit of the train station.

Back to Verdon.

Chapter 64

Cole

Rogan's Audi purrs a steady, soothing hum as we travel back to Verdon, my hand clasped firmly in his, atop the center console. The fingers of my other hand absently traces along the lines of his tattoos that peak out just below the cuff of his jacket.

"I met your husband today." He says, breaking the silence of the ride. My heart ratchets up a notch and I feel his fingers tighten around mine.

"You what?" I whip my head around to face him, my eyes flaring wide as my heart slams against my rib cage.

He met him?

He glances at me, molten silver eyes locking on mine briefly before returning to the road ahead.

My chest tightens painfully at the thought of Rogan and Cain in the same room together.

"How?" I croak out, my voice a broken rasp as an unbidden tightness in my throat threatens to suffocate me.

"That was the meeting I took in London. I think he was trying to check me out. To size me up, so to speak."

My thoughts start to spiral...

Does he know who Rogan is?

Has he figured out where I am?

Does he know I've slept with Rogan?

Is he coming for me?

Did the sick bastard lure him there? But for what?

I blow out a few slow breaths and try to calm my racing heart, trying desperately to convince myself the meeting was just a fluke, a random coincidence.

No, if Cain knew who Rogan was to me, he would have killed him on the spot. It's got to be just a coincidence that the meeting he had was with him. I keep the thought close, praying that if I wish for it hard enough, it might just be true.

My mind won't stop spinning, my panic ratcheting up more and more with each second that passes. Unable to take it a moment longer, I break and finally ask the question I'd been avoiding.

"Do you think he knows I'm with you?"

My voice sounds meek as terror grips my throat, nearly preventing any words past my lips.

He's quiet for a minute, a severe look on his face. When he finally turns his attention to me, there's a dark look in his eyes that makes my blood run cold.

"Yes, I think so."

I feel my insides turn to liquid and bile burns the back of my throat as my stomach churns.

"Cole, listen to me." He squeezes my hand. "There's not a doubt in my mind that he's an absolute fucking monster," Rogan continues, "but I want you to know... he doesn't scare me."

He locks his eyes to mine again, making sure his intention is clear.

"In fact, it took every ounce of willpower I have not to go back in and kill the fucking piece of shit once I figured out who he really was!"

I study him, trying to get past the fact that he'd just come from a meeting with Cain. He glances at me again, giving me a reassuring smile before returning his attention back to the road.

I want to believe him, I do.

But how can I when I know what Cain is capable of? When every nightmarish thing he's ever done to me lives just at the edge of my mind, constantly nagging at my psyche. Knowing full well the measures he'll take to get me back.

I've seen it before... there's nothing he won't do to get what he wants. He won't let anything stand in his way. He's got too much power. Too much pull. Too much ego to let me go.

We pull into the drive of the Manor and Rogan parks the Audi. He brings my knuckles to his lips and presses a soft kiss to them.

"Stay right there, my love." He says softly, looking deeply into my eyes.

He exits the car then walks around the front and smoothly opens my door for me. Taking my hand, he helps me to my feet, then reaches into the back to grab my bag. Pulling me to his side again, like two magnets attached at the hip, we start up the steps to the Manor.

"Rogan?" I ask, looking up at him as we make our way up the stairs.

"Yes, my love?" He smiles sweetly down at me.

"How on Earth did you find me?"

His smile is huge, his white teeth sparkling as a dimple pulls into his cheek, just beneath that perfect line of stubble.

"I've got a surprise for you, Little Fawn," he beams.

Just as we reach the top step, the door swings open. James waits patiently for us as we approach.

Stepping into the foyer, my mouth opens wide in shock.

"Maria! Juan Carlos!"

I squeal, running across the expanse of the entry, as Maria, supported by her grandson, gingerly rises to meet me.

"Oh my God! What happened?"

I step back, taking in her black eyes, her split lip and the way she's holding her side, as if it pains her just to breathe.

"Mija...," she whispers, a watery smile breaking across her battered face as she raises a quivering hand, her voice thick with emotion as she softly strokes my cheek.

I turn into her gentle touch, cupping my hand against hers and close my eyes, leaning into the warmth, the love, in a touch I thought I might never feel again.

"Mr. Cain is what happened!" Juan spits out.

"He did this to *mi abuela*!"

His dark eyes flit between us, landing on Rogan standing behind me. "You promise, we will be safe with you, *si*?"

"Sí, amigo mío." Rogan assures him, slipping seamlessly into Spanish. "Nos aseguraremos de que las Víboras de Sangre no te encuentren. Estarás a salvo en Verdon."

-We will make sure the Blood Vipers don't find you. You'll be safe in Verdon.-

"*Gracias, señor Rogan*." Maria replies, her hands gripping my arms. "And thank you for looking after Miss Nicole." Her hand strokes my cheek again. "I did no think I would see you again, *Mija*." She says, her voice breaking as she gazes into my eyes.

Her smile brings a fresh wave of tears flowing down my cheeks again.

"The doctor has been alerted, Your Grace," James intones.

"He will be arriving at the Manor within the hour."

"Thank you, James." Rogan replies, threading his hand around my waist again and motioning us into the parlor, as Juan helps his grandmother cross the room.

Once they're settled in, James brings them some drinks and food while we wait for the doctor to arrive. Maria catches me up on what happened with Cain, including the fact that he has a private investigator looking for me.

"He wanted me to tell him where you are, Miss Nicole, but I no tell him nothing!" She snaps, slicing her hand through the air in a no-nonsense sweep, her anger with him radiating off her. The little woman always had a fire in her that impressed me to no end.

I take her hand in mine, squeezing it gently. "I'm so sorry, Maria. This is all my fault. He never would have come after you if it wasn't for me."

"No!"

Her response is so loud, so strong, she actually makes me jump.

"He try to kill you, *Mija*! You had to go, to get away from him. He do no scare me and I no afraid of him! Mr. Cain is a bad man. This no your fault!" She slices her hand through the air again, emphasizing her point.

I nod, pulling her into a light hug, so worried I'll hurt her if I squeeze too hard.

There's a light tap on the door and James clears his throat.

"The doctor is here, sir."

I kiss Maria on the cheek, giving her hand another gentle squeeze, then head out of the room with Rogan so the doctor can check her out and tend to her injuries.

He wraps his arm around me, guiding me down the hall.

"You're really prepared to help them?" I whisper.

He looks down at me, his eyes darkening, growing intense as they stare into mine. His voice deepens and I can feel it thrumming through my body.

"Of course I am." He says without blinking. "Maria... Juan Carlos... They're your family. Maria literally saved your life, Cole. For that, I will be forever in her debt. Without her, you wouldn't even be here right now."

His hand gently cups my chin and I turn my face up to his. I feel my legs weaken, his hand around my waist, pressing me into him—the only thing holding me up.

I'm lost in the soft look of love in his eyes as they lock onto mine. The truth behind his words, shining into me, radiating off him like the sun.

"Can't you see, Little Fawn? There isn't anything I wouldn't do for you. I would tear this world apart for you, watch as it crumbles, then build it back again, carving your name into its bones. There is nothing and no one that I'll ever allow to come between us. No matter what happens. You have to believe that, Cole."

My eyes scan his face, taking in his severe expression, the commitment he's making to me with those words. Everything in me wants nothing more than to believe him.

"Okay." I whisper, nodding as I smile up at him and pull his lips down to mine.

As he holds me to him, as I drown in his kiss, I truly believe that he would.

Chapter 65

Cain

I walk into the dimly lit pub in a dump of a town a few miles outside of Verdon-on-Wye. The smell of stale beer and old smoke hangs heavy in the air. Based on what my PI had uncovered, this is where I would be most likely to find Zavier Johnson.

The place is a total shit hole. I had hoped he might be at the same pub where the viral video had been shot, but he never went back there after that night.

Fucking pussy. One little ass kicking and he's got his tail tucked firmly between his legs.

I scan the dimly lit room. A handful of patrons are slumped in their seats along the bar, shadows draped over their hunched forms.

My gaze settles on a broad-shouldered man. A shock of greasy blonde hair veils his eyes as he throws back a tumbler of amber liquor, the glass clinking softly against his teeth.

As I approach, the details of his features sharpen—deep bruising beneath swollen eyes, a bandage stretched across the bridge of his nose, and a raw split carving through his lower lip. His icy blue eyes, bloodshot and dulled by drink, flicker toward me as I approach him.

I sidle up next to him, unwilling to sit on the sticky looking stool beside him.

"Zavier Johnson?"

His eyes narrow as he slowly looks me up and down.

"Yeah... who's askin'?"

He immediately turns his attention back to the bartender and raps his knuckles obnoxiously on the bar.

"Another one, Frank!" He barks at the man.

Clearly irritated, the bartender makes his way over and refills Zavier's glass with whiskey. He immediately knocks back the new drink in one big mouthful, grimacing slightly as he swallows past the burn. The bartender huffs, rolling his eyes in disgust.

I throw several fifties onto the bar and nod to the bartender.

"Keep them coming."

His eyes drop to the money and widen, snapping back to me before snatching them up quickly.

"You got it, boss." He says, pulling a fresh glass out for me and filling it with the same, then refilling Zavier's once again.

Zavier straightens, a greedy smile lifting half his mouth.

Taking a big mouthful of the newly poured glass, he sits back in his chair, turning to face me. He rolls his tongue over his split lower lip before saying, "Alright friend, you've got my attention. Who the fuck are you and what the fuck do you want from me?"

He watches me—eyes bloodshot, unfocused—his drunken glare laced with skepticism.

"We have a mutual... *friend*." I let the word 'friend' hang in the air, as he looks at me curiously out of the side of his eye.

"We do, huh?" He snorts a disbelieving laugh, then tips his glass up, emptying its contents once again. He burps, then motions a couple fingers in the air at the bartender to refill his glass.

Frank comes over with the bottle in hand, ready to pour, but I place my hand over the opening before he can tip the liquid into the glass.

Zavier's eyes shoot angrily to mine. "The fuck?" he spits.

"This *friend* owes us both something, and you're going to help me make them pay."

He holds my stare, interest slowly taking shape behind the drunken haze in his eyes as he studies me. He drops his chin, barely a nod, an acknowledgement.

I move my hand away from his glass, allowing Frank to pour. My eyes stay locked on Zavier's as I say, "Leave the bottle, Frank."

Frank grunts, but drops the bottle loudly to the bar top beside me and shuffles off to the other side of the bar, busying himself wiping the countertop down with the filthy rag he's pulled from his hip.

"So, who's this... *friend?*" Zavier asks, his full attention locked on me now.

"She goes by a couple different names, but I think you know her as "Cole Allbright.""

Chapter 66

Cole

The evening becomes a quiet ceremony of repair—a reforging of bonds, a reaffirmation of love and trust between friends who had long since become my chosen family. I tearfully apologize for my behavior, for the way I'd left, words tumbling out between sobs and shame.

Kya, ever fierce in her affection, scolds me through her own tears, pulling me into tight, trembling hugs. I've never felt more deeply cared for by another woman—even my own mother, than I do in her arms, as she sternly reprimands me, but holds me close with all the tenderness of someone who refuses to let me drift too far away again.

Brick laughs. "Well at least you gave me a good workout!" he teases, chuckling as he pulls me into one of his bear hugs. "God knows I've needed a good run for a while now."

Laughing too, my cheek pressed against the solid wall of his broad chest. The muscles beneath my cheek speaking volumes about how little he actually needed to exercise.

Rogan watches each pairing in turn, a small, knowing smile softening the harder edges of his face. He waits patiently for me to reunite with my friends, for them to convince me to forgive myself, assuring me they understand why I had chosen to leave, but never want me to do that again.

Later, we sit at the kitchen table, my chair drawn as close to his as humanly possible. The weight and warmth of his hand never leaving my thigh, grounding me. The conversation shifts to next steps, to the security measures we'll need to put into place to keep Cain from reaching any of us.

Ideas pass across the table, alternatives weighed, scenarios played out.

I lean my head against Rogan's shoulder, my eyes heavy, my lashes eventually fluttering closed, as the exhaustion that had been haunting me finally settles into my bones.

I feel his strong arms scoop me up and tuck my head beneath his chin as he settles me against his chest. My fingers find the buttons of his shirt, tracing them lazily, nails lightly grazing the skin beneath. The moment transporting me back to another time, another place—where he'd held me close to his heart for the very first time. Where he made me feel safe in a world that had been dark and unforgiving for too many long years.

Laying me down on the bed, he carefully strips me down to my t-shirt and panties, pulling back the duvet so I can slip beneath it. Athena leaps up gracefully, circling twice, then curling into a tight ball at the foot of the bed. Her golden eyes watch me closely, as though she too fears I might vanish again.

Moments later, Rogan slides into the bed beside me, his body fitting mine perfectly, the missing piece to my puzzle, the other half of my soul. The warmth of his body settles me in a way nothing else ever has.

I shift closer, molding my back to his chest, melting into his embrace. I fall asleep to the rhythm of his heart as it drums softly against me, his breath a warm, gentle caress against my neck. His strong arm slung over me, his hand cupping mine against my breast, our legs threaded together entwined in an embrace all their own.

Both of us drifting off into blissful, dreamless sleep, simply basking in the quiet calm of each other's presence, an unspoken safety held within the arms of the love we've found with one another.

We spend the next day toiling away in the bookstore, readying it for opening day. The four of us work companionably, our laughter and chatter a soft veil over the quiet worries none of us dare voice.

I can't help but smile as a shiver of excitement runs through me as I think of what's coming—the grand opening.

A milestone.

A reclamation.

To think I nearly gave this up—my friends, this dream, my love—what once felt so impossible, unimaginable, is now my new reality.

Kya and I giggle as we sort through boxes of the new spicy titles we've chosen to stock. Athena, my constant shadow, leaps in and out of the cardboard boxes like a feline jester, her antics drawing more laughter from us as we work.

At the other end of the room, Rogan and Brick hang signs and adjust wall fixtures, their voices low and deliberate. I catch fragments of their plans, the deep timbre of their words threading through the store like distant thunder.

They're preparing for what we all know is coming.

The threat of my husband lingers, a darkness overshadowing light, marring the atmosphere with its quiet menace.

Later, we'll head to the dojo.

It couldn't hurt to train a little more, sharpening our reflexes, keeping our self-defense skills honed and at the ready.

Just in case.

With my confidence renewed after an epic night of practicing both offensive and defensive techniques, we leave the dojo, Rogan's arm around my shoulders, as we step out into the cool night.

The light coating of sweat on my skin causes it to pebble in the chilly air, but it feels amazing, my adrenaline still high from the workout.

Brick and Kya linger in the doorway. While Brick tries to lock the door, Kya teases him, stalling his efforts with playful blocking techniques. I hear his warm laugh mingling with her giggles and give Rogan a knowing smile. He grins down at me, taps his finger to the tip of my nose, then pulls me tightly to his side, leaning down to press a kiss to my lips.

I was so wrong to try to leave this behind. This moment proves this is exactly where I belong, where I'm meant to be. I can't believe I almost gave all of this up, could have lost it all.

All because of that son of a bitch.

I feel myself relax as I sink into Rogan's side and breathe in deeply. That's when I smell it...

Smoke.

I had smelled it when we first stepped out of the dojo, but thought it might just be someone having a small bonfire, enjoying the clear night. But no... this doesn't smell like a bonfire.

It's not just wood smoke. It's dense... heavy... hanging in the air and I realize my eyes are burning. I glance up to the night sky that had been peppered with bright stars when we'd entered the dojo earlier, but now they're invisible, blocked out by a dark cloud.

"Rogan..." I start, but he's noticed it too.

Brick and Kya quickly come to stand beside us, our eyes searching the nearby village.

That's when we see it...

The glow of flames lapping at the darkened sky, just up ahead.

Just above Lover's Lane.

"Fire!" Rogan yells, and we bolt.

The four of us sprint toward the direction of the flames, Brick grabbing Kya's hand and pulling out his phone at the same time to call for fire rescue as we run.

As we get closer, we see it.

It's the Terrace...

Kya's home.

Flames and smoke billow out the windows and up the side of the building. The tattered remnants of her once colorful curtains flip wildly from the torrent of heat pushing past them.

She lets out a blood curdling scream, her hands reaching up, clawing at her face as she collapses to her knees. Brick reaches for her, going down with her, his arms encasing her, trying to hold her up.

"Noooooo!! Not again! *Not again!*"

Even in the light of the flames, I can see her normally honeyed complexion has gone stark white. Tears stream down her face, an inconsolable terror in her eyes.

She's frantic, lost to fright, tugging at the roots of her hair. She wrenches herself free from Brick and gets back to her feet, pacing back and forth like a caged animal.

Suddenly, she spins toward Brick, her eyes wide with horror.

"Oh my God! Grumbl! Brick, Grumbl is in there!" She pleads. "We need to get him out! We need to save him! I can't lose him too! Not like this, Brick! Not fire... *anything but fire!*"

Her voice breaks more and more as her words turn to anguished sobs.

"I'll get him!" He assures her, before barreling toward the flaming cottage.

"Brick, no!" Rogan bellows after him. But he's already through the door, knocking it down with a single, powerful kick. The sound of sirens can be heard in the distance as I rush to Kya's side, pulling her into me. Rogan holds us both as we watch the door... waiting.

"Not again, not again, Oh my God, not again..." The words fall from Kya's lips in a steady chant as she continues to tug at her hair and claw at her face. Her whole body, shaking violently.

We watch the door, our fear for Brick and Grumbl's safety growing worse and worse the longer they're in there.

"It's been too long!" Rogan says, tugging a towel from his bag and pouring water on it. "I'm going in."

"Rogan, no!" I scream, grasping for his arm. His head swivels between the flaming house and me, then back again as he wars with his decision.

His expression tense, his eyes lock onto mine.

"I can't let him do this alone..."

My throat tightens as I hold his stare, but I nod. I won't make him choose. He leans down, kissing me hard then breaks away, running toward the house, pressing the wet towel to his mouth and bolts straight through the flaming door.

Finally, fire rescue arrives, tugging hoses and equipment off the trucks and hurrying to get water onto the flames. A large man in uniform rushes over to us, shouting over the roar of the flames and commotion, the entire village gathering nearby.

"Is everyone out?"

"No!" I shout back. "There are two men in there, and our dog."

"Damnit!" The man barks.

"Alright, we've got this. You ladies stay back now and let us get them out!"

I nod, squeezing Kya tightly to me, her eyes wild and unseeing. I think she's in shock. We huddle down to the ground, clinging to one another, our eyes never leaving the door.

There's a loud explosion near the back of the property and both Kya and I duck down and scream.

A moment later, two large, dark forms barrel out the door, soot covered and coughing. Brick holding something large wrapped in a blanket close to his chest.

Choking on smoke and running his hand down his blackened face, Rogan gives the fireman the okay to start putting out the flames and they hit the building hard with several hoses spraying a torrent of water onto the fire.

Kya's face crumples when she sees the bundle in Brick's arms, launching into a fresh wave of wailing tears.

The paramedics rush over to help, quickly getting to work providing oxygen masks and water to the men, checking their vitals. Another immediately starts working on Grumbl's unmoving form.

We rush over, holding each other as we stand nearby.

Rogan and Brick brush off the paramedic's ministrations to stand with us, waiting, praying they can save our little friend, while Kya's house turns to ash. It's a scene straight out of a nightmare, come to life.

"I've got a pulse!" One of them shouts.

"O2, one hundred percent, NOW!" She bellows.

Finally, his little round sides begin to rise and fall on their own. He moves to sit up and coughs a few times, swaying groggily. Kya's whole body shakes, as she practically screams a sob of relief, running to his side—kissing him and holding him tightly.

The lead paramedic keeps oxygen pressed against his nose and mouth, and strokes a soothing hand down Kya's back.

"He should be okay, love."

"Thank you, thank you, thank you!" She cries.

"He'd wedged himself under the sink." Brick says, his voice scratchy and dry. "Took a bit to get the smart little bugger out of there." He chuckles, then coughs, a painful hacking sound.

Kya turns to him; huge tears welled in her eyes. She rushes him, colliding into his body hard enough to knock him back a few steps.

He wobbles a bit, but quickly regains his footing, wrapping her in a tight hug.

"God bless you, Brick! You saved him. You saved him..." Her voice trembles, barely more than a whimper, her body sagging under the weight of all the trauma she's endured.

She raises her tear-streaked face to look into his eyes and he cups her face gently in his hand, his thumb wiping away her tears.

I sniff and lean into Rogan, watching them in this raw moment, when a weak shout pierces the air from somewhere just beyond the smoke...

"Over here!"

Old Tom. He's carrying a limp body out of the house next door, as flames lick at the back of the property. The paramedics rush to help him, taking the frail, unconscious body from his arms, and placing her on a gurney. I recognize the colorful, hand knitted cardigan hanging off of her loose limbs...

Edna... Tom had gone into the fire to save his love.

I run to Tom's side as he sways on his feet, black soot surrounding his mouth and nose.

Wrapping his arm around my shoulder, I let him lean his weight onto me, leading him farther away from the smoke. The third paramedic brings over an oxygen mask, deftly securing it to his face.

I hear one of the machines hooked to Edna start squealing, an alert that something has gone wrong.

"I'll be right back," she says, shooting me a look, imploring me to keep watch on Tom until she can get back to him.

I nod, and she races over to help with Edna.

Tom smiles at me beneath the mask.

"You really do look so much like your mum." He says, his cloudy eyes bloodshot and watery as he takes me in.

He sways weakly, so I guide him down to the ground to get him off his feet.

"You think she's gonna be okay now?" He asks, his worried stare locked on Edna, the paramedics working feverishly to keep her breathing—when he falls into a fit of soupy coughs.

"You did so good, Tom." I tell him, drawing his attention back to me, rubbing circles across his back, trying to help him shift the smoke that must be settling in his lungs.

"You're gonna be the talk of the whole village! You're a hero." I smile proudly at him.

"You think?" He beams, but his coughs quickly overtake him again. But this time, they don't let up. He can't seem to catch his breath. I move to flag down the paramedic, but he grabs my hand.

"Let them take care of Edna, dear."

I shake my head, "What about you, Tom? You need help too."

"I'm all good now." He wheezes between wet coughs.

The paramedics start shouting, moving quickly to revive Edna with more urgency than before.

"Tom, let me get you some help." I move to get up again, but he grips my arm with surprising strength.

"Let it be, dear." He says firmly. "Edna needs them more than me. Ain't got much time left anyway."

"What?" My eyes snap back to his. "What do you mean, you don't have much time?"

"Cancer...," a cough, blood and spittle splatters the inside of the mask he's still wearing. "Final stages... only got about two or three weeks left now anyway."

The coughing overtakes him again as I feel my heart crush inside my chest.

"Oh Tom..." I weep, pressing my forehead to his, tears burning my eyes.

Rogan, Brick and Kya—Grumbl held tight to her chest, come over, crouching down with me and Tom as I cradle him on the ground. They kneel around him, each of them reaching out a hand to rest on his arms and legs.

Quietly telling him they're there. That he's not alone.

"There's something else you need to know..." He says, pulling the oxygen mask from his face.

"It's okay, Tom. We don't need to talk about it now." I tell him, trying to take the mask from him to secure it back over his nose and mouth.

He holds it away from me, shaking his head, working to regain control from another bout of wet coughs.

"No. It has to be now, dear." His grip holds firm on my wrist. I lean my head closer, tipping my ear toward his mouth to hear him better.

"It was Zavier." He whispers on a pained breath.

"He did this. He set the fire."

Our eyes all go wide as we look from Tom to each other, then back to Tom again.

His gaze moves to Kya, "I saw him going 'round your cottage with a can of petrol. The bastard set fire to your house and could have taken out the whole damn village." He wheezes, chest rattling as I finally get the oxygen mask back onto his face.

His cloudy eyes track back to me. "He ain't done either. Saw the slimy son of a bitch heading in the direction," he pauses to work through another bout of coughing, struggling to take in a breath, "in the direction of your bookshop."

His voice is muffled by the mask, but there's no mistaking what he's just said.

My eyes fly to the group.

"Jesus." Brick says, running a hand through his hair.

Tom's grip loosens on my wrist, snapping my attention back to him.

He smiles at me, for a moment the look of pain gone from his watery eyes.

"You look so, so much like Mary… Just like…your mum…" his voice trails off, his mouth slackening as I watch the last bit of light fade from his eyes—his final breath escapes him as, what makes Tom the incredible man he is, quietly slips away.

"Tom? Tom…" I call to him softly, giving him a gentle shake, unwilling to believe the reality of what's right in front of me. His eyes half lidded and unseeing as his body lies slack and unmoving in my arms.

Rogan moves in and lays him down, removing the oxygen mask, preparing to start CPR, but Brick grabs his shoulder, tugging him back gently.

"I'm sorry, but you can't do that, mate." His face is somber as he looks down at Rogan's confused stare.

"What do you mean, I can't?" Rogan says, his tone incredulous.

"Tom has a DNR. He doesn't want any life saving measures taken. He set it up with me a few weeks ago."

"What…?" I feel my heart shred as Brick's words sink in.

We can't save him.

We have to let him go.

That's why he wouldn't let me get the paramedics to help him.

It's what he wanted.

This was his choice.

I grip his wrist, checking for a pulse, "Tom?" My voice comes out as little more than a whispered squeak, barely a sound at all, as I realize my dear, sweet friend is gone.

"She's back! We've got her! Get her into the ambo! Let's go, let's go, let's go!" The paramedics shout as they scramble to ready Edna for transport to the hospital.

I look from them to my friend, lying unmoving on the ground, his hand still gripped in mine. I lean in to kiss him gently on the cheek and whisper in his ear. "Well done, Tom. You saved her. You really are a hero."

Chapter 67

Cole

The fireman who was the first to arrive at the scene makes his way back over to us, crouching down next to Tom's still form. He looks grimly at the unmoving man in my arms and gently presses two fingers against the side of his neck, checking for any signs of life.

His face is somber and after a long moment, he shakes his head, confirming what we already knew.

"I'm so sorry folks, but I'm afraid he's gone."

I nod, my hand still holding tightly to Tom's, as a fresh flood of tears spills down my cheeks—although I honestly don't think they've ever really stopped.

He pulls out his radio to contact the ambulance, requesting a return time.

"ETA two minutes," is the echoing reply.

"The paramedics will take care of him." He says gently, placing one big hand on my shoulder.

Rogan crouches beside me, his hand replacing the fireman's, as I press Tom's hand to my cheek. Closing my eyes, I let my tears fall, as I say goodbye to my friend.

The peace of the moment is shattered when we hear a loud braying in the distance.

Hannah.

All four of our heads whip in the direction of the bookshop,

"Fucking Zavier!" Rogan spits, quickly getting to his feet, taking my hand to pull me up with him.

"Go. I'll stay here with Tom and Grumbl and wait for the paramedics to get here." Kya says, holding her pup close to her chest, lifting her chin toward the lane leading to the shop.

Brick stands at her side, a protective arm wrapped around her shoulders. He looks anxiously down the lane, his arm pulling her tightly to him.

She studies his face, knowing he's struggling with going to help his friend or staying with her in her time of need.

"Brick, go with them," she gives him a gentle nudge.

"Just please be careful, all of you."

His jaw tightens, the muscle feathering, as his decision to leave her behind is made. He steps into her, lifting her chin. Without any preamble, his mouth crashes down on her lips. She stiffens slightly and a small squeak escapes her throat, but then she relaxes into him, her lips moving softly against his as she welcomes his kiss.

"I'll be back, Sunshine. It's gonna be alright. Be safe." He says, softly kissing her one last time, before the three of us move to sprint toward Hannah, the bookstore, toward Haven.

Hannah's frantic braying echoes through the trees, the forest lining the river and village acting as a natural funnel, amplifying her frightened bellows.

As we round the bend, the buildings come into view and we see the first small curls of smoke behind Haven as they start to travel up into the air.

Brick somehow doubles his speed when he spots Zavier stepping out from beside the building, can of gas in hand, making his way toward the bookshop, oblivious of our approach—his soul focus locked on destruction.

His long legs eat up the distance between them as he barrels toward Zavier. Brick drops his chest low, widening his stance, aiming his head and shoulders straight toward Zavier's hips.

Zavier's head snaps up in Brick's direction mere seconds before impact, the bulk of his shoulder slamming into Zavier's pelvis as he wraps his big arms around the backs of his knees, driving him up, only to slam him back down into the ground, executing a perfect rugby tackle.

The can of gas flies off to the side and Zavier grunts, as the air is driven out of his lungs by the impact of Brick's shoulder.

Rogan races to Brick's side, throwing his own weight on top of Zavier, his arms and legs thrashing and flailing as he tries to wriggle out of Brick's hold.

Rogan deftly snares Zavier's wrists, locking them together in a one handed, iron-fisted grip, while tugging the cord out of his hooded sweatshirt with the other.

Within seconds, he's fastened it around Zavier's wrists in a tight bowline knot as he squirms, spewing profanities at the men.

He kicks his legs at them, landing a solid kick to Rogan's knee, dropping him down to all fours next to Zavier. Fury blazes in Rogan's eyes and he slams his fist into Zavier's face—once, twice, a third time.

With one last, brutal punch, Zavier's head lolls to the side, his eyes rolling back as he loses consciousness.

The flames lick along the back wall of the cottage and grow rapidly as they catch onto the dry materials nearby.

I sprint to grab the hose—hoping to put the fire out before it causes too much damage to the cottage. I yank at the coil, but in my hurry, I end up jamming it in on itself, the knot only tightening down further, the harder I pull. I tug at it feverishly, and curse, anxiety shredding through the last dregs of my patience. I glance back toward the cottage to see the flames licking up the sides of my grandparents' home, threatening to catch the thatched roof alight.

I snarl and yank furiously on the tangled hose, desperation making my movements futile.

Rogan and Brick join me, Brick heads to the side of the building to turn on the spigot, while Rogan nudges me aside to take over the hose retrieval.

He scans the knot, quickly figuring out the best way to approach it, then gives the reel a hard crank in the opposite direction. The backward turn allows for a bit of slack in the line, finally unjamming the hose from its tangle.

When he tugs it again, the reel unravels easily and I blow out a breath of relief as he snakes the hose around the side of the cottage to attack the fire.

Brick grabs Hannah's empty feed pail and scoops at a pile of soil nearby, tossing it onto the flames, while Rogan opens the hose to full blast, soaking the dry surfaces of the building closest to the flames to prevent the fire from catching any further before it can be fully extinguished.

Hannah is still braying with fear as she paces frantically back and forth in front of the bookshop, her tether not giving her enough slack to run far.

There's not much more I can do to help put out the flames, so I hurry to her side to try and soothe her. She's bucking wildly and carrying on something fierce. I grab at her harness to try to settle her, pulling her down and speaking to her in as calm a tone as I can muster.

Her bucking eases a bit at my touch, her eyes still wild as she grunts, chuffing as she stomps the ground. I run a soothing hand down her nose, whispering soft words of praise to her. She buries her nose into my chest, finally calming down.

"Good girl. That's it. Easy now, it's all going to be alright, girl." I coo, leaning back to look her in the eyes.

She chuffs again, her eyes wide and nervous. Then, without warning, she bucks back, letting out a loud bray, knocking me back a couple steps.

I reach for her again when a hand clamps over my mouth from behind, tugging me back into a large, hard chest.

The cold bite of sharp metal presses against the skin of my neck as hot, fetid breath coasts across my cheek.

"Hello...*wife.*"

Chapter 68

Cole

My blood turns to ice as I feel the sharp edge of the knife biting into my neck.

I want to struggle, to break free of his hold, but when I attempt to pull at his wrists, he only presses harder, the blade digging deeper into my flesh and I wince at the sharp sting of pain.

"Thought you got away this time, huh *whore*?" He hisses against my cheek, his stinking breath skating along my skin.

"I think you and I should have a little chat, don't you?" He runs his hot tongue up the side of my face and I cringe, bile rising in my throat.

"Let's go inside, shall we?"

He tips his head toward the bookshop door—the door I now realize is standing ajar, the handle hanging, the door frame smashed in and broken.

Hannah brays and bucks wildly, kicking her back hooves toward Cain, but he's hauled me just beyond her reach, her tether keeping her at bay.

I dare a glance toward where Brick and Rogan are still struggling to put out the flames on the cottage, but they don't see us—they're too focused on the fire to realize I'm not with them.

"Your little boyfriend is too busy for you, Nicole," he sneers, "but don't worry. I'm sure he'll come looking for you soon and when he does, *I'm going to gut him.*"

He laughs coldly, his tone promising the hell I've been dreading, as he drags the tip of his nose along my jaw, his hot breath ghosting across my skin.

He pulls me with him, backing us through the door of the bookshop, the knife held tight against my skin. I feel a warm, wetness trickle into the collar of my hoodie, his blade slicing deeper with each step we take.

He kicks the door shut and pulls me deeper into the darkened space, the room lit only by a few dim nightlights in the reading alcoves.

"Now, you're gonna be a good girl and keep your fucking mouth shut if I take my hand off your mouth, right? Because you know what will happen if you scream... don't you, bitch?"

I don't dare move to nod, but let out a soft whimper of agreement.

He slowly peels his hand back off my mouth, but snags a fistful of my hair instead, wrenching my head back. I gasp as he uses my hair to haul me further into the rows of books lining the shop.

He spins me, slamming my back into a bookshelf, driving the air out of me, as multiple copies of books fall to the floor. Pain streaks up my spine as it connects with the unforgiving wooden shelf.

Deftly spinning the knife in his grip, he presses it back against my neck, using his body to pin me against the bookshelf.

Raw terror seizes me when, for the first time in months, I'm staring into the cold-hearted, soulless eyes of my husband.

I claw at his wrist, trying to pry the knife away from my throat, but the angle of the blade is so close to slicing through my jugular, I'm terrified to try to twist out of his hold. He leans into the blade, the razor-sharp edge splitting my skin further. I recoil, trying to press myself harder into the bookshelf.

He releases my hair, snaking his hand down my body, groping me as he grinds his hard cock against my hip, mercilessly squeezing my flesh through my clothes.

He presses his thigh painfully against my waist, using his bulk to hold me in place. He drags his nose along my cheek, his words a stinking, rancid venom as they drip from his lips.

"Mmmm... I'm going to enjoy fucking you again." He runs his tongue along my jaw and squeezes my breast hard, giving it a painful twist through the fabric of my shirt.

I cringe as his hot breath runs along my neck and jolt when he bites down hard. His teeth break the skin and I cry out, unable to hold it in—my tolerance to Cain's abuse lowered having gotten so used to Rogan's gentle touches.

His head draws back, outrage flaring in his hard eyes. My head smacks back into the shelf, dazing me as pain sears across my cheek, when the back of his hand cracks across my face before I even realized it was coming.

"I told you to keep your fucking mouth shut!" He snarls through clenched teeth, his fist squeezing down on my throat. He shifts the knife to my side, digging the point between my ribs.

Spots dance before my eyes and I claw at his hand, but my vision starts to swim, his tight grip on my neck unflinching.

I feel my consciousness starting to slip away, my eyes rolling back in my head, my body slowly going slack in his grip. He quickly releases my throat and I suck in a sharp lungful of air.

Choking and spluttering, I drag in several quick breaths, each one feeling like razor blades in my throat. My vision swims and my head throbs as oxygen floods back into my system.

"Oh no you don't." He barks. "I want you awake for the fun we're gonna have, you fucking little cunt!"

He slaps me so hard across the face, the bitter taste of copper coats my tongue as my mouth fills with blood.

He crushes his hips against mine again, repining me to the shelf. His nostrils flare as he grinds his rigid cock against me, his cold, black eyes vacant of any emotion.

He always did enjoy it more if I was in pain, better still if I was bleeding.

He claws at the waist band of my leggings, but I shove his hand away. He growls and thrusts the knife back against my neck and I wince as the sharp edge slices into my skin again. He grinds his hips against me even harder.

"I'm gonna fuck you in every hole you've got and then I'm gonna make you watch while I kill your precious fucking *Duke.* Then, I'm gonna fuck all your holes again, right on top of his rotting fucking corpse!" He snarls, roughly shoving his fingers down the front of my leggings.

I whine and buck my hips, trying to get him away from me, but it's no use. The sharp blade of the knife only cuts into me deeper the more I squirm.

He's struggling to get his fingers past my underwear, when a loud yowl from over my shoulder catches his attention.

Athena lashes out from between the books on the shelf behind me, hissing as she slashes her claws across the hand he has holding the knife at my throat.

He screeches, yanking his hand back, the knife dropping to the floor between us. Blood instantly bubbles up from the four jagged slices along the back of his hand.

She got him good.

Taking advantage of his disorientation, I drive the base of my palm up into his jaw with as much force as I can. He staggers back, stunned by my blow. I've never once stood up to him before and he clearly wasn't expecting me to retaliate.

Finally free from his grip, I take advantage of his momentary confusion to push myself off the bookshelf and step to the side.

Instinct takes over and I settle into my ready stance, bracing myself as I lower my center of gravity, my hands bracketing my body protectively.

His tongue trails out, licking at the bloody split in his lip, studying me with a glimmer of curious interest in his cruel eyes. He chuckles coldly, a condescending smile playing at the corners of his mouth.

"Oh, you think you can fight me, little girl?" He taunts.

"Come on then, bitch! Let's see what you've got."

I hold my stance, unmoving, patiently waiting him out as I steady my breathing and watch him closely.

His eyes flare as his patience finally snaps and he lunges for me, roaring as he throws out his fist in a brutal arc. I dodge his punch and grab his arm as it sails past my face, pulling him downward and driving my knee up into his ribs. He stumbles forward letting out a surprised, "Ummphf!"

I quickly move out of his reach, dropping back into my stance again.

His rage is palpable as he roars, charging toward me like an angry bull. I easily avoid him, stepping aside at the last second. He barrels past me, his anger making him clumsy and erratic, and slams into a stack of boxed books—the pile toppling down, books scattering across the floor.

He scrambles back to his feet, instantly lunging for me again. But I spin on my back leg and drive my heel into his groin, his body colliding into the same bookshelf he'd had me pinned against. He crumples to his knees, gripping his crotch, writhing on the floor in pain.

"Fucking bitch! Cunt! Whore!" He spews his vitriol at me, a long line of spit running off his bottom lip.

I head for the door, my sights set on escape, but he grabs my ankle as I move past him, wrenching me down to the floor beside him. I flip onto my back and try to kick out at him, but he drags me beneath him, his huge frame pinning me down.

He grabs my head in both of his hands, lifting it toward him, before slamming it down hard on the floor, once... twice, a third time, maybe more... my vision begins to fade. Dazed by the countless blows, I'm barely aware of his hand coming around my throat, squeezing down hard to cut off the last of my air.

"I'm done playing around with you, you fucking cunt! This time I'm gonna make sure you're fucking dead!"

Time stands still as he slams the blade of the knife into my side.

Chapter 69

Rogan

Finally dousing the last of the flames, Brick and I pant and cough as we circle the cottage, making sure there's nothing else on fire. Thick smoke hangs heavy in the air, dark tendrils curling around the blackened sides of the building.

Hannah brays wildly at the front of the bookshop. I look around and realize I don't see Cole. She's probably struggling to calm the beast down.

"I'll find Cole and see if I can help her calm Hannah down." I tell Brick, hooking a thumb over my shoulder toward the bookshop entrance.

"Call the police and tell them where they can find this fucking prick." I lift my chin in Zavier's direction, as he lies beneath one of the apple trees, tied up and snoring loudly, still knocked out cold from the beating I'd given him.

As I make my way to the bookshop, Hannah is frantically bucking and braying, gnawing determinedly at her tether and pulling against it with all her might. I quickly glance around looking for Cole, but don't see her anywhere.

I grab Hannah's harness and shush her, trying to get her to settle. She pulls and chuffs, her braying subsiding just long enough for me to hear the commotion coming from inside the bookshop.

I hear a roar and a loud grunt, then an even louder crash. I race to the door, only to see the wooden frame smashed and broken, the handle hanging.

Fuck!

I push through the door and Athena scrambles past me as I hear more grunting and slamming sounds coming from somewhere between the shelves. I struggle to get my eyes to adjust to the dim light.

"Cole? Cole!" I shout.

That's when I hear him. I'll never forget that fucking voice.

"I'm done playing around with you, you fucking cunt! This time I'm gonna make sure you're fucking dead!"

I race to the back of the shop, slipping on the books scattered across the floor and round the corner to see Cole on the floor.

Cain's dark form looms over her, pinning her in place. She's bloodied and dazed as she weakly claws at his wrist while he crushes her throat in his fist.

But time stands still when I see him ram the long blade of a knife right into her side.

"NOOOOOOOOOOOOOOO!!!"

My roar echoes in the space as I barrel toward him.

Leaping into the air I tackle him off of her, my fist closing around his throat as I slam him down, following him to the floor. I'm barely aware of the scream erupting from my chest as I unleash the torrent of my unending rage, ruthlessly pummeling my fist into his face over and over again. My knuckles split against his teeth as I drive my fist into his mouth, but the pain only fuels my fury as I crush my fist against his skull.

"You couldn't just leave her alone! You couldn't just let her be happy. You had to come back, had to ruin everything for her. You're done you miserable piece of shit! I'm going to fucking kill you, you rotten mother fucker! Do you hear me? *I'm going to fucking kill you!*"

The crazy son of a bitch only grins up at me, his teeth coated in blood, the skin of his face splitting and tearing with each punch I land—his dark eyes, wild and empty, not a shred of remorse in their vacant depths.

He almost seems to be enjoying the pain of the assault.

When he drives his knee up into my ribs, I'm stunned by his sudden movement and he manages to knock me off of him. Grabbing the corner of a large bookshelf, he drags himself up and pulls it down, tipping the entire thing, books and all, on top of me.

The heavy shelving slams against my skull, nearly knocking me unconscious.

Dazed, I struggle beneath the weight of the shelf, trying to push it off of me.

Cain rises to his full height hovering over me. He presses his foot down on the shelf, crushing me further beneath its hold, his hand disappearing into his pocket.

A malicious smile slides across his lips as he clicks the safety off of the gun he now holds pointed directly at my head.

He slips his finger over the trigger.

"Kill me? I don't fucking think so..."

"Fuck you, *Your Grace.*"

Chapter 70

Cole

Pain.

Everything hurts. My head is swimming, but my side is screaming. I reach down, my fingers trailing along my ribs. The material is wet and sticky, but there's a hot pain deep inside me.

Probing lower, I feel something hard sticking out of my side.

A wave of nausea rolls through me as the memory seeps back to the surface... *Cain.*

It's the handle of Cain's fucking knife.

My vision fades in and out as I try to get my bearings. I can hear voices shouting, the sounds of a vicious fight. Sometimes it feels close, other times the room fades around me and it all seems so, so far away.

The room grows dark.

I'm just so tired.

Bone deep exhaustion.

I'll just close my eyes... sleep for a little while.

Then I can figure this all out.

My mind drifts as I let myself sink into sleep.

Away from the pain.

Away from the nightmares.

Away from...Cain.

But then I hear a deluge of anger, words being bellowed and fists hitting flesh...

Rogan.

"You couldn't just leave her alone! You couldn't just let her be happy. You had to come back, had to ruin everything for her. You're done you miserable piece of shit! I'm going to fucking kill you, you rotten mother fucker! Do you hear me? *I'm going to fucking kill you!*"

I peel my eyes open, another wave of nausea rolling over me as I lift my head. I choke back the bile creeping up my throat and reach down, gripping the handle of the knife.

I close my eyes and grit my teeth as I tug, crying out as searing pain rages through my side as I manage to slide the blade halfway out. My head swims and the edges of my vision blacken as my consciousness threatens to leave me.

My head drops back, the ceiling above me spinning so hard I have to close my eyes before the vertigo consumes me. Swallowing against the nausea, I summon the courage to try again. With a final hard pull, I tug the blade the rest of the way out.

A rush of hot blood pours from the wound and my vision swirls, the room spinning above me as I fade again.

A loud crash pulls me back and I twist my head in the direction of the sound.

Books are scattered everywhere and a large bookshelf is slanted on its side.

Breathing hard, I press my hand to my side, trying to staunch the flow of blood as I roll over.

Weakly, I push myself up onto my knees and sway slightly before dragging myself up the rest of the way, using the bookshelves for support, leaving bloody handprints in my wake.

I look over to see Cain; his attention focused on the floor in front of him. His back is to me, but I see him slip his hand into his pocket. I pull myself along the shelf, fighting against the waves of nausea, dizziness clouding my vision as blood continuously pours from the wound in my side.

I shake my head trying to clear away the fog that's creeping along the edge of my vision, threatening to pull me under. I push past the weakness, ignore the pain. Clinging to a shelf, I come up behind Cain, his foot holding down the bookshelf Rogan is pinned beneath. Rogan's muscles strain as he struggles to shift the weight pressing down on him.

Cain moves, the flash of metal in his hand drawing my attention back to him. Back to the gun he's holding—the barrel pointed directly at Rogan's head.

Terror floods my veins at the sound of the safety clicking off, watch as his finger wraps around the trigger, hear the words he spits out like venom...

"Kill me? I don't fucking think so..."

"Fuck you, *Your Grace.*"

My pain forgotten, I scream, launching myself at Cain. I leap onto his back and drive the blade of his own knife straight into the side of his neck, burying it all the way to the hilt.

The gun fires as it drops to the floor, the bullet sinking harmlessly into one of the boxes of books. The loud bang rings in my ears as I fall from his back.

He staggers sideways, clawing at the handle protruding from his neck. Blood gushes down his chest, a look of surprised disbelief in his eyes, his mouth gaping open in a silent scream.

Rogan pries himself free from beneath the shelving. I grip my side and stumble over to him. He catches me as I fall against him.

Cain grabs the handle of the knife, ripping it out of his neck, blood spraying in wide arcs across the room.

He loosely clasps his hand over the wound in a futile attempt to quell the flow of blood. He sways, stumbling into a bookshelf, his eyes rolling back in his head before collapsing, falling to his face on a scattered pile of books—a large, dark pool of blood ebbs from the wound in his neck, soaking into the pages.

His leg kicks out once, and then he's still.

His evil reign of terror, finally at an end.

Chapter 71

Rogan

Cole's fingers fumble over the material of my shirt, her other hand clutching tightly to her side as she collapses against me. Blood pours from between her fingers as her grip weakens, no longer able to apply the pressure needed to hold the wound closed. Her eyes find mine before rolling back in her head, her body going slack in my arms.

"Cole baby, NO!" I cry, lying her down, replacing her hand with my own, pressing hard to staunch the blood.

"BRICK!" I scream. Within seconds he barrels through the door, followed closely by the detectives—Olubanjo in the lead, Kerr soon after.

"Holy fucking shit!"

Kerr swears under his breath, his wide eyes taking in the carnage of the bookshop. His face turns a ghostly shade of white when they lock on Cain's unmoving form, lying face down in a large puddle of his own, cooling blood.

Olubanjo smacks him in the shoulder, "Snap out of it and get your shit together, Kerr! We have work to do! Call the team and get everybody down here, now!"

She rushes to my side, dropping to her knees and quickly assessing Cole's injuries.

"She... she saved my life." I gape, tears rolling down my cheeks as my Little Fawn lies pale and motionless on the floor beside me.

A few seconds later, the paramedics rush through the door, taking over Cole's care.

"She's still got a pulse. It's weak, but she's a fighter." Olubanjo tells the paramedics.

They cut away her blood-soaked shirt and quickly start applying first aid to her wounds. Once she's stable, they get her onto a gurney, and rush her out to the ambulance.

Olubanjo stands beside me as I watch them lift her into the back of the ambulance, my hands coated in her blood.

I feel numb, lost.

What will I do if she doesn't make it?

I must speak this out loud, because I feel a gentle squeeze on my arm. I look down to see Olubanjo, her fingers wrapped around my bicep. Her eyes kind as she tries to offer me some sort of comfort, knowing there's little she can do or say that will help me right now.

"She's strong, Rogan."

Her tone is soft as she addresses me by name instead of by title.

"She'll pull through this. I just know it."

I finally drag my eyes off the ambulance as the doors slam shut. The sirens blare as they take off, heading as quickly as they can in the direction of the nearest hospital.

My fingers instinctively curl over the top of Olubanjo's.

I look down at her, as more and more tears streak down my face, my lips tight, my face grim.

God I hope she's right.

When we arrive at the hospital, they've already taken Cole into surgery.

I pace in the hospital waiting room, Kya and Brick sit huddled together, Brick's arm holding her close as she cries softly against his shoulder. Several of the villagers stop by to check in, to see if there's been any news, any updates on Cole's condition, offering up any semblance of comfort they can in a time like this.

My Little Fawn is so loved.

In such a short time, she managed to rally an entire village—each villager pulling for her, offering whatever support and prayers they have to give, each and every one of them needing her to be alright.

There's been so much loss already tonight.

We simply can't lose her too.

It's almost three o'clock in the morning before the doors swing open, a tired looking doctor stepping through.

"Cole Allbright?" He says softly to the room. Every head in the room swings in his direction.

I step over to him; Kya and Brick quickly follow and stand at my side. Kya clings to my arm as Brick stands behind her, bracing her shoulders. Our terrified, yet hopeful gazes lock on the doctor as we await the news of how Cole has fared.

"The surgery went well."

He finally says and I feel my knees go weak. Brick throws a strong arm around my shoulders, keeping me upright—always a dependable wall of strength when I need him the most.

I hold my fist against my lips and brace for the details of her surgery.

"She lost a lot of blood so we had to give her several transfusions and we had to remove her spleen. She'll need some time to recover, but she was very lucky. The blade missed hitting anything vital. A fraction of an inch or so in any other direction and we'd be having a very different conversation right now."

I drag in a ragged breath, my chest squeezing tight. I nod as he reaches over and gives my arm a reassuring squeeze, his kind eyes finding mine.

"She's gonna be okay, son." He says, smiling warmly at me.

"Th-Thank you...," I manage to stammer, relief flooding my body as more hot tears flow down my cheeks.

"Thank you so much for saving her!"

He dips his chin and gives my arm one more gentle squeeze, then heads back through the doors.

I spin into the arms of my friends as we hold each other, embracing the surge of relief and happiness at the news.

My Little Fawn is going to be okay.

Chapter 72

Cole

I wake in an unfamiliar room. Bright sunlight floods through large windows and there's a soft beeping sound coming from somewhere behind me. My head is foggy, my throat is sore and my eyes and mouth feel like they're coated in sand.

Weighted warmth blankets my hand and my head feels like lead when I try to turn it. Slumped forward from his chair, his head resting on the mattress beside me, Rogan snores softly, his large hand covering mine.

I try to sit up, but a flash of pain tears into my side. Sucking in a sharp, gasping breath, I quickly give up, dropping my head back down on the pillow.

Rogan's head snaps up, his grip on my hand tightening. His sleepy, bloodshot eyes find mine; his whole face is lined with exhaustion and worry. His beard has grown out, and his hair hangs loosely across his brow. He somehow looks older and younger all at the same time.

A wash of relief floods his features when he sees I'm awake.

"Cole..." The timbre of his voice is deeper, gravely from sleep.

"Don't," he clears his throat shifting closer to my side, "don't try to sit up. Just take it easy."

His hand shakes as he holds mine against his lips and peppers tiny kisses along my knuckles.

I grimace, swallowing against the painful rawness in my throat. Rogan pushes up out of his chair and hurriedly grabs a cup of water, tipping the straw down to meet my lips.

The cool water feels divine and I drink greedily, but the sudden rush of liquid makes me cough and I'm hit with a flare of pain shooting up my side. I gasp as the pain takes my breath away, my head falling back against the pillow.

"Easy there, Little Fawn." Rogan says softly, his tired eyes looking worried as he waits for my pain to subside, lightly brushing back the hair that's fallen across my face.

Taking a few shallow breaths, the pain finally eases enough for me to be able to talk.

"What happened?" I rasp.

Rogan takes his time as he recounts the events of that night, filling in the details where my memory fails me. He explains what the doctors had to do to save my life, his voice gentle when he tells me they had to remove my spleen, but he quickly assures me I'll be just fine without it, but I'll need to rest while I recover.

"I'm sure Dick will appreciate his break from your brutal ass kickings." He teases, a playful edge coloring his tone.

"I'm all but certain I saw him cowering in the back corner of the dojo the other day. Poor bastard still hasn't recovered after the last time you kicked the shite out of him." He chuckles softly.

I chuff a small laugh, but regret it immediately, wincing and grabbing my side. His smile falls away, his lips flattening into a grim line, a deep groove sinking between his brows.

He leans down and presses his lips against mine, his eyes falling closed. He lingers there—his lips quivering slightly and I feel the warmth of his tear as it hits my cheek.

I lightly run my fingers through the rough stubble lining his jaw, thicker and unkempt from days of sleeping at my side in a hospital chair.

"You scared me, Little Fawn." His voice breaks as he rests his forehead to mine, his words, barely a whisper against my lips.

"I thought I'd lost you for a moment there."

The next few days are a blur of doctors and nurses fussing over me, police interviews and insurance people hounding me.

Rogan refuses to leave my side. But instead, lies beside me in my hospital bed in a private room he secured. He barks angrily at anyone who even hints at suggesting he should be anywhere else.

Olubanjo and Kerr return, this time a welcome sight.

They confirm, with the combination of Rogan's report, the discovery of Cain's gun—covered in his own fingerprints, plus my blood mingled with his on the blade of his knife are all more than enough proof to back my claim of self-defense against him.

Even Zavier, grasping at the last threads of his freedom, didn't hold back when he threw Cain under the bus. Claiming he was the reason he'd set fire to the cottages.

As if that even matters. It's not like it will save him.

The list of charges against him is a long one:

Second-degree murder.

Arson.

Intent to kill.

Oh, and let's not forget the several counts of sexual assault.

He'll spend the rest of his life behind bars.

There's also been a wealth of eyewitness reports, evidence uncovered by detectives from the Met—the force that polices Greater London—having raided Cain's offices and home.

They found reports from his PI, countless unsolicited pictures he'd hired him to take. My original hospital report from London which listed all the previous injuries I'd sustained at his hands, including the cuts to my wrists. Cuts that couldn't possibly have been made by my own hand. Not to mention a litany of the many years of systemic abuse.

Now that he's dead, Cain's staff finally broke their silence, no longer in fear of what he could do to them in retaliation. They spoke of the horrors they'd endured under his tyrannical reign.

Several women have come forward claiming he raped and abused them, including his last temp, evidence from his assault still marring her face and body. Further proof of his brutality against her was found coating his stapler, the detectives having recovered it from his trash can during the raid of his office.

Fearless Maria... she didn't hold back in giving her statement either. She and Juan Carlos are now under witness protection, tucked safely into the spare wing of the Manor.

Rogan offered them a home, employment and security here, where they'll be surrounded by love. By family. By the kind of people who will cherish them, fiercely, without condition, ridicule or abuse.

Do I feel guilty for having taken a life?

That Cain died by my hand?

My subconscious tells me I should, but I can't seem to find it in me to feel any type of remorse.

I'm simply relieved he's dead.

Gone.

And most importantly, that he'll never be able to hurt me or anyone else, ever again.

There was something wrong inside him. Something broken and depraved. Something that drove him to crave the pain he inflicted on others. He thrived on the torment, the suffering feeding some sick desire within his twisted mind.

My therapist calls him a psychopath.

He hid his true nature so well, I never saw him for who he truly was before I married him. How he ever convinced me to love him, I'll never fully understand. Not now, when I've experienced what it means to be truly loved, cherished and respected by a man.

I know now, love isn't supposed to hurt.

I know Rogan is no saint. He has his own darkness in him from the things he's had to endure in his own life—the things he's had to do to survive. But I also know he'll never unleash that darkness on me.

His wrath is reserved for the protection of those he loves, for safe-guarding his own and for defending them against the evils of the world.

I know with everything I am; I'll never have a reason to fear my dear, sweet Duke.

Chapter 73

Cole

The sky is a brilliant blue on the day of Tom's funeral. The soft rays of spring sunshine kiss the petals of the daisies and buttercups lining the path to the gravesite, the tiny flowers dancing lazily on a warm breeze.

Rogan spared no expense, quickly offering to cover all the costs for his services. The church was standing room only, as villagers lined the walls and doorways, standing shoulder to shoulder as they paid their respects and said their final farewells, drawn together by love, loss and legacy.

Tom's heroism echoed through the chapel, while Edna wept into a handkerchief—nestled between Kya and her own daughter, Briannah. Three women, three lifelines, their hands entwined—grief braided across blood and memory.

As his simple wicker coffin was lowered into the earth, the Vicar recited the Committal softly and reverently, while a group of local singers murmured 'Amazing Grace' in quiet harmony nearby.

We cast white roses onto his coffin—our final gesture of thanks and farewell to the man who welcomed me without question, and who always looked at me and defended me as though I was his own flesh and blood.

Rogan slipped his arm around my waist, drawing me into his side. No words were needed. The grief settled heavily between us, silent and understood.

Brick and Kya approached the grave; her arm looped through his as she dropped in the roses. He placed his palm gently at the nape of her neck, then turned her into him, pressing his lips to the top of her head, her arms looping around his waist as she cried against his shoulder.

After the funeral, we gather at the Wye Inn for a few drinks and to share memories and stories of the good times we remember at the hands and heart of this wonderful man.

We all take a moment to lift our glasses in the air...

To Tom.

The Hero of Verdon.

Chapter 74

Cole

With Kya's cottage burned to the ground—now nothing but ashes and soot—Brick insisted she and Grumbl move into the Gatehouse with him, while Athena, Hannah, and I have officially settled into the Manor with Rogan.

I love watching Hannah roam the expansive lawn at the front of the house, lavishing in her vast new space. No longer tethered to the bookshop, her new found freedom feels like a reflection of my own.

Thinking back to the day I first arrived here in Verdon and learned of her impending demise—had I rejected the terms of my grandfather's will—I realize just how much we've actually saved each other.

I think I see a bit of Sundance in her—his grace, fierce loyalty, and protectiveness over me. Sometimes I wonder if a part of his spirit was reborn in this donkey, allowing us to find each other again in this new, happier life.

Kya and Brick's relationship seems to be something of a question mark. She swears they're still just friends and they aren't sleeping together. But there's no denying their relationship has shifted.

They think they're being sly, but whenever they're together, they're constantly touching, stealing flirtatious glances and, when they think no one is looking—stealing kisses.

The spring morning air is cool and crisp, as Kya and I stroll arm in arm through the woods. She pulls me close, grinning like the Cheshire cat.

"Can I tell you something?"

She giggles, lowering her voice conspiratorially as a deep blush creeps into her cheeks.

"I'd be upset if you didn't at this point."

I say, wide-eyed—curious of what could make this confident woman turn this particular shade of red.

"Okay, so I know I've said Brick and I are *just friends*, but...," she trails off, her teeth sinking into her bottom lip, "I've just got to say, the man kisses like a fucking god!"

She looks completely giddy, as she shakes my arm excitedly.

My laugh echoes through the wooded trail and I face her with a knowing grin, having seen how much she adores the man for so much longer than she's been willing to admit.

"Mmmm... and the way those big hands feel on my skin."

She purrs, her head thrown back, her eyes closed as if she's practically feeling his touch right now.

"I can only imagine how they might feel in... other places."

She shoots me a devious look, waggling her eye brows at me.

"Kya!" I scoff dramatically, feigning a shocked expression.

She squeals and we both fall into a fit of giggles, our laughter carrying all the way across the river.

Once our laughter subsides, we continue our walk.

I take in the happiness radiating off her and the beautiful, contented smile on her face. I love seeing my best friend this happy.

I know she's experienced darkness in her past. Things she'll never be able to completely heal from. The emotional scarring, a pain I'm all too familiar with and understand all too deeply.

It's the type of pain that never, truly goes away.

It just becomes a quiet part of you.

One you have to learn to live with.

But it's always there.

Always lingering just beyond the edges of dreams, waiting to resurface, unbidden as the nightmares inevitably creep back in from time to time—reminding you of its existence from where it lurks in the deepest recesses of your mind.

For everything she's done for this town, for everyone she loves, and especially for me—she deserves so much in this life and I'm beyond grateful to be able to see her this way.

She's lost so much.

But there is something... one little thing I can do, to begin to repay her for everything she's done for me—for taking me in when it felt like the rest of the world had thrown me away.

As we step out of the soft shadows of the woods, and walk into the village, we settle down onto a bench overlooking the Wye. The same bench we sat on together, the day I revealed my truth to her about Cain—about how I came to Verdon.

Taking her hands in mine, I tug them into my lap, turning her to face me.

"There's something I want to do for you."

She looks perplexed and starts to shake her head, clearly already trying to dismiss any attempt I might make toward restitution.

But I give her an insistent look, lightly squeezing her hands.

"Please."

She studies me, then gives me a resigned nod, her face softening.

"I want to give you Haven."

Her eyes flare wide and she starts shaking her head again, more vehemently this time, but I raise a hand.

"Please, Kya. Let me just get this out."

A deep furrow forms between her brows and her lips pinch into a tight line. Her shoulders lift on a deep breath, but then she dips her chin in a shallow nod.

"Grandpa Jesse left me that cottage to do with as I see fit. I don't have a use for it since I'm living at the Manor with Rogan."

"He loved you, Kya. You were there for him when I couldn't be after Grandma Maggie died. You took care of him and Hannah when he was all alone. And you took care of his property for him, even when he was gone—even when you didn't have to."

Her eyes shimmer, unshed tears welling along her lower lashes.

"He would want you to have it, especially now after you've lost everything. Let's face it, your home is gone, because of me. It's the very least I can do."

Her eyes darken, ready to protest again, but I give her hands another squeeze and lock my eyes with hers.

"Kya, I *need* to do this for you. Please." I continue, softer now.

"Your home is gone. Everything you've worked so hard to build... I want you to have somewhere you can feel safe. Where you can thrive."

"And since we've only just begun working on repairs, you'll be able to make it entirely your own."

Her throat works, her chin quivering as one large tear spills down each of her cheeks.

"I've already asked Brick to sort out all the paperwork, to be able to put it into your name. All you need to do is sign, and it's yours."

There's a long silence that hangs in the air between us, until a quiet acceptance seeps into her gaze—more tears coating her cheeks.

I sniff, just now noticing I've been crying too.

I smile at the thought of how much we feed off of each other's emotions and how alike we actually are for two women who were complete strangers, from two totally different worlds, not so long ago.

She pulls me into a tight hug, squeezing me so tightly my side aches where I'm still healing, but I ignore the pain and hug her back, relishing in the warmth of my best friend's embrace.

"Okay."

She finally says, nodding as she sits back, wiping her palms across her cheeks and sniffing loudly.

"That actually does sound pretty wonderful."

Her watery eyes meet mine again.

"Thank you, Cole."

I nod, smiling at her warmly.

Her gaze fixes back on the Wye, admiring the dappled light of the slowly setting sun as it dances across the gentle ripples of the river.

We laugh as Grumbl grunts, pouncing on top of a fern that had been bobbing lazily in the light breeze, then stomps off clumsily through the undergrowth in search of his next conquest. Leave it to our little wrinkly, comedic companion to lighten the mood.

She turns back to face me, "I have two conditions, though."

"Oh yeah? What might those be?"

I raise a curious brow at her, smirking as I await her terms.

Her face is serious when she speaks.

"Promise to let yourself be happy with Rogan. He's a good man and I know he'll treat you the way you deserve to be treated. I know he can be a grumpy bastard sometimes," she feigns annoyance with an eye roll, but her smile returns as she continues, "but he'll never hurt you and he'll give you the world, if you let him."

"You deserve that, hun. You deserve to be loved, respected and treated like a bloody queen."

My throat feels thick and I have to swallow hard past the lump that seems to have made a home there during this conversation.

I smile and nod. "Okay." I croak, the word sticking in my throat. I clear it then ask, "What's your other condition?"

She takes in a deep breath.

"You have to promise you'll never leave Verdon again." She hits me with a no-nonsense look, as if daring me to argue with her.

"This is your home, Cole, and I can't imagine my life without you in it." She sniffs, tipping her chin up in mock indignation.

"Oh, and one more thing!"

I chuff a laugh, "What happened to only two conditions?"

"Pssh! You should know by now I don't stick to the rules, love." She swats a dismissive hand in the air between us.

"Alright then. What's your third condition?" I ask, chuckling.

"Promise me you'll come 'round for lunch when you're working at the bookshop. I'm gonna be missing my bestie with you living the high life over there at the Manor with Mr. Fancy Pants." She plasters on an over-the-top stern expression and mimes tightening her tie.

Laughter overtakes us again and I agree easily to all of her terms.

Once our laughter fades, we settle into a comfortable silence and watch as Grumbl chases a colorful butterfly on the trail in front of us.

I bite the corner of my lower lip and shift my gaze slightly, looking at her guiltily through the side of my eye.

Without turning her head, she calls me out.

"Spill it, Cole. What's going on in that head of yours?"

"Well, there is one other thing I wanted to talk to you about..."

She turns to face me, her expression curious.

"I wanted to make you part owner of the bookshop with me."

Her jaw practically hits the forest floor and her eyes flare as wide as saucers as she stares at me disbelievingly.

I grin widely at her expression, unable to hold back my excitement anymore and quickly begin to chatter out the speech I'd planned to use to convince her of the idea.

"You've put in as much time and heart as I have, into making the bookshop what it is today. It just feels right, we should run it together. Think about it! You'd be able to give up some of your other jobs... you'd only have to focus on one... Grumbl could be with you all the time, and we could work side by side and have lunch together every, single...,"

I trail off, suddenly aware I'm rambling.

Her look of shock quickly morphs into a delighted smile. A smile that lights up her whole face. I've clearly already won her over and relax a bit when I realize I don't have to sell this idea as hard as I'd initially anticipated.

"Deal."

She says softly, her eyes brimming with fresh tears. She bats them away with annoyance and sniffs loudly, a much more serious look crossing her face.

"I think that would be brilliant!" She beams.

"However...," she trails off, her expression turning philosophical, pointing a finger up as if she's just had a profound thought, "If we're really going to do this, then I think the romance section needs to be *much, much* larger!"

I throw my head back and laugh, nodding my head vigorously in agreement.

As we resume our walk, I have no doubt the villagers can likely hear our animated chatter as we discuss our plans for the cottage, the bookshop and our futures.

Chapter 75

Cole

Several weeks pass as we settle into our new lives together. After a fun night out of dinner and drinks at the pub, Rogan and I say our goodbyes to our friends at the gatehouse, then make our way up the drive to the Manor—to our home.

The door opens as we approach the top step, James waiting stoically to greet us. The moment we're through the door, Rogan sweeps me up into his arms, carrying me into the foyer and up the stairs.

It's been weeks since we've been intimate. He'd refused to do anything that could possibly hinder my healing, but my doctor told me today I was well enough to go back to my daily activities; which we've both taken as permission to get back to the spicy stuff too.

When we reach our suite of rooms, he holds me close as he slides me down his body, setting my feet to the floor. I breathe him in, lost in his clean scent, as the bright notes of bergamot and warm spice fill my nose.

His touch is light as it coasts along my skin, gliding down the zipper of my simple black dress. The fabric falls open, exposing the bare flesh of my back. He hums appreciatively at the absence of a bra.

He slips the straps of my dress down my arms, grazing his lips across my shoulder as the material slides away, the dark silk pooling around my feet like liquid night.

Backing me toward the bed, he lifts me onto the mattress, then slides my stockings down my legs, one by one, kissing his way back up. The glide of his tongue drives me wild as it teases along my skin, followed by the slight sting of his teeth as he lightly nips the soft flesh of my thigh.

His breath is a steamy caress as he hovers his mouth over the apex of my thighs and I wriggle beneath him. His dark laugh proves he knows exactly what he's doing to me.

He runs the tip of his tongue over the material of my panties, already soaked in anticipation of his touch, giving me a tiny taste of what he's got planned for me and my hips lift to meet his mouth. His grip tightens on my thighs, holding me where he wants me as he buries his face against my center, groaning as he draws in a long, slow breath. The deep vibration sends an ache through my core, tearing a gasp from my throat. I arch into his touch as he drives me ravenous with need.

Snagging a fistful of his hair, I pull him against my pussy. He pinches the material of my panties between his teeth, dragging them off of me, his fingers dimpling my skin as he tugs them down my thighs.

He towers over me, his dark eyes scorching a blazing path across my skin, charting his course as they rove over my naked body, brimming with voracious desire.

His weighted stare sends a shiver through me, goosebumps erupting across my skin. His pace unhurried, he takes his time unfastening his shirt, the material falling open one button at a time—a tantalizing unveiling of his sculpted chest and carved abs.

Need tugs at my core, the ache elicited by the deep grooves and muscles lining his toned body, the dark whorls of ink snaking across his chest and the perfect V disappearing into his waistband, pointing me toward the hardened evidence of his desire, straining against his fly.

Just the thought of his cock, hard and ready for me, has a flood of wet heat slickening my thighs.

His cocky smile proves he knows what he's doing to me. He takes his time unclasping his belt and pants, exposing the swollen crown of his cock, the tight material of his briefs unable to contain him when fully erect.

My mouth waters at the sight of the prominent outline of his hardness and the thick vein running along his shaft.

An ache throbs deep within my core, remembering the feeling of him surging deeply into me over and over again. It's actually painful, how badly I want him inside me right now.

"Tell me your safe word," he commands.

"Rogan...," I whine, wiggling my hips impatiently, desperate to feel the heat of his naked body against mine. He lets his pants drop to the floor and grips his length over his briefs. His tendons flex and the tattoos snaking out from beneath his sleeve ripple, as he squeezes his prominent erection. I lean up on my elbows, enjoying the view.

He pulls his briefs down his legs, his hard cock rising upward with its new found freedom.

"Your safe word, Little Fawn. Say it."

"Sundance." I whisper.

"Mmmm... that's my good girl." He growls, hunger flaring in his eyes as he lowers down over me. The hairs on his chest tickle my skin with each heavy rise and fall of his breaths.

He begins his torment, hovering his lips over me, nearly, but not quite touching me—drawing out each and every movement into torturous, blissful agony.

His hot breath skates over my skin and his body trembles as he braces himself above me, a palpable desire radiating off of him.

His mouth moves over my body. His lips, his teeth barely a whisper against my flesh, edging my want for him until each light touch makes me flinch.

His monstrously slow descent only heightens each glimmer of contact he allows me, his mouth never quite touching, nor leaving my skin. His fingers lightly flank his mouth, barely adding a hint of pressure as they skate across my skin and my need for him becomes a live wire beneath my flesh.

I cry out at the sudden firm contact when he drops his mouth over my breast, sucking and swirling his tongue over my hardened nipple. The light drag of his teeth as he releases it, combined with the cool air hitting my dampened flesh, sends a shiver through me.

He dips down below my breast, his thumb gently stroking beneath the new red scar along my ribcage. I run my fingers through his hair, watching as he lingers there, feathering a reverent kiss over the tender skin.

But soon his attention shifts back to the heat of the moment and he resumes his maddening trek, slowly lowering himself down my body, toward my aching, needy pussy—soaked as I writhe in anticipation.

Pushing him down, I urge him closer to where I want—*no need* to feel him most. His lips lift into a devious smile, and he chuckles low in his throat, the heat of his breath sending a flurry of goosebumps over me.

"What is it, Little Fawn? Is someone getting impatient?"

"Yes, Rogan, please." I whine, lifting my hips and nudging his head down again. But he resists, teasing me—his lips and tongue only ever hovering in the vicinity of where I want him.

After weeks of missing his touch, the added torment of his teasing only builds the momentum to a fever pitch.

"All in good time, my love. I'm going to savor you tonight.

I want to enjoy every...," his tongue skims along my inner thigh,

"last...," his teeth graze over my lower lips,

"drop." His tongue lightly swirls over my clit, then dips shallowly into my sex.

A loud gasp tears from my throat and I fall back on the mattress. He stiffens his tongue, pressing it in deeper, finally giving me the much-needed pressure I've been craving.

Lust overtakes him as he shoves my legs wide, throwing them up over his broad shoulders as he settles himself between them, his mouth descending with ravenous abandon.

He grips my ass, lifting my pussy to meet his mouth, sinking his tongue into me. He groans as he delves his tongue deep into my center, his hunger insatiable as he devours me.

Wild with need, pressure begins to build in my core and my spine tingles as my climax quickly swells, but the moment he senses my impending release, he draws back, lessening his touch—taunting, teasing, keeping my orgasm just out of reach.

"More...," I plead, spurring my heels into his shoulders. Desperately trying to pull him further into me. I tug at his hair, but the harder I pull, the lighter he licks me and laughs low in his throat.

Frustrated, I growl at his infuriating taunt and he gives my pussy one more maddeningly slow, shallow lick all the way up my center, nipping lightly at my clit—those steel gray eyes finding mine, a devilish smirk teasing the corners of his mouth.

Instead of resuming his feast, he makes his way back up my body. I squirm as he stalks above me—a panther hunting its prey, his muscles rippling as he moves at a glacial pace.

His shirt hangs loosely over his shoulders; his hard cock hanging heavy between us. He settles down on top of me, grinding his length against my pussy, his mouth finding mine.

I taste my own arousal as he plunges his tongue between my lips, dragging the hard length of his cock against my soaking center, his tongue dancing feverishly with mine.

I raise my hips to meet his, matching his pace.

But I need more. I need him inside me.

It's been too long.

Enough.

He's had his fun—*now it's my turn.*

I break the kiss, shimmying out from beneath him. He lifts up, watching me with heated curiosity as I kneel on the bed in front of him. His nostrils flare and his breath quickens; his eyes are dark with desire as he waits to see what I've got planned.

I smirk, biting my lip. He surges forward, chasing my mouth, but I lean back, keeping him at bay with a gentle push. I grin devilishly and shake my head.

Backing down, he licks his lips and gives me a knowing nod.

I'm in charge now.

I flick my eyes toward the pillows, indicating where I want him. He eagerly complies, quickly rolling over and settling himself against the headboard.

Lightly trailing my fingers across his chest, I sweep his shirt off his shoulders. It drops down his back and he tugs his arms out of the sleeves, removing it from his large frame, then tosses it to the floor.

My mouth waters and I fight the sudden desire to bite into his thick biceps. I rake my nails over his skin, his flesh twitching under my touch. His breathing deepens as he watches me, his look a combination of excitement, pride and fascination.

I glance over the side of the bed to where his pants lie in a pile on the floor next to his shirt.

His gaze follows me as I slide off the bed.

He tilts his head curiously as I climb back up, straddling his lap, his belt in my hands.

I meet his stare—a silent question residing there.

His eyes darken, a wry, knowing smile playing along his lips. He dips his chin in the barest nod and holds out his wrists.

I'm hit with a momentary wave of trepidation, but push past it, ignoring that inner voice—my biggest critic. That damn voice that's riddled me with doubt my whole life and made me question my own worth, my own thoughts, my own value.

I need to prove to myself I can recognize my own needs, my own desires. And right now, I need to have this control, to be in charge of my own body—*of his body*. To experience what it feels like to be the one holding the power.

He allows me to slip the belt over his wrists. Threading the leather through the buckle, I fasten it tightly, then push his hands up over his head, settling the loop over one of the posts on the headboard.

His hungry eyes explore my body, his irises a thin steel ring swallowed by the fathomless depths of his blown pupils.

Mimicking his earlier ministrations, I leisurely peruse his body, letting his anticipation take the front seat, while I drive *him* wild with need.

Breathing as if he's been running, his abs ripple with each rise and fall of his chest. The head of his cock weeps with precum and his hips writhe beneath me, his desire consuming him.

"Alright, Little Fawn. You've got me at your mercy now."

He grins wolfishly at me; his eyes filled with a ferocious hunger.

His next words are slow, baiting, taunting.

"What... pray tell... will you do to me next?"

A blush creeps across my cheeks, but the growl in his tone sends an ache to my core. I bite my lip and trail the tip of my finger slowly down his shaft, then drag it back up just as slowly, only to torment him further by just barely skimming it over the crown.

His hips buck and his head slams back against the wooden headboard, the leather belt creaking as he strains against its hold. I grin at him wickedly, enjoying the feeling of having this kind of control over him.

He watches me eagerly as I grip him, flicking my tongue, lightly licking the precum from his slit, swirling it over the tip, then easing the swollen head between my lips.

He groans, the muscles in his neck straining as his hips buck again.

"Jesus, Cole! Y-your mouth. I need your fucking mouth."

There's a loud crack as the wooden headboard threatens to give way as he strains against his tether.

Unbothered, I tease, "What is it, Your Grace? Is someone getting impatient?"

I smirk playfully, using his own words against him.

His eyes snap to mine, wide and disbelieving, his mouth agape, then he grins, his face shifting from surprise to pride.

"You never cease to amaze me, Little Fawn."

I smile up at him, preening at his praise.

Without any warning I drop down, quickly sliding my lips down his shaft. He gasps as his cock disappears deep into my mouth.

Remembering his lesson, I relax my throat so I can take him deeper—my hand making up the difference for the remaining length of him that doesn't fit in my mouth.

He moans when my cheeks hollow as I suck. Sliding my mouth up and down his length, he grunts and pants. I can feel his eyes on me and he starts to ramble—chanting words of praise, spurring me on. His hips move beneath me, thrusting up in time with my movements.

"That's it, Cole. That's my good girl. God, yes, let me see you take my cock. Suck hard baby... just like that. Mmmmm..."

The drive of his hips starts to falter, becoming erratic and his legs begin to shake. The wood of the headboard cracks again as he tugs at the belt looped around his wrists. His muscles strain, a look of pained ecstasy on his face as his wild eyes implore me—a fine sheen of sweat glistening across his skin.

"Stop. Please, please, Little Fawn," he begs, his breathing a ragged staccato as he struggles against his restraints, "You're gonna... make me come."

Barely able to form full sentences, he pleads, struggling to fight against his own desire, his hips pulsing upward of their own accord as his body involuntarily chases release.

"I *need* to fuck you!" he demands.

Relishing the pleasure I can pull from his body, I smile.

Deciding I've tortured him sufficiently, I slide my mouth off him with a pop, licking my lips as I move up his body.

I straddle his lap, and take his mouth, slipping my tongue between his lips, sliding my soaking center along his dick.

He rocks his hips, slipping his steely length through my wet folds, coating himself in my arousal.

The feel of his hot cock against my slickened pussy feels divine against the hyper-sensitized skin and we both moan, writhing in time with one another—the heat, the need, building to an aching crescendo between us, edging each of us closer and closer to sweet oblivion.

The need to feel him inside me, consumes me. I need his hot cock thrusting into me over and over again, filling me, stroking that spot within me that will make me come undone. The thought of that feeling alone sends an aching need to my center and I grind myself down even harder against him.

"Now, Little Fawn. Need... to fuck you... please. Now!" He pants heavily, gasping for air between biting kisses.

I lift up on my knees, the head of his cock rising to meet my dripping center. Holding his gaze, I slowly lower down onto him, the fat head of his cock stretching me with a delicious ache as I take more of him. Inch by inch I ease down, his size daunting in this new position.

I take my time, working him deeper, both of us groaning as I push myself down the rest of the way, taking him fully to the hilt.

I have to take a few shallow breaths, giving myself time to adjust to his size—the stretch, the fullness overwhelming me in the best way.

His cock pulses a slow, steady beat within me, the need to move, to roll my hips and feel his shaft slide along my inner walls almost more than I can take. I succumb to the need, moving slowly at first, gradually getting used to the feeling of being on top of him.

He rolls his hips in time with my movements, easing me into a sensual rhythm and then his words—Jesus, his fucking words...

"That's it. That's it, baby. Ride me, Cole. Take your pleasure from me. Take what you want... what you need. All of me, everything I am, everything I've ever been and everything I will ever be... take it all."

I reach above him to unfasten the belt. He growls as I lean forward, his tongue circling my nipple before greedily sucking it into his mouth. I arch my back, pressing into him and fumble with the buckle until I manage to release his hands.

Finally free of his restraints, he tosses the leather to the floor, immediately finding my hips, his fingers digging into the flesh of my ass as he eases me up and down on his cock, grinding his hips up into me each time he pulls me back down.

"I'm yours, Little Fawn. There's no limit to what you can take from me. Nothing I wouldn't give you. Nothing I wouldn't do to see the pleasure in your eyes, to see the smile on your lips.

"Nothing I wouldn't do to hear my name on your tongue, the sounds of your moans as I bring you to sweet rapture."

Each sweet phrase, each loving thought he utters is met with a decadent upward thrust of his hips. I curl my body into him, his strong hands squeezing my ass, sliding my wet pussy along his hard, throbbing length again and again.

"You want the sunrise? It's yours. The clouds in the sky? You can have them. The air in my lungs... you've owned since the moment we met, when you took my breath away."

The soft ridge of hair that trails down his abdomen teases my clit as we move. He drives up into me, each time he pulls me down. His cock gliding in decadent strokes, sends heat up my spine and my orgasm quickly starts to build.

I chase the feeling, moving faster, building up the pace and lean in to capture his mouth. He devours me hungrily and we lose ourselves to each other in a clash of lips, teeth and tongues.

Pressure builds within me, my inner walls beginning to quiver as my orgasm swells. Rogan, feeling my climax beginning to crest, increases his pace, wrapping me in a tight embrace, his eyes locked onto mine as he thrusts up into me harder, faster.

He reaches between us, pressing his thumb against my clit, the added pressure driving me higher with each indulgent stroke of his cock.

"I belong to you, Cole. You are my everything. So take it. Take it all. All of me belongs only to you."

Rogan's low growl in my ear is the last thing I hear before ecstasy overtakes me.

"Come for me, Little Fawn."

All at once, I break, my head thrown back as I scream my release. My pussy clamps down hard, pulsing over and over as Rogan continues to drive his steely length up into me.

Just when it feels like my climax is about to subside, he shifts his hips, hitting me at a whole new angle and rolls his thumb over my clit, causing yet another wave of pleasure to crash over me.

"Don't stop!" I beg. I never want this feeling to end. Every inch of him feels so goddamn good as he continues to slide his dick in and out of me. I can feel the thick ridge of his crown as it caresses my quivering inner walls, drawing out my release, making me come again, even before my last orgasm can fade.

But still, I want more.

"Harder," I plead, almost whining as I continue to grind my pussy against him.

My pleas spur him on and suddenly, he rears up, flipping me beneath him. He grips the headboard, bracing himself above me and grabs my thigh, opening me to him as he continues to fuck me. He drives into me, grunting as he slams his hips against mine.

The force of his strokes push me up the bed, closer and closer to the headboard. I grasp at his sides, searching for a place to grip onto him, but I can't get purchase against his sweat slickened skin.

Instead, I reach above my head, bracing myself against the headboard, holding myself in place while he continues slamming into me, our wet skin slapping loudly between us.

I follow his stare to where his eyes are locked, watching our bodies connect. His cock is slick, glistening as it plunges in and out of me.

I hook my leg around his thigh, urging him on. He shifts slightly, his cock striking a spot deep within me, making yet another orgasm begin to rise.

I tense, my breath catching in my throat on a silent scream as stars explode behind my eyes.

He drops down over me, his mouth pressing against my neck, his teeth grazing my flesh as he keeps up his punishing pace. He kisses me, his tongue pushing through my lips, molding me, remaking me. Turning me into something entirely new.

Entirely his.

"I'm there, Cole," he grunts, his hips starting to lose rhythm, "I'm going to come."

I lift my hips, meeting each of his thrusts.

"Come for me, Rogan." I command.

His hips falter, his breath hitching at my words. A low growl builds in his throat as he pistons into me, until his whole body tenses. He drops his forehead to mine and releases a loud roar, locking his hips against me—his cock pulsing deep inside me, heat spreading throughout my core.

The rigid muscle ripples and pulses, throbbing as he pours himself out completely.

Spent and gasping, his body shakes as he braces himself above me. Both of us breathing hard, he gently rubs his nose against mine. His lips find mine in a tender kiss as one more, final pulse rocks through him, making him shiver.

I giggle and we grin at one another.

We continue to kiss, tangled in each other, unwilling to separate even now.

"I love you, Rogan." I whisper against his lips.

"And I You, Little Fawn."

Chapter 76

Rogan

It's been two months. Two months that have simultaneously felt like an eternity and have also somehow flown by, all at the same time.

But the day is finally here.

Cole's—and now Kya's, grand opening of the bookshop.

I can already tell it's going to be a perfect day, as the sun crests the horizon, casting a warm amber hue across the floor of our bedroom as it peeks through the slight openings in the new drapes.

I wasted no time having them installed after the detectives showed us the salacious photos Cain's PI had taken of Cole and I standing in front of the large floor to ceiling windows.

Between the sheer terror and chaos Cain had inflicted on so many levels, the destruction and heartbreak Zavier had caused with the fires, and the time it took for Cole to recover from the stabbing, we were all starting to feel like this day might never come.

With everything that's happened, we decided it was best to take our time—to let Cole heal, to rebuild and recover as much as we could from all that was lost.

To give Kya the time she needed to grieve her losses as well as adjusting to her new role as co-owner of the bookshop. Brick, ever the solid wall for all of us to lean on, has been there for her, supporting her at every turn.

With so many changes, we all just really needed to take the time to acclimate into the rhythm of this new life.

It also felt important for Cole and I to take some time to just enjoy each other. To appreciate the simple act of being together, without the foreboding black cloud of Cain or Zavier hanging over us.

Cole yawns, cooing as her back bows, stretching out long like a cat, then curls back against my side. She drapes her arm and leg over me, snuggling her head against my chest and I relish the warmth of her naked body, the touch of her soft skin, divine against my own and my cock stirs to attention.

"Mmmm... five more minutes," she purrs, tightening her hold on me.

I chuff a soft laugh, and kiss the top of her head, hugging her body against mine, then slowly trail my fingers along her spine. She wiggles, her skin pebbling into goosebumps at my feather light touch.

"Time to get up, Little Fawn," my voice, a teasing sing-song. "Your future awaits..."

She blinks her eyes open, her lashes brushing against my chest. As she tips her sleepy face up to mine, I'm greeted by her beautiful smile.

I press my lips to hers, and guide her onto her back, my tongue parting her lips as I deepen the kiss. I feel my way down her body, my fingers deftly mapping over each of her now familiar curves. She melts into me as every part of her body surrenders to my touch.

I tease my tongue down to her neck and nip lightly at her skin, tasting and kissing my way down her sweet body.

Breathless, she threads her fingers into my hair, her nails lightly grazing my scalp.

"Mmmm... Rogan, what are you doing? We need to get up."

"Oh, but I am *up*, my love." I hum against her skin, my grin widening. I gently scrape my teeth on the soft flesh of her breast before sucking it into my mouth. Her nipple responds, instantly hardening as I swirl my tongue over the stiffening peak.

She giggles, moaning softly as she writhes beneath me, rocking her hips toward me, searching for touch, for friction, for pressure. She holds me in place, arching into my mouth as I continue to lave and suck at her nipple.

"But we need to get ready to go to the... ahhh!" She cries out, her words lost, melding instead into a gasping moan as I slip two fingers into her already soaking center.

Always so wet and ready for me.

"Again, Little Fawn, I am getting ready." I trail my lips lower down her belly, licking along her soft flesh, moving lower, inching ever closer to where I want most to be.

"I haven't had my breakfast yet."

I meet her stare as she watches me, grinning wolfishly as I lick my lips, then drop my mouth over her clit and suck.

"Ahhh... Rogan!" She throws her head back, bucking her hips beneath me. Gripping her hip, I hold her right where I want her and begin my feast, lapping at the sweetest nectar I've ever tasted, as if I've been deprived of drink.

Pumping my fingers inside her, I curl them to rub at the spot deep within her I know will send her spiraling over the edge of ecstasy. Her inner walls start to ripple as I lick at her, sucking and swirling my tongue against her clit, just the way I know will make her beg for my mercy, but keep her pleading for more, just the same.

She moans, crying out in pleasure, her soft body writhing beneath me. Her breaths ragged as she pants, chanting my name with each pump of my hand, each flick of my tongue, as I coax her body closer and closer to sweet release.

"That's it baby. Come for me, Little Fawn."

Wet heat rushes over my hand as my words hit their mark, sending her over the edge. Her pussy grips my fingers as I continue to thrust them in and out of her. I devour her, never stopping, licking and sucking at her hot center, greedily lapping up every drop, while the pulses of her orgasm slowly begin to ebb.

"Rogan, please. I need you..."

She whines, tugging at my hair.

I know what you want, Little Fawn.

I slip my fingers from her, meeting her eyes as I suck them into my mouth. I hold her stare and slowly lick them clean before lowering back down. Taking my time, I press the flat of my tongue firmly against her glistening pussy, tasting her again in one, slow, leisurely stroke, licking her from bottom to top.

My cock hangs heavily between my legs, as I stalk up her body. Bracing myself above her, I lower my hips and slide into her in one smooth thrust. Her pussy—slick, swollen and ready, welcomes me as I begin to pump my hips. She rolls her body in time with mine, as I sink in and out of her tight heat.

She cries out, as another orgasm barrels through her, her pussy squeezing down hard on my cock. Her legs tighten, gripping my hips, her nails clawing at my back. The tight grip of her perfect cunt as her climax ripples deep within her, makes my cock swell, growing impossibly harder.

I groan as the feeling of her pleasure triggers my own release and I spill into her, stalling only for a few moments—the force of my orgasm seizing every muscle in my body.

Once I'm able to move again, I continue to rock my hips, leisurely grinding out the last pulses of our combined pleasures.

"Good morning, Little Fawn." I say, breathing hard as I grin down at her, both of us trying to catch our breath.

Her own smile shines back at me and she giggles.

"Well, I'd certainly say so!"

Chapter 77

Rogan

Looking at the shop now and seeing what Cole and Kya have worked to sculpt it into, I can't imagine it as anything else.

How I ever thought I might turn it into an outdoor center feels absurd and laughable now.

The old swept away by the new, this place has become a hearthstone for the village—a wellspring of hope, of stories untold and, with the light Cole's brought to it, of belonging.

This quaint little shop has managed to change so many lives for the better.

My own included.

It is, and always will be, the village bookstore.

The stories following the fire, have drawn an intrigued crowd.

Cole, no longer in fear of being discovered, has encouraged Kya to work her magic on social media, spreading the word about the grand opening date and upcoming events. Even being so bold as to pose with Kya for photos, next to the new displays inside the shop.

To Kya's credit, the bookshop page has been blowing up with interested and excited villagers, curious to see just what the girls have in store for them, when they finally open the doors on the big day.

They seem especially drawn to the enticing teaser posts, cleverly flaunting the new 'spicy books' section.

Posts stating they'll be stocking a wide range of romance books—from dark, kinky tales, to even darker romantasy—where creatures of myth and folklore break through the pages, ramping up the spice to heights untold—imagination and magic making all things possible.

And I do mean *ALL* things.

I have to admit, I myself was intrigued by the stories in some of these books. When I asked Cole what it meant exactly, when she talked about the *spicy book section*, without a moment's hesitation, she grabbed one of the books off the shelf, quickly flipped to a chapter somewhere near the middle and read a couple passages aloud to me—blushing furiously the whole time, of course.

I suddenly realized I was staring at her, completely entranced, as the sensual words poured off her tongue, portraying highly descriptive, elicit scenes where the characters did incredibly licentious things to one another.

As her voice trailed off, the last of the sex scene wrapping up so salaciously, I realized I had a raging hard on and my heart was racing.

Thank God we were alone in the shop, because I basically tore her clothes off and took her right there on the cushioned bench of the alcove. I also insisted that particular book was to come home with us that night.

But as much as Cole loves her spicy books, the section she seems to be the most proud of is the section for local authors—small indie writers hoping to get their books recognized.

Cole and Kya are in talks with a few who've eagerly accepted the opportunity of them hosting a 'Cocktails and Smut' evening, complete with readings and perhaps even a guest from one of the high street shops, specializing in erotic toys and apparel.

"Can I come?" I tease, pressing my face into the space between her neck and shoulder, breathing in her familiar sweet scent of apples and patchouli. I'm addicted to her—to the glow and vitality radiating from her.

She arches her neck, allowing me better access. Permission granted, I suck lightly on her soft skin and she slips her hand around my neck, pulling me into her.

"Mmmm... of course you can *come*..." she laughs, her voice dripping with innuendo.

I hug her tighter, grinding myself against her perfect ass and growl low in my throat, purring into her ear, "We'll need to bring home some of those *toys* too. Find out which ones will make you scream."

"What's this I hear about toys?" Brick interrupts, entering the dining room, his plate piled high with buttery toast.

Kya rolls her eyes, her forehead dropping into her hand. She puts on a show of looking scandalized, but struggles to hide her grin.

She snatches a slice of toast off his plate.

"Those 'toys' are only for the grownups, Brick. You wouldn't have the first clue what to do with them." she snarks.

"Wanna test that theory, Sunshine?"

He waggles his eyebrows at her and winks, leaning in to peck a quick kiss to the tip of her nose. Then, keeping his eyes locked on hers, he bites the slice of toast that now hangs loosely between her fingers and grins devilishly at her as he chews.

She gapes up at him, her cheeks blazing a bright shade of pink as she fights to hold back her smile.

Brick's being uncharacteristically coy about their relationship, which I take to mean they haven't slept together. But it's quite something to see my best friend—the serial-playboy, finally reigning in his rakish ways.

I haven't seen any of the usual ladies he always used to have hanging around him, for months now.

I feel a surge of pride when I look at him. After all the bullshit he's been put through by women, I honestly didn't think he had it in him anymore. I thought the hopeless romantic inside him had been driven away entirely with the amount of times he's been used for his looks and his money, only to have his heart broken time and time again.

But then again, I didn't think I had it in me either.

It's incredible to think just how much Cole has changed me... and every last bit of it has been for the better.

Chapter 78

Rogan

My nerves roil as the words I want to say to her play on repeat in my mind. Palming the small box in my pocket, I stroke my thumb over its velvety surface, my eyes fixed on the freshly painted exterior of the bookshop.

Cole chose the bright turquoise color to symbolize protection, wisdom and healing—the rich color representing overall tranquility and her own spiritual growth.

A chuff of hot air blows across the back of my neck and soft lips and prickly whiskers tickle me, as Hannah nuzzles her nose into me.

Turning to face her, I give her a scratch against her cheek. She groans, enjoying the feel of my fingers as she gazes at me, blinking her wide, wise eyes. I get the feeling she's reading me.

The farrier's been out—trimmed her hooves, tidied her up. Then Cole and I gave her a bath, though I swear we ended up with more water on us than she did.

I won't deny, it was fun getting Cole out of those wet clothes and laying her down to worship her beautiful body beneath the trees in the orchard.

Hannah nudges me again, shaking me out of the sweet memory.

I place a hand flat against her neck, giving her a gentle pat just below the ridiculously oversized turquoise bow Cole insisted on tying around her.

She looks like a gift.

And maybe today, she is.

"You ready for this, girl?" I murmur, watching as the bookshop door swings open, my breath catching in my throat as she steps out beside the storefront sign—still hidden beneath its cloth, awaiting its big unveiling.

Sunlight catches on the auburn strands of her hair, her eyes sparkling as the rays illuminate the green of her irises, making my heart do its usual stutter. The same one that happens every, single time I see her.

She simply overwhelms me, in the best ways possible.

The warm, spring breeze pulls a tendril of hair loose from her French braid and it flutters across her cheek. She tucks it back behind her ear, giving me a glimpse of the tattoo inked over the scar Cain left on the side of her neck.

An apple blossom.

I watched the artist trace the delicate shape into her skin as Cole explained the powerful meaning behind the simple flower. I had never realized just how much depth it could have, how profound that one little symbol could be.

It's a tribute to her mother and the time they'd spent together reading in the orchard when she was a child.

A mark of hope and survival.

New beginnings and prosperity, and most importantly, a link to the memory of what she found in me—on the day we met—as I gathered her into my arms, recovering her from beneath the apple tree in the orchard of her new home.

Cole has this uncanny ability to take things that are broken, scarred and ugly, and turn them into something beautiful.

That's just what she does.

She takes the unloved, unwanted and abandoned—the ruined, heartless soldier, weighed down by duty and loss—subsuming them into her world as if they should have been there all along, turning them into something worthy, something deserving of love.

I've found being a part of her world is one of the most precious gifts I could ever dream of earning.

My Little Fawn's past may have scarred her, but it did not break her.

The true beauty of her scars lies in the fact that they only made her stronger—didn't make her callous to the world—still able to see the beauty in the life around her.

My fists clench slightly as these new emotions well up, threatening to spill. Emotions I've never dared to let myself feel.

I was taught to avoid them, to hide them away, to see vulnerability as weakness. But she's rewritten that script.

I vow here and now to fight every day to continue to be worthy of her. To ensure she knows nothing but love and security. That she is always the one in control of her life—and I'm just the bastard lucky enough to get to walk alongside her as she lives it.

She smiles the moment her gaze catches mine, and the vision causes my heart to hammer in my chest, my thumb stroking once more against the velvet box in my pocket.

"You all right, mate?"

I jump, startled from my reverie, and huff an embarrassed laugh before turning my attention to my best friend and the roly-poly dog waddling along beside him.

"All good..." I say, drawing in a deep breath and rolling my shoulders back.

He snorts, tapping his knuckles hard against my shoulder, "Yeah, right. I don't think I've ever seen you look more nervous than you do now, pal."

"Shut up, you bloody wanker." I grin at my friend—who sees far too much—knocking my knuckles into his shoulder a little harder than neces-sary.

In an attempt to steer the conversation away from the topic I know he's just dying to broach, I ask, "How are things in Dublin?"

My gaze follows Cole as she moves across the temporary dais with Kya, shaking the mayor's hand and greeting local business owners who've agreed to partner with them to bring more customers into Verdon.

"Fine. Everything's running smoothly for now."

"Good."

I drop my chin in a quick nod, my eyes never leaving the small stage, where Cole and Kya stand beaming as they turn to face the crowd of villagers gathered around them, awaiting the big grand opening.

After the incident, I bought out Abelridge and folded it into Cavendish Holdings. I kept on anyone who had stood against their former employer—rewarding them for their loyalty.

The rest?

The ones who stood by him. Defended his actions, helped him cover up the atrocities he'd been committing for years.

I fired them all. Their names blacklisted across every company that matters in London—and by extension, the world.

I even brought charges against several who had participated in his crimes, effectively dismantling his entire evil enterprise.

"Keep a close eye on Dublin and let me know if anything changes. We may need to act fast."

"Don't worry," Brick replies confidently, folding his thick arms across his chest. "She has everything under control. Always has. She's keen to come over. To meet you."

I feel his eyes rest on the side of my face.

I shake my head subtly. "Not yet. It's too soon."

I watch as Cole steps up to the microphone, her hand shaking slightly as she reaches for it, and clears her throat.

Brick nods, turning his attention back to the stage, my eyes never having left the vision of my beautiful Little Fawn.

She's positively radiant. The constant fear now banished from her life, there's a newfound confidence shining in her. She looks so much healthier, eating more, smiling more—her body forming delicious new curves.

My cock twitches in my pants and I mentally tell it to stand down.

Not right now, fella. I promise, we'll get to play with that later.

"Welcome," Cole's voice rings out across the crowd, her arms opening wide and the whole crowd erupts with thunderous applause.

"Thank you all so much for coming today. Kya and I have so many people we want to thank. I'm sure you'll probably be rolling your eyes by the time we're through."

The crowd chuckles.

Her eyes drift to the pub across the river. "But I promised Greg, I'd encourage you all to head to the Inn on the Wye for a celebratory drink"—a loud cheer erupts from across the water, the speakers carrying her voice clearly— "*after*," she stresses, "you've been inside the bookshop and bought something."

Mock boos and laughter ripple through the crowd.

Cole laughs good naturedly with them, waving her hands to settle them down.

"I know, I know." She teases, rolling her eyes as if the thought is atrocious to her too. "But, since you all mean so much to us, we're throwing in vouchers for a free drink at the pub with every purchase made today."

The crowd roars again, clapping and cheering, Brick letting out a loud whistle beside me.

Her eyes find him in the crowd and she grins widely at him.

"That's one per customer, Brick." She says sternly, waggling a finger at him and giving him a wink.

He winks back at her and I elbow him in the ribs.

"Oi! She did it first, mate!" He laughs, rubbing at his side and we both turn our attention back to the stage.

"Now, before we open the doors, there's a few things I need to say to you all.

"Today is the beginning of a future I never dreamed I could have. I was a stranger to you all when I arrived, but from the very first day I came to Verdon, this village has welcomed me. You all took me in. Accepted me as one of your own and made me feel like I belong here, right from the start. There's never been a time I've felt like an outsider. I'm beyond grateful to you all, my new friends, my new family."

Applause ring out across the crowd and is echoed across the river from the pub. I watch her as she takes it all in, her warm smile lighting up the stage.

She turns to a group of men off to the side, clapping her hands in their direction.

"Now, let's hear it for all those who helped get the shop up to snuff."

The workmen smile proudly at her—clearly as entranced by her as I am—and the crowd cheers loudly.

"To Kya, for agreeing to take this journey with me."

Kya beams, reaching out to link hands with Cole.

"To my dear, sweet Maria, for all your love and support over the years. I truly wouldn't be standing here today if it wasn't for you."

Maria sniffs and dabs at her eyes with a tissue.

"You're my guardian angel…" Cole's voice catches in her throat as she struggles to regain her composure.

"You saved me, Maria. I love you."

"Te quiero, Mija." Maria calls back, her voice carrying across the now silent crowd. All eyes turn to find the small woman, her arm looped through her grandson's as he stands tall beside her, gazing down with pride into his grandmother's eyes.

Then Cole turns her attention back to Brick. She lifts her chin, straightening her back, making herself taller and stoic as if she were a soldier standing tall, and salutes—a wry smile teasing at the corners of her lips.

"To Lieutenant General, Thaddeus Brickton the Third—"

"Oi!" Brick shouts, the whole crowd bursting out into laughter, Brick laughing louder than all of them.

She breaks into a wide grin, laughing along with the crowd and relaxes her stance.

"To *Brick*, for sorting out the legal stuff and for helping us to rebuild the bookshop, proving just because you're a lawyer with soft hands, doesn't mean you don't know how to use a screwdriver."

Brick continues laughing, his calloused, bear-like hands—the complete opposite of soft, lawyerly ones, never having conformed to that particular mold—grip the shiny turquoise leash of the little round bulldog, who's snuffling along the ground by his feet, unbothered by the large crowd of people around him.

"Seriously though, Brick," she smiles warmly at him, her tone softening, "thank you. Not just for that, but for your unwavering friendship."

"Anytime, Red." He gives her a little salute and I catch him flash her his signature wink again. I don't give him shit for it this time though, because I can also see the fierce loyalty burning behind his eyes.

Cole returns her focus to address the whole crowd again, letting silence hang in the air for just a moment.

"To Tom."

The crowd falls silent, a collective breath held, as she lets the name of the true hero of our story hang in the air.

"Kya and I have decided to dedicate the bookshop's tea room to his memory—*Tom's Butty.*"

A pleased hum of approval ripples through the people—the dedication, a clever nod to the Forester's term for friend—and Tom's favorite pint at the pub, the Butty Bach.

"His memory will live on here and in this village. He will never be forgotten. We've also set up a charity in his name, with all funds raised going to the local fire station. I hope we make you proud, Tom..." she adds, her voice breaking, trailing off as she takes a moment to brush a tear from her cheek.

A soft applause flows through the crowd, a warmth felt in the sound.

Finally, Cole shifts her gaze to find me.

"And my final thank you is to Rogan, Duke of Wyeholme.

"My partner. My life."

She draws in a breath, the sun glinting on an unshed tear in the corner of her eye. It sparkles before spilling over her lashes.

"My love."

A gentle applause rises from the crowd and they sigh collectively.

But all I see is her beauty. All I hear are her words. Everything else fades into the ether.

"You have proven to me that love *is real.* A gift, not an obligation. You have been my rock. My constant supporter. My beacon of light in a world that had left me alone in the dark. Thank you for showing me what it means to be truly loved."

My breath stills in my chest, my throat tight as I try to choke back the tears burning my eyes—my vision blurring as I lose the battle.

Placing my fist over my heart, I hold my chin high, keeping my eyes locked on hers. A silent promise to hold her close to my heart forever.

When the applause quiets down, she steps toward Kya, taking her hand.

"Kya, you took me in when I had nothing. You believed in me and supported me even though you didn't have the first clue who I was. Now, you're my business partner, but most important of all, you're the very best friend a girl could wish for. Will you please help me do the honors?"

Kya's chin quivers and she pulls Cole into a tight hug, then steps toward the microphone.

"It is my job, my duty and my greatest honor and privilege..."

Together they step forward, an oversized pair of scissors held between them, and cut the large turquoise ribbon, signifying the official opening of the book-shop. The crowd roars as the two ends of the ribbon part, fluttering to the ground.

I give Hannah a gentle swat on her backside and she snorts, trotting off to the side of the shop. The tarp covering the bookshop sign—connected to the huge ribbon around her neck—slips off to reveal the sign over the door.

The girls squeal, hugging each other again before proudly leading the crowd, as many as can comfortably fit at a time, into the shop.

Chapter 79

Rogan

Guests fill the bookshop for hours, their arms overflowing with books and other bookish items like specialty bookmarks, t-shirts and library decor. The girls work side by side to help each person finalize their purchases, taking turns to help them find the perfect books for their tastes, while the other hurries to restock the items that have quickly flown off the shelves.

A couple of the ladies from the village had volunteered their time to work the tea room, helping to keep the coffee and tea fresh and the trays filled with sweets and treats from some of the local shops.

It's not until around midday that the crowd of shoppers slows down.

I make my way past a group of ladies, giggling as they discuss the spicy books they're holding, in search of Cole. When I find her, she's focused on reorganizing some books on a shelf that had gotten a bit disheveled during the crowd's excitement, in their search to find just the right book.

She startles a bit when I quietly slip my arms around her waist from behind, pulling her back against me, but instantly sinks into me the moment she realizes who's holding her. I nuzzle into her neck, breathing her in—the scent of apples and patchouli immediately filling my senses.

"I'm so bloody proud of you, Little Fawn," I purr into her ear.

She shivers, her body melting into mine, her hands locking mine in place where I've encircled her waist. Her head falls back heavily against my shoulder, exposing her neck to me and I take it as an open invitation to feather light kisses along her smooth, pale skin.

"Do you think you could take a little break? There's something I wanted to talk to you about."

"Mmm hmm…," she nods, turning her smile up to me—her emerald eyes sparkling as they meet mine.

"There's actually something I wanted to talk to you about too."

Cole gives Kya a heads up, letting her know she's stepping out for a bit. Kya nods and gives her a confident wink, grinning brightly as she tucks a drink voucher into a bag and hands it over to the customer she'd been checking out at the till.

I crook my elbow toward Cole and she loops her arm through mine. We stroll down the forest path beneath the shelter of the trees, the late afternoon sun dancing through the leaves across the ground.

We stop in the clearing where the sun glitters off the water of the small stream nearby. I turn her to face me and slide the stubborn tendril of loose hair away from her face, tucking it behind her ear.

I curl her in close and struggle to swallow past the lump in my throat as I stare at her.

I lightly graze her skin, tracing along all of her features—her cheeks, her jaw, her lips, allowing myself to become completely subsumed by her.

She smiles up at me, but the longer I stand there, lost in her—my hands now visibly shaking; her smile falters, her brow furrowing with concern.

"Rogan? What is it?"

I suck in a quick breath and smile, shaking my head.

Get it together, Ro!

Choking back my nerves, I take one step back, pressing my lips to her fingers as I lower down to one knee.

Her breath stills in a silent gasp, her eyes sparkling as unshed tears pool above her lower lashes. She trembles, her hand clasping tightly over her mouth, as I flip open the little velvet box and lift it between us.

The ring, once my mother's—a diamond surrounded by sapphires—gleams between us in the warm rays of the afternoon sun.

"Little Fawn…,

"I realize now, I've loved you since the very first moment I saw you. Since you came into my life and turned my world upside down."

Large tears spill down her cheeks, her lower lashes unable to contain them any longer.

"You are my everything, Cole. You are the air I breathe. The beat of my heart. The very essence of who I am, who I want to be as a man.

"I promise to strive every day to be the type of man you deserve. Someone who knows your worth. Who will cherish you, worship you, protect you, *love you*, for the rest of our lives and beyond."

I lift the box higher, my meager offering in exchange for her promise of an eternity by my side. The sunlight reflects across the facets of each of the gems in a brilliant kaleidoscope of color.

"Promise to walk beside me for as long as we have breath in our lungs. And dance with me in the afterlife, when Earth no longer holds us."

"Nicole Allbright... will you do me the greatest honor of becoming my wife?"

Tears stream down her face, her head bobbing as she nods. She pulls me to her, her lips dropping over mine, kissing me like it's the first time.

Grabbing her waist, I pull her into me and kiss her deeply.

Sobbing, giggling and breathing hard, she breaks the kiss only long enough to answer me.

"Yes, Rogan. I will marry you!"

"Thank fuck!" I laugh and blow out a heavy breath, my hands shaking as I slip the ring onto her finger, then pull her in to kiss her again, excitedly peppering her with even more kisses all over her face and neck.

She lets out a squeak as I quickly stand, hugging her tightly and lifting her feet from the ground, giddily spinning us both around, our laughter echoing through the trees.

As I set her feet back to the forest floor, we cling to each other and I smile down at my beautiful fiancée.

Her eyes, still glistening with happy tears, find mine and, though she's still smiling, a flicker of concern crosses her face.

"What is it, Little Fawn?" I ask, smiling warmly at her, running the pad of my thumb along her wet cheek.

She draws in a steadying breath. Her voice is hesitant at first, but then she rushes her words out in a flurry, as though afraid if she doesn't say them now, she never will.

"Rogan...I'm...ummm... well... You're gonna be a daddy."

It takes a moment for her words to sink in and all I can manage to do is blink at her dumbly.

"The doctor confirmed it yesterday and said I'm about eight weeks along," she continues, while I stand there gaping.

Silence hangs heavy in the air and she wrings her hands and watches me nervously.

My teeth click together as I snap my mouth closed, realizing it was hanging wide open and my eyes flicker between hers—the reality of the news she's just shared finally hitting home.

An overwhelming sense of euphoric joy floods through me and my stunned look of shock softens into a dopey grin.

"Say something," she giggles, laughing at the look on my face.

My knees hit the ground at her feet and I grab her hips, pulling her body close. She threads her fingers through my hair, holding me to her as I press my lips to her belly.

I look up to see her eyes shining with new tears.

"A baby?" I ask, sounding as if I'd never even heard of one before.

She sniffs, laughs, and nods.

"Yep. A baby."

"So... you're gonna be a mum... and... a-and I'm gonna be a dad?"

"Yes," she giggles, nodding and cupping my face in her hands.

"That's usually how that works with these things."

"Little Fawn," I breathe, pulling her down into my arms, "you have no idea how happy you've made me today."

I kiss her, gently at first, but the kiss quickly turns heated when she opens her mouth for me, her tongue teasing the seam of my lips beckoning entry.

I don't know how long we stay here—Cole held tight to me as I kneel on the forest floor, kissing each other until our lips are numb, as if the rest of the world doesn't exist.

What I do know is, however long it is, will never be long enough.

Eventually, we come back to ourselves, realizing we've got a whole life to return to.

As we walk back toward the bookshop, I pull Cole to me, tucking her into my side, our fingers laced together and we make our way back to the world.

Back to our friends.

Back to our family.

Back to the bookshop.

Where beside the door, a new sign welcomes...

Little Fawn Books
Open To All

Chapter 80

Epilogue – Cole

ABOUT SIX MONTHS LATER

Juggling my bag of snacks—because I swear, I'm constantly hungry these days—and three different beverages, I waddle into the bookshop. My feet are swollen, and I feel like I'm roughly the size of a baby elephant.

Kya greets me with her usual cheer and runs to help me empty my hands. I really don't know how I would have survived the last six months without her undying support.

"Alright, hun?" She asks, perpetually checking up on me as she gauges my expression today.

The doctors have told me it could be any day now. I'm officially past my due date and I feel like everyone's watching me like I'm a ticking time bomb, about to explode.

"Just a little tired." I try to reassure her, but this is starting to feel like my usual response. It's pretty much what I've told her every day this week.

"You know, you don't have to keep coming in. I can handle things. You should go home and put your feet up."

"I'll be gone enough once this little one gets here," I say, stroking my hand over my swollen belly.

I'm so excited to be having this baby, but I have to admit there's a small part of me that's worried I'm going to be leaving the bookshop for a couple months for maternity leave. I have no doubt Kya's got it completely under control and I'm leaving it well-tended in her more than capable hands, but this bookshop is also my baby and it just makes me irrationally anxious.

"I'll just stay for a few hours today." I promise, giving her a smile that I hope will assuage her worry, and reach out to pluck my coffee cup from her hand.

Feeling positively huge as I toddle around the shop, straightening books and refilling shelves—my belly getting in the way of me being anywhere near able to add anything to the higher shelves no matter how hard I try—I reluctantly begin to wonder if Kya is right, and perhaps I should consider heading home and let her run the show for today.

Plus, I keep getting a tight cramping in my lower back every so often and I haven't dared to mention that little tidbit to anyone quite yet.

At around eleven o'clock, the bell over the door chimes and I grin when I see my handsome hubby stroll through it. His gorgeous steel gray eyes, lined with worry, find me immediately—the look of concern changing to relief the instant he spots me.

I roll my eyes and shift my attention over to my devious best friend, looking guilty as hell where she stands behind the cash register, trying to look busy.

"Kya..." frustration lacing my tone, "You called him, didn't you?"

"You can be as angry with me as you want, but I knew that was the only way you'd go home, hun. You're dead tired and I can tell you need to put those feet up!"

Damn it, that girl really doesn't miss a thing.

"Alright, alright you two. Consider your conspiracy to extricate me from the bookshop a success, because I have to admit, my back is really killing me today."

Oops... now I've done it.

I cringe when I look back to see Rogan's temporary look of relief has once again returned to his, more usual as of late, incessant look of panicked observation. The same one he's been watching my every move with lately.

He doesn't hesitate as he takes several long strides across the room to get to me, stepping behind me to wrap his long arms around me, lifting my belly up, giving me instantaneous relief from the weight of our sweet baby growing within. I sigh and let myself sink back into his chest, relishing the blissful, yet momentary reprieve.

"Mmmm... you live here now." I purr, smiling up at him through heavily lidded eyes.

He kisses my temple and rocks me gently, "Let's head home, Little Fawn. You need your rest."

"Okay, just let me grab my things." I slowly make my way around the counter to gather my bag and travel cups, but as I bend to reach beneath it, a sharp, stabbing pain sears into my side and I cry out, doubling over.

Kya is at my side in an instant. I grip her hand tightly and squeeze as another wave of pain hits me again.

Groaning and panting hard, I look up just in time to see Rogan, vaulting over the counter. The next thing I know, he's gently but swiftly scooping me up into his arms.

"About that time?" Kya suggests, cocking an eyebrow at both of us.

I look at Rogan and even though he's as white as a sheet, he's beaming. I smile back at him and grimace a little as another pain begins to roll through me.

"Yeah..." I blow out a breath.

"I think she might be right."

Twenty-Three and a Half Hours Later

Monitors are beeping, the nurses all seem to be talking at once and everything seems to be moving too fast and too slow, all at the same time.

I've been in labor for hours that feel like days and it's just not progressing. I heard one nurse say she's worried about the baby's heart rate, another expressed a concern over my blood pressure. All I know is I'm beyond ready to be done with this delivery, because I don't know how much more I can take.

The drugs have had little effect, even though they've given me two epidurals. Rogan has been my rock, but I'm not blind to the dark circles under his very worried eyes.

Finally, the doctor comes into the room, and takes a look at my chart, reviewing all the details, then checks the tape scrolling out of the fetal monitor.

"Alright folks, I don't want to alarm anyone, but your baby's heart rate has dropped into a range I'm not comfortable with and Cole, your blood pressure is not in a good place either. So I think it's time to change things up a bit."

She turns to look at Rogan, taking in his protective presence over me and begins calmly, but firmly laying out the plans for the next steps, quickly taking control over the situation.

"Dad, you're going to go with these nurses here and they're going to suit you up into the proper apparel and Cole, my dear," she shifts her attention to me and gives me a reassuring smile, resting her hand on mine, giving it a gentle squeeze.

"We're going to move you into the operating room. This baby is going to have to be delivered by C-section."

A gasp escapes me and I feel a new flood of terror come over me. Her smile softens with kind understanding, her eyes crinkling at the corner, and she gives my hand another gentle squeeze.

"Now, I don't want you to worry. I do this all the time and I can have your little one out and safely in your arms in as little as two minutes, if need be. Everybody is still okay here and we're going to make sure it stays that way, alright?"

"Rogan?"

I glance over at him as tears roll down my cheeks.

"It's okay, Little Fawn. You heard the doctor. Let's get our little one out of there and into your arms, yeah?"

I can see he's terrified, but he's being so strong, so reassuring for my sake, and I absolutely adore him for that. He moves across the room, placing a loving kiss on my brow, his thumbs softly sweeping the tears from my cheeks.

"I'll see you in a minute, alright?"

I nod, but I'm scared shitless...

From then on out, things begin to move fast.

Wires and lines are draped across me and they start moving pieces of my bed around as if it were a Transformer from that movie. The next thing I know, I'm being wheeled down the hall, through a set of double doors and into a freezing cold operating room.

Rogan is already there, his hair covered with a cloth cap, a hospital gown and a mask over his face. All I can see are his beautiful, worried gray eyes.

The doctors and nurses quickly set up the room around me and erect a cloth in front of my face—blocking my view of what they're about to do to me.

I have to assume they gave me something to numb the area, because I can't feel a thing below my ribs.

"Alright, Cole. I'm going to deliver your baby now. You shouldn't feel any pain, but you'll feel some pressure. Right, then. Here we go."

Rogan grips my hand and locks his gaze to mine. I can only feel the movement beyond the screen and the pressure the doctor told me to expect, but I'm so fucking scared. Tears flow unbidden from my eyes and track toward my hairline, also covered in its own cloth cap.

Rogan kisses my hand through the mask, "You're doing so good, love. I'm so damn proud of you, Little Fawn. Just look into my eyes. Everything is going to be just fine."

I nod, and try to believe his words, but the fear is overtaking me. I can hear the doctors and nurses talking, their voices low and urgent.

"The cord... watch the cord."

"The cord is around the baby's neck."

"Careful, it's wrapped around twice."

"Get the oxygen ready... start compressions."

"Rogan...," I cry, terror consuming me as I see a tear slip from his eye too, but he doesn't look away. Doesn't break my stare. Just holds my hand to his cheek, stroking his other hand down my arm in a gentle attempt to try and soothe me.

Time feels as though it's standing still.

And then—there's a cry...

The most beautiful sound I think I've ever heard in my life.

Rogan drops his forehead to mine and we cry together, my hand still firmly gripped in his.

Finally, the doctor brings our baby over, wrapped in a blanket, and places the little wailing bundle gently on my chest.

"It's a boy!"

The doctor beams, "Seven pounds, eight ounces and very healthy. This little man had his cord wrapped around his neck twice, so it's a good thing you didn't get to pushing, Mummy."

"A boy?"

I weep, gazing at our son, then back to Rogan, tears spilling from my eyes. But this time, they're happy tears.

"A boy."

Rogan sighs, breathing out a long, slow breath, his shoulders finally relaxing as he smiles down at our little treasure, then—pulling the mask from his face—places the most gentle, tenderest kiss onto my lips.

"I think...," I start, but then hesitate as I gaze up at Rogan.

"What is it, Little Fawn?" His smile is soft as he admires the face of our tiny little boy.

"I think we should call him... Devon. Devon Thomas."

Rogan's throat works, swallowing hard as his eyes return to mine and then—he nods, a soft smile forming on his lips.

"Devon Thomas." He says the name, testing it out.

"You know, I think they both would have loved that."

The next few days, the hospital staff is giving us all kinds of tips and advice, showing us how to do things neither Rogan nor I have ever done before.

Maria is beyond annoyed, shooing them away.

"Aye! Dios mio! I will show her what to do. Go away!"

Rogan and I lock eyes, shooting each other a knowing glance. laughing at how feisty this sweet looking little woman can get.

Finally the day comes we can go home from the hospital. It will take me a bit longer to heal since they had to do the C-section to deliver Devon, but I guess this is one scar I'm not all that upset about.

I think about all the scars I have, each one having shaped me into who I am today. Each one giving me a life lesson, one cold, hard truth at a time.

I didn't ask for them, nor did I deserve them. But then again, does anyone deserve to be abused, mistreated, neglected, *raped*...?

Absolutely fucking not!

Everyone deserves to be treated with love and respect.

To be loved.

To be respected.

Not everyone finds that the first time around.

But when we persevere, when we find our inner strength... that strength lives inside all of us, if we just have the courage to look hard enough...

That's the person we were always meant to be.

When we rise from the ashes of our own personal hells and are able to look back on it and say...

I survived.

That's when our life can truly begin.

With everything packed up, Brick and Kya carry arm loads of gifts and bags out the door, Maria hot on their heels barking orders in Spanish. I grin up at Rogan from my wheel chair, little Devon sleeping soundly in my arms.

There's a soft knock on my door, pulling our attention from each other to the woman peeking her head inside.

An older woman, auburn hair with light lines of white running through the strands, her green eyes sparkling with unshed tears, an apprehensive smile on her lips.

She offers a timid wave of her fingers.

My mouth drops open and my eyes flare wide.

"Mom??"

THE END...

?

Bonus Chapter – Kya

PROLOGUE, BOOK 2 - SCARS OF THE PHOENIX

Not much in this world scares me. I've never really been someone who fears anything. But there is *one* thing that absolutely terrifies me...

Fire.

Sometimes I still wake up smelling the phantom stench of smoke, choking my lungs. The acrid combination of burning wood, plastics and fabrics—the scent of memories turning to ash...

Then there's the smell of burning hair and flesh, the scent branding itself into my nose, and searing into my nightmares.

The sound of their screams will haunt me for the rest of my life. Sounds that have scarred me deeper than any injury to my skin.

Yes, I've learned to live again—slowly, painfully, but the past continues to haunt me, reminders creeping in, tormenting me when least expected.

He took everything from me that night...

Things I can never get back.

But his biggest mistake...

I survived.

And now, I'm going to make him pay...

From the Author

This story was created on a whim, sparked by a seemingly innocuous conversation between two unlikely friends, an entire ocean between them, who somehow managed to find one another through the magic and mystery of Booktok.

Through many iterations and countless brainstorming sessions, this story has evolved, morphing from something playful and silly, into a much deeper, darker tale. I pulled elements from my own life experiences and mixed them with the liberties provided by creative license, to craft them into a heart wrenching, in-depth dark romantic thriller, full of mystery, intrigue, heartbreak, hope and of course, spicy romance with a bit of playful banter sprinkled in to balance out the heavy.

As an avid reader of spicy novels, I made sure to thread plenty of spice of my own into this, as well.

Many of the characters were born with a nod and hat tip to several people IRL who have been my unwavering supporters throughout my journey as a brand-new indie author.

I want to thank all of my Booktok Besties in the indie author community. (You all know who you are and I would have to write another whole book, just to thank you all individually.) This community has been the very reason I've been able to chase this dream and wouldn't be possible without each and every one of you.

That being said, I do need to say a special thank you to my besties, Athena, Jen and Kim. You ladies have been my rocks through this entire journey and I am forever grateful to you. You inspired me, encouraged me, pushed me. You believed in me whenever imposter syndrome inevitably chose to rear it's ugly head from time to time. Your support means the world to me, but your steadfast friendship and unwavering confidence in my abilities, even when I thought I couldn't do this, has been more appreciated than I could ever put into words.

Now, of course, I need to thank my family. You've all listened to me chatter on about my adventures in writing and only rolled your eyes a few times when I wasn't looking. (Yes, I heard them roll!)

And finally, to my handsome hubby, you've never doubted me. Through all the crazy ideas I've had, you've always backed me 100%, having faith that I'd be able to pull off whatever plan I'd concocted regardless of how outlandish it was. You've always, ALWAYS believed in me, even when I doubted myself. None of this would be possible without you. *Have I told you lately that I love you?*

I hope you'll enjoy Scars of the Fawn, the first book in the Beyond Her Scars series and hopefully, the first of many more books to come from me, NJ Colle, in the future.

Happy Reading, and Keep it Spicy!

About the Author

NJ Colle, a serial entrepreneur with a passion for spicy books, now the debut author of the dark romantic thriller Scars of the Fawn, the first novel in the spicy contemporary romance series, Beyond Her Scars. Colle has plans for at least two other books in this series.

Other books on the horizon for NJ Colle will delve into the spicy romantic fantasy genre, with another series coming soon.

As a self-proclaimed 'word-nerd', NJ Colle has always had a love for the written word, escaping into fictional worlds that come alive through paper and ink. Composing her own works was a natural transition, writing what she loves and creating characters she craves from her experiences as a reader.

When not writing, NJ Colle enjoys reading, spending quality time with her family and cuddling with her puppy, who fancies herself her co-author.